SEASON OF THE WITCH

Book One of The Penumbra Papers

by

SILVER JAMES

SEASON OF THE WITCH is a work of fiction. Names, characters, places, and incidents are either the product of the author's imagination or are used fictitiously, and any resemblance to actual persons living or dead is entirely coincidental.

Cover design by *Clary Carey*, clarycarey@gmail.com
Cover Image: © Robert Anderson, Jr., www.bigstock.com
Edited by Alan Gregory

Print ISBN: 978-0-9899217-3-2
ISBN-10: 0989921735

Published in the United States of America
9 8 7 6 5 4 3 2 1

Chapter One

Hello, Darkness

HIS HAND CARESSED her throat and lingered on the soft skin stretched over her carotid artery. Her pulse thrummed beneath his fingertips and his heart quickened to match its fluttery pace. Her eyelids opened. He noted an innocence in her gaze uncommon in this day and age and he watched her eyes widen in recognition—of him and her situation.

"Why?" She mouthed the word rather than saying it out loud. Even so, her question hung between them, begging for an answer.

Though he owed her no explanation, he answered. "Because it has to be." She shook her head even as his fingers tightened around her throat. "Don't fight me, Cynthia Celeste." There was power in names so he used her full one instead of the idiotic nickname everyone called her. CeeCee. That wasn't a proper name at all.

She whimpered, tears welling in her eyes before one spilled down her cheek to leave a silvery trail. "Will it hurt?" Her whispery voice choked on the last word.

He considered the question, weighing his answer. "Probably. Birth. Life. Death. Each transition comes with its own pain. Close your eyes." He didn't smile. This was a solemn occasion, one he wanted to mark with proper dignity.

She vehemently shook her head, dragging her fingernails across his wrist and forearm hard enough to leave bloody tracks.

"Bitch!" He spat the word and drew back his other hand now tightly curled into a fist. *No,* a voice whispered in his head. *There can be no marks.* He squeezed her throat hard enough to cut off oxygen and blood yet with a gentleness meant to prevent bruises. Didn't she realize the honor he paid her?

Fear and anger battled in her expression. Her nostrils flared as she attempted to suck in air and her mouth gaped in a silent scream. Arms and legs flailed for a few short moments then stilled. The innocence in her eyes faded as darkness consumed her.

"There now," he soothed. "That wasn't so difficult. Your name will live on, Cynthia Celeste, honored as a sacrifice for the cause."

University of Chicago

JUST AS HE tucked his lecture notes into his briefcase, the door to his classroom banged open. A squad of burly men, halogen lights blazing in their hands and wearing all manner of religious objects, stormed in.

"Kristian St. John, you're under arrest!"

Since the Veil ripped, legislation had been enacted, and he now had rights and protection under human law. This wasn't like the Dark Times. Or so he thought as two men grabbed his arms and forced silver handcuffs around his wrists. The silver stung a little but not so much he couldn't escape. He went along with the farce, believing there'd been a mistake and he would be freed once they arrived at the police station. Glancing at one of the uniformed officers, he couldn't help but chuckle. The man wore three crosses, a Star of David, a star and crescent, and even a yin yang pin. The cop was nothing if not prepared. Too bad the religious icons would protect nothing if Sinjen decided to escape. He'd chosen to live as a law-abiding citizen for his entire life. That wasn't about to change now.

He blinked against the blinding light and tilted his head. "Under arrest? For what crime?"

"Murder." A man in an ill-fitting overcoat pushed to the front.

"Murder?" A sharp bark of derisive laughter escaped before Sinjen could catch it. "Who are you and who have I allegedly murdered?"

The cop glared, his lip curled into a reasonable facsimile of an Elvis sneer. "I'm Detective Richard Kowalski. Chicago PD. We'll stake you right here, you sonavabitch, if you don't cooperate."

He slowly extended his hands, shaking off the uniformed officers as easily as drops of rain. At his age and power, there wasn't much that threatened him. "I ask you again. Who did I murder?"

"Just shut up."

All but one of the officers refused to look him in the eye. He tilted his head to get a better look at the one.

"Cynthia Celeste Adams." The uniform uttered the words and then cringed as the detective whirled on him, sputtering and cussing.

Sinjen ignored the argument between the two cops. CeeCee murdered? She'd been one of his best students; had gone to work for the government, he thought. She'd also had a crush on him, as so many of his coed students did. Bright. Pretty. And her death was a complete waste of human potential. Anger flared and he tensed. That these mundanes thought he would willfully end so vibrant a life rankled. Distracted by his own musings and the dust up between Kowalski and the uniformed officer, Sinjen didn't realize a third man stepped within reach until the cop jammed an electronic taser against his chest. White-hot pain shot through him and he crumpled. His brain struggled to comprehend what just happened, even as his muscles twitched. Sinjen focused on Kowalski as the detective leaned over him, lips curled into a parody of a smile. The last conscious thought in his head wondered if he would live to see another night.

Washington, DC, three days later

FBI DIRECTOR GEORGE BAILEY didn't need directions. He strode down the hallway to the Oval Office with an assurance born of familiarity. The door was open, waiting for him. He stepped across the threshold into the inner sanctum of the President of the United States and paused. The handsome man seated behind the desk smiled but he wasn't fooled. By the time the President requested his presence, things had already gone to hell.

Waved to a chair positioned in front of the desk, he sat but didn't get comfortable. He studied the man across from him before speaking bluntly. "The glamour seems to be working better I see."

President Rhys Wynne chuckled, the sound ominous rather than humorous. "How many years since the Big Rip? Yes, some of our abilities have returned." The President swiveled in his chair to stare across the frozen lawn outside the windows. "I sometimes wonder if the world is better off knowing of the existence of magick kind."

George knew magicks had regained far more of their talent than they revealed to humankind. His right shoulder lifted in a shrug but he made a conscious effort to stop the reaction even as Wynne continued.

"You mortals are so prejudiced at times."

The comment rankled but he did his best to hide his reaction. Despite being an elf, the being behind that desk was the Commander in Chief. Under normal circumstances, the elongated ears and the ethereal beauty remained hidden behind a magical facade—a glamour. The Big Rip stripped that ability, leaving preternatural beings exposed, until recently. The magic was returning slowly.

"You magicks have had millenniums dealing with humans behind your glamours, Mr. President, while we've known of your existence only a few short years." George didn't finish his thought aloud. *And the magicks have preyed on humans since the beginning of time.*

The President swiveled back to face him. "You are thinking too hard, George." His smile reached his eyes, warming their mossy-green depths. "How is the MAGIC unit working out?"

This was safe ground. The Magical Activities, Grievances, and Inhuman Crimes Unit was a topic they could discuss without rancor. "Recruiting is coming along. I currently have one agent undercover on a case."

"And our human member? Agent Marquis. How is she managing?"

George inclined his head, a smile twitching at one corner of his mouth. "Special Agent In Charge Marquis is nothing if not…resourceful."

Wynne pushed a folder across the desk. "She needs to be in Chicago by nightfall."

He didn't pick up the folder, watching the President's face instead. "Must be something big if you're directing my operations personally, sir." He schooled his voice and expression. A Washington veteran, George knew how to play the game. A veil clouded Wynne's eyes. That wasn't a good sign. A moment later, light shimmered between them and he got a good look at the President's true form: pointed ears, sharp features a bit reminiscent of a fox, slightly tilted eyes that currently bored right through him. He fought the urge to gulp, unsure if he would ever get used to seeing magicks in their real guise.

"Yes. I am being presumptuous, Director Bailey. This is a matter requiring some…diplomacy."

The snort escaped before he could stop it. "A matter requiring diplomacy and you want to send Marquis?" He didn't miss the switch from familiar to formal in Wynne's address. Wary now, he watched closely.

The air shimmered again as the President's glamour settled back into place. "Yes, well. Despite her proclivity for…speaking plainly and acting somewhat brash, she is the right agent for this case." Wynne paused, glancing out the window again.

The wintery landscape hadn't changed and George wondered what held the President back. What kept him from full disclosure? He'd been in law enforcement his entire life. He knew reluctance to tell the whole truth when he saw it.

Still staring through the window, the President continued. "You are aware of the continued astral and planetary disturbances. They have been accompanied by darkness of a sort none of us can explain."

"*Us?* I presume you mean magicks."

Wynne nodded. "I do. And if we cannot explain it then we must leave it to you mortals to investigate."

"So that's why you want Marquis on this? Because she's human?"

The President remained silent. An antique clock across the room ticked away the seconds, the sound a soft echo of George's heartbeat.

Several minutes passed before Wynne spoke. "She is. But she is also more."

He laughed and then sobered. "More? More than my best agent? More than a smart-mouthed…" George trailed off as Wynne swung around to glare. "Dammit, sir, there isn't a diplomatic bone in her body and you know it. She doesn't take shit, she gives it. If she's going into a dangerous situation, I want to know about it."

Something that sounded suspiciously like a harrumph exploded from the president's mouth. "Every time we send a MAGIC agent into the field, it is a dangerous situation, George. That's the whole point. I worked damn hard to get the legislation passed that keeps our kinds safe from each other and the MAGIC Unit is a key component. Giving those agents complete jurisdiction is counter-intuitive to more laws than I want to consider. And you well know it! I handpicked you when your former boss elected to retire. You are probably the only human who can accomplish our mission." He suddenly looked very tired, and very old given he could pass for a youthful forty-five. Closing his eyes, he rubbed his temple. "I need her in Chicago by tonight, Director. And I trust her to do the job." He pushed the file forward again before turning his attention to a second folder at his elbow.

George snatched the file and stood, recognizing a dismissal when he got one. "Thank you, Mr. President. I will keep you informed." Turning on his heel, he strode toward the door. He might be merely mortal, but there was nothing wrong with his hearing. Behind his back, the president lifted the phone receiver and punched out a number.

"Tell him it is done."

George resisted the urge to turn around. He doubted that bit of information was meant for his ears, but who the hell was *him* and just what the bloody blue blazes had Wynne done?

Chapter Two

Charlie Foxtrot

"Sit."

Sade Marquis stared at the man behind the desk before perching on the edge of a chair. An angry buzz spilled from the telephone receiver in his hand, though not loud enough for her to understand the words. From the irritated look pasted on the director's face, the caller was chewing some federal ass. Wondering how long the Old Man would put up with it, she made a bet with herself. George Bailey was not a patient man. He wasn't particularly polite when pissed either.

"Troll," he mouthed at her, rolling his eyes.

Sade choked back a guffaw and returned her gaze to the Washington cityscape visible through the window. Shadows still lurked beneath the pallid winter sunshine and she fervently wished for a cup of coffee. Hot. Black. Chicory. Yeah. Chicory would do the trick. Her day started at the butt crack of dawn and she'd had no time for caffeine. Contemplating a road trip to Chicago without caffeine could make a girl cringe.

She studied her boss as he continued his phone conversation. He was relatively new to the office. His predecessor abruptly retired after the moon and a wild star called The Flyer aligned during a lunar eclipse. That was the first tear in the Veil. The solar eclipse two weeks later ripped the hole bigger. In fact, a whole slew of veteran agents retired. This brave new world was one the old-timers just couldn't—or wouldn't—face. Bailey had earned the fond "Old Man" moniker from his subordinates. Whether his agents loved or hated him, they all respected him.

The door opened and his secretary slipped in carrying two official mugs—navy ceramic with the Bureau's emblem embossed in gold leaf on the side. Steam wafted above the rich, dark liquid as Sade took a sip. Chicory. She wondered, and not for the first time, whether Alice had a touch of magical blood. The woman seemed downright prescient at times. Sade herself was proof that preternatural beings could not procreate with humans. Her mother had certainly tried hard enough with the faerie king, Oberon. However, witches and wizards were closer to humans genetically.

"Yes," the Old Man growled into the phone, breaking her reverie. "I will see to it personally. My agent will be there this afternoon and I expect full cooperation from local law enforcement." Bailey glanced at her, the grimace on his face replaced by a wicked smile. "Trust me, Mr. Mayor, your cops do not want to cross my agent."

Mr. Mayor. Sade was absolutely positive he'd mouthed "Troll" earlier. She coughed to cover her laughter. The director had a sense of humor after all. Who knew?

"She *will* be there this afternoon, Mayor Dandridge," her boss asserted. "Someone from our field office will meet her at the airport. Your people will brief her as soon as she arrives."

As Sade watched his face, she noticed the man's color darkening. If the vein on the Old Man's forehead started to throb, she was headed for the door. He slammed down the phone before he lost his temper. Almost.

"Frickin' alpha hotel," he snarled. He grabbed the mug Alice left at his elbow and gulped. Almost immediately, the secretary reappeared, not bothering to knock this time. She retrieved the director's empty mug, handed him a fresh one, passed Sade an envelope, and sedately retreated, all without saying a word. The envelope contained an E-ticket, round-trip to Chicago with an open return date.

Sade glanced up and met the Old Man's gaze. He didn't call someone an asshole, even using the military "code" for it unless every one of his buttons had been pushed. His anger was back under control. She relaxed—slightly. She never let down her guard completely in his presence. Too many agents had, only to be bitten in the ass. She'd been there, done that, and had the tee shirt to show for it.

Before he could start the briefing, Alice buzzed in. "Sorry to disturb you, Director, but Senator McMahon is insistent."

With an exaggerated sigh, he acknowledged her message. "Patch him through." When the light for the correct line blinked, he stabbed the button. "Director Bailey." He sounded like a junkyard dog ready to fight over a bone.

"George, I want something done," the senator's adamant voice echoed from the phone console.

That surprised the hell out of Sade. Bailey put the senator on speaker-phone? She sat up to listen, paying close attention.

"Senator—" The Old Man started to reply but he was cut off.

"Don't start with me, George," McMahon barked, his midwestern drawl evident. "I was lucky to get a line out of my office. My switchboard is lit up like the fuckin' Christmas tree in Rockefeller Center. I've got little old church ladies calling me, for Chrissakes."

"Calm down, sir," the director ordered, his voice cutting through the senator's tirade like a hot laser through cold metal. "I just got off the line with Mayor Dandridge. I'll tell you what I told him. I'm sending my best agent to deal with the situation. In fact, she would have already been on her way if my briefing wasn't constantly interrupted by these inane phone calls."

The next few words the senator uttered were unintelligible gibberish as he sputtered and spit in anger. Sade tilted her head in an attempt to decipher what the man said. Only the swear words came out plainly. She looked up to catch the Old Man rolling his eyes and snickered before she caught herself.

The senator stopped stammering and took a deep breath. "Dammit, George, I don't think you grasp the seriousness of this." He was all but shouting now. "The gawddamned Tribune is threatening to run this as a front-page story. This despicable creature needs to be dealt with immediately. The sweet Lord only knows how many fuckin' virgins he's sacrificed on the altar of his sins."

Her mouth gaped as she listened to the angry diatribe. She closed it with a snap. Alex McMahon, darling of the extreme religious factions in the country, certainly knew how to sling the vernacular. That profanities so liberally spiced his language rather shocked her.

"Frankly, Senator, I don't give a damn."

Before the man could respond, the director hung up on him. Sade snapped her mouth shut a second time and exhaled slowly through her nose. Her boss had brass balls for damn sure. Whatever was happening in Chicago made the hairs on the back of her neck stand up—not a good sign. She might not have an ounce of magical blood but given the marks placed on her as a toddler and the environment she'd grown up in, she figured some of the magic had rubbed off. Her gut was seldom wrong. At the moment, it scribbled a paperback novel of warnings and dire predictions and relayed the rough draft to her brain.

The Old Man leaned back in his chair, which creaked as he rocked back to the very limits of its hydraulics. He steepled his fingers across his massive chest and then tapped his forefingers against his bottom lip, staring at Sade the entire time. Like a schoolgirl called to the principal's office, she squirmed in her chair.

"We have a situation."

Marquis D. Sade

SADE MUTTERED THE name scrawled on the cardboard sign under her breath. This whole trip was shaping up to be a Charlie Foxtrot—military slang for a cluster fuck. She leaned against the wall of the airport concourse at Chicago O'Hare as the passengers who'd deplaned with her surged forward. She'd wait for the tide to ebb and used the time to study the rookie agent holding the sign. The kid shifted his weight from foot to foot, scanning each face as they walked up the concourse. Yeah, he was an FBI agent. She could tell by the ill-fitting black suit, white shirt, and the tiny bit of toilet paper stuck to his throat where he'd cut himself shaving. The problem was Richie Cunningham looked older than this kid. Hell, Opie Taylor looked older.

"Absolute cluster fuck." Two men and a woman cut their eyes in her direction even though she'd muttered. When the crowd thinned to a trickle, she walked up and stopped right in front of the kid.

"You!" Sade stabbed her finger at the redhead. He glanced around, blinking rapidly as his prominent Adam's apple bobbed convulsively. "Yeah, you. Richie Cunningham."

"My name isn't Richie," he stammered, still swallowing hard.

"Could have fooled me." She rolled her eyes. On the flight from DC to Chicago, she'd been crammed between the used car salesman from hell—figuratively, not literally—and the little old lady from Pasadena returning from a visit with her 2.5 perfect grandchildren. Sade was not in the mood for fun and frolic and she'd played this game before. Some poor rookie agent drew the short straw, which sentenced him to chauffeur duty. She had a reputation in the Bureau and with a name like hers, the pranksters just couldn't resist.

"Let's go," she ordered, striding past him. Her booted heels clacked on the scarred linoleum of the concourse. When no answering echo of footsteps followed, she glanced back over her shoulder. Like a sculptor's bad joke, the rookie stood rooted to the floor—Alfred E. Neuman in gargoyle guise. "I'm Marquis, kid. Special Agent Sade Marquis." She snapped the words out. He blinked. And blushed. Color suffused his face, clashing with the carrot-top red of his hair. She sighed. "Heaven help me, but you're my ride."

She pointed her chin at the stupid piece of cardboard he still held up in front of his chest. "Lose the sign." Sade didn't believe it possible for him to get redder but he did. He stammered all the way through the terminal and out to the plain-Jane black sedan parked in a No Parking Zone. There were perks to being a federal agent—not many, granted, but a few. The uniformed airport cop standing guard over the sedan was one of them. Not all feds drove around in shiny black SUVs with tinted windows despite what

TV portrayed. In the real world, they drove four-door sedans with cheap, plastic seat covers.

The uniform reached to open and hold the passenger door for Sade. Something about her demeanor, or the arched eyebrow she raised, made him nervous. He backed up about three feet and stayed out of her way. She threw the little wheeled weekender in the back seat. The rookie still carried the damn sign. He put it in the car. Carefully. Like it was precious or something.

"I told you to lose the sign, Richie."

He straightened his shoulders and actually had the balls to retort, "It's government property."

"Oh, right. Yeah. We all know you can't just throw away government property—not without doing paperwork, in triplicate, and then it's voted on by Congress. Even if it's just a piece of cardboard scribbled with magic marker."

Sade wasn't sure which worried her the most—the fact he wouldn't throw the sign away or the fact he didn't recognize sarcasm. Raising her eyes to the sky in supplication for patience, she climbed into the front seat. The passenger side. She'd already embarrassed the kid enough. She wouldn't give fodder to the motor pool troglodytes. It was bad enough the kid looked like Howdy Doody. They didn't need any more reason to make fun of him.

Chicago just before noon was like any other big city—busy. She settled back and let the kid drive, hiding her white knuckles and the bracing of her feet against the floorboard by checking the file she'd brought with her from DC The kid was a meticulous driver—turn signal on by the middle of the block, gentle rolling stops with plenty of space between the sedan and whatever vehicle stopped in front of it, a speed five miles less than the posted limit. Sade hoped to hell Ritchie had more than his learner's permit and that she wasn't his licensed driver. What the hell was the Bureau coming to?

Chapter Three

SNAFU

WE HAVE A SITUATION. That's Old Man speak for the shit has hit the fan and things have gone to hell in a handbasket. In Sade's life, that meant Situation Normal—All Fucked Up. His words to her in Washington resonated as she opened the case notes. The file reminded her of a bad *Dragnet* episode: Just the facts, ma'am. Cynthia Celeste "CeeCee" Adams, congressional aide to Senator McMahon, had been found dead. Cause of death? Exsanguination—her body had been drained of blood. Initial DNA testing hadn't come back yet.

If people had known about vampires back in the day, there would have been no need to develop DNA testing. A vampire's palate can't be fooled. Not when it comes to blood and genetic typing. Her godfather, Mathias, knew from the barest taste of her blood that his accountant, William Marquis, was her father. That her mother, Tracie, had been the mistress of King Oberon at the time of her birth didn't help matters. Of course, the King and Queen of Glitter Land weren't satisfied with the outcome. Oberon and Titania, the most royal of the royal Seelie Court. Faeries. Sade's life would be so much simpler without the fae mucking about in it.

"Can you go any slower?" She glanced at her driver. He studiously ignored her.

He waited until he stopped the sedan at the next stoplight before cutting his eyes in her direction. "I...uhm...I..." He sucked a deep breath and let it out with a rush as the light changed to green and he eased the car forward.

Sade stared at him. Evidently, he couldn't speak and drive at the same time. Half-tempted to tell him to pull over so she could drive, she resisted. Since she hadn't had the chance on the plane, she still needed to analyze the thin file before she got her briefing with the local field office and Chicago PD. Information about the alleged perpetrator was slim at best. No name, rank, or serial number. Except that he was a vampire. Curious.

Two blocks further on, she was glad she kept her feet braced against the floorboards and her seatbelt tightly fastened. The light turned yellow while the sedan was still in the intersection. Ritchie panicked, especially when a large yellow truck bore down on them from the cross street. He slammed on the brakes and the truck barely scraped by the sedan's bumper. Sade hoped the rookie had a strong sphincter. Amid honks and curses from other drivers, the kid managed to maneuver the car through the intersection. She hoped the steering wheel didn't crack under his death grip.

"Don't drive much do you, kid." It wasn't a question. Sade sighed as he stammered without producing a coherent reply. "How the hell did you ever get through the academy?" she muttered.

Back in her day, agent trainees competed tooth and nail for slots. She closed her eyes for a moment as memories intruded. Slim. Caleb always called her Slim, especially when he joined her class at the FBI academy. And he had Bogart down pat. *You know how to whistle, don't you, Slim? You just put your lips together and blow.* Their code phrase for trouble.

Her heart felt like a block of stone in her chest. Sade would never admit to anyone how much she missed Caleb. Foster brother. Best friend. Guard dog. Werewolf. Squaring her shoulders, she looked up to discover Ritchie pulling into the drive of the Chicago Hyatt. The sedan jerked to a stop under the portico at the front entrance as the kid tapped the brakes unevenly.

Once the car stopped rocking, a man in a green livery coat opened the door. When she didn't move, he stared down at her, his face pinched and his expression sour. He appeared more than a little perturbed when she didn't jump right out.

Sade peered down her nose at Richie. "This isn't the FBI building."

The rookie agent looked uncomfortable and refused to meet her gaze. He actually raised his hand and ran his finger around the collar of his dress shirt as if trying to loosen it. "I…uhm. Well, you see—"

"Spit it out, Richie."

"My name isn't Richie. It's David Michaels."

Sade blinked. Was the kid finally growing a pair? She arched one eyebrow, waiting to see if there was more bravado to come.

"I was told to bring you here, that you have a reservation, and you're to wait in your room until Agent Burrows calls you."

Her expression never changed as she mulled over the possibilities presented by David's declaration. A – The local boys were pissed she'd been called in and were trying to stall her; B – The local boys were relieved she was here and were trying to keep that fact a secret; C – Someone highly placed in government circles was involved; D – None of the above; E – All of the above. The Hyatt was a little swank for government rates and she certainly hadn't made reservations. Sade wondered who was picking up the tab.

The doorman, uncharacteristically rude for his position, snorted. "Lady? You getting out or what?"

"Or what," Sade retorted. Her gaze rested on David again. "If I get out to check in, you're going to take off like a scared rabbit." She watched his Adam's apple bob as he gulped. Two and two weren't adding up to four. If the locals thought she would sit back and wait, they had another thing coming. She glanced up at the doorman. "My bag is in the back seat. I'll take the laptop case." Glancing at David, she muttered. "You, I'll deal with later." He gulped again, his face paling to the point his freckles stood out in stark contrast. Sade didn't feel bad about scaring him.

She swung her legs out and the doorman scuttled to get out of her way. As she stood up, she stared down at him. Almost six feet tall in bare feet, in heels she made most people look short. The man stuttered something that faintly resembled, "Yes, ma'am, right away, ma'am." He snatched her bag, stumbled to the front door, and grabbed the handle, all but pushing her inside.

The desk clerk, an older man with distinguished silver hair at the temples, was the model of a modern major general. He stood behind the marble battlements of the counter, framed by an impressive skyline etched in glass forming a backdrop to the reception desk. He checked her in with an economy of effort. Despite her insistence she could manage her meager luggage, a bellboy took the bag from the doorman and waited. Expecting a message to be waiting, she asked. Twice. So much for being contacted, right? Answer A looked more and more like the sure bet.

Sade and the bellboy stepped off the elevator into the Regency Club. She looked around, stunned. Oh yeah, Uncle Sam definitely wasn't picking up the tab for this trip. On the penthouse level of the West Tower of the Hyatt, this special little enclave sported its own concierge, continental breakfast, hors d'oeuvres in the evening, and late night desserts. She listened to the bellboy's spiel with just enough interest to realize she could graze up here. She hated eating alone—restaurant or home, it didn't matter. Her room was a king in earth tones and quiet. It would do. No messages waited there either. She tipped the bellboy to get rid of him and tossed her bag and laptop case on the bed. Pushing open the curtains, Sade stared out at the cityscape. Her perp would be down for the count until sunset. Somebody didn't want her snooping around the FBI offices and now she wondered if Chicago PD even knew she was in town. She had way too many questions for her peace of mind and the time for answers was long overdue.

She hit speed dial number one on her cell phone.

"Director Bailey's office, Alice Cooper speaking."

Alice's curt tone reassured Sade as she checked in. "I'm at the Chicago Hyatt."

"Oh? A bit ritzy for your per diem, Agent Marquis."

"That's what I thought. My ride dropped me off here. I had reservations, only I didn't make them."

"I had you booked at the Holiday Inn Express. A moment…"

Sade listened to keys clicking and the occasional "hrm" followed by a short intake of breath.

"Curious."

The hairs on the back of Sade's neck bristled. Anything Alice found curious got her investigative antennae quivering. "How so?"

"Your account at the Hyatt was paid in cash, with a large deposit. Your reservation is open-ended. No check-out date."

Her brow wrinkled as she considered the possibilities. "Very curious. I'm headed to the field office. Tell the Old Man I'll be in touch." Sade broke the connection and headed out.

Stepping outside under the front portico, the cold wind hit her like a blast of liquid nitrogen, despite her long, fur-lined, black leather coat. She found her gloves stuffed in one pocket and pulled them on. A different doorman hailed her a cab. Traffic was a bitch but she managed not to shoot the cab driver just because. He let her out at the FBI office building on Roosevelt. She paid and he took off. They both survived the encounter.

The guards at the front doors eyed her badge and ID, exchanged suspicious glances, but cleared her to enter with her weapon still on her hip. She'd done this dance before, so she ignored them as an elevator dinged open. Without appearing to rush, she stepped on-board and doors whispered closed behind her.

After an express ride, she stepped off and directly into a waiting area. Looking like a cardinal hopping along a fence, the receptionist stood behind her desk, anticipating Sade's arrival. Sade figured the guards called up the moment she stepped on the elevator. Without breaking stride, she headed down a side hall, leaving the pert little brunette wearing a red blazer to scramble after her.

"Wait. Wait! Please wait!" The receptionist wailed in Sade's wake, her voice rising in pitch and volume like an air-raid siren.

Sade read the names on the doors she passed. *Edgar R. Burrows.* This was the place. She didn't knock. She opened the door, stepped in, and shut it in the brunette's face. The man behind the desk looked disgruntled and sloppy, his tie halfway undone, shirtsleeves rolled up his beefy forearms, and his greasy brown hair mussed as if he'd continuously pushed his fingers through the short thatch.

"Get the hell out of my office."

"Nice to see you too, Ed." For a split second, Sade considered sinking into one of the chairs in front of the desk. She liked having the height advantage, though, so remained standing. "You know why I'm here."

"Big fucking deal. If the Old Man had called me first, I could have saved you the trip." Burrows pushed back in his chair, glaring up at her. She didn't even blink. "Look, we have the perp. It's a slam-dunk case. I closed the file the minute they had St. John in custody. The chick was found in his apartment. Drained. He's guilty."

Now she blinked, one corner of her mouth lifting into a snarl. "The file isn't closed until I say so. That's the way it works. I want the Bureau's file, any files Chicago PD might have, and I want to interview this *alleged* perpetrator." Her voice curled around the word "alleged," emphasizing it.

"I'm telling you—"

"No." She pitched her voice low but her tone cut across Burrow's, stopping him cold. "I'm telling you. I'm in charge. You want to argue, you have the director's number." No agent who'd been called on the carpet by the Old Man ever wanted to repeat the experience. Sade knew for a fact Burrows had been there enough for permanent rug burns. She took two steps, put her hands flat on his desk, and leaned toward him. "Tell little Miss Sunshine out there in the hall to get the files ready to go. Then call Chicago PD and tell them I'll be interviewing the suspect as soon as the sun goes down. I want to meet with their investigator and whichever DA filed the charges by mid-morning tomorrow. We clear?"

Burrows sputtered and spit. He bitched and moaned under his breath, but he finally nodded curtly. "We're clear. Now get the hell out of my office."

Sade turned on her heel, and three short strides later, jerked open the door. She didn't bother to hide her smile as she caught a flash of red darting around a corner. She wondered how long she'd have to cool her heels before the case file appeared.

Ten minutes later, the file tucked under her arm, she pushed through the doors of the glass and steel building housing the FBI offices. A sudden burst of mid-afternoon sunlight bounced off the windows before scudding clouds muffled it. She huddled deeper into her coat, the cold wind's bite vicious. A cab pulled up to the curb and stopped, though she hadn't raised a hand to summon one. Sade climbed into the back seat and answered the cabby's look of "Where to?" through the rear view mirror with an internal shrug.

"Head toward the Hyatt. I'll let you know if something changes." She opened the file, flipped through a couple of pages. "Scratch that. University of Chicago."

Curiouser and curiouser. Turned out her murder suspect was a college professor. Dr. Kristian St. John. Vampire. How the hell did a vampire live with that name? Did the other vampires make fun of him at the Conclave? She kept reading until the driver slowed and jerked the wheel toward the curb. The winter slush sloshed around the vehicle's tires as Sade slid out in front of the University's Quadrangle.

She walked around to get a feel for the place before finding a bench sheltered in the lee of a building and sat down. She had no real idea why she'd come here. A vague idea niggled at the back of her conscience but she couldn't coax it into the light of day. Staring up at the grotesques and gargoyles on the buildings around her, she battled feelings of loneliness and isolation.

"I miss them." The wind snatched her whispered words and drove them like snowflakes in a blizzard. Chicago was called the Windy City for a reason and sitting there huddled in the cold, its gusts chilled her to the bone. "Damn. It's colder than the balls on a brass monkey at the North Pole." Her breath puffed out with each word, framing them in ice crystals. Better to concentrate on the frigid weather than the reason her heart felt frozen. She didn't want to admit she missed both Caleb and Roman, though it was true. She'd been with them her entire life, her rebellion when joining the Bureau notwithstanding.

She looked up as one of the gargoyles moved, stretching his wings just a little, and her heart quickened for a beat or two then returned to normal. Not Roman. She didn't recognize the creature perched on the building but she blew him a kiss anyway. He almost fell off his perch. Chilled to the bone, she stood and headed toward the street to catch a cab back to the Hyatt. She still wasn't sure why she'd stopped there, other than to feel nostalgic for old friends.

Back at the hotel, she tossed her coat on the foot of the bed, stripped down, and ducked into the shower. Hot water and steam went a long way toward warming up the bone-deep chill. Before she could get dressed for a visit to the Cook County Detention Facility, the room phone rang.

"Marquis."

"Did you enjoy your afternoon, Agent?" The disembodied voice on the other end of the phone line sounded way too sure of himself for a stranger.

Okay, so maybe that gargoyle at the University of Chicago wasn't a fluke. Maybe he'd been keeping an eye on her after all. She was a very curious cat now, though a little voice in the back of her mind whispered something about curiosity and dead cats.

"Enough." Her reply remained intentionally cryptic.

"Did you happen to bring evening wear with you, my dear?"

Sade laughed, the sound loud and raucous. "Excuse me?" She sputtered the question through her laughter.

"The question is simple enough, Miss Marquis." He sounded affronted by her reaction.

"*Agent* Marquis and I'm here on assignment. That means work not fun."

"I strongly suggest you acquire formal attire and be downstairs by eight o'clock sharp."

Sade bit back her initial retort of *fuck you*. Swallowing the expletive, she turned on the charm. "Thanks, but I already have a date—with a suspect."

"Ah, our esteemed Professor St. John," he gloated. "He is innocent, you know. Just as you suspect." The mystery man sounded as smug as Burrows had when he'd insisted the vampire was guilty. "Though no one will ever be able to prove him so." The caller's voice took on a hard edge. "Eight o'clock, Agent Marquis. You will not see St. John otherwise."

The jerk beat her to the punch—he hung up first. She hadn't worn a formal gown since ball when she debuted as a debutante and Sade debated about wearing one now. However, the mystery man on the phone intrigued her enough she was half tempted to meet his deadline. Dragging a brush through her hair, she eyed her reflection. "Oh, who the hell am I kidding?" She snagged the room phone, dialed the concierge, told him her vital statistics, and that she needed a black evening gown and heels ASAP.

"Very good, madam."

The concierge broke the connection and she shuddered. Damn. He sounded so much like Hoskins, Mathias's butler, her skin crawled. She and Hoskins had issues—stemming all the way back to her childhood. Opening the file on St. John, Sade only read a page before the scudding clouds of the Chicago winter lured her eyes to the window. A storm had been brewing that day too, and she'd had trouble concentrating on her schoolwork. When her tutor threw her puppy, Caleb, out of the room, she'd been hurt in the struggle. The damn butler didn't help her. She shook the memories out of her head. She had no time for the past, even though it intruded at every opportunity. If she let it.

Sade rubbed her temples. Why the hell was she missing Caleb so much? He was the one who'd gone feral. Turning on the desk lamp, she concentrated on the file.

"What the fuck?" She blinked and reread the paragraph. CeeCee Adams had a boyfriend. Richard Dandridge III. And the autopsy report revealed something *very* interesting. Before she could get a complete grip on that idea, someone knocked on her door.

"Delivery, Ms. Marquis."

Chapter Four

Just Blow

AT 7:59, Sade stepped off the elevator to the strains of "You're So Vain" piped in over the hotel's sound system. The irony wasn't lost on her as every male in the lobby stopped and stared, their eyes following her progress to the front doors. A doorman hustled to open the doors and then scurried out to the luxury car waiting under the portico.

"Your car, Miss Marquis." He gestured toward the vehicle and all but bowed.

She eyed the black and silver Rolls Royce Phantom. "Yeah, I wish."

While the doorman held open the back door of the car, Sade took her time eyeing the driver and checking the back compartment to make sure no one hid there. This escapade tallied in the Really Dumb Idea column since she had no clue who had so imperiously summoned her. A magick wouldn't be dumb enough to mess with her. One, they couldn't hide what they were and two, Mathias and Oberon would not be happy campers. Mother Nature might be a bitch when pissed, but it took a true idiot to cross a master vampire and the High King of the Fae.

She slid into the back seat and settled a dress bag next to her. The concierge had done a bang up job on the dress—a sleek little Vera Wang number with a single shoulder strap and a pencil skirt with a side slit that would allow easy access to her weapon. Sade looked up and met the driver's eyes in his rear view mirror. He looked down his nose at her, which was quite a trick in a car mirror. Hoskins could do it too, so maybe it was a retainer-to-the-rich-and-famous thing.

Without turning around, he archly informed, "You are underdressed, madam."

"No shit, Sherlock. What was your first clue?" Sade stared at him through the mirror. The man actually sniffed at her. "You're taking me to Cook County Detention Center and don't spare the horses, James."

He sniffed again, still glaring. "My instructions are to drive you to the Drake Hotel."

Her expression remained noncommittal. "Fine. Head to the Drake. I can catch a cab from there back to the jail. I told your boss I was going to interview Kristian St. John first."

The chauffeur made a phone call while the fancy car idled and blocked the drive at the Hyatt, much to the doorman's consternation. After snapping his cell phone shut, he put the Rolls in gear and smoothly pulled into traffic. Sade leaned back against the soft-as-buttercream-icing leather seats and chuckled. She couldn't wait to pull up at the jail in this baby. The fourth time she caught the driver scowling at her through the mirror, she sat forward and rustled the dress bag.

"I promise I have a little black dress in here, James. And I promise to be wearing it before we get to the Drake. None of the other chauffeurs will make fun of you because your passenger is socially inept."

Her sarcasm was obviously lost on him. Sade wondered if she was losing her touch or if the men of Chicago were simply that dense. She shook the bag again to emphasize her point. Jewel tones were all the rage in evening gowns but a girl could never go wrong with a little black dress, except maybe at her debut. Sade couldn't keep the sardonic smirk off her face. She still remembered that night and oddly enough, most of the memories were fond ones.

Still grumbling, the driver parked the Rolls in front of the detention center. Sade got out and headed in before he made a move to get out. "Just blow, Slim," she muttered, preparing for the upcoming interview.

Inside, a bespectacled corrections officer stared at her from behind his wall of bulletproof glass. He studied her ID, her badge, and then studied the ID again. With his thick glasses and thin countenance, the guard looked like a fish in an aquarium. Sade stood on the other side staring at him the entire time. He stared back, unblinking.

"You can't see him until his lawyer gets here."

She tapped her ID on the glass, drawing his eyes. "This says I don't have to wait." She'd been in the Cook County Detention Center before. She knew her way around.

Her long legs ate up the distance of the hallway that led to the holding cells. She didn't wait for the elevator, instead taking the stairs down to the "extraordinary prisoner" holding area. The guard on duty looked up and started to stop her until she flashed her badge.

"Don't even think about it," she barked as she brushed past him, preempting any protest he might have made. She left him flustered and a bit awed in her wake.

"THE DEVIL TO PAY INDEED," the man in the glass-sided cell muttered darkly. At the moment, his voice was the only dark thing about the place. The cell had been illuminated by halogen lights since his incarceration three nights ago. It was bad enough he was on display like a freak under glass 24/7 but his captors seemed to think they could wear him down with the constant bombardment of radiance. The mundanes never had figured it out. Light wasn't a vampire's Achilles' heel, although the sun's radiation seared them like raw steak on a grill. Being soulless, the dark nurtured and consoled them, gave them life. Daylight simply illuminated the secrets he and those like him preferred to hide. The sun sucked their life away, made them weak. Humans were afraid of things that went bump in the night and so slept away their fears during the darkest hours. Vampires slept away the day.

Despite their fragility and occasional stupidity, Kristian St. John actually liked humans. For the most part. He would, however, exclude present company from that assertion. An armed guard remained on duty at all times with orders to keep his back to the prisoner so he couldn't pull any of those nasty vampire mind tricks, like hypnotizing the guard to unlock the cell. Sinjen wasn't that stupid. He remembered the days of hiding and persecution right after The Big Rip all too well. And he was old enough to remember the Dark Days a millennium before. If he did escape and the authorities caught up to him, they'd wait until daylight and stake him where he slept.

His fondness for humanity had led him to academia and teaching—among other things. Under the flurry of laws passed in the wake of The Big Rip, as the magicks referred to it, a vampire could only feed from a willing donor or make a withdrawal from a blood bank. The role of college professor put Sinjen in the right place to cross paths with lots of willing donors. His position, and the honorary PhD that accompanied it, meant a great deal to him. As an ancient, he taught history from firsthand experience. He always had waiting lists for his classes despite them being taught after sundown. Knowledge was important. He merely wanted to pass his along.

To while away the time of his incarceration, he'd been soliloquizing Shakespeare's plays during his waking periods. Once a frequent and honored guest at the Globe Theater whenever the Bard previewed a new play, several of the leading actors at the time had been willing playmates after the performances.

"And now, my children," Sinjen murmured, "Old Scratch comes collecting."

Leaning his hands against the thick glass of his cage, Sinjen closed his eyes for a moment letting the words form on his tongue. As each one spilled out, he savored and tasted it. "To be or not to be, that is the question," he began in a whispered tone. "Whether 'tis nobler in minds of men to suffer the slings and arrows of outrageous fortune, or to take arms against a sea of troubles, and by opposing end them?" The staccato tap of heels on concrete broke his concentration. He lifted his head.

Sinjen was aware of his looks—tall, dark, and handsome in what might be considered a clichéd Hollywood way. Add the innate sexiness all vampires shared and there wasn't a female within a hundred miles who'd be immune. At least not until the tall, dark-haired beauty with the bottle-green eyes burst through the door and stalked toward his glass cube. He "sat up and took notice" in all the wrong places—places that should have been long dead. Without the kick-start of a fresh feeding, his cock shouldn't respond. Sinjen looked down. And smiled.

He watched her approach and appreciated the abrupt way she brushed past the guard. The man stammered an order to stop but she never broke stride.

"Special Agent Marquis, FBI."

Her voice washed over him, deep and warm like an intimate caress. Once again, he marveled at her build. If they stood toe-to-toe, she would be almost as tall as Sinjen himself. Curious, he glanced at her feet. The woman wore heeled boots but those heels weren't extravagant. Letting his gaze trail up the long length of her, he determined she would be close to six feet tall even in stocking feet. Streaks of mahogany highlighted her dark hair as it lay in loose waves across her shoulders. Dressed completely in black—silk and leather from head to foot—she was the stuff of Goth wet dreams. Something shiny fastened on her belt caught his eye. The gold shield hanging at her waist elicited a quirked eyebrow.

His voice deepened and he drank in the sight of this woman as he told her, "To die, to sleep no more; and by a sleep to say we end the heartache and the thousand natural shocks that flesh is heir to, 'tis a consummation devoutly to be wish'd. To die, to sleep; to sleep, perchance to dream. Aye, there's the rub; for in that sleep of death what dreams may come when we have shuffled off this mortal coil, must give us pause."

The vampire's voice was like hot caramel dripping over a scoop of ice cream—slowly, inexorably coating that cold mound, pushing sweet, melted cream before its deliberate seduction as he emphasized all the right words. His eyes bored into hers but Sade met his gaze dead on and it was St. John who blinked first. A small smile teased the corner of her lips as she stepped closer to the glass. She tilted her chin just a hair. "There's the respect that makes calamity of so long life," she murmured. "For who would bear the whips and scorns of time, the oppressor's wrong, the proud man's contume-ly." She glanced down and changed a teasing smile into a knowing one as she continued, "The pangs of despised love."

"The law's delay," Sinjen asserted, rocked back on his mental heels, sur-prised and delighted the woman knew her Shakespeare. He looked her over from head to foot once more. She didn't flinch, didn't even blink. He acknowledged her with a slight nod of his head. "The insolence of office and the spurns that patient merit of the unworthy takes, when he himself might his quietus make with a bare bodkin?"

The nearest guard moved a step closer, watching from the corner of his eye. Sade ignored him, concentrating on the vampire in the glass cage. Her eyes narrowed. *Oh, this guy is very, very good.* A shiver skittered down her spine as he continued in that same hot caramel voice—a voice that left no doubt as to the directions of his thoughts.

Capturing her gaze with his, Sinjen persisted, intrigued by this turn of events. "Who would fardels bear, to grunt and sweat under a weary life, but that the dread of something after death, the undiscover'd country from whose bourn no traveller returns, puzzles the will and makes us rather bear those ills we have than fly to others that we know not of?"

She continued staring into his eyes and recognized the moment he per-ceived who she was—by name and reputation. His eyes turned to sapphires, glittering midnight blue.

Despite identifying her, he never missed a beat. "Thus conscience does make cowards of us all; and thus the native hue of resolution is sicklied o'er with the pale cast of thought, and enterprises of great pith and moment with this regard their currents turn awry, and lose the name of action." His nostrils flared slightly. "Soft you now! The fair Ophelia! Nymph, in thy orisons be all my sins remember'd."

She was willing to play this scene out. The hidden meanings and innu-endos flew fast and furious without fear of discovery from either of the guards standing flat-footed by the door, still in shock from her brusque treatment of them, or anyone else who might be watching. They were under surveillance by video cameras but she doubted there was an English Lit major among the guards. To discover where this conversation was headed, Sade would play Ophelia and she would listen closely to St. John's insinuations. "Good my lord. How does your honour for this many a day?"

With a little quirk of his eyebrow, Sinjen continued. "I humbly thank you; well, well, well."

So he hadn't been abused. So far. Sade remained true to the Bard's words. "My lord, I have remembrances of yours, that I have longed long to re-deliver; I pray you, now receive them."

Sinjen shook his head almost imperceptibly, believing they were indeed reading from the same script. "No, not I; I never gave you aught."

She blinked slowly and knitted her brows. This was no game of seduction played by a master. This war of Shakespeare's words had become her interrogation. She stared at him for a long moment. Had he killed the girl? She had doubts beyond the hints from her mystery caller. Doubly intrigued, she pushed a bit. "My honour'd lord, you know right well you did; and, with them, words of so sweet breath composed as made the things more rich. Their perfume lost, take these again; for to the noble mind rich gifts wax poor when givers prove unkind. There, my lord."

Snorting, his face a mask of disdain, Sinjen actually laughed. "Ha, ha! Are you honest?"

"My lord?" Sade pitched her voice in such a way to keep true to the scene and to confirm what he was asking.

"Are you fair?" He stared at her unblinking.

Sade nodded, the merest dip of her chin. "What means your lordship?"

Intrigued and relieved, Sinjen relaxed the muscles in his face, softening the hard planes. "That if you be honest and fair, your honesty should admit no discourse to your beauty."

Sade's brain rifled through possible meanings. "Could beauty, my lord, have better commerce than with honesty?" She kept her face blank even as her brain pushed and shoved the facts to make them fit the narrative. Why had CeeCee Adams been in his apartment? If she'd been murdered by humans, why set up the vampire? Sade had too many questions and not nearly enough answers.

Sinjen lowered his voice to a whisper soft exhalation before hardening it. "Aye, truly. For the power of beauty will sooner transform honesty from what it is to a bawd than the force of honesty can translate beauty into his likeness. This was sometime a paradox, but now the time gives it proof. I did love you once." The word *proof* tasted sour on his tongue.

Sade nodded. "Indeed, my lord, you made me believe so." She emphasized the word *believe*.

Shaking his head, he turned partially away from her. "You should not have believed me; for virtue cannot so inoculate our old stock but we shall relish of it. I loved you not."

Sade took a long breath, considering the possible meanings of that passage. She continued the scene in a soft voice. "I was the more deceived."

Pushing off the glass, Sinjen whirled and stormed to the far side of the cell. He turned back, his face a mask of distrust. "Get thee to a nunnery! Why wouldst thou be a breeder of sinners? I am myself indifferent honest; but yet I could accuse me of such things that it were better my mother had not borne me." In three strides, Sinjen was back across the cell and staring at her through the glass. "I am very proud, revengeful, ambitious, with more offenses at my beck than I have thoughts to put them in, imagination to give them shape, or time to act them in. What should such fellows as I do crawling between earth and heaven? We are arrant knaves, all. Believe none of us. Go thy ways to a nunnery." He paused for several beats, his eyes boring into hers. "Where's your father?"

Sade pondered his actions for a moment. She gnawed on her lower lip then continued the scene, hoping she would be able to figure out *which* father Sinjen referred to—the Old Man, Mathias, or perhaps her biological father. "At home, my lord." Which was true for all of them.

"Let the doors be shut upon him, that he may play the fool nowhere but in his own house. Farewell." St. John turned his back to her.

Her gut twinged so she took a slow breath before answering. "O, help him, you sweet heavens!" Sade whispered, unsure of who she meant—Mathias or St. John. The Old Man didn't belong in this conversation.

Glancing over his shoulder, his voice returned to the decadent tones he'd used at Sade's appearance. "If thou dost marry, I'll give thee this plague for thy dowry: be thou as chaste as ice, as pure as snow, thou shalt not escape calumny. Get thee to a nunnery, go. Farewell. Or, if thou wilt needs marry, marry a fool. For wise men know well enough what monsters you make of them. To a nunnery, go, and quickly too. Farewell."

She shook her head from side to side, the movement slow and deliberate. "O heavenly powers, restore him!"

Sinjen kept his back turned and his face averted, fighting the need to see her, to touch her. "I have heard of your paintings too, well enough," he murmured before whirling to look at her again, unable to resist. "God has given you one face, and you make yourselves another. You jig, you amble, and you lisp, and nickname God's creatures, and make your wantonness your ignorance. Go, I'll speak no more on it; it hath made me mad. I say, we will have no more marriages. Those that are married already, all but one, shall live; the rest shall keep as they are. To a nunnery, go."

Turning away again, Sinjen, with all the boneless grace of the magical races, sank down on his cot. The interview was over. Hamlet had exited upon that line, in the play and here as well.

TWO MEN WATCHED the scene unfold from the darkened space of the video control booth. "Fuckin' Shakespeare," one growled. "They're quotin' fuckin' Shakespeare to each other."

"Yes," the second man agreed, his voice hushed. "Very curious indeed. You are sure they have never met before?"

The first man nodded. "Yeah. I'm sure. My snitches said the two vampires clashed about 1812. And then in the thirties. St. John and DeVries haven't crossed paths since. I can't find anyone who can put the bitch and St. John in the same place at the same time."

The second man slipped out, a cell phone to his ear. The first one flipped off the sound and glowered at the scene on the video monitor.

"Fuckin' fangers," he snarled. "Shoulda staked the bastard when I had the chance."

SADE RODE THE elevator this time. As the doors opened, she came face-to-face with a blast from the past. The startled fae stared at her.

"Are you the FBI agent who just violated my client's rights?" When she simply stared at him, he continued. "I am Robin Goodfellow IV of Winkyn, Blynken, and Noddingham, attorneys at law. How dare you question my client, Agent Marquis!"

She blinked. He'd pronounced her name Mar-CUE-is. He had no clue who she was because the guard who called couldn't pronounce her name. She smiled, knowing exactly who he was. Dressed in a tux, he tried his best to look down his nose at her. In his current glamour, though, Sade was at least a head taller. She wondered where he'd been headed before rushing to the jail. He was off balance and she was glad to have any advantage over Puck. Yes, *that* Puck, aka Robin Goodfellow, Peasblossom Pucke, and Will Wisp among other *noms de guerre*. What was the world coming to when someone like Puck could pass a bar exam and become an attorney?

He launched into a tirade, spouting a case citation and then a heap more in shotgun fashion, evidently hoping to impress her with his command of legalese. Puck also tried to glamour her. Yeah, like that was going to work.

Checking her watch, she tapped her booted foot in a not-too-subtle display of impatience. She had a date with a mysterious voice that had truly piqued the curiosity of her particular cat. She was already aware of the life expectancy of inquisitive felines. Even so, Sade wasn't overly concerned about her safety. She stared at Puck, wondering how long it would take him to remember her face. Granted, she'd been about twelve the last time they'd met, and back then she had frizzy hair. And fat cheeks. Hell, she'd been encased in baby fat. Her own mother wouldn't recognize her these days and she'd seen Tracie far more recently than Puck. But then again, Puck was fae. He should know better.

When he finally sputtered to a stop, she brushed past him. "I dare because I can, Puck." Sade grinned, a momentary curl of her lips, as she heard the patter of expensive Italian shoes tapping up the hall behind her.

Puck grabbed her arm to stop her. "Who the hell are you?" he hissed.

She snickered. "The last time I saw you, a gargoyle named Roman was tossing your pansy ass out my godfather's front door."

"Oh, shit." Puck groaned and slapped his forehead à la the V8 commercial. "I didn't recognize you."

Laughing, Sade let him stew for a moment. "You feel so damned superior to us mundanes you didn't bother to actually find out who I am after you asked." She shook her head and made *tsking* noises. "You're slipping, Puck." Without waiting for his reply, she headed to the front entrance and pushed out the door into the frigid Chicago night. She had a ball to attend and she felt a lot more like one of the wicked stepsisters than Cinderella.

Chapter Five

Three Hour Tour

SHE STEPPED INTO the backseat of the Rolls and bathed in its shadows. Without looking back at her, the driver put the luxurious car into gear and its engine purred with the touch of his foot on the accelerator. Intermittent ambient light from streetlights and storefronts coupled with the occasional glance from the driver drew a sharp order from Sade.

"Eyes front."

Black Vera Wang replaced black slacks and blazer, stilettos for boots. A quick upsweep of her hair and a strategically placed hair stick held the dark mass in place. Once she was presentable, she leaned her head back, closed her eyes and finished Hamlet's Act III in her head.

> "O, what a noble mind is here o'erthrown! The courtier's, soldier's, scholar's, eye, tongue, sword. The expectancy and rose of the fair state. The glass of fashion and the mould of form, the observed of all observers, quite, quite down! And I, of ladies most deject and wretched, that suck'd the honey of his music vows. Now see that noble and most sovereign reason, like sweet bells jangled, out of tune and harsh. That unmatch'd form and feature of blown youth blasted with ecstasy. O, woe is me, to have seen what I have seen, see what I see!"

"O, woe is me, to have seen what I have seen, see what I see!" The words tripped off her tongue and stuck in her head. If she hadn't known better, the Bard had been talking about her. Even though she studied the dude in both high school and college, she still didn't fully understand him. She'd wondered a time or two if the man wasn't more than he seemed. He knew way too much about the fae, for one. And what was the deal with the three hags in MacBeth?

She could go toe-to-toe with Professor Fang in the quote department, but she was far from being a Shakespearean scholar. She had a photographic memory. All she had to do was read something once, or see it or hear it. Ever after, that bit of information knocked around in her memory waiting for a game of Trivial Pursuit, Jeopardy, or a case with clues strung from here to there and back again. She'd once suggested that Shakespeare used his historical plays as political commentary and cited Henry IV, Part II as an example. In that paper, she had the audacity to suggest that Henry had been presented as a surrogate for Elizabeth I.

Her thoughts came full circle. Politics. It all returned to politics. Hamlet, a political pawn, was ultimately murdered. A lecturer in forensics at Quantico once insisted Horatio was the first CSI. Hamlet asked his friend to discover who had murdered him as he lay dying from poison.

The victim in this case was practically drowning in human politics. But why involve the magicks? Why frame an innocent vampire? Her gut insisted Kristian St. John was innocent. He didn't kill CeeCee Adams. He wasn't some newly turned vampire unable to control his urges. The man had been around at least 400 years and if he wasn't a master vampire, she'd eat her leather coat. He wouldn't arbitrarily decide to drain the girl and then leave her in his apartment to be found.

Vampires weren't nearly as bloodthirsty as literature and the modern media painted them. And they didn't go around changing every *victim* either. Sade snorted softly. Really, if vampires changed everyone they fed from, there'd be nothing but vampires by now. Well, vampires and the other magical races, she mentally amended. She didn't even want to contemplate a vampiric elf...or a fae vampire. That was just...wrong. On so many levels.

She watched the street scene rolling past as she continued to nudge the puzzle pieces of St. John's case into some semblance of order. If humans tried to cover their tracks by involving the magicks, they were just plain stupid. When push came to shove, the magicks would come out on top and in charge. Period. Didn't matter that humans outnumbered them about a hundred to one.

While magicks weren't squeamish when it came to taking a life, even a human one, it really wasn't their *modus operandi*. But why Kristian St. John? A vampire who had mainstreamed so well he became a celebrated expert in academic circles didn't seem a logical fall guy. And why pick a high-profile victim? She worked for Senator Alex McMahon. And dated Mayor Dandridge's son. And was having his baby. Or somebody's, according to the autopsy report. Nothing added up.

The case had everything the tabloids or Hollywood could want—drop-dead handsome perp, sweet young virgin—allegedly. He was preternatural. She human. And there was that whole Svengali thing. He had been her professor. From the case notes she'd been able to scan, she'd bet CeeCee took every course St. John taught. Sade made a mental note to grab the papers and see what the local media coverage was like. According to the frantic calls to her boss, the media was all over the story.

She chewed her bottom lip, ignoring the waxy taste of lipstick. There were far too many loose ends to suit her. Did the boyfriend know he'd taken a nosedive into the gene pool, albeit only a brief swim? She made a note to interview him. Alone. Without his father or his father's handlers present. This incident wouldn't be the first time murder was used to cover up sexual misbehavior. She also wanted to know who invited her to this shindig. At one of the oldest luxury hotels left in Chicago.

The Rolls purred to a stop under the portico of The Drake Hotel. The doorman, his uniform and cap reminiscent of an old-time train conductor's, scurried to open the back door. He looked startled when Sade shoved a dress bag into his arms.

"Hold that at the front desk for me," she ordered.

He nodded and stepped back as she emerged. Black heels swung to the pavement, followed by legs—long legs, one bared by the slit in the black silk gown she wore. As she stood, the doorman had to look up to meet her eyes. Without a backward glance, she strode toward the door and kept a straight face as the doorman scrambled to keep up with her and get the door open in time.

Sade swept up the stairs from the street level to the lobby. There were others, couples and singles, in formal attire. She watched them funnel toward a short flight of stairs beyond the elevators then joined the stream. At the top of the stairs everyone turned left to follow the promenade past the Drake Room. In the foyer area between the Palm Court and the entrance to the Gold Coast room, a musician softly played a baby grand piano. Sade hummed a few bars, trying to place the tune. "Someone to watch over me," she sang under her breath. Gershwin. She liked Gershwin.

Most of the crowd moved to the right toward the magnificent formal hall. Joining this queue, Sade studied the people around her. A few were magicks and for a moment, her breath caught in her chest. A dark-haired man with a familiar lope joined a woman standing next to the piano. Caleb? She blinked. No. He wasn't tall enough. The strains of another familiar song, *A Kiss is Just a Kiss*, wafted above the conversational buzz and the clink of glasses. Her vision darkened and that long-ago scene replayed like a first-run movie.

SADE SAT OUTSIDE the rather run-down apartment building, waiting. Caleb had done everything possible to throw her off his trail and she figured if she simply went up and knocked on the door, he'd refuse to answer. Her patience finally paid off just after dusk. She recognized Caleb's lanky gait as he walked up the sidewalk. She stepped out of her rental car and walked toward him.

Stopping dead still, Caleb stared at her as she approached. "Took you long enough," he stated softly when she was close enough to hear him. He pivoted sharply and headed into the building, Sade close on his heels. She wasn't leaving until she got to the bottom of things.

They made the elevator ride in uncomfortable silence. After several jerks and jumps, the elevator ground to a stop and the doors rumbled open. They stepped off and Sade followed Caleb down the hall. He stuck his key in the door and opened it. He stepped inside, leaving her standing in the hallway.

"You wouldn't take my calls and then I got shipped out on assignment," Sade told him, her voice low and urgent. "And you'd moved by the time I got back. It was like you dropped off the face of the earth, Caleb." He hadn't slammed the door in her face so she walked into his apartment. The place was plain and sparsely furnished, much like the man himself. Sade shut the door behind her and leaned up against it. "I was afraid you'd gone feral, Caleb, and you were trying to cover your tracks."

"Feral?" Caleb snorted. He tilted his head as he growled, "Cover my tracks? Jeez, Sade. I'm living in a studio apartment working as a security officer on the graveyard shift. I don't hunt chickens except the ones that come sealed under plastic, and I certainly don't run around naked under the full moon, although I could tell you about some very nice Wiccan folk I met at a party who do. What tracks do I need to cover? I'm not *making* any." He tossed his keys on the small wooden desk shoved under the window and hitched a hip on the corner of it as he stared at her. "What are you doing here?"

Sade sighed. "You're my brother, Caleb. You quit the Bureau and then dropped out of sight. I was worried. I...Dammit, Caleb. What the hell is going on with you anyway?"

Caleb glanced down and to the left. "Watch your language, Sade. Besides, what does it matter? You're the star, the water-walker. You're right where you've always wanted to be. You don't need me pushing you, challenging you, making you be all you can be. It was time for you to be on your own. Time for me to back away."

Sade stared at him like he'd grown a second head. "I don't need you backing away, Caleb. I'm perfectly capable of making my own name, thank you very much. I've never ridden your coattails and I don't intend to start.

Don't leave the Bureau because of some whiney-assed excuse about not holding *me* back."

Caleb shrugged, pushed off the desk and padded into the tiny kitchen. "Fine," he tossed back over his shoulder as he ducked into the fridge. Straightening, he popped the top on a beer and took a long swig. "Then call it not wanting to wear a suit and tie for the rest of my days when I can get along just fine in denim and cotton. I'm an individual, not a nameless buzz-cut *agent*." Caleb leaned against the door jamb between the kitchen and the main room. "Look, Slim, maybe you're into that Fox Mulder and Dana Scully thing, but for once in my life, I don't want to be the Fox to your Hound."

Sade sighed. "Dammit, Caleb. Are you ever going to get over the fact that I made you sleep at the foot of the bed?" She tilted her head and stared at him for a long moment before comprehensive finally dawned. "This isn't about me at all, is it? What's really going on with you?" She pushed away from the door and stepped closer to the man who meant more to her than she wanted to admit.

Caleb narrowed his eyes—that predator look Sade recognized immediately. "It's all about you and me. And there not *being* a you and me for a little while. We're not equals because of how we grew up. I'm not your brother, Sade. If I follow where you go, I'll just be dogging your heels for however long you decide you want to be a spook. I mean, fighting crime? That's straight out of the Girl and Her Dog stories you used to read to me when you had trouble finding friends in grade school. What's really going on is that I need to find my own direction. To *be* wild for once with-out...well, without losing you for good."

Sade stared at him, her mouth opening and closing a few times before she realized she was impersonating a fish gasping it's last breath on the bank of a muddy river. Her cheeks flushed as her temper rose. "Fine," she snapped. "So you don't want to play Lassie running home to tell Dad that Timmy's fallen in the well. That's just...fine." Sade blinked rapidly, fighting the tears welling up behind the sweep of her lashes.

"Just fucking fine," she repeated. "I never asked you to follow me anyway." Turning on her heel, her back ramrod straight, she marched to the door. "No skin off my nose. You want to embrace your wild side, go for it. Who the hell am I to stand in your way?" She paused at the door, one lone tear leaving a thin, silver trail down her cheek. "You'll never lose me, Caleb," she whispered. She jerked open the door and rushed out, all but slamming it behind her.

"Watch your language, Slim," Caleb told the closed door, his voice breaking.

SADE SHOOK HER HEAD, consigning her memories to the cold lump in her chest—the one that always formed when she thought about Caleb. The unknown werewolf and his date moved off. She shuffled along with the fashion parade of plain old human beings. She was tall enough to see the front of the line and the guests filing between metal detectors. The smile on her face turned caustic. This could be fun. She had a Beretta 25 strapped to the inside of her thigh, just above her knee. From the outside, the strap looked like a garter and there had been more than one man who thought he'd found the Promised Land only to realize his ass was about to get filled with lead when she'd worn her weapon this way.

The strains of "Puff the Magic Dragon" filled the air. People turned to stare and she backed out of the queue. Dammit. What did that damn dragon want? She opened her text message app.

You came to Chicago and didn't tell me? I'm hurt, Sade.

What the hell? Nikos Constantine, Drakon of the Kholkikos Clan was in Chicago. Her night just got better. Not. Sade's thumbs flew over the virtual keyboard. *I'm busy. Go away.*

But you are dressed for dinner...

Holy crap! Her head snapped up and she gazed across the crowd until she found his arrogant face. There he stood, surrounded by his watch dragons, Stavros and Xan, ignoring all the deep, feminine sighs of the ladies vying for their attention.

Take your mouseketeers and get lost. Busy working here. Scram.

She heard his laughter above the crowd noise and risked looking at him again. Nikos offered a jaunty, two-fingered salute before leaving. A few moments later, her phone dinged again.

As you wish, but you still owe me dinner. I shall be collecting this trip. Antío, khriso mou.

"Note to self, get that friggin' Greek dictionary sooner than later." Sade muttered the reminder under her breath then glanced to up make sure no one was paying attention. They weren't.

Like lemmings headed toward a cliff, the people in front of her trundled forward. Sade had two problems—the Beretta automatic between her legs and the fact the muscle up ahead asked for invitations as they scanned for weapons. The woman in front of Sade wore a coat hundreds of little critters had sacrificed their skins for. She also wore the equivalent of a small country's GNP around her neck and chubby wrists. The woman puffed and surged forward like the Titanic on dead slow. Sade watched the woman's little husband push her forward like Scuffy the Tug Boat. The two guys on security detail at the metal detector stopped the couple and asked for their invitation.

The woman bristled. "I am Eunice Wentworth Thurston. This is my husband, Howell J. Thurston III." She paused to take a deep breath in preparation of launching into a full-blown tirade.

"Now, now, lovey." Mr. Thurston tried to soothe his wife.

Sade stepped up behind the woman and as soon as she determined all attention was focused on Mr. and Mrs. Thurston, she managed a bit of sleight of hand. The heavy gems weighing down the woman's ample bosom took a sudden nosedive for the floor. Mrs. Thurston gasped. One of the guards made a grab for the necklace and clutched more than he bargained for. The woman howled and beat the hapless guy with her meaty fists while her husband ineffectually tried to calm his wife and retrieve the necklace. Sade slipped out of line, ducked around the metal detector and slid into the Gold Coast room.

Inside the ballroom, she paused a moment to get her bearings. Two colonnades of ornate columns bisected the room. A spiral of vines layered in tones of cream and gold climbed each pilaster in Art Nouveau grandeur. Across the room, a row of stately windows opened up the view of East Lake Shore Drive, a small park, and the surface of Lake Michigan where icy whitecaps glistened in the moonlight. Tennessee marble gleamed in the center of the floor while period carpeting softened the outer edges. The room had been religiously maintained to preserve its elegance and it formed a plush and fitting background for the chic crowd gathered there.

With her "Spidey" sense working overtime, Sade hoped to remain unobtrusive. A small combo played on the stage to her left and a wannabe Frank Sinatra clone crooned a ballad into an old-fashioned microphone like one a forties-era torch singer would make love to when singing.

Cocktail glasses clinked, high heels tapped across the marble, and the murmur of myriad conversations all created a syncopating harmony of sound that blended into a soothing hubbub. A waiter carrying a tray loaded with champagne flutes waltzed by and Sade lifted one. Her gaze wandered across the room but she picked out only a few magicks. She had their flavor. The majority of the people in attendance were human, just as they'd been in the line waiting to get in.

Working her way down the room, Sade stayed close to the wall. She recognized a few familiar faces here and there—the humans from the society pages, the magicks from intelligence reports. And then she spotted the ringers. She even pegged the ones wearing tuxedos and pretending to be guests rather than employees. A man with a big weapon holstered snug under his armpit was as hard to miss as a man with a loaded weapon tucked into his britches, if you knew the signs to look for.

One face stuck out in the crowd. Headed toward middle age but youthful in appearance and attitude, a circle of mostly female admirers fawned over Senator Alex McMahon, a notorious bachelor. "Curiouser and curiouser," Sade muttered softly. Just that morning, the senator had allegedly been calling from his Washington office. Granted, there were almost hourly flights between DC and Chicago but she was suspicious by nature.

Sade stepped toward the senator but two men in hand-tailored suits of the expensive Italian variety swooped down on either side of her. Instinctively, she widened her stance—for balance and for ease of draw. One of the men grabbed her right arm. She stood dead still, staring at his hand before she slowly raised her eyes to meet his. Hard as glass, her green eyes bored into the man's brown ones.

"Move it or lose it." She keyed her voice low, husky, like velvet over steel and sexy as all get out but there was nothing flirtatious in her words. A little smile quirked her lips and made the beauty mark on her cheek dance.

"You're not an invited guest," the other suit growled. "You need to come with us." He reached for her other arm.

Both of the guards were human. Sade's smile grew a little wider but it never reached her eyes and the mark at the corner of her mouth put a period on things. She stepped away from the second man and directly into the one whose hand remained on her arm. Her left hand griped his wrist, her nails sinking into the tender flesh underneath. She twisted, giving him, what appeared to witnesses, a gentle hip-bump. The man landed almost lightly on the floor staring up as her spike heel left its imprint on the tender flesh under his jaw. Her fingers curled around the Beretta hidden by the softly draped folds of her dress as she grabbed the second man by his shirtfront.

"Oh, but I am a guest," she asserted. "And this is where I get to say, take me to your leader." There was no semblance of a smile on her face now. Sade was all business and it was obvious her business could turn deadly in a heartbeat.

A squad of security guards, all in those expensively tailored suits, swarmed to the little scene. Three peeled off to huddle around the senator, the rest surrounded Sade and her two adversaries. She moved her right hand just enough to let the hired guns know she was armed but not enough to send the rest of the guests into a panic. Because this all occurred near the wall, behind one of the columns, not many people had tumbled to the fact something was amiss.

The proverbial noose tightened around Sade's neck but she never blinked. "Easy there, boys," she told them, coating her words with Texas honey. "The hotel will keep the damage deposit if y'all make a mess all over the pretty carpet." She flashed them a tight smile. "And since it's not my money, I don't mind if things get messy."

The only one of the bunch dressed in a tux held up his hand. "Now miss," he cautioned. "Let's not do anything hasty. This is a private party. You're not on the guest list. If you leave now, we won't call the authorities."

Betting Tux Man was the head of the security detail, Sade chuckled, the sound a dry whisper of amusement. "I *am* the authorities."

"And Miss Marquis is an invited guest."

The voice echoed from behind her and she recognized it as one and the same as her mysterious caller. The security guards stepped back, deference written all over their faces. The hair on the back of her neck prickled. "That would be Special Agent Marquis," she amended with a smirk. "FBI." She refrained from a fist pump when each member of the security detail took another step backwards. "Everybody take a deep breath," she suggested, her voice still pitched low. With a flick of her thumb, Sade engaged the safety on her automatic and with a flip of black silk, she holstered the weapon. Turning, she faced her host. "You have the advantage, mister..." The curious expression on Sade's face added a question mark. "Hannibal Crowley, at your service."

She stared at the man, her right eyebrow quirked. Not quite sure what she'd expected when she turned around, this dapper beanpole of a man wasn't it. Hannibal Crowley was several inches taller than Sade but she probably outweighed him. Long, spidery fingers uncurled from his bony wrist as he extended his hand to shake. With reluctance, Sade held out hers. When Crowley's hand touched hers, it was all she could do to keep from flinching. The man's dry skin felt reptilian. Withdrawing her hand from his clasp, she resisted the urge to wipe her palm down her thigh to rid it of the sensation.

The hired guns filtered through the crowd to take up unobtrusive positions. Sade made note of where each one settled, along with those who had not responded to the little standoff. The knot of people around Senator McMahon loosened and Crowley, with a hand on her elbow, did his best to covertly steer her away from the other man. She glanced at her host from the corner of her eyes then narrowed them slyly. Hannibal Crowley did not want her to speak to the honorable senator from Illinois.

"Excuse me a moment. I see Senator McMahon is free now." She didn't give Crowley time to respond but turned and headed directly toward the politician.

Alex McMahon looked up as she approached. She saw his reaction and could almost read his mind. She knew what she looked like—tall, shapely, eyes a startling bottle green. His gaze raked her mouth and lingered on the little mole at the corner. He wet his lips as he glanced at her hands. She wore no wedding rings. In fact, she wore no jewelry at all.

Plastering on her Washington game face, Sade fixed a noncommittal smile on her lips. "Senator McMahon."

"Please, call me Alex," he murmured capturing her hand and lifting it to his mouth for a kiss. "I don't believe we've met…Miss?"

"Marquis. Special Agent Sade Marquis."

McMahon all but jerked his hand away from hers. She watched his reaction, carefully noting the slight narrowing of his eyes, the almost imperceptible flare of his nostrils, the faint dilation of his pupils. Sade caught movement in her peripheral vision and a woman about half McMahon's age joined them. She guessed the newcomer to be in her mid-twenties. The girl slipped her hand onto the senator's arm, the gesture both familiar and possessive.

"Are you going to introduce me to your friend, Alex?" Her soft, little-girl voice matched her heart-shaped face. Like a china doll, her ivory complexion was porcelain smooth and silken curls of strawberry blonde capped her head. Petite, perfect, wearing pale pink velvet and white lace, the young woman looked like a Victorian valentine.

Sade beat the senator to the punch. "Sade Marquis."

McMahon smoothly slid into the breach of Sade's brief introduction. "Ms. Marquis works in Washington."

"Oh." The full lips of the girl's little bow mouth forming a perfect 'O'. "A lobbyist."

Sade snorted a rather inelegant sound at the assumption. "Quite the contrary. I'm with the FBI."

The girl blinked, long lashes fluttering against her cheeks, before her face changed. Her expression and words dismissed Sade as being beneath any further notice. "My apologies. Simply a secretary then." The girl stood up on tiptoes to whisper something into McMahon's ear.

Tilting her head, Sade observed the senator, ignoring the Kewpie doll at his side. "I believe Director Bailey told you I'd be in touch." After a few moments, she glanced at the girl in a rather negligent perusal. Everything in her attitude gave the girl a brush-off even more cutting than the "just a secretary" remark. Her gaze returned to McMahon's face. "I'll call your local office in the morning. I want to interview your staff. All of them. And you, yourself, Senator. I'll be talking to you too," Sade promised.

The girl batted long lashes up at McMahon. Sade could almost feel the backbone ooze out of the man. This little slip of a girl had Washington's most eligible bachelor completely pussy whipped. When the girl turned a baleful glare on Sade, the hair stood up on her arms.

Hannibal Crowley slithered up beside the couple facing her. "Agent Marquis. May I present my daughter, Eugenia."

"Eugenia Crowley," the girl added. With a glance up at Alex, she continued. "Soon to be Eugenia Crowley McMahon."

Eugenia Crowley, Sade thought. *Witch.*

Chapter Six

Déjà Vu

---

*E*UGENIA CROWLEY, WITCH. Sade wasn't too surprised she hadn't recognized the girl. The last time Eugenia's face appeared in the news she'd been a moppet in Muppet brand clothing. Her father filed a lawsuit against a local school board claiming the school discriminated against his daughter. They'd made the rounds of talk shows: Today, Tonight, Good Morning, Late Night, and the Noon Report in Poughkeepsie. That was before the Veil ripped.

The limelight eventually dimmed, and the Crowleys were banished to has-been purgatory. Then the Big Rip sent everything to hell in a handbasket. Crowley reappeared and proclaimed that as high priest of some obscure religion, he had all the answers. He did, if you didn't listen to the question. The guy was a scam artist from way back, but he was sure running with the cream of Chicago's crop.

The space between Sade's shoulder blades itched. Two plus two supposedly equaled four. But not with this case and not with the people in this room. She didn't trust any of them but she had no way to tie them directly to CeeCee's murder. And tying them to St. John was tenuous at best. She couldn't go to a judge with an anonymous phone call.

People like Eugenia Crowley and her father made her twitchy but she wasn't scared of them. Had she been an old-school FBI agent, she might have been unnerved by the look Eugenia leveled at her. Red sparks shone in the depths of the petite doll's eyes and a dark shadow passed across those cherubic features. The girl exhibited something very *otherworldly*. Seeming to ignore Eugenia for a moment, Sade favored McMahon with a smile. "Well, Senator, this news will break the heart of every society hostess in Washington. Congratulations."

"Oh, yes. Quite. Indeed." McMahon stammered.

"And a pleasure to meet the girl who finally lassoed one of the country's most eligible bachelors," Sade continued smoothly, flicking her gaze over Eugenia again. "You must be quite special, Miss Crowley."

Turning to the girl's father without giving Eugenia a chance to respond, Sade's expression maintained her Washington game face—the polite, noncommittal one all public servants learned to wear when dealing with elected officials. While she wasn't quite sure what category Hannibal Crowley fit into, Sade would play the game. He might not be a king but in every likelihood, he was a king maker. At the very least, he had a US Senator in his pocket. Movement by the door caught her eye before she could follow through with a question for Crowley. Mayor Richard Dandridge arrived with his entourage, including a young man who was definitely his father's son. In twenty-five years, Trey Dandridge would be the spitting image of his old man.

The fact that Dandridge III wore a tuxedo with a drink in one hand and a smile on his face didn't escape Sade's notice. The kid sure didn't look or act like he was in mourning. She decided to dump her present company and move on to the Dandridges, but they saved her the trouble by strolling over. The mayor looked like he was on the campaign trail as he approached, hand out and a huge smile pasted on his jovial face.

"Hannibal," the mayor bellowed genially, pumping the scarecrow's hand. "And the lovely Eugenia." Dandridge leaned in and kissed the petite girl on the cheek. He offered his hand to the senator then realized Eugenia had both arms wrapped around McMahon's right forearm. In a smooth, continuous movement, the mayor bypassed shaking hands and patted the other man's shoulder instead. He was nothing if not the consummate politician. He eyed Sade appreciatively and then smiled as he worked up another head of steam to greet her.

Sade could almost see the wheels turning in the mayor's head as he tried to put a name with her face. She let him stew for a long moment before she introduced herself. "Special Agent Sade Marquis, Mayor Dandridge." She enjoyed the look of surprise on the mayor's face almost as much as she was intrigued by the quick look he exchanged with Hannibal Crowley. No matter what else Crowley might be, he definitely held some power behind the throne. She shifted her attention to the mayor's son.

"I'm sorry for your loss, Mr. Dandridge," Sade told the younger man.

"My loss?" Dandridge III looked baffled.

Sade stared without blinking. "CeeCee Adams? Your fiancé?" The boy still looked clueless.

"CeeCee?" he asked, completely perplexed. "She's in Madison. She went up to visit and to get her wisdom teeth taken out."

Sade managed to hide her surprise even as she wondered whether the kid truly was as dumb as a stump or if he was as accomplished an actor as his father was a politician. Glancing at the others standing in the little group, she focused on the senator. In her cop voice, she said, "You told the Director this story was all over the news. How is it that her fiancé hasn't heard?" Sade turned back to Trey. "Did CeeCee herself tell you she was going home to see her parents?"

Trey shook his head, glancing at his father for guidance. "No," he finally replied. "One of her friends called and told me." The kid's eyes cut to Eugenia as he continued. "I knew she hadn't been feeling well. Throwing up and such. When Eugenia mentioned that CeeCee was going home to get her teeth done, I didn't think twice about it."

CeeCee's pregnancy might not be known and that fact troubled her. Besides, wisdom teeth and upchuck? That made no sense to her but to a clueless young man, it might. Sade turned her attention to Eugenia. "You and CeeCee were friends?"

The girl lifted her shoulders and dropped them in an elegant motion. "CeeCee worked for Alex. I knew her. She was…" Eugenia's voice trailed off and she let out a very theatrical little sigh. "CeeCee was rather gregarious. She thought everyone was her friend."

A dry chuckle escaped before Sade could choke it off. "Well, obviously, not everyone was." *Curious,* she thought. Trey spoke of CeeCee in the present tense and Eugenia in the past.

Sade's words finally penetrated Trey's alcoholic buzz. "My loss?" He turned to stare at his father again. "Dad? What's she talking about? Why is the FBI asking about CeeCee?"

Sade decided the kid probably was as clueless as he appeared. She glanced at his father. "I'm guessing you have decided to tell your son gently, Mayor Dandridge. Me? I'd rather just rip the Band-Aid off than work at peeling it back a little at a time."

The mayor puffed up like the popinjay he was. "This is hardly the time or the place, Agent Marquis. In fact, what are you doing here?"

Inclining her head toward Hannibal Crowley, Sade's mouth formed a little moue. "You might ask Mr. Crowley that. I'm here at his insistence." Her eyebrows danced, adding emphasis to the last word.

Both politicians hit Crowley with what could only be described as baleful glares. Trouble in paradise. That was always a good sign. The mayor stepped away for a moment and spoke to a young guy who was probably a gofer on his staff. Sade's eyes followed the man as he hurried off, intent on an errand of some apparent importance, given his gait. She smirked when first a woman and then, a few seconds later, a man slipped out through the service area. She'd bet dollars to donuts she'd just witnessed the hasty retreat of a certain assistant district attorney and a grizzled veteran of the Chicago Police Department's homicide squad.

Sade decided Kristian St. John needed to be released on bail before he suffered some unforeseen accident in police custody. She had a few trump cards to play in that regard. Any further time spent here would be an exercise in futility and diminishing returns. She'd learned all she could without further research. It was time to hit the road.

Facing Hannibal Crowley, she flashed her best cop smile—the one hinting she knew everything but gave nothing away. "Thank you for the invitation, Mr. Crowley. It has been a most…" She paused a beat for emphasis. "…interesting evening. Senator, Mayor, I'll be in touch." Turning on her heel, she headed toward the exit, her long legs eating up the distance with each stride.

The head of the security detail caught up to her at the door. "I'll see you to your car, Miss Marquis." He took her arm.

Staring for a moment at the hand gripping her biceps just above the elbow, Sade then raised her eyes to meet his. He turned loose like her skin burned his hand. Without a word, she swept from the room, a little smile niggling the corner of her mouth as the man stumbled in his effort to keep up with her.

The bell captain saw her coming down the stairs and he hurried to grab her hang-up bag. She figured the doorman must have given a really good description of her. Sade extracted a ten-dollar bill from her evening purse and exchanged it for the bag. "Nearest ladies room?"

He pointed toward the Palm Court. "Take a left at the top of the steps."

Turning to her escort, Sade explained, "I'm changing back into my street clothes. If you've got the balls, you can come into the ladies room and watch." The man blushed. "I thought not," she murmured as she pulled away from him and paced across the lobby. She dashed up the steps to the Palm Court and was halfway to the hallway leading to the ladies room before the guy reacted.

It didn't take long to change back into her silk shirt and tailored slacks. Boots replaced heels and she pulled out the hair stick so her hair tumbled past her shoulders again. She tucked the formal dress and heels into the bag and startled two college girls as she clipped a holster on her belt and adjusted it as she settled the Beretta into its accustomed place.

Shrugging into her black wool blazer, she folded the hang-up bag into her long black leather coat and draped it over one arm. She waited for the next group of women to emerge—professionals who'd stopped for a drink on their way home. Sade attached herself to this group and headed back into the Palm Court with them. Her escort hovered at the top of the stairs, staring at the door to the restrooms. Ducking behind a voluptuous redhead,

Sade kept the women between her and the hired gun. Once past him, she broke off and headed toward the foyer between the Palm Court and the Gold Coast room. Changing her gait and rolling her shoulders forward, she kept her eyes lowered as she dodged through the crowd along the Promenade.

Rounding the corner and skipping down the stairs, Sade jumped on a just-arrived elevator and rode down to the street level with the other passengers. Clearing the elevator, Sade headed in the opposite direction of the lower lobby, following another group headed to the Cape Cod Restaurant for a late dinner. They strolled down a hallway lined with businesses and shops, Sade tagging along. As they passed through the restaurant door, she kept going, pushing through a revolving door into the cold January night and the bustle of East Lakeshore Drive. Flagging a cab, she hopped into the back seat. "Hyatt Regency."

For a brief moment, Sade considered heading straight to the jail but without a court order in hand, she'd be unable to spring St. John. Once in her room, she'd be safe to make the needed phone calls. Leaning back against the seat of the Yellow Cab, she wondered how long Crowley's security chief would wait until he figured out she'd given him the slip. She chuckled, the dark, rich sound making the cabbie glance at her through the rear view mirror.

The vehicle caught green lights at every intersection and Sade briefly wondered about that. This was Chicago, a place not necessarily famous for smooth traffic flow. The two hotels were just over a mile apart. Under different circumstances, she would have been tempted to just hoof it. Tonight, though, with way too many people interested in keeping her occupied and under surveillance, she'd caught transportation. Her leather coat lay across her lap, still wrapped around the dress bag. Wearing just a blazer, she was thankful the heater blasted in the chill, even though the air freshener dangling from the rear view mirror made the enclosed space smell like some demented chemist's idea of a forest. At the Hyatt Regency, the doorman opened the back door as Sade handed money through the safety screen to the cab driver.

Inside the hotel, Sade caught the elevator up to her floor. Card key in hand, she approached the door to her room. The key disappeared, replaced by her pistol. The door looked closed but wasn't. She nudged it with her toe and it opened a few inches. She nudged it again and dropping low, slipped into the room. The place was empty but someone besides the maid doing turn down service had been there. She didn't holster her gun as she checked the bathroom, the closet, and the separate work area behind the low wall at the head of the bed. Her laptop was open on the desk. On a hunch, she flicked the on button. The computer hummed, fizzed and whirred but the screen remained an ominous shade. She picked it up and shook it gently, as if that would clear the blue screen of death.

Whoever had sabotaged her laptop sure didn't know her very well. With a grin, she retrieved her case file from the bottom of the dress bag. The red roped packet held not only hard copies, but a memory stick and a plastic bag containing a backup hard drive. "My daddy didn't raise no foolish children," she murmured out loud.

Snagging her cell phone, Sade hit a speed dial number and let it ring.

"What do you want?" a voice finally snapped.

Sade just managed not to chortle. "What? I can't call my godfather just to say hello?"

On the other end of the phone, Mathias snorted but he made it sound refined. "Sade, you don't call just to say hello. Ever. What do you want?"

"Winkyn, Blynken and Noddingham," Sade told the vampire. "When did they become an equal opportunity law firm?"

There was a pregnant pause before Mathias replied, "What do you mean?"

Sade could tell from his voice that she had his attention now. "When did the illustrious fae firm start representing vampires who have been accused of murder?"

"Who?" he snarled.

Oh, yeah. She had his attention now—his undivided attention. "Kristian St. John."

Mathias snorted again, only this time it was a sound of disgust. "Sinjen? Murder? I don't believe it."

Sade sighed. "Neither do I, Mathias. But that doesn't answer my question. Why would the fae be involved?" She could almost feel his shrug through the phone lines.

"If the retainer fee is high enough, they'll represent any of the magical races," Mathias finally replied.

Sade shook her head even though the man she was talking to couldn't see the gesture. "Mathias, I'm talking Puck himself, though he's using his Robin Goodfellow glamour."

"Puck? That good for nothing pile of…" Mathias didn't finish the sentence. The weight of his thoughts filtered through the phone connection. "Why are the human authorities involved, Sade? We never take our disputes into the human realm. Ever."

Sade remembered the battle once waged over her custody. "St. John is accused of murdering a human—a girl who worked for a US Senator. Said girl also just happened to be engaged to the son of the Mayor of Chicago." Sade squinted and then cringed as a long series of words in Dutch and French poured from the phone, expletives deleted all.

"He's safe for the moment, Mathias." Sade quietly interrupted the vampire's tirade. "I've seen him. Talked to him. My next call is to arrange bail and get him some place safe where no accidents can befall him." Sade knew the vampire population was small enough they all had at least a passing acquaintance with each other. Sade wasn't sure she wanted the answer but she had to ask anyway. "Mathias? You called him Sinjen. That's pretty personal. Just what is he to you?" The pause lasted long enough she wondered if she'd lost the connection.

Mathias finally replied, his voice a distant whisper. "My savior."

Something in his voice made the breath catch in her chest and she had to clear her throat before she could continue. "What does that mean, Mathias?"

The vampire remained silent for a long moment. "It is a lengthy story, child."

Sade sucked in a breath. Mathias never called her child, hadn't used the term in—she couldn't actually remember the last time. "I have time to listen."

"Unfortunately, I don't have time to tell it." He sounded gruff. "Suffice it to say I owe Sinjen a debt that cannot be repaid." Mathias hung up abruptly, his final words echoing in her ear. "Take care of him, Sade."

Chapter Seven

Promises, Promises

TAKE CARE OF HIM, SADE. That final request caught her completely off guard and she found herself promising, "I will, Mathias. I will," to a dead connection. This whole deal felt like a bad acid trip and she identified far too easily with Alice after she'd fallen down the damned rabbit hole and awakened in Wonderland.

She called the Old Man's private number, briefed him, and then asked him to call in some of her favors. Like a spoonful of sugar, a late-night phone call from the Director of the FBI helped the medicine go down. She figured a call from some poor assistant US Attorney saying she could go pick up Sinjen would come sometime between then and dawn. Her instincts insisted she didn't want to leave him in Cook County even one more day.

In the meantime, she needed to line up all the facts in this case and push them around until they made sense. Maybe it was all in her head but this situation seemed a bit personal and that idea didn't sit well at all. These people did not want to make it personal. She never played nice when it was.

She had quite a to-do list. First thing was to follow up on the "get out of jail free" card for Kristian St. John. A trip to the morgue, Chicago PD homicide, the DA's office, and a little visit with Trey Dandridge rounded out her dance card for the next day. She added research on the Crowleys to her list. There was something just not right about them. Their actions had her Bullshit Meter jumping off the chart.

Much sooner than anticipated, her cell rang. She listened, snapped it shut, checked her weapon and grabbed her coat. Hurrah for the swift wheels of justice.

THE ASSISTANT US ATTORNEY waited for Sade on the front steps of the Cook County Detention Center. He looked miserable despite the heavy overcoat he wore. She stepped out of the cab and hurried up to him. "Carl Johansen?" At his nod, she held out her hand. "Sade Marquis. Sorry to get you out in the cold."

"I'd sure like to have your connections, Marquis," Johansen growled. He stuck out a gloved hand for a brief shake. "What's the big deal about this guy anyway? What makes him so special that a federal judge doesn't even blink about signing a release order in the middle of the night?"

"Need to know basis. If I told you—"

"You'd have to kill me." Johansen rolled his eyes as he finished for her. "Can't you *Feebs* come up with something more original?"

The two of them headed inside. Sade liked Carl. Sarcasm was a good trait for a federal prosecutor in Chicago. They stopped at the front desk. Mr. Limpet, the fish-eyed guard, had gone off duty. She was thankful his replacement didn't even blink at the federal court order. He simply called down to have the prisoner brought up and returned to the book he was reading. Sade glanced through the window at the title—American Constitutional Law. Interesting.

WHEN THE DOOR to his glass cage popped open, Sinjen didn't move. He'd anticipated some sort of attack since the squad of cops had shown up in his classroom four nights ago and informed him he was being arrested for murder. Instead of being taken to police headquarters, they'd brought him straight to the detention facility. Sinjen kept his smirk to himself as he remembered how much religious bling the men wore. They'd even put him in a pair of handcuffs with crosses etched into the silver metal. No one had interrogated him. They'd tossed him into this fish bowl of a cell and left him.

As old as he was, Sinjen didn't have to collapse at the stroke of dawn and he had fought the drag on his senses for as long as he could, anticipating he'd be staked once he was incapacitated. Unable to resist the day sleep any longer, he'd finally collapsed. About an hour before sunset, he stirred. As the sun slipped below the unseen horizon that first night of his captivity, Sinjen slowly returned to full cognizance. To say he was surprised to be alive to see another night was an understatement.

The guards stood outside his cell waiting but Sinjen still didn't move. He ruminated over his captivity. That first night, he'd awakened to find a bag of blood from the Red Cross left for him. As it was for most vampires, the act of feeding was intensely personal to him. Agitated he had no privacy for it, he sank down on the rough cot, thankful they hadn't actually supplied him with a casket. Sinjen had hunkered in on himself as his fangs pierced the blood bag. The blood tasted like plastic but it would keep his strength up.

He had not expected the fae lawyer who showed up about an hour after sunset. Goodfellow claimed to represent him and told him to keep his mouth shut except to say, "I want my attorney." Five minutes later, the fae was gone. That's when Sinjen started reciting his repertoire of Shakespeare's plays. The second and third days and nights had passed just as the first one had. And then the fourth night arrived. If he hadn't expected a fae attorney, he definitely did not expect the federal agent with legs that went from here to there and a voice that was a heady mix of whiskey and honey.

The memory of the woman brought an involuntary smile to Sinjen's face. She had real curves despite being lean. And those legs? He all but sighed at the fantasy those legs evoked. He found society's current fascination with what he considered to be little more than skeletons bizarre. He wanted a woman with breasts that filled his hands, with thighs that cushioned his thrusts, with firmly rounded buttocks that were a pleasure to watch walk away.

Technically, the fed was a little on the skinny side for his tastes but her hair and eyes? Those full lips with their little punctuation of a beauty mark, plus the way she walked? All brash self-assurance with a dash of smirk. Sinjen was a connoisseur of the way women walked and the fed had the sexiest one he had ever seen. The sentiment was not an exaggeration. All his blood had pooled low the moment she'd appeared and had stayed there long after she'd gone. She'd noticed his reaction despite the loose-fitting slacks he wore. If he'd had more blood in his system, and been more of a gentleman at that moment, he would have blushed.

He'd finally recognized her name. Sinjen always wondered what prompted Mathias to wage war with Oberon. Had the other vampire known what a beauty the baby would grow up to be? Was Sade his lover now? The thought churned his stomach and he clenched his teeth. That he was angry at the thought amused him. He hadn't suffered a fit of jealousy in... He actually laughed aloud, a short bark of sound that caused his guard to turn around and stare for a moment. With an evil grin, he stared at the man. Then he said, "Boo." The man jumped and quickly turned his back. Sinjen laughed again. He might pay for his games in the morning, once he was vulnerable, but the look on the guard's face was worth it.

"Is there a reason the door has been opened?" Sinjen finally asked. "If you anticipate me trying to escape so you have reason to stake me, it won't happen."

"You're free on bond," an unfamiliar voice echoed from some hidden speaker.

"Did Mr. Goodfellow post my bail?" This sudden turn of events presented an intriguing puzzle.

"Own recognizance," a familiar voice replied. "There is a US Attorney on his way in, Mr. St. John. You've been remanded to federal custody and a federal judge has agreed to the O.R. bond."

Sinjen smiled, as much at hearing her voice as the thought of being free. He relaxed and shrugged into the suit jacket he'd been wearing when arrested—mainly to cover his reaction to her voice. A few moments later, a man appeared. Middle-aged, bald and with a small paunch, he glowered.

"Why are all of you the stuff of magazine covers?" the man groused. "Damn glad you aren't coming home with me. My wife would put me on the couch. Carl Johansen, by the way." Johansen stuck out his hand but Sinjen didn't move. "Marquis? Tell your pet fang that I'm one of the good guys. I left a warm bed for this."

Arching an eyebrow, Sinjen stared down at the US Attorney. "I am no one's pet."

"Yeah, yeah, whatever." Johansen continued to grumble. "Get your un-dead butt in gear, buddy. I have court in the morning and my wife did *not* have a headache when I left the house. Marquis has your personal belong-ings. She'll meet us in the hallway."

Sinjen finally stepped out of the glass cubicle and shook Johansen's hand. "Kristian St. John, though most people call me Sinjen. If it makes you feel better, not all of us look like fashion models."

Johansen shook his hand and headed back toward the door leading to the bank of elevators. "Yeah, well, I'd like to say it's a pleasure to meet you but it's so cold outside my nuts are freezing and my wife doesn't get hot very often. Forgive me if I don't stick around."

Sinjen chuckled, his long stride keeping up with the rotund attorney easily. Considering his own discomfort at the moment, he did indeed understand Johansen's eagerness to return to his wife. A guard waited at the elevator, holding the door open. The deputy stepped into the car with Sinjen and Johansen.

"Agent Marquis will be waiting on the main floor," the deputy told them. "Scary bitch," he murmured under his breath.

"No shit," Johansen agreed affably. "Judge Wilcox got out of bed to sign the orders. On her say so." His voice sounded full of wonder as he shook his head. "Judge Wilcox," he added again for emphasis.

"No fucking way," the incredulous deputy challenged.

"Yes, way," Johansen asserted. "I'm the one who went by his house for his signature. Talk about brass balls." The elevator doors slithered open just as he made that statement. He looked up at Sade and audibly gulped.

"Yeah, I do," Sade replied, her tone conversational. "Have them," she clarified, waiting for Sinjen and Johansen to step off.

The deputy remained where he was. "Don't turn your back on her," he advised in a loud whisper as the doors closed.

Carl stared at the FBI agent. "You have a helluva rep, lady. Why do I get the feeling you nurture it?"

Sade's lips pursed as she tilted her head to stare at him. "I haven't killed anyone." He chuckled at her sarcasm. "This week," she added a couple of heartbeats later.

Carl laughed until Sade stared at him, her right brow arched. His laughter trailed off to a hesitant intake of breath. He blinked, sobering. "You…aren't kidding, are you?"

Sade shook her head. "I never kid, Carl." She looked dead serious.

Making a note to check his sources in Washington, he checked out Marquis's cool demeanor. Carl didn't doubt for a minute that she'd pull the trigger in a heartbeat. When they'd walked in to spring the vampire, he simply stood back and let her take the lead. Like a steamroller over hot asphalt, the agent had flattened all protestations. She verbally castrated several of the deputies when Sinjen hadn't appeared immediately and after that, the rest of the staff had simply gotten out of her way. Carl never, ever wanted to piss off this woman.

The three of them stepped out into the frigid wind. "My car's around the corner. Can I give you two a lift?" He hoped they'd decline and let out a sigh of relief that was caught by a gust of wind when they did so.

Sade offered her hand. "We'll grab a cab. Get home to your warm bed, Carl. Thanks for getting out in the cold."

With a quick shake and a wave, Johansen trotted down the steps and faced into the wind, head down and huddled within his overcoat. Without looking at Sinjen, Sade headed down the steps. Traffic remained fairly heavy and within moments, a Yellow cab pulled up to the curb. As Sade reached for the door, Sinjen beat her to it.

"After you, lady fair," he offered with a quick dip of his head.

It was cold enough that the warm air escaping from the back of the cab appeared as steam. Sade slid in and scooted across the seat to make room. The cab driver stared at them through the rear view mirror waiting for a destination.

Sade cocked an eyebrow at the vampire. "Your place or mine?"

"You have a place here?" Sinjen was surprised. Surely he would have known if Mathias' goddaughter lived in Chicago.

"I'm staying at the Hyatt Regency."

Sinjen leaned forward. "Central Station," he told the driver. "The twelve hundred block of South Michigan." Settling back against the seat, he faced Sade. "I hope you don't mind. I've been in that place four nights now and I would like to bathe and change clothes."

Sade flashed a tight smile. "No problem. I want a look at your place anyway. That's where the body was found, right?"

Closing his eyes, Sinjen rubbed at his temple. "If you say so. I was teaching a class at the University when they arrested me and they didn't tell me much. I suppose that means my apartment is now a crime scene. I still need clean clothes even if I move to a hotel for the duration." He opened his eyes and stared at her. "You believe me to be innocent." It wasn't a question. A slight smile hovered around his lips as he continued. "And you look me in the eye without fear." One corner of his mouth curled tighter as he blinked, which left his eyes half-lidded. "You are either very brave or very foolish, Special Agent Sade Marquis."

"I am neither, Mr. St. John." Sade's voice matched her expression—cold and unemotional.

"Please. Call me Sinjen." His voice almost a purr, he hoped to tease a smile from her.

"I'm not buying whatever it is you're selling, Mr. St. John."

Wordlessly, she handed him the plastic bag with his personal belongings. The rest of the trip continued in silence until the cab pulled up in front of a new forty-story building. Sinjen paid the driver even as Sade dug in her pocket for cash. When she opened her mouth to protest, he held up his hand.

"I am a lot of things, Agent Marquis. A gentleman happens to be one of them. And a gentleman always pays a lady's way." Sinjen turned his attention to the cabbie. "Keep the change." He climbed out of the vehicle and offered his hand to help her exit.

Sade hesitated a moment then placed her hand in his. Her eyes widened as magical energy danced across the skin of her arm, making the hair prickle all the way to the back of her neck. She stared into Sinjen's eyes and realized that he'd felt it too, and was just as surprised. That didn't bode well. It wasn't one of his vampire tricks. Sinjen took her elbow without really touching her and Sade suddenly got a sense of the strength of the man, both physically and psychically. Stopping dead in her tracks, she twisted to face him.

"Even if they'd been decked out for a visit from the Pope, you could have walked away from those cops." She didn't express her next thought out loud. Not since Roman or that damned dragon had Sade felt *petite*. She allowed him to escort her inside.

Like most luxury apartment buildings, Sinjen's had both a concierge and a doorman on duty. As the outside door blew open, catching both men flat-footed, they exchanged nervous looks. "How did you get—" the concierge began and then stopped. "Uh, ma'am..." Again, his voice trailed off.

"Special Agent," Sade corrected him. "FBI." She tried not to smirk as the men now exchanged relieved glances. "Has anyone been up to Mr. St. John's apartment?"

The doorman, about thirty-five and good-looking in a toothy Italian way, shook his head. "Not since the cops and the...the coroner." He grinned suddenly. "It was just like an episode of CSI around here."

Sade rolled her eyes. "Well, I hope the local boys aren't quite so Hollywood," she muttered under her breath. She scowled at Sinjen's echoing chuckle.

The doorman hit the button for the express elevator and held the door for Sade and Sinjen to enter. "I know you didn't do it, Mr. St. John." The man whispered, attempting to look and sound conspiratorial as the vampire brushed past him.

Leaning her shoulder against the door to keep it open, Sade stared at the doorman. "Oh? And you are so positive of that how?" She paused just a beat before the last word.

"She wasn't his type." The man sounded confident. "Too skinny. He's like me. Mr. Sinjen likes 'em round and full with places to squeeze. That little gal looked like a stiff breeze off the lake would've snapped her in half."

Sade stared at him a long moment. "You saw her come in?"

The doorman nodded. "Well, duh. I'm on duty from five p.m. to one a.m. That night, I was workin' a double for George, the guy who handles the graveyard shift. Just like I'm doin' tonight. I was here until nine that next morning. I usually see who comes in an' Frank and I compare notes. Never hurts to know who's spending the night, if you know what I mean."

Glancing at Sinjen, Sade frowned. "You have somebody in your life you trust enough to spend the night?" She realized she shouldn't have been so happy when the vampire shook his head. She returned her attention to the doorman, reading his nametag. "Have you ever seen Miss Adams here before, Chuck?"

The man suddenly turned into a bobbin-head doll as he nodded vigorously. "Yeah, two or three times a week at least. She works...worked for Senator McMahon. He keeps a flat here." Chuck turned to stare at Sinjen, a light bulb going on in his head if the stunned expression on his face was any indication. "Just down the hall from Mr. Sinjen, in fact," he articulated his thought. He then stopped nodding long enough to stare at Sade. "I hadn't thought of that 'til just now." He perked up. "S'pose that's important?"

Sade stared at Sinjen for a long moment. "We need to talk." Her blunt tone left no room for discussion. Turning back to Chuck, she nodded. "It very well could be. Can you put together a list for me? Everyone who was in and out of this place that night and the approximate time if you can remember?"

Chuck nodded. "I can do that," he replied and then looked perplexed. "How come the cops didn't ask me to?"

At that bit of news, it took some effort but Sade managed to keep the surprise off her face. She stared at the doorman for a long moment. "Perhaps they asked the concierge or the other doormen?"

Shaking his head, Chuck declared, "Nope. We would have all compared notes. Just like I'm gonna do now. We're a team around here."

Sade nodded and finally stepped into the elevator to let the doors slide to a close. "Let me know when you've got the list," she ordered just before the elevator sealed shut. Sinjen started to speak but Sade shook her head. With a slight cut of her eyes, she pointed out the security camera.

The express elevator zoomed to the penthouse floor. The uneasy heaviness combined with a sense of sterile air pressing against them ended with a moment's rise in the soles of their shoes as the car glided into position, followed by the kiss of cooler, fresher air when the doors opened. Sade stepped out first, her right hand, while not really hovering near her holster, was close enough to be effective if a threat presented itself. The well-appointed and, what mattered more to Sade, empty hallway stretched out in both directions. She motioned for Sinjen to join her and noticed the rather bemused expression on his face.

"What?"

The vampire chuckled, the rich dark chocolate and hot caramel sound again doing something funny to Sade's insides. "I'm not used to being protected, especially by either a human or a woman, but most especially not both at the same time. The sensation is a new one for me and I am quite flattered."

Sade snorted. "Don't be. It's all just part of the job, Sinjen." She was too busy looking for traps to see the slow smile light up the vampire's face as she used his nickname.

He moved down the hallway toward the door to his apartment. "I believe the senator's flat is the other direction," he told her, his voice one notch above a whisper.

Sade noticed he acted wary now. She followed, looking for any telltale signs of hidden cameras. If the building had high tech security the tenants were unaware of, perhaps they'd captured images of who had dumped the girl's body.

When Sinjen stopped at the door to his apartment, Sade was more than a little surprised. No yellow crime scene tape criss-crossed over the door-frame; no notice of the place being sealed stuck to the dark wood. That was highly suspicious in and of itself. If she hadn't already decided Kristian St. John was innocent in CeeCee Adams' murder, this latest discovery would have tilted the odds in his favor. The deeper she delved into this investigation, the more it smelled like a frame job. Learning that Senator McMahon kept an apartment down the hall made her want to sniff around. Had the real murderer gotten confused? Broken into the wrong apartment thereby implicating the wrong man? Sade decided something was certainly rotten in Denmark and it smelled a lot like red herrings.

She wasn't quite certain what she expected when she stepped into Sinjen's lair, but this tastefully furnished apartment wasn't it. The kitchen, a combination of stainless steel, granite, and rich, dark cherry cabinets opened to the right as she paced down the short entry hall. The hall opened into a living area with a gently curved wall of windows that gazed out over a vista of shoreline, lake, and cityscape. The impression she'd gotten of the vampire had been one of urbane sophistication, of glass and metal not the leather and stone that set the decorating tone. A few discerning pieces of original art were elegantly displayed. The large, leather couch looked both stylish and comfortable. A chunk of marble, used as a coffee table, anchored the couch to an overstuffed chair and ottoman upholstered in a rich but subtle burgundy and gold plaid.

Gesturing with one hand, Sinjen explained the layout. "My office and the guest room with a bath are that way," he said sweeping his arm to the right. "My room is through that door."

Sade turned, taking a slow look around as she absorbed every nuance in the room. She walked the length of the living room and poked her head into the office/den and then the guest room. Sinjen's office was book-lined with a fairly modern computer desk holding a sleek LCD monitor and keyboard, the CPU hidden somewhere out of sight. Another large, overstuffed chair that looked like it had seen many nights of comfortable reading squatted in a corner with a small side table and reading lamp.

The next door opened to a three-quarter bath off a short hallway that then spilled into a fairly small guest room. A double bed, covered with a comforter of French blue, beige, russet red, and sage green stripes, fleurs-de-lis and paisley prints, sat at an angle in the far corner of the room. The closet was empty. Sade returned to the living room and found Sinjen standing in the doorway to the master bedroom, his back to the living room.

"Is this where they found her?" Sade asked in a quiet voice as she walked up behind him.

Sinjen turned his head to stare at her a moment. "I actually have no idea where the body was found," he admitted. "Frankly, I expected to return to a mess. You know—black fingerprint powder all over everything. Drawers ransacked. Bed linens stripped and tossed across the room." He looked around. "It almost looks like the maid has been here."

Sade nodded. She'd been thinking precisely the same thing. Tilting her head, she tried to see around Sinjen's impressive body. "Do you mind?" she asked.

With a slight smirk, Sinjen moved on into his bedroom, Sade close on his heels. A sliding glass door opened onto a cozy balcony. Discreet metal shutters folded flat against the wall on each end of the door. Sade nodded her approval.

"I take it you aren't the only magick in the building?" she asked.

Sinjen headed toward the door to the walk-through closet and the master bath beyond, stripping out of his jacket as he went. "There are a few," he called from the closet. "A werewolf couple, several elves. A few fae trip in and out from time to time. I believe, however, that I am the only vampire in the building."

Sade snorted a wry chuckle. "That's convenient." Sinjen stepped back through the door from the closet and Sade almost choked. He was shirtless. Her mouth went dry. Dark hair feathered lightly across his muscular chest.

His abdomen wasn't a washboard of ripped muscles but it was damn sure close enough for government work. She forced herself to look at Sinjen's face. His cocky smile almost undid her. He knew. He knew exactly where her thoughts lingered. She took a long, slow, steadying breath and used her cop voice to continue. "Dead girl, drained of blood. Only one vampire in the building. Almost too convenient."

"I did know her." Sinjen's voice held regret. "I believe she had a...crush? Yes. A crush on me. She took all of my classes. A sweet girl if a somewhat mediocre student."

"I thought you were going to clean up?" Sade hinted and hated that her voice came out low and husky.

The man unleashed his sinful laugh and Sade told her girly bits to calm down and quit clamoring for his attention. Turning on his heel, he called over his shoulder. "And no, until now, there has been no one I trusted to spend the night."

Sinjen disappeared back through the door of the closet and within moments, Sade heard sounds in the bathroom. Crossing closer, she listened to the noise from behind the closed bathroom door as she searched the closet. She wasn't too surprised when she found nothing incriminating. At the sound of a zipper, Sade sucked in a slow breath. Moving quietly to the door, she put her ear to the jamb to listen. She caught the whisper of cloth against skin and then cloth against...something. She thought a moment. He'd stripped off his slacks and tossed them into a hamper of some sort. Running water. The sound of a razor scraping against skin. The man was shaving? She blinked at the sound of the glass door to the shower opening. Spray from the shower. Sade could picture Sinjen naked, those broad shoulders and sculpted chest tapering to a "West Point" waist and hips above long, muscular thighs and calves. Sinjen had come to manhood in a time when strength meant survival. He had been a warrior—and a magnificent specimen of one at that—much taller than his peers at the time.

Reminding herself to breathe, Sade heard the shower door close. It occurred to her that she should get away from temptation. She pictured him soaping his...manly bits. Fighting the urge to charge into the bathroom, she retreated to the bedroom in self-preservation. Never had she felt an attraction for a man like this. Ever. A part of her knew the allure was dangerous while another part of her was ready to strip down and join him.

In the bedroom, she took a long look around. The king-sized bed sat at right angles to the glass patio doors. Silk sheets, a rich, iridescent midnight blue shimmered beneath a pale lavender microsuede comforter. Thick, white pillows looked like snowdrifts against the sleek wooden headboard. A Monet landscape—softly blurred flowers and sunlight—hung on the wall over the bed. Sade figured it was an original.

Wandering around the room, she picked up a small box on his dresser. Crudely made, there was a coat of arms carved into the lid. She was far from being an expert in heraldry. Unconsciously, her finger traced the design. To the uninitiated, it looked like a winged lion. At least Sade knew it was a griffin. Standing on all fours, the creature looked like it was on point like a bird dog on a covey of quail. She thought the pose indicated the creature was *rampant*. Mathias attempted to teach her once upon a time but she'd tuned him out. There was a Maltese cross behind the griffin and small nicks in the wood had worn down to smudges. Someone had spent countless hours tracing the design with a fingertip and she wondered what story the box would tell if it had a voice.

Setting it back in its place, she wandered to the window. A single teak deck chair and small table graced the balcony. The view was magnificent, a sweeping panorama of lake, parks and boulevards and the sparkling city skyline. Sade got the impression Sinjen spent many a night sitting there, staring out across a city he could own if he put his vampiric powers to the task. For the first time, she realized she'd met a vampire who was at least equal in power with Mathias. It was a sobering moment.

The longer she stared out at the city, the more she wondered about the magical races. They were so much more powerful than humans yet in all the millennium they had co-existed with mankind, they'd never tried to take over. They played their petty political games with each other but for the most part, the magicks never truly involved humankind in their squabbles— her childhood notwithstanding.

A wave of sadness washed over Sade as she wondered just how often Sinjen stood here. Alone. Watching a life he could never fully partake of again. She'd watched Mathias once, when she was a child, hiding behind a chair as he slipped into the small death the sun brought. The man who always seemed so strong, so invincible had looked so terribly sad and alone as the stillness crept over him and his last breath sighed out from between his lips.

The child she'd been sobbed uncontrollably until Roman appeared. The gargoyle led her out to the garden, picked a daffodil and then turned to stone before her very eyes, the daffodil still cradled in his hand. Moments later, he resumed his more human-like glamour, handed her the flower, and kissed her forehead.

"Just a different guise, Lady Sade," Roman explained. "Mathias will return as the sun sinks." Sade the child hadn't known how to explain it wasn't the death that upset her, it was the profound sadness on her godfather's face that broke her heart. That's when the full import of Sinjen's words sank in. *No, until now, there has been no one I trusted to spend the night.* She repeated the words in her head. "Damn," she muttered. "He's fuckin' dangerous."

Chapter Eight

Danger Will Robinson

---

*H*E'S FUCKIN' DANGEROUS.

Sade repeated that phrase over and over in her head to remind herself. Standing there looking out over the lights of Chicago, she had an epiphany of sorts. She'd always thought that at the top of the magical food chain, vampires and the fae were fairly equal on the power scale. She realized in that moment, though, that vampires were much stronger than faerie. The reason? Vampires could and, more importantly, *would* kill humans. The magical races might all gleefully slaughter each other but when push came to shove, the fae would hesitate to pull the trigger, allegorically speaking, when it came to humans.

Memories—half buried, half forgotten—surged to the surface with that realization. She remembered a conversation between Titania and Roman, overheard as she hid behind curtains in lieu of getting caught when the two of them came in. Holding her breath, she'd listened.

"He would see her dead, Titania," Roman had said.

"You would do this at his order, Roman?" the queen demanded. "You would steal her life with your own hands?"

Peeking out from the edge of the curtain, Sade watched Roman shake his head. "Not by my hand, Titania, by his own. Death is something intensely personal to him."

Horrified, Titania fled from the room and Roman called Sade out from her hiding place and set her in the middle of Titania's bed. "Stay," he'd ordered before going to the balcony and launching himself into the starry sky.

Later, after Roman had delivered Sade to the place that would become her home, she'd been put to bed. Supposedly asleep, she watched through her lashes. Mathias stood beside the bed gazing at her. Roman appeared at his side. Though it was night, the moon filtered in through the wide windows and she could see both of their faces clearly.

"Did you mean it?" Roman asked, his voice soft, like a boot scuffing through gravel. "Or was that simply Black King's Bishop to G4?" He didn't look at Mathias as he added, "Checkmate."

"I do not play games, Roman. I would see her dead before relinquishing her and therefore the battle to Oberon."

She hadn't understood the words at the time and Mathias's bland tone of voice didn't really register in her child's brain. It stuck, like every other conversation she'd ever heard, but it didn't register until later. The man she adored, the man she thought would protect her and keep her safe from all harm would have killed her like an unwanted puppy to keep from losing.

Sade rubbed her chest, hoping to ease the ache that developed every time she remembered that episode in her life. The man who is more than a father to her would have sacrificed her life for his honor. Talk about a kick in the ass. And for some reason, the life of the man—the vampire—in the other room was important to Mathias. That detail made Sinjen powerful. That made him more than dangerous. In fact, it made him terrifying.

"I can be," Sinjen chuckled. "Terrifying."

"Crap. Did I say that out loud?" Sade muttered. She caught his reflection in the patio door. "Clothes," she ordered. "Put some on."

After slipping from the shower, he'd wrapped a towel around his waist. Padding quietly into the closet, he discovered Sade standing at the window in almost precisely the same place where he watched the first fingers of dawn dance across the water of Lake Michigan. Of all the things gone from his life, he missed true dawn the most. Watching the pale peach and lavender watercolors wash across the midnight blue of the heavens had once filled him with peace. Now it filled him with dread. Until he thought of wrapping his arms around the woman who stood across the room—of holding her as the lethargy stole his breath and he died with the day. A woman such as Sade Marquis could make *la mort d'aube*, the death that came with dawn, bearable.

Sinjen stalked across the room, the towel slung low on his hips. Sade turned but with the preternatural speed inherent in his kind, he blocked her against the window, a hand on each side of her head effectively pinning her without actually touching her. He leaned in as if to kiss her but only brushed his cheek against hers. "Why are you here?" he whispered against her hair.

"I told you, Mr. St. John," Sade replied, retreating back to formality and using it as a shield. "I'm the preternatural liaison officer for the FBI's MAGIC unit. If there's a crime involving one of the magical races, I'm sent to investigate."

"Why will you not call me by my given name?" Sinjen murmured, his lips nuzzling her earlobe. He felt her reaction but his own response to her surprised him once again.

The shiver that betrayed her stiffened her resolve, and her body. Sade closed her eyes. The sexiest seducer in the faerie kingdom had tried to get between her sheets. Repeatedly. Even as a randy teenager, she'd managed to hold Ariel, the King's Seducer, at arm's length. And ever since New Orleans, she'd had a sexy dragon pursuing her yet she'd resisted his charms.

She inhaled and Sinjen's unique scent filled her lungs. Leather-bound first editions. A cold breeze blowing in off the ocean. And something else. She breathed again. Musk. He smelled rich and sexy and she wanted to rub against him like a cat. Good grief. All she had to do was take a deep breath of this particular man's scent and her knees buckled. Then, to add insult to injury, her traitorous girly bits all lined up to scream, "Do me first!"

"Shut up," she muttered.

Sinjen leaned back just enough he could study her face. "I beg your pardon?"

"Not you," Sade replied. "I was…" Blushing, she vacillated. "Never mind." She attempted to step back, to put more room between them, forgetting the glass patio door at her back. She collided with it and her breath whooshed out.

"But I do mind, Lady Sade." His sibilant voice washed over her skin, raising goosebumps on her arms. "Especially when the woman is as beautiful as you."

She stared at him, her upper lip curling into a snarl. "No one calls me that."

Sinjen offered a lazy smile. "The gargoyle does."

Planting her palms in the middle of his bare chest, Sade pushed. Trying to dislodge the vampire was like trying to shove a brick wall. "Anybody ever teach you about invading personal space?" she groused. "And nobody but Roman is allowed to call me that. We clear?" Sinjen chuckled and she could almost taste caramel on her tongue. "You're wasting your time." Deep down, she wasn't sure who she tried to convince with her protestations. And a little voice in the back of her mind nudged her, though it felt more like a Gibb's slap to the back of her head. How did he know about Roman?

That lazy smile curved the corners of his full mouth. "Your wish is my command, Lady Sade," he murmured as another chuckle followed his words. "And I never waste time." Abruptly, Sinjen stepped away and turned his back. Striding off, he paused at the closet door. "I will have you, Sade Marquis," he promised. "Sooner than later."

Before she could retort that he wasn't the first to declare such, he disappeared into the closet, closing the door behind him. "Damn," she muttered, her hands curling against her thighs in lieu of trailing her fingers across the hard, muscular planes of his back. She'd just thought his chest was a piece of art.

"Don't curse," his voice called from behind the door. "It doesn't become a lady."

"Fuck you," Sade grumbled.

Rich laughter spilled from behind the door. "Yes. You will."

Drake Hotel

EUGENIA STARED AS fire flickered in the small brazier. The yellow flame turned to blue under the intensity of her gaze. "No," she whispered. The flame extinguished and she shrieked.

In the other room, Hannibal slammed down the phone, a grimace twisting his features. He glared at the man standing back in the shadows. "Explain yourself," he barked.

The man cut his eyes toward the bedroom door as the shrieks grew in intensity. "Federal judge signed the release order. There wasn't anything we could do." He shrugged. "The fed outfoxed us." The man relaxed slightly as the screaming in the next room moderated to a low moan. "Besides, it's not like he can leave town or anything. He's just out on an OR bond."

Hannibal stared at the man, both incredulous and angry. "How stupid are you?" he sneered. "The man is a vampire. Do you really believe civilian authorities could stop him? *Human* authorities?" The visitor opened his mouth to reply but Hannibal cut him off. "Shut up. Just...shut up." He marched over to the bedroom door and banged on it. "You too, Eugenia. Just shut up." The sounds emanating from the other room ceased and Hannibal rubbed his forehead. "Think. I must think. We are so close," he mumbled, pacing once again. "Plan B. Must think of Plan B."

In the bedroom, Eugenia rekindled the flame in the brazier. She set a marble mortar and pestle on the table next to it. From a drawer, she withdrew a large leather roll, untied the strings binding the roll, and laid it out flat. Contemplating the selection of herbs and spices contained in small silver tubes, she pulled out a few and set them aside. She reached for another tube, this one glass and containing a dark liquid. Holding the tube by the glass stopper, she gently swirled it in front of the small flame. The liquid glistened like rubies on black satin. Her hand shook and Eugenia quickly slipped the cylinder back into its padded pocket before she dropped the vial and its precious contents. Her hand continued to shake for a few moments even after she clasped it with her other.

"Too much," she whispered, wrapping her arms around her middle. "I can't hold it. Too much."

The flame in the brazier flared, turned green, and then changed to a purple so dark it was almost black. Eugenia moaned as the flame burned itself out again. She looked up, staring into the mirror above the dresser. Her pupils were so dilated her irises looked black. Her eyes remained fixated on the mirror as her hands added pinches of the aromatic herbs from the silver vials to the mortar. Her lips moved in a silent incantation as she ground the mixture with the pestle. Eugenia withdrew a small square of silk from another pocket sewn into the roll. Very carefully, she upended the mortar and dumped the mixture onto the silk.

Reaching up, she plucked a long hair from her head. She tied one knot in the exact center. "Birth," she intoned. She tied a second knot approximately an inch away. "Death," Eugenia pronounced. She tied a third knot about an inch further along the hair shaft. "Life everlasting," she promised.

The brazier leapt to life, flames dancing across its surface. Eugenia gently curled the hair into the center of the silk and using utmost care, folded up the square. Clasping it gingerly pinched between thumb and forefinger, she held it over the fire until it burst into flame. She let go of the silk bundle and it fluttered into the flames, leaving a comet trail of sparks in its wake. A thin plume of black smoke undulated above the brazier. As the delicate cloud dispersed, Eugenia's eyes returned to normal. She smiled at her reflection. "Life everlasting," she repeated.

Buckingham Fountain, Grant Park

THE MULTI-TIERED FOUNTAIN glowed against the darker vistas of Grant Park. White spotlights lit the center spray and three tiers around it. The icy water turned the lights golden. Yellow-gold spotlights painted the verdigris sea horses as they undulated in the frigid liquid, the spray from their mouths looking more like frosty breath than water. The far-off hum of traffic masked the soft plop of something dropping into the dark water of the huge basin surrounding the fountain's structure. A dark shape floated on the surface, bobbing like a piece of flotsam until the waves pushed it against the curled tail of one of the horses where it stayed, gently bumping the green metal. The ambient white and yellow lights dimmed as a soft red glow crept in, slowly brightening until scarlet overtook gold, bathing the whole fountain in blood-red light.

A couple, both of them bundled up against the midnight chill, walked hand-in-gloved-hand along the path leading to Buckingham Fountain. The man leaned down and whispered something in the woman's ear. She laughed at his words, the sound floating through the glacial night air. They stopped at the fountain, marveling at the magnificent sight.

"I've never seen red lights on it before," the woman murmured, her voice filled with wonder. "It's beautiful."

Her companion turned to face her and pulled the woman into his arms. "Not as beautiful as the woman I'm about to kiss," he declared. He kissed her then, his lips sealing against hers, his tongue probing, his arms pressing her against his chest. "I have a warm bed waiting," he whispered against her cheek after he broke the kiss.

The woman smiled and nodded. "Home, Jeeves," she agreed.

Arm-in-arm, they headed across the fountain plaza. Their leisurely stroll now had a bit of urgency as they made a beeline for the nearest cabstand. The couple had a night of lovemaking ahead of them and they were both anxious to be home. As they circled the fountain, something in the water caught the man's eye. "What's that?" He slowed down for a closer look.

"Where?" The woman glanced at him. The man pointed toward the base of one of the sea horses and her eyes followed his gesture. She blinked and squinted, moving closer to the rim of the basin. The wind whipped up little waves on the water's surface and the thing bobbing in the shadows floated closer. Transfixed, the couple watched the object drift nearer. When it was only a few feet away, the thing suddenly rolled in the water. The couple found themselves staring at the pale, dead face of a young woman. Empty eye sockets stared up in mute supplication. The woman screamed…and screamed and screamed.

Chapter Nine

Blood and Turnips

SCREAMS ECHOING IN THE NIGHT.

Something about screaming sirens set Sade's teeth on edge. Beneath their wail came the heartrending sound of a human scream and that was the worst sound of all. An ambulance, parked just outside the crime scene tape, idled amid the grumbling exhaust of a diesel engine. The shrieking came from inside the back of it. Standing there freezing her ass off, watching her breath leave a cloud of crystallized frost with each puff, Sade tried to figure out why the local boys had tracked her down.

The screaming woman and her boyfriend—the poor guy wrapped in a blanket with his hands over his ears huddled in the back of the squad car parked behind the ambulance—had found the body. Turning around, she could see Sinjen's building. His windows overlooked Grant Park. With a good set of binoculars, she would be able to see Buckingham Fountain in minute detail from his balcony.

Sade attempted to leave Sinjen at his place but he wouldn't hear of her traipsing around Chicago in the middle of the night all by her lonesome. Yeah. All alone in the middle of a working crime scene. Right. There were more uniformed cops than she could shake a stick at and despite the fact she arrived in one of their patrol cars, they all seemed intent on asking what she was doing there. Her badge and ID hadn't left her hand. She dealt with every attempt by the local cops to stop Sinjen with a brusque, "He's with me."

The night was cold enough to freeze a witch's tits and she still hadn't figured out why she was there. From what she'd learned so far, boyfriend and the screamer found the body of a female victim floating in the fountain. The woman had screamed hysterically—like she was still doing—until somebody finally called the cops to complain about the disturbance.

The first uniform on the scene called for backup, detectives, and EMS for the woman—the screaming woman, not the dead one. Even the rookie cop was smart enough to figure out the victim was dead. The uniform giving Sade the run-down was showing the whites around his eyes, but she figured that had more to do with the vampire at her side than the crime scene. This was Chicago. Murder happened. A lot. Standing face-to-face with a vampire? Not so much.

A knot of people gathered near the fountain—a couple of uniforms, at least two detectives, evidenced by their clothing, and a guy Sade suspected belonged to the Medical Examiner's office. Another group huddled a few feet away—two transport guys from the morgue and a pair of crime scene investigators. One of the CSIs snapped pictures of the fountain.

The place was an impressive site—a huge, pink marble wedding cake surrounded by green seahorses. Water shot from too many jets to count and the red lights gave the scene an ethereal glow. Sade studied the water, surprised it hadn't frozen. For a brief moment, she wondered how much it cost the city to heat the fountain's water for year round use.

One of the detectives motioned Sade over and she headed his direction, Sinjen half a step behind her. "You the special Fed?" The cop's voice sounded hoarse in the frigid air. "Bobby Franks, Chicago Homicide." He didn't offer to shake hands. Both of his remained fisted deep in the pockets of his down jacket.

Sade nodded, flashing her badge and ID. "Sade Marquis. I'm the Special Agent in Charge of the MAGIC unit." She glanced around. "Frankly, Detective Franks, I'm not sure why you called me."

"This is most odd," Sinjen murmured in Sade's ear before the detective could reply. She glanced at the vampire, an eyebrow quirked in question. "The fountain," he explained in a whisper. "It is only in operation from April until October. It should not be activated. And…" his voice trailed off as his nose twitched. "Blood."

A vampire's nose was better than a bloodhound's when it came to sniffing out blood. Sade, about to retort something snide to that effect, remained silent when one of the technical investigators retched. The guys from the ME's office both looked green around the gills too. Sade stared at Sinjen.

"Blood," he reiterated. "That isn't water in the fountain. It is blood."

Okay, Sade thought. *That explains why they called me.* She watched the reactions of the investigators around her and then made a quick eyeball measurement of the fountain. She guessed the wedding cake tiers rose between twenty-five and thirty feet and that the bottom pool of the fountain measured between 250 and 300 feet in diameter. The forensic tech who wasn't sick recited the pertinent facts from memory as she jotted them down in a notebook.

"I used to work for the Parks Department. The base pool is two hundred and eighty feet in diameter. The lower basin is a hundred and three feet, the middle basin is sixty feet and the upper basin is twenty-four feet. The lip of the upper basin is twenty-five feet above the water in the lower basin. The pumps circulate over fourteen thousand gallons a minute." She paused to take a long breath. "The fountain holds one-point-five million gallons of water." The whites showed all the way around her pupils as she gulped and stared at the detectives. "Where the hell do you get a million and a half gallons of blood?" It wasn't a rhetorical question.

Sade stared at the answer gal. She just thought her brain was stuffed with trivia and she, too, wondered how the hell 1.5 million gallons of blood materialized in the dead of winter.

"Fuckin' A," Franks swore softly then turned back to Sade. "I knew you were in town because of the Adams murder. I called you because of the state of my vic." He shook his head. "She was warm. Floating in liquid that should be frozen solid and she was warm. And her eyes." The detective shuddered, "Her eyes had been plucked out but..." His voice died.

"There was no obvious trauma to the eye sockets or the skin around them," the ME added. "No blood. No bruising. Even the best surgeon in the world would have left marks."

"Okay. That's pretty creepy," Sade admitted.

The ME snorted. "And one point five million gallons of blood isn't?"

Sade shrugged but before she could say anything, she realized Sinjen had moved closer to the basin. Steam rose from the surface of the pool. Something Sinjen said finally registered. "Wait. Let me get this straight," she began. "The fountain shouldn't be working at all?"

Franks nodded. "Correct. City shuts down mid-October to mid-April, depending on the weather. Even if it were in season, the light show shuts down at eleven o'clock."

Watching Sinjen, Sade nodded absently. "So why didn't our couple figure out something was screwy? Tourists maybe?"

"No. Locals," Franks replied. "The man says it didn't even occur to him. He only wanted to get his girlfriend home and in bed. She'd been complaining they never did anything romantic so he figured a walk through the snowy park would do the trick."

"Some trick," Sade muttered. Something about Sinjen's posture caught her attention. She moved closer. "What is it?" She pitched her voice low so only he could hear.

Sinjen stared down at the body floating in the blood bath. "Miriam." The sadness in the vampire's voice was palpable. "Miriam Goddard. She was one of my students."

Movement in the corner of her eye made Sade hold up her hand. "Back off, Franks," she ordered. "I was at Cook County when the assistant US Attorney hit them with the court order and I've been with Professor St. John ever since. He's not a suspect."

"Not in this one anyway," the homicide detective muttered.

"Not the other one, either." Sade snapped the words out.

"Bullshit," a third voice chimed in.

Sade looked the newcomer up and down. Something about him niggled the back corners of her memory. Short, wide, middle-aged, balding, with a paunch overhanging his belt, the man's eyes were narrow and rather piggish. He carried himself like a cop but Sade saw Franks stiffen beside her. She got the distinct feeling Franks did not like this guy.

"Fuckin' vampire's guilty as sin," the man continued, assessing Sade much as she'd appraised him. "You must be the hotshot Fed," he snarled. "Go back to Washington. We don't need you stickin' your nose in where it isn't needed or wanted. 'Specially not a monster lover like you."

"Don't be a dick, Dick," Franks retorted.

The light bulb went off in Sade's head. "Detective Kowalski, I presume." Her voice dripped sarcasm. "Fancy meeting you here." *And I'm sorry I missed you at the party.*

"What's the bloodsucker doing here?" Kowalski stabbed his index finger in Sinjen's direction.

"He's in my custody, Kowalski, and has been since his release from the detention facility earlier tonight." Sade took a great deal of delight in the effect that piece of information had on the cop. She enjoyed the sour look on his face as she added, "You've been avoiding me, Dick, but since you're here now, let's talk about CeeCee Adams."

"I don't have to talk to you, bit..." Kowalski clamped his mouth shut before going too far, but he continued to glare at her and Sinjen both.

Sade laughed. "Sticks and stones, Kowalski. It's true. You don't have to talk to me here." She shrugged, a negligent lift of one shoulder to match her intentionally bored look. "I'll call your captain in the morning and request a formal interview and your case file."

"You...you can't do that," the heavy-set cop sputtered.

Flashing him a smile as frigid as the night air, Sade nodded. "Yes. Yes, I can. It's a federal case now." She turned to face the fountain, effectively dismissing Kowalski. "Oh, Dick?" she called over her shoulder. "Don't fuck with the files. I'll eat your balls for brunch if you do." She glanced at Sinjen as he cleared his throat and gave her a disparaging look. "What? I will. Right after I cut them off and sauté 'em in bacon grease."

While Sade dealt with Kowalski, the ME, the two CSIs processed the scene. The crime scene tech with the weak stomach recovered enough to go through the motions mechanically. The other CSI took a couple of samples of the viscous liquid in the fountain while the first took pictures.

The ME shook his head as his two transporters hauled the body out of the basin. "Ambient liquid temperature is ninety-eight point seven," he muttered. "There's no way. It just isn't possible." The men laid the naked woman down on the open body bag and the ME knelt beside her. After his initial assessment, he looked up at Franks and Sade. "No visible wounds. Just the missing eyes. I can't tell you how long she's been dead. Floating in—" he paused to jerk his head toward the pool, "—*that* kept the body warm. Hopefully, I'll know something after the autopsy." He gestured for the transporters to zip up the bag as he regained his feet. "I've never seen anything like this. I was here for the ghoul attacks so it's not like I haven't been around."

Sade remembered that incident well. A nest of ghouls appeared in an old cemetery called Bachman Grove. The ghouls split up with half of them infesting Resurrection Cemetery and the others moving into Graceland Cemetery. Ghouls normally didn't attack live creatures. They preferred dead flesh and dark places. No one ever figured out what caused them to chew on live people. Sade nodded in sympathy. Ghouls were messy eaters. She'd been on a case in Seattle at the time and missed the fun and games in the Windy City. Eventually, the governor called out the National Guard and the nests were burned out. Pulling a business card out of her pocket, Sade passed it to the ME. "Would you give me a call when you find something?"

The coroner flashed a lopsided smile. "When not if? I appreciate the confidence. Will do." He stared at the dark ruby waves shimmering across the torpid surface of the pool. "Gotta be magic," he muttered.

Sade glanced at Sinjen. "Yeah," she agreed with the ME. "Magic. But no magic I'm familiar with. This is bad mojo shit."

The transporters loaded the body onto a gurney and wheeled it toward their van. The ME had to force himself to turn away from the fountain. "I'll be in touch." He acknowledged both Sade and Franks but brushed past Kowalski without a word.

Franks stared at Sade, his face looking tired and gray. "Why do I get the feeling that when *you* say it is bad mojo shit it's really-*really* bad nasty magical shit?"

"Because I'm the preternatural expert?" she quipped with only a hint of irony in her voice. A moment later, her expression settled into a blank mask. She was too good a poker player, having learned from the best—Roman and Caleb—to let the locals know that not only was she completely baffled but that she was worried too. Sade had been exposed to magic her entire life— the good, the sexy, the evil. And this had her stumped.

"It is dissipating," Sinjen murmured so only Sade could hear. She glanced at him, a question in her eyes. "The magic…the spell. It's wearing off," he explained.

As she watched, the deep red lights on the fountain faded to pink and then clear. The water stopped looking like rubies on black satin, reflecting the lights now in silvery shimmers across its surface. Icicles formed on the tiers and the muzzles of the seahorses. Sade turned to him. "How the hell is this happening?"

Before Sinjen could reply, a civilian jangling a huge ring of keys trotted up. "The mechanical room is locked up tighter than a drum. There's no way water should be pumpin' or the lights be on. There shouldn't even be water in this thing. We drain the system when we winterize it." He sounded breathless and confused.

Everyone exchanged uneasy glances. "I've heard of water into wine," one of the techs mumbled. "But water into blood?"

"And the Lord spake unto Moses," Sinjen intoned, his voice quiet and reverent. All eyes turned to him, even Kowalski's. "Say unto Aaron, take thy rod, and stretch out thine hand upon the waters of Egypt. Upon their streams, upon their rivers, and upon their ponds, and upon all their pools of water, that they may become blood; and that there may be blood throughout all the land of Egypt, both in vessels of wood, and in vessels of stone."

"Armageddon?" Kowalski's voice cracked and he croaked like a toad trying to clear it. "You talkin' about fuckin' Armageddon?"

Sinjen, his expression calm, regarded the cop who had arrested him. "No. That would be the Book of Revelations. Water to blood was one of the plagues God visited upon Egypt. Old Testament."

"Great," the second crime scene investigator snarled. "When it starts snowing frogs, we can blame all this on God and go home to bed." His sarcasm was difficult to miss.

"Do not take His name in vain!" Sinjen's voice rang in the cold air.

Everyone turned to stare at him. The cops all exchanged uneasy looks and then stared at Sade. "I thought the bloodsuckers were allergic to religious shit," Kowalski finally said.

"Depends on the vampire," Sade replied after a slight hesitation. She still watched Sinjen. "I mean, the guy's name is Kristian St. John, for cris…" Sinjen's glare caused her to amend what she'd been about to say. "Yeah. Whatever. There's a lot of hype about vampires and other magicks floating around out there on the web. Believe all of it with a grain of salt." Sade wasn't about to tell them all the secrets she was privy to. "Of course, the converse is true. If you have true faith, that never hurts."

"Remind me to start going back to Mass," a uniformed cop muttered as he genuflected.

"No shit," the other CSI concurred. "And I'm not even Catholic."

Sade watched for Sinjen's reaction and she noticed the narrowing of his eyes and the way he pressed his lips together. He was angry and trying very hard not to show it. Talk about still waters running deep. There was a great deal about this man she didn't know but she would damn sure find out—starting with why Mathias thought he owed Sinjen his life.

She turned to Franks. "I'd like to see a copy of all your forensic reports as soon as they become available." Without warning, she whirled and stabbed a finger into Kowalski's chest. "And I want to see you and the ADA who filed the charges against Professor St. John first thing in the morning. No ifs, ands, or buts, Kowalski. And no ducking out the back exit."

Sade grinned toothily. Oh, yeah. She would have fun with Dick and Jane in the morning. She extended her leather-gloved hand to the other cop. "Wish I could say it was a pleasure, Detective Franks, but under the circumstances…" She dipped her chin in his direction while lifting one shoulder to indicate the events surrounding their meeting sucked.

"I hear that." Franks shook her hand. "You'll keep me in the loop?"

Sade nodded. "For now, it's still your case, Detective. I'm just here to help." Kowalski sputtered but Sade cut him off. "You'd already made an arrest, Kowalski. I automatically get jurisdiction when that happens. Besides, you're a dickhead." With an arched-brow glance in Sinjen's direction, Sade headed back toward Columbus Drive. She sensed his shadow following behind her.

The two of them ducked under the yellow crime scene tape in unison and walked to the street. Sade's long legs set the pace; Sinjen matched her stride for stride. Any other night, he would have walked the several blocks back to his apartment. Tonight, he hailed a cab. Though a patrol car had picked them up, none seemed available to return them to his building. Settled into the back seat, he draped one arm around Sade's shoulders and tucked her into his side.

"Take your gloves off," he ordered in a quiet voice. When Sade flashed him an angry look, he shushed the retort forming on the tip of her tongue by laying his index finger against her lips. "Shh," he murmured. "Your hands are cold. I only intend to warm them."

Before Sade could react, he'd peeled one of the gloves off her frigid hands. Sinjen folded his massive paw around her slim fingers. Pulling that hand to his lips, he gently kissed the back of it. Almost immediately, warmth returned. "The other glove, Sade."

"Can't." The word sighed out with her exhalation, a soft rush of the breath she'd been holding. "Takes two hands and you've got that one." Her green eyes glittered as she spoke and the mole at the corner of her mouth threatened to change from a period to an exclamation point.

He stared at that small black mark and fought the urge to taste it with the tip of his tongue. He had every intention of wooing and winning this woman but like a spirited horse, she would need to be gentled rather than broken. Sade Marquis was a legend in the preternatural world—the Holy Grail of sexual unavailability, the only human woman who could resist the allure of the King's Seducer.

The fact that Ariel still tried to warm her bed was a perennial wager among the magicks. Her capitulation was a trophy all of the legendary lovers coveted. Even Oberon had remarked that he would have deflowered the girl had not Titania ensorcelled his cock causing it to go limp whenever Sade was near. He tucked her bare hand into the crook of his arm and worked off the glove on her other hand. This one he simply held between both his hands, chafing it with gentle strokes.

The cab pulled to the curb at Sinjen's building. Chuck, the doorman, was Johnny-on-the spot and opened the car door even as Sinjen leaned forward to pay the driver. With an elegance of motion inherent in his breed, he exited the cab and held out his hand to help Sade out. Without gloves, her hands chilled again—until she placed one in his hand. Warmth immediately spread through her. Her eyes flashed as she stared at him and flexed her fingers. He knew warmth spread up her arm, just as it radiated up his own.

Chuck slammed the cab's door and scurried to get the building's door opened. He followed them into the warmth of the lobby. "I have those security tapes you asked for, Agent Marquis. Want me to bring them up to Mr. Sinjen's?"

"Miss Marquis will pick them up on her way out in the morning, Chuck," Sinjen answered before she could reply. "She's off duty at the moment."

"I'm never off duty," she retorted.

Chapter Ten

Nothing to Fear but Fear Itself

I'M NEVER OFF DUTY. The words ricocheted through the silence enveloping the elevator. She wasn't, Sade admitted. Ever. But riding up in the small, enclosed space as she stood next to Kristian St. John, her girlie bits threatened mutiny. She didn't have time in her life for girlie bits...or for the manly bits they clamored for. Men just complicated things. Sex just complicated things. And love? Oh, man, she damn sure didn't want to go there. Lust was bad enough but when emotion got stirred into the mix?

That was the rub. She didn't know Sinjen well enough to be emotional about him. But her libido shifted into overdrive to convince her that she did know him and that she wanted to be *emotional* about him. *Stop*, she argued with herself. *I don't know anything about him and I don't want to know anything. Okay, so that's a lie. I want to know all sorts of things.*

Mainly, she wanted to know about Sinjen's link to Mathias. Her curiosity had nothing to do with it. Her gut insisted both vampires were up to their fangs in this mess. Vampires had their own brand of magic but none she knew could have pulled off that deal at the fountain. Any master vampire could create the *illusion*, but that had been real. Hell, the fae weren't even powerful enough to fill an empty fountain with over a million gallons of water, turn it to blood, and then back into water in the dead of winter. In Chicago. When the temp was fucking negative twenty outside.

King Obi-wan and Queen Tittyfae and probably most of the Seelie Court could have managed the illusion too. But Sade was positive this was no mass hallucination engineered by a magick. She'd seen the blood, making it impossible to be anything but real. Magic didn't work on her. Any magic. She couldn't be hypnotized, spellbound, bumfuzzled, enthralled or otherwise messed with thanks to the marks left by both Mathias and Oberon when she was a child.

Sade refused to look at the vampire beside her, even as she unconsciously rubbed her temple with fingers that trembled. What role did Hannibal and Eugenia Crowley play? Why would someone want to frame Sinjen for murder? The murder of a girl who worked for Eugenia's fiancé at that. A girl who was engaged to the son of another political mover and shaker?

What about the second girl in the fountain? Was her murder tied in with CeeCee's? They'd both been Sinjen's students. No one could have known she'd be getting the vampire out of jail. Either way, he had a helluva alibi for the second girl's death. There was more going on here than she or Sinjen knew, and her job was to figure things out. The weight of responsibility pressed against her chest making it hard to breathe. Two young women dead—and grotesquely murdered. Would there be more? She was determined to stop the perpetrator here and now.

Sinjen didn't speak. He stared stonily ahead when Sade glanced at him. She wondered if the amount of magic involved at the fountain freaked him out as much as it did her. Once she was in his apartment, with the door closed to the outside world, she hoped to put the whole situation into perspective. She glanced at him again and chastised her girlie bits as they clamored again. She had to keep her mind on the case, had to stay focused. Loosing another victim on her watch was unacceptable.

She closed her eyes for a moment. She didn't have a clue about the motive, but she did have a passel of politicians, vampires, self-professed witches, two dead girls…and a partridge in a pear tree. Plus girlie bits standing up to be counted every time her arm brushed against his. Damnation. This was so not good. There was some bad nasty magic in town and she needed to focus on finding out who, what, where, when and how. She did not need distractions. Didn't want distractions. All six feet plus of him. Yeah, buddy. Kristian St. John was one helluva distraction.

The doors to the elevator opened.

"Dammit." She stepped into the hallway.

"Why do you persist in using foul language, Sade?" He leaned against the elevator door, keeping it from closing.

She turned to stare at him. "Why do you care? Besides, you're a vampire, Sinjen. We all know vampires belong to the dark side." She tossed her shoulder up in a little shrug. "And since you walk in the shadows a few cuss words shouldn't get your panties in a twist."

Sade headed up the hallway toward his apartment and missed the sudden gleam that lit his eyes. In fact, she wasn't looking at him at all. The nonchalance with which she consigned him to the dark was a mere irritant. Despite the twinge of anger, a pleased glow spread through him but Sinjen let no sign of his delight show. She had called him by his familiar name.

"It is the principle of the thing, dearest Sade," he explained, striding after her. He brushed past her to unlock his door. He pushed it open and stood back to let her enter first. "You are a lady and a lady's words should be as fair as her face." Genuinely puzzled, he added, "Why does being a vampire mean I am evil? I don't understand this logic."

Arching one eyebrow, Sade stared at him. "Vampires are evil. Didn't they teach you that in Vampires 101? Or did you just read the 'Vampires For Dummies' version?"

The only outward sign he gave that his anger had overtaken his delight was the slight flaring of his nostrils. "Raised by Mathias and yet you know nothing." His frosty voice could have hung icicles on the words.

Sade stared at him. He stared back, watching as her eyes widened when she recognized the cold anger behind his words. It was almost palpable and she stepped back from him, as if to fend him off. "Whoa, dude. Where'd that come from? You don't know me well enough to be familiar with my upbringing." He stalked across the room toward her as she backpedaled. Red sparks flashed in the depths of his eyes to be mirrored in hers.

"Back off, St. John."

Sinjen didn't. He backed her up until the glass of the wide window in his living room stopped her. "And you know nothing of mine, Sade Marquis," he growled.

No one had ever accused Sade of knowing when to back down. "How many people have you killed, Sinjen?" she demanded, taking an aggressive step into him. "How many women have you seduced?" He didn't back up so Sade got right up in his face. "How many?"

"Enough to last several lifetimes." His anger stoked a fire under his words. "I was a warrior, Sade. I killed to stay alive. I killed because it was my duty." He took a long breath, his chest swelling enough that it brushed against hers. "As for the other, I was a knight. A Templar."

Looking completely dumbfounded, Sade stared at him until she found her voice. "You aren't that old. You can't be." She shook her head, still disbelieving. "That would make you over seven hundred years old. That's older than Mathias and that's just not possible."

Sinjen sighed. "You think you know so much and yet you are such a child. Marking you as they did has done you more harm than good, Sade. You don't have the sense of wonder needed to keep yourself safe. How old do you believe Mathias to be?"

"I know how old Mathias is. He was born in the fifteen hundreds."

"Ask Mathias, Sade. Ask him about Richard." The heat left Sinjen's voice, replaced by cold resignation. "Ask him about the battles he fought at the side of the Lionheart."

Sade's mouth gaped. He watched the wheels turn in her head. Finally managing to close her mouth and find her voice, she whispered, "That isn't possible."

Sinjen stepped away from her then turned his back. "You have talked to Mathias since we met. What did he tell you about me? About him and me?"

Her knees shook, the muscles in her thighs danced under her slacks, yet Sade managed to sink semi-gracefully onto the arm of the leather side chair. "Nothing. Not really. He told me..." She paused to consider just what Mathias had told her. She should have been able to read between the lines. "He told me that it was a long story and that he didn't have time to relate it.

He told me to take care of you." Sade took a deep breath. "Coming from Mathias—"

Sinjen interrupted her. "Mathias cares for no one." His shoulders raised, then lowered, as if he took a deep breath—or sighed. "Not even you, Sade. You have always been just a pawn." He turned around to face her.

Sade twisted her mouth into a hard, grim line as she glared at the vampire standing across the room. "You think I don't know that? When I was three, he would have killed me with his own hands, Sinjen. He didn't go to war with the Seelie Court out of love for my father or for me. He did it simply to fuck with the fae, because he wanted to win."

"Language."

"Fuck you, Kristian St. John. I want to know why Mathias cares about *you* when he cares for no one else. I want to know why he called you his savior." Heat rose in her cheeks. She didn't care if her anger translated to a red face. She pushed off the chair, her fury propelling her across the room. She jabbed her index finger into Sinjen's chest. "I want to know why a creature incapable of love loves you."

Before she could react, Sinjen pulled her into his arms and kissed her— deeply, one hand at the small of her back, the other tangled in her hair. After a long, breathless moment, he released her so suddenly she fell back a step.

"Why do you persist in believing that we are incapable of love?" He panted like he'd run a marathon. "We loved as humans—fully and passionately. Because the sun can no longer shine on us, this makes us evil?"

Sade wiped her mouth with the back of her hand, noticed a little smear of blood. Using her tongue, she licked at the small cut on her bottom lip. Caused by one of Sinjen's fangs, it stung as her tongue teased it. Every nerve ending in her body popped and sizzled. "I never said you were evil. Vampires have no conscience. If they act with honor, this does not become a problem."

"You believe there is no honor among *thieves*, yes?" Sinjen's voice dropped to a husky whisper.

Tilting her head to look up at him, Sade replied. "I believe *thieves* are only honorable when it suits them."

Sinjen reached out to brush her cheek with the knuckles of two fingers. His voice dropped to the merest whisper. "Mathias and the fae have done you a grave disservice, Lady Sade."

Her cheek burned from his touch. "Don't," she hissed, jerking away from the contact. She struggled to control her emotions; forced her breathing to remain slow and steady. She prided herself on her ability to maintain control. She didn't love. She didn't lust. She didn't get mad—she got even. "Just don't," she repeated, unaware of the pleading tone in her voice.

"What are you afraid of, Sade?"

"Nothing!"

Sinjen shook his head, a hint of sadness revealed before he blinked and erased the emotion. "You should be, Sade, you should be very afraid."

"Because you say so?" She snorted, the sound crude and inelegant. "You know nothing about me, Sinjen. I'm not afraid of you. I'm not afraid of Mathias. I'm not afraid of the fuckin' fae." She sneered at the expression of dismay that crossed his face. "And I will cuss any damn time I feel like it, even if it upsets your delicate sensibilities."

Sinjen schooled his face into a bland expression but he couldn't keep the quizzical tone of his voice when he asked, "Why do you persist in trying to antagonize me, Sade?"

She laughed, the sound dry and mirthless. "Antagonize you? You make it sound personal, Professor St. John. Trust me, it isn't. I'm just doing my job."

The expression on Sinjen's face didn't change, didn't flicker or waver, but his eyes filled with a sadness so profound it brought tears to her eyes. "Yes," he agreed. "It is never personal for you. And they call me the monster."

"I never called you a monster, Sinjen," she murmured. "I've never called any of your kind monsters."

"My kind?" he growled. "Just what is my kind, Sade?" Sinjen brushed past her and went to stand at the window. "Undead? Evil? Seducers of virgins? I am a vampire. Now. I wasn't always. I was once a warrior, a knight. I was also a young man who loved a beautiful young girl. I buried her...and my son with her. I fought a war against the Saracens. I became a Templar. And I sacrificed myself to save a man whose life was more important than my own. I died and I was reborn. Where is the evil in that, Sade Marquis? What is there in my life that makes me a monster?" Sinjen stood feet apart, his back stiff, broad shoulders straight, midnight blue eyes staring unseeing into the predawn cold outside the window.

Sade took a step toward him, her hand out, reaching. She touched his back and he flinched. With a sigh, she turned and headed for the hallway door. "I'll be in touch. Make sure your doors are secure." She opened the front door and stepped out. Pausing, she turned back. "I'm sorry, Sinjen. I'm not sure what you were expecting from me."

"I wasn't expecting you to be a coward."

Chapter Eleven

Coward of the County

I WASN'T EXPECTING YOU TO BE A COWARD.

Those words stung. She was not a coward. Absolutely not. She didn't care what Sinjen thought. And it *wasn't* personal. It couldn't be. It had to be all about the job. It had to. She didn't have room in her life for personal.

Shut up! The internal command did nothing to still her thoughts. Her psyche insisted this was not a case of the lady doth protest too much. Sade hadn't joined the FBI for it to get personal. She was good at what she did. Damn good. "Yeah, another four letter word. I'm just full of the damn things, Kristian St. John. To hell with you." Her words echoed hollowly as the elevator doors closed.

Chuck, true to his word had burned a disk of the security tapes. As soon as she stepped off the elevator, he hustled to get them for her.

"I burned two DVDs 'cause I figured you'd need it original, ya know. I kept a copy for here too."

She barely slowed down after snatching the disks. Chuck hustled out the door and whistled like a construction worker eyeing a leggy blonde. A cab pulled up at the curb, and Sade climbed in while Chuck held the door for her.

"The Hyatt on Wacker."

The cabby floored the accelerator and the vehicle lurched. Sade simply pressed back against the seat and braced. This guy might actually survive the drive too. Checking her watch, she planned the upcoming day. A couple of hours until dawn. She'd check the DVD, grab some sleep then head to Chicago Homicide.

As the sun rose across Lake Michigan, *l'morte d'aube* would claim Sinjen. Sade closed her eyes. Why even think of him? This case was not personal. Hell, Ariel was better looking. Caleb had more animal magnetism. Roman's body put everyone's to shame. Nikos oozed sex appeal. So why was it when she closed her eyes, Sinjen haunted her thoughts? She sneezed a disgusted snort. The obvious solution would be never to close her eyes again.

The case. She had to focus on the case. Two girls. One drained of blood. One bathing in it. Both were students of Sinjen's. What else did they have in common? CeeCee Adams was blonde, blue-eyed, pert in all the right places. The cheerleader next door in a "Debbie Does Dallas" kind of way. Miriam Goddard was dark-headed and…no-eyed. She made a note to find out the color of Miriam's eyes. Both girls were nude. She'd bet dollars to donuts CeeCee was killed elsewhere then moved to Sinjen's apartment. Had Miriam been killed at the fountain? And damn it all to hell, where did all the blood come from?

Sade squinted her eyes, rubbed her temple, braced as the cab careened around a corner just ahead of a red light. For a moment, the light bathed the pavement in glimmering ruby, just like the water at the fountain. *Okay*, she admitted to herself. The only possible explanation meant someone…or some *thing* changed the water to blood. The removal of Miriam's body broke the spell and the liquid reverted to water. Holy fuck. She combed fingers through her mop of hair.

Who or what could do bad-nasty enough magic on a body to create an enchantment that powerful? And would silver bullets kill it? Yeah, she had a clip loaded with silver bullets and one that had modified bullets carrying high explosives. She had another loaded with 9mm Parabellum hollow-points. Luger first manufactured parabellum bullets in the 19th century. The name came from the company's Latin motto. *Si vis pacem, para bellum*. If you seek peace, prepare for war. Sade nodded in agreement. The phrase fit her philosophy and reminded her of that old adage: Don't bring a knife to a gunfight.

Raised in a vampire's household, she didn't exactly receive a religious upbringing. College philosophy classes failed to answer the eternal debate—did God create man or did man create God? If a human had faith in holy religious symbols, did it help keep a vampire at bay? Sort of like voodoo, maybe. She'd been told if a person didn't believe in voodoo, it wouldn't work.

After her stint in New Orleans, a plethora of voodoo dolls with her likeness littered the streets down there. She certainly couldn't tell any difference in her day-to-day life. Sade put her faith in silver bullets and wooden stakes, though warding off the fae created a whole different set of magical woowoo. And dragons. The only way to kill a dragon was to shred its heart.

Most humans were way too enamored of the magicks to suit Sade. Magicks were the rock stars of the new millennium. Everyone wanted to be a groupie. Except her. She wasn't anyone's groupie. Not Ariel's. Or Oberon's. She shuddered at the thought. That would be too much like sleeping with Mathias. That was doubly icky. Ewww. Just ewwww. She shuddered again. Caleb. Too frequently of late, he filled her thoughts.

They'd shared a bed for most of their lives. Granted, he'd been in wolf form until puberty. After his change, all the debutantes in her social set thought he was wild and sexy. 'Course they never knew just how *wild*. She steadfastly refused to dwell on the sexy part. Playing doctor didn't count when the patient could turn furry at any moment. Not to mention the fact that familiarity breeds contempt and sibling rivalry. Any affection beyond that bordered on feelings more incestuous than their comfort zone allowed.

Roman. She'd had a crush on the gargoyle since the age of three. He was her rock, no pun intended. Roman arrived for good after Mathias found Ariel in her room for about the tenth time. Gargoyles protected cathedrals and other important buildings for good reason. They didn't take shit off anybody. And they didn't take sides. A tenuous thing, their loyalty—getting and keeping. Roman was the only person allowed to call her Lady Sade. Period. No ifs. No ands. No buts. No matter what that damn vampire insisted.

Her phone dinged with the opening notes of "Puff the Magic Dragon." She considered letting the call roll over to voice mail. Then again, Nikos might get her mind off a certain elegant vampire. Sade could sum up Nikos with one word—impeccable. Ariel's word was frivolous, though after that case in New Orleans, she might have to rethink that. She also had one word for Sinjen. Delicious. And sexy. Okay, two words. She answered her phone.

"I told you, I'm working."

Drake Hotel: Dawn

THE SUN PUSHED up past the horizon on the far side of Lake Michigan, sending deep rose fingers through the clouds. Traffic trickled toward rush hour and the cold wind chilled everyone to the bone. Eugenia Crowley finally slept quietly, the demons and visions of the dark put to rest at last. The dreams of blood and sightless eyes were swallowed by the warmth of the pale winter sun kissing her even paler cheek.

Hannibal Crowley stood in the doorway watching his only child sleep. Her moans and whimpers had kept him awake and he was concerned even now as she slept peacefully. He knew what was happening—had in fact anticipated it. In the beginning, he'd been willing to sacrifice her. Now he realized he would not have to. His daughter, the fruit of his loins had been chosen a fitting vessel for *O Kim Bkze Bedoaru Gelmek*—for She Who Is To Come. It was time, finally. *Mevsim in belgili tanamlak büyücü* was here. The season of the Witch had arrived. And the Witch was making her wicked demands known.

Hyatt Regency: Dawn plus one hour

SADE CALLED THE Regency Club concierge and left a wake-up call for 9:00 a.m. sharp. She planned on playing with Dick and Jane before noon. After making certain the curtains were drawn tight, she punched up the pillows on the king-sized bed and settled back against them. With luck she could snatch a couple of hours of sleep.

Anatolia: Then

THE MAN, his face gaunt and his eyes sunken, stared at the woman. Hers was a lush beauty. Jet-black hair caressed rounded shoulders, and teased the firm mounds of her breasts. Knowing brown eyes watched the fallen warrior, a small smile teasing her lips.

"Why do you persist, sir knight?" the woman purred. "You should be comforted that I have kept you here with me, underground." She patted the cushion beside her, tempting the man to join her. He didn't move. "Why do you fight me, Mathias? You know your capitulation is inescapable." She rose to her knees and reached over to stroke his chest. Her eyes glittered like frozen coffee, her smile hard and brittle. "I will own your life."

"No, Sahirah, you will not," Baron Mathias DeVries replied. Though his voice was hushed, there was absolute conviction behind his words.

The woman huffed out her breath, a derogatory sound. "Oh, but I will. Your life is more important to you than your honor, your nobility, even your oaths and vows." Her eyes narrowed in speculation. "Your life is more important than your soul, Mathias, and thus will you give that last bit of yourself to me." With the grace of a dancer, she leaned against the mass of pillows at her back. "It is just a matter of time before you submit. You will be begging me when the hunger takes over. You will give me whatever I ask and more. Why not surrender now? Save yourself the suffering, my poor, doomed knight."

Mathias didn't move a muscle as he continued kneeling beside Sahirah's bed. The woman clapped her hands and two robed soldiers entered, dragging a young girl between them. Mathias schooled his features. He knew what was to come. This virgin was not the first the witch had sacrificed to her perpetual youth. While he mourned the loss of a life so innocent, there were no guarantees the girl would live to see any sort of advanced age. Disease, war, famine—the very times themselves conspired against her ever growing to true maturity.

His expression didn't change as Sahirah slit the girl's throat. Despite the hunger clenching his belly, he did not succumb to temptation as the scent of hot, fresh blood washed over him. He forced his hands to stay at his sides rather than reaching up to catch the glob of blood that landed on his cheek. Mathias would not give the witch the satisfaction.

Drake Hotel, Chicago: Morning

"YOU ARE SURE?" Hannibal Crowley barked into the phone. He heard the brush of morning stubble against the phone receiver as the man spoke, as if he were nodding.

"Yes, Master Crowley. I'm sure. The woman left the vampire's lair and returned to her hotel. She's in her room. I'll wait here in case she leaves later."

Crowley rubbed his forehead. "No. She's a smart one and if you're seen, she will know we're watching. As long as she and the vampire are apart, our preparations can progress as we've planned. Return to the Sanctuary. I will be in touch with further orders."

Hannibal hung up and paced over to the window. Staring out over the frigid landscape, he knew he needed to sleep but he was too keyed up. He had waited his whole life for this one moment in time and the anticipation sent tingles along every nerve ending in his body. When Eugenia wed Alex McMahon, he would become the power behind the throne. The elfin president, fool that he was to have revealed his true nature, was likely a lame duck. Humans would not reelect him. That meant McMahon was poised to take the nomination and with the help of his future father-in-law, would win handily.

But *O Kim Bkze Bedoaru Gelmek* had her own agenda and she had not deigned to enlighten her high priest. This disturbed Hannibal more than he would admit to anyone. After all, he had been the one to find the prison where her soul had been entrapped all these centuries. He had been the one to bring forth the vessel to receive her, to give her new life. Him. Hannibal Crowley. He had planned and put things in motion for all these years. He peeked in at Eugenia again. The curtains remained open to embrace the morning sun and the expression on her face was one of peace.

Perhaps, Hannibal thought, it was time to assume control once again. He had summoned the Witch. She should be his to command, not the other way around. Crowley continued staring out the window. The first sacrifice should have been left on the altar at the Sanctuary, not in the vampire's lair to draw attention. When that FBI agent arrived, things spiraled out of his control. He suspected the Witch wanted the agent as her sacrificial lamb.

A calculating smile played about his lips. Millennium-old feuds did not concern Hannibal Crowley. Only the present and future did. If Agent Marquis was *prematurely* dispatched by accident, the Witch would be his to rule once again. Hannibal would have to think on this. He had much to contemplate.

Shutting the door to Eugenia's room, he returned to the living area of the suite. "She is not to be disturbed," he told the matronly woman waiting there. The woman nodded. "I'm going to the Sanctuary. Call me there if anything occurs."

Again, the woman nodded but this time she also replied, "As you command, Master Crowley." With her head bowed she murmured, "Your will is mine to do."

Hannibal shrugged into his overcoat and stepped out into the hall. When he got to the Sanctuary, he would meditate. Destiny would reveal its plans for him. Destiny would bathe him in its glory.

Sinjen's apartment: Morning

ACCORDING TO MYTH, vampires died with the sun. While all signs of life disappeared, they weren't technically dead. Granted, they did not breathe. Their hearts did not pump blood through their bodies. Their brains, however, could and sometimes did continue to function. The very oldest of them could be cognizant of their surroundings though unable to interact. The inertia brought to the "undead" by the rising sun paralyzed the body if not the psyche.

Such was the case for Sinjen this dawn. Thoughts of Sade and his parting words to her whispered incessantly in his brain. And with those thoughts came others, darker and unbidden. Thoughts of times and places and faces he'd long ago relegated to some far corner of his memory. As he lay paralyzed under the burden of the sun's rays, Sinjen tried to reconcile his feelings. Mention of Mathias had dredged up memories best left long buried.

"He called you his savior," Sade said.

Sinjen both loved and despised the man who was his sire. At the time, it seemed a small sacrifice to trade his life for that of the great knight imprisoned with him in that dank dungeon near the Holy Land. Sir Kristian St. John, Knight Templar, had been shocked at first to discover just what sort of creature his cellmate was. But as the long nights stretched and they passed the time in quiet contemplation of their fates, Sinjen discovered not a monster but an honorable man.

Day after day, he watched the brave knight weaken. Then the time arrived when one of Queen Sahirah's viziers came to them with a plan to entrap the woman who held them captive. This vizier, a sorcerer in his own right, wanted her power for himself. He promised to free the prisoners and set their feet upon the homeward path if they but aided him in defeating the evil witch.

Thinking to give up his life to make Mathias strong enough to defeat the queen, Sinjen became the blood sacrifice needed to seal the witch's fate. He died, only to be resurrected by the man he thought to set free. The shock eventually wore off and Sinjen managed to reconcile with the abomination he had become. As it turned out, the vizier was just as evil in his way as the

Queen had been. That situation left a bad taste in his mouth and after a time, he and Mathias returned to Anatolia to finish the job by assassinating the vizier.

As Sinjen lay unmoving, the sun climbed higher in the sky and he longed for the death that should have been his. When a young vampire, he'd decided the death sleep was the universe's way of compensating a vampire for cursed longevity. With the sleep came forgetfulness. This was no longer case. He vainly tried not to think of a pair of long legs, of startling green eyes that bored fearlessly into his own, of a little beauty mark that put a period at the end of each of her smiles. He would have Sade Marquis before all was said and done. Of that he was certain. Sade would either be his salvation or his true death. That was his last thought as he finally succumbed to the false death of day sleep.

"To sleep, perchance to dream," his psyche murmured to the cosmos.

Chapter Twelve

Doctor Who?

To sleep, perchance to dream. "Yeah, dreaming totally fucks up sleep." Sade rubbed her temples. The raging headache pounding behind her eyes didn't lessen despite the handful of aspirin she'd choked down earlier with three glasses of tepid water from the faucet. "To be or not to be and why the hell am I stuck on Shakespeare?"

She stumbled out of bed and found the bathroom by instinct. Popping the light switch with one finger and squinting against the glare, she stared into her reflection. She stuck out her tongue in a fit of juvenile pique then shuddered at the thick coating layered on it. She rubbed the offending appendage across her teeth and gagged.

"Eww." She screwed up her face and shuddered. "Yeah. I am feeling rather Hamlet-ish today. Prince of Denmark, the original emo kid." Unwilling to deal with the bright light, she flicked it off, turned on the shower, and stripped.

Standing under the stinging spray as steam filled the room, she let her mind wander even further afield. Why not Hamlet, she decided, since Horatio was the first CSI. Her case was a mess, with too many loose threads to tie up neatly. Grabbing the metaphorical end of one and unraveling it only led to the short end of a stick. She grabbed another before abandoning what was now an exercise in futility.

A case like this one made her homesick for Caleb. The werewolf was part bloodhound when it came to sniffing out magical trails. He explained it to her once. Evidently, to an educated nose, magic did indeed have a scent—a touch of brimstone, of swamp, of wind blowing across new snow— all depending on the type of magic.

Caleb was good enough that once he sniffed out a spell, he could track it back to the spellcaster. From then on, he recognized a caster's signature scent on any new spells. Sade could have used him out there at Buckingham Fountain. That was major bad mojo magic. She puzzled over the implications. Was the girl killed to set the spell? Or was the spell set because the girl was killed?

The old chicken or egg argument. Did the spellcaster need the death of the girl to create the magic? Or, conversely, was the magic spell triggered because the girl was killed? Death magic was evil shit and it took something really powerful to control it. As Sade understood the concept, death magic could be worked with blood and—well, she'd heard sex worked too. That whole *petite morte* thing from orgasm. She'd never had one so she was way out of her league there. And why the light show at the fountain? Was it just a big, badass statement? Done only for effect?

That's what bothered her. Magicks tended to hide their crimes. They didn't want the mundanes involved. Public relations and all that—especially after the dark days right after the Big Rip. So why go splashing evil intentions all over the front page of the Chicago Tribune? It just didn't make sense.

Finally scalded enough she could function, Sade climbed out of the shower. Using a towel, she rubbed a circle on the steamed mirror. In the dim light, all she could see was her eyes. Eyes. Why were Miriam's eyes taken? Blood, eyes...what next? But the definitive question still remained. Chicken or egg?

Something buzzed in the other room. Her cell phone. She stumbled into the bedroom and glanced around. Where the hell had she put the damn thing? She found it vibrating across the file she'd left open on the bed. Snatching it, she answered before the call rolled over to voice mail.

"Marquis."

Oak Woods Cemetery

OH YEAH, she should know better than to ask the kind of questions plaguing her that morning. It never boded well. Two uniformed cops stopped her cab at the gate. Sade paid the driver and swung out of the back seat, all legs and long, black leather coat. Her badge case was already open in her hand as she strode up to the first cop. The cocky grin on his face faded as he noticed the badge in her hand and the gun on her hip. "Which one of you boys is going to volunteer to drive me to the scene?"

The second cop turned to stare at her. Female, she gave Sade a jaundiced look and turned her back again, watching the scene in the cemetery.

"Oops," Sade muttered, nothing sincere about the word or her reaction. The woman had cropped her hair short and was trying to come off as big and tough—and failing miserably. The cop simply looked like a woman trying to look like a man. Sade smirked. Even under the best of circumstances there was just something about her that pissed off female officers on every level. In fact, there seemed to be something about her that pissed off a lot of people. She arched an eyebrow at the male cop. "Guess that leaves you with the short straw, slick."

The cop gestured for her to follow and headed toward the squad car parked to partially block the entrance. Sade passed by the female officer. "You really should see about getting that stick removed." She kept her voice low on purpose. A few steps past the woman, Sade added a bit louder, "You and everyone around you will be a helluva lot more comfortable."

The woman snarled as Sade climbed into the front seat of the patrol car with a sardonic grin plastered on her face. It was all she could do to keep from laughing as the male cop almost ran off the narrow lane. He was so busy watching her out of the corner of his eyes he almost took out a large granite tombstone. "Eyes front, slick." Sade's quiet command snapped his eyes forward and he didn't look her way again.

Mercifully, the crime scene wasn't too far into the large cemetery. The car rolled to a gravel-crunching stop and Sade was out of the vehicle even as little puffs of dust dissipated in the frigid air. She stood for a moment, surveying the scene. A brown tarp covered a mound of fresh soil. The sides of a white canvas tent popped and flapped in the wind. A group of people huddled nearby. Sade recognized the detective from the scene at the fountain.

"Franks." She acknowledged him with a quick nod as she walked up. "Don't you ever sleep?"

The man shook his head. "I wish, Marquis. What do you make of this?" He stepped back so Sade could approach the open grave.

A female victim, her pale flesh ghostly against the rich brown loam of the soil at the bottom of the hole, was posed lying on her back, legs together, arms crossed over her chest. She glanced over at a woman wearing a navy windbreaker with the initials of the Cook County Medical Examiner's office on the back.

"There's a lot of blood soaking in down there," Sade stated.

The woman looked a bit startled. "Most likely," she agreed. "You have good eyes."

Sade shrugged. "Cold enough the body's probably frozen. Even so, not much lividity."

The assistant ME nodded. "Good guess. Heard about the case last night. Do you think this is a serial killer?" A shiver, visible to everyone standing there, coursed through the woman.

Unsure of an answer, Sade turned back to Detective Franks. "You got called in special on this one," she surmised. Before he could reply, she noticed the granite statue that appeared to stand guard over the grave. Narrowing her eyes, she stepped closer to read the bronze plaque set into the statue's base. "St. John the Baptist," she read softly. "Fuck." Taking a deep breath she immediately regretted as cold air seared her lungs, she coughed before turning to Franks.

The detective already had his hands up in a gesture of surrender. "He's not even a suspect. But that's why they called me. I called you because of this." The stocky man dropped to one knee and pointed to a spot about six inches from the lip of the grave.

Squatting beside him, Sade peered at the spot where he pointed. "Salt?" She cocked her head then bent over for a closer look. She stared into the grave, her brow furrowed in concentration. "Salt?" she repeated. "No one but a novice uses salt for a spell." Looking around, she noticed a faint trail of salt encircling the open grave. "To keep in or keep out?" she wondered mostly to herself.

Sade looked up as a fire truck rumbled to a stop with a squeal of air brakes. Two firefighters climbed out, wearing bunker gear to help insulate against the cold. They grabbed a ground ladder and carried it over. A CSI and the assistant ME helped them position it in order to disturb the scene below as little as possible. As the AME and CSI climbed down, Sade stood up and cast about, much like a hound looking for a scent.

"Her clothes?" Sade asked over her shoulder. "Did you find her clothes?"

Franks shook his head. "Not yet."

She nodded and ambled off, quartering the area. She found the neatly folded pile of clothes about the same time she heard the assistant ME gasp. Looking up at the serene face of the statue of Mary, Sade muttered, "Gawddammit." She sighed and called louder. "Her clothes are over here. Check missing persons for a teenage runaway wearing a school uniform."

A second CSI trundled over to take charge of the garments as Sade returned to the graveside. Glancing down, she looked into the angry eyes of the pathologist. Sade arched an eyebrow.

"This is beyond rape," the ME spit. Her flushed face and clenched fists left no doubt as to the depths of her anger. "This is mutilation."

Sade could picture the horror the ME found between the girls thighs. Her gut already knew there was more. "It's clean? Surgical?"

The doctor glared up at her. "Yes, even though the scalpel was wielded by a butcher."

Sade avoided lifting her shoulders in a shrug. Anyone performing surgery in the bottom of a grave met that classification. "When you get her back to the morgue, you'll find vagina, uterus and most likely, the fallopian tubes gone. Surgically and cleanly removed in one piece. The perp wanted virgin equipment. This girl will only be about fifteen or sixteen.

"Monsters," the ME spat out.

"People are," Sade agreed before moving back from the edge. She glanced over at Franks. "Tell Kowalski and the district attorney to back off Professor St. John. This has gone well beyond him now."

The Chicago cop nodded. "Already have." Glancing around, he gave a little toss of his head to indicate Sade should follow as he stepped back and walked several yards away.

Curious, Sade followed. Once they were out of earshot, Franks turned his back to the wind and hunched his shoulders. "Internal Affairs has had Kowalski on their radar for quite some time." His low-pitched voice had just enough volume for the wind to carry it to her.

Sade nodded, watching the group still gathered around the grave. "When did Kowalski become an acolyte of Crowley's?

The detective's eyes widened and he crossed himself quickly. "He's not," he whispered and then gulped audibly. "Is he?"

Sade stared at Franks for a long moment. "You really didn't know." She nodded once, a curt bob of her chin. "I'm positive Crowley is tied up in this mess somehow but I can't put my finger on why. Did you know his daughter is engaged to Senator Alex McMahon?"

If possible, the cop's eyes widened even further. "No official announcement. At least not here anyway." He shook his head in wonder. "You haven't even been in town twenty-four hours. How do you know all this shit?"

Sade flashed the detective a sour grin. "Crowley sent a car for me last night, with an invite to his little soirée over at the Drake. The senator was there, with Eugenia hanging on his arm." She barked out a dry laugh. "She informed me she was going to be Mrs. Alex McMahon to put me in my place." Sade couldn't help but roll her eyes. "As if I'd be interested in that sleazeball."

Despite the gravity of the situation, Franks snickered. "Jeez, Marquis, I can't imagine why another woman would see you as a threat." He looked around, not quite meeting her eyes. "Shit, I'm a guy and you intimidate the hell out of me." Sobering, he scuffed the dulled toe of one shoe against the winter-browned grass. "So, any ideas? About who or what we're dealing with?"

Sade shook her head. "Unfortunately, no. It's not a vampire. Hell, it's not any of the magical races I'm familiar with." She stared off into the distance, her insides twisting with the regret brought by the end of another innocent life. "It's almost like someone's building Frankenstein's monster." She tasted the idea on the tip of her tongue as she said it. It didn't prove unpalatable.

Franks gulped audibly. "That's just...fuckin' creepy."

Her lips pursed, Sade blinked against the weak winter sun. "Think about it, Franks. The first victim was drained of blood. The second had no eyes. This one's minus her girlie bits." She blinked again. "What color was the second victim's eyes?"

The detective shook his head. "I don't know. I was still waiting for some records from the university when I got called out on this one." Franks shrugged, a gesture that conveyed both his frustration and his helplessness. He cleared his throat and continued in a matter-of-fact tone, "She hasn't even been reported missing yet. No reports for a girl matching her description."

To a civilian, the detective's offhand tone and bland face might prove upsetting. Sade understood. The job couldn't be personal. Ever. If it got that way, a cop would be eaten alive from the inside out. She acknowledged the information. "Find out about this vic. There's something special about her. I'm betting she was snatched because she was a virgin, but my gut says there's something else too. Someone...or some *thing* is creating a vessel."

"Vessel?" Franks asked, his brow knitted in consternation. "Out of human parts?" The man shuddered. "That's just—"

"Fuckin' creepy," Sade finished for him. "Yeah." She lifted her shoulders in an elegant shrug. "And very, very human."

Franks shook his head. "Don't say that. That'll mean you won't have jurisdiction." He looked around, as if embarrassed by what he said next.

"We need you on this case, Marquis. I don't care what any of the others say. I'm cop enough to admit I'm in way over my head here."

Sade patted his shoulder in commiseration and then watched the fire-fighters lower a Stokes basket into the grave. Two of them scrambled down the ladder after it. Four live bodies and a dead one would make the grave a very tight fit. "No worries, Franks. The only place I'm going is to the bottom of this thing. There may be human agents but whatever is employ-ing them is magical. With a capital M."

Letting out a relieved breath, Franks squared his shoulders and shuffled back toward the scene, Sade hard on his heels. The two of them stood at the foot of the grave waiting as the people below dealt with the body. With his hands shoved deep in his coat pockets, Franks again hunched his shoulders against the cold and probably the enormity of the situation. Sade knew the feeling.

A raucous laugh caused her to look up. An old cedar tree stood silent vigil not far away and a huge crow, shiny blue-black even in the weak winter sun, hopped among its lower branches. As soon as the bird knew it had Sade's attention, it stayed on one branch, its coal-black eyes fixed on her. The wind didn't even ruffle its feathers. Sade stared back, one eyebrow arched as if to say, "What?" The crow, as still as if it had been stuff by a taxidermist, watched unblinking.

"He's not done yet, is he?" Franks murmured.

Sade shook her head. "Not by a long shot."

Chapter Thirteen

One Crow For Sorrow

NOT BY A LONG SHOT. That had to be the understatement of the week, if not the year. Odds were they'd find a long trail of bodies before everything was said and done. Sade's head pounded as her instincts insisted the local cops would find more bodies or missing parts. Was it possible they were dealing with some sort of mad scientist wannabe trying to bring the spark of life to his creation? But why not just grab the whole body? Why the individual parts?

The first girl—CeeCee—was gorgeous in a cheerleader-next-door kind of way. And the second, Miriam, was the nerdy-girl-next-door. This one was the virgin-next-door. Any of the bodies would do for reanimation. What was it about each of these girls—and their missing parts—that was so damned special they had to die? She winced inwardly, wondering if these victims were truly damned.

Sade backed away from the group and paced toward the cedar tree. "What am I missing?" she muttered. "Forget the chicken and the egg. I'm stuck with the forest and the trees. And the birds have eaten whatever breadcrumb trail was left behind. Poor Hansel and Gretel aren't going to be rescued from the wicked witch. They'll end up in a pie and she'll bake them in her oven." She stared the crow. "Or was that the four and twenty blackbirds?" The crow rustled his wings and cawed. "See? Birds. It always comes back to birds and to you, you fucking crow, sitting there laughing your ass off." She planted her fists on her hips. "Sh'up, you."

Franks walked up behind her, a puzzled look on his face. "What?"

Sade pulled her gaze away from the tree and the raucous crow. She stared at the cop for a long moment. "What?" she echoed.

Knitting his brow, Franks replied, "Thought you said something."

Sade's lips pursed and she blinked a couple of times. "Wasn't me," she murmured. For a moment, she watched the activity in and around the scene. The rest of the firefighters on the engine arrived to help lift the Stokes basket out of the grave. Sade looked up, her eyes going straight to the cedar tree. The crow was gone—it had disappeared without a whisper of flapping wings. She glanced at Franks out of the corner of her eye. "There will be at least one more." She rolled her shoulders to ease the tension. "At a minimum."

Franks tilted his head as a long sigh escaped. "You know something or is this just your gut?"

Sade flashed the man a half-hearted smile. "Does it really matter which? The perp is going to want either a body with a head or more pieces for his sick jigsaw puzzle."

She turned away from the grave. It had revealed all the secrets it held. Sade headed toward one of the unmarked cars parked nearby. After a few moments, Franks backed away from the scene and followed her. He had to stretch his legs to catch up to Sade's long-legged stride.

"So?" he asked as he drew up even with her.

"You headed back to the office?" Sade asked without breaking stride.

"I can be."

"Good. You can drop me off at the University of Chicago. Which one of these heaps is yours?"

Franks pointed her to a tan Crown Vic sedan. Sade opened the passenger side door and slid in. Watching her, he couldn't help but admire the fluid grace of the woman. Getting behind the wheel, he carefully backed out and around the other vehicles. The gravel that had been scattered along the single-width lane crunched beneath the car's tires as he negotiated the road back toward the main gate.

In a few hundred yards, the tires rolled up onto pavement and as the vehicle headed down the pavement, a piece of gravel lodged in the tread of one tire *snicked* against the hard surface with each turn of the wheel. As the sedan passed the two uniformed cops on guard duty, Sade flashed the female a sardonic smile and a two-fingered salute. The cop returned the gesture with one a bit ruder. Sade just grinned.

Driving toward the center of the city, Franks took a moment to glance at his passenger before returning his eyes to the road. "Why the University?" he asked, hoping to sound less curious than he was. "Going to interview some of St. John's colleagues?"

Sade shook her head. "Nope."

After a few miles of silence, Franks decided to try again. "You gonna tell me why you want to go there?

"Nope," she replied again.

"Are you trying to cut me out of the investigation, Marquis?" Frustration edged into his voice.

"Nope," Sade replied a bit distractedly.

"Dammit, Marquis," he finally growled.

Sade chuckled, her eyes showing some life as she glanced at him. "If I find out anything, you'll be first to know, Franks. Promise. I'm not even sure what it is I'm looking for." She glanced out the window as the car approached the quadrangle. "Stop here." He steered to the curb. As the sedan rolled to a stop, she opened the door and stepped out, her leather-booted foot sinking into the slush running along the gutter. "I'll catch up to you later," she promised and shut the door.

Franks hit the button to roll down the electric window. He leaned over in the seat. "Hey, Marquis," he called.

Sade stopped and leaned in the window. "Yeah?"

"Call me. I'll come pick you up when you're done," he offered.

"Thanks." She walked away a couple of steps and then turned back. "I'm here to see a man about a crow," she told him, leaning forward from the waist to look in the still-open window. Sade chuckled at his look of consternation. "Don't ask," she added with a wry smile. Turning on her heel, she crossed the sidewalk and headed into the main quadrangle.

In the cold light of the winter noontime, the bas-relief faces and gargoyles carved in the stone façades of the various buildings stared unblinking down at Sade. Returning to the bench she'd occupied previously, she pulled her leather coat tightly around her even though the buildings blocked most of the blustery wind. The overcast thinned and the winter sun poked frostbitten fingers through the hazy layer of clouds. She closed her eyes and raised her face to the chilly caress.

"You are a long way from home." The deep basso voice grated in her ear.

Sade nodded without opening her eyes. "Yes. I am. As are you, Crevan."

The gargoyle's breath exploded in a deep rumble as he grunted. "I was called."

Making note of the slight nuance in Crevan's voice, Sade kept her eyes closed. When dealing with the stone creatures, she knew to listen, not see. "Who is bold enough to call one so great as you, Crevan?"

The gargoyle expelled another puff of air that sounded suspiciously like a snort. "If I knew, I would complete my business and be gone. I have no appreciation for the cold."

Sade chuckled, a dry, rustling sound from the back of her throat. She heard the sharp intake of the gargoyle's breath and held up a restraining hand. "Neither do I, Crevan." She let the small smile fade from her lips. "I've been called also, Old One. There is much magic here. Bad magic. Death magic."

She heard the leather rustle of his wings when the gargoyle shifted his weight from one foot to another as he stood behind the bench. "We do not work death magic."

"Most magicks don't, Crevan," she agreed. "Humans who want what they should not have. Wizards. Witches." Opening her eyes, Sade cranked her head around to look up at the grotesque creature squatting behind her. "I fear one with the power to command you, Old One."

The gargoyle stared at her, unblinking. "No one commands me, *tödlich*. I was called. I was not compelled. Curious, I came."

Remaining silent but still staring at him, also unblinking, Sade waited for him to continue. To get information from a gargoyle was to play a game of verbal chess. Composing her face, she arched her left eyebrow, knowing the beauty mark at the right corner of her mouth added a little "Oh really?" to her expression.

"Why have you come?" the gargoyle asked, the mental equivalent of blinking first.

"To stop the evil, *Le Vieil*," Sade replied, using his formal title. He had called her "mortal" before, to remind her of his status. "Before it grows so big it cannot be stopped and both magicks and humans suffer for it."

Craven stared. Sade stared back. She could almost read his thoughts and recognized his dismay that a mortal woman dared face him unafraid.

"Yes," he finally agreed. "What is it you require?"

Relaxing her expression, Sade dipped her head in formal acknowledgement. "I thank you, *Le Vieil*."

"Roman taught you well."

"I require information, Old One. Who or what? I will discover the why."

Crevan stretched to his full height—well over seven feet. Leather wings folded at his back and a spike-tipped tail lashed back and forth like an angry whip. "I have not discovered who. Without that knowing, I cannot tell you the what." He walked several long paces away from her, turned and strode back, his anger radiating like a hot stone next to a roaring fire. "The *enfant de l'homme* who meddles knows not what he does."

Sade curled her lips back against her teeth and gave the gargoyle a curt nod. "They seldom do, Crevan." Her gaze slid across the massive being to the traffic sloshing by on the street. Neither spoke for several minutes. This time, Sade broke the silence. "Hannibal Crowley? Or his daughter, Eugenia?"

The gargoyle laughed. The harsh sound panicked the pigeons roosting on the roof line above them. With a rush, they all took flight, their wings sounding like gunshots in the cold air. "Meddlesome fools. He thinks to control. And cannot. He thinks the seed of his loins can contain. She is already broken." Crevan shook his massive head. "No. It was not he who called. Nor was it your vampire." The gargoyle stared at Sade for a long moment. "There is a debt there to be repaid," he told her. "A sacrifice willingly made." Before Sade could ask, he continued. "Do not ask me. The story is not mine for the telling."

Sade watched the pigeons circling overhead. *The story is not mine for the telling.* How many times had she heard that phrase growing up? From Mathias. From Roman. Even from Caleb, once he could talk. It meant the speaker knew what was going on but would not explain. Frustrating, but Sade knew from experience she'd not get an explanation from Crevan until and unless the gargoyle was ready to divulge. Pulling her gaze back to the bizarre figure beside her, she schooled her voice. "Whose story is it then?"

The sound that rumbled deep in the gargoyle's chest might have been laughter. "You are the investigator, Child," Crevan rumbled. "But perhaps the crone will have some questions for which you have answers."

Sade stared at him, trying to decipher the nuance in his words. The crone. A title? Or merely a description? "And where might I find this crone?"

Her answer was once again that gravelly rumble that passed for his laughter. "So impatient are the children of men. We are sentinels, Child. Neutral in the petty disputes that plague magick and man alike." He stretched his wings as if to take flight but after a moment, the gargoyle continued. "Riddle me this, Child. What do you call a gathering of crows?"

She blinked, letting her lids cover her eyes for a moment before opening them. Even sorting through the bits of magic trivia stuffed into every nook and cranny of her brain, nothing sifted out that made sense so she shrugged. "I have no idea. Crows aren't my thing."

The gargoyle's face transformed from its mask of patience. "So you have sought me out? Because they are mine?"

Sade resisted the urge to say something snide about pigeons. Instead, she shook her head. "No, Old One. I didn't know you'd be here. But I've asked you because you are *Le Vieil*. The Old One. Because you have knowledge forgotten by most others."

This time, Sade was sure the gargoyle laughed at her. "You have spent too much time in the company of polite society," Crevan snorted. He spat out the word *polite* like it tasted foul on his tongue. "Fae and vampire think to be cunning and speak in riddles."

Answering with her own snort, Sade shook her head. "And gargoyles don't?" She laughed, a short bark of merriment. "All the magicks cloak themselves in pomp and circumstance, Crevan. I've never gotten a plain, simple answer from any of you. Riddle me this, riddle me that. Replies that are not answers veiled in pretty language and vague gestures." She pushed off the bench and started for the street.

"Why are you so curious, Crevan?" she asked without stopping or turning around. She knew instinctively he paced right behind her. A sensible person simply did not get up and walk away from a gargoyle, leaving their back unprotected. Sade never once claimed to be sensible. "Why would you answer a call without being compelled? Who summoned you, Crevan, that you could not resist?"

Sade felt the rush of wind lift her hair as Crevan swung his massive paw at her head. It took every ounce of resolve she had to keep her spine ramrod straight, chin up, and not a tremble showing. She'd seen the aftermath of a gargoyle attack. What little that remained wasn't a pretty sight. "Pushed a button, did I?" she murmured, continuing to walk.

Crevan gripped her biceps and spun her around. "Do not trifle with me, *tödlich*!" he roared. The pigeons shot into the air again and Sade watched several of the gargoyles on the surrounding buildings cringe.

Jutting her chin up at the creature, Sade's anger flashed. "Do not ever touch me again without permission, Crevan." Her voice grated, sounding much like the gargoyle. "I know your secrets, Old One, and I will hunt down your nests." There was no threat in her voice, just icy promise. Very slowly, the stony fingers gripping her upper arm loosened and then fell away. "If you know what evil walks this place, tell me."

For the first time in her life, Sade saw a gargoyle blink—actually, physically blink. The realization that Crevan had did not make her feel better. In fact, it scared the shit out of her. She had never met something that actually frightened a gargoyle and she damn sure didn't want to start now.

"If I knew, I would rid this place of it, *tödlich*," Crevan rumbled. "'Tis why I came to this forsaken city. It sought to control me. It cannot do so. Not yet."

"Damn," Sade sighed. "So its power is still growing?"

Crevan nodded imperiously. "With each act of evil."

"Damn," Sade said again. "I have to go, Crevan. I'll be in touch." She turned, walking with determined strides toward the street, intending to catch a cab to the police station.

"Child," the gargoyle called after her. "A gathering of crows is called a murder."

Chapter Fourteen

Two Crows For Joy

A GATHERING OF CROWS IS CALLED A MURDER? What the bloody hell?

Sade rubbed her forehead. She'd had no clue but by the time she turned around, Crevan had already disappeared. Typical gargoyle. They just had to get in the last word. So. A gathering of crows was called a *murder*. Appropriate, given her case at the moment. Her skin prickled, as if her hair stood on end. Reaching back, she brushed her palm across the back of her neck to smooth away the feeling as she considered her next step. Despite her earlier thoughts, she really didn't want to go to police headquarters to see Franks. At the curb, she raised an arm and a cab splashed to a stop beside her.

As she climbed in, the cab driver watched her through the rear view mirror. Sade pulled a twenty dollar bill out of her pocket and passed it to him. "Drive until that's gone, then I'll tell you where else to go." He shrugged, steered into traffic and ignored her. She leaned back, lips pursed as she worked through the facts.

Something tried to bend Crevan to its will. Was that the reason for the spell at Grant Park? Crevan was *Le Vieil*. That was like…the Grand Duke High Muckity-muck of gargoyles. Dammit. She should have asked him how long he'd been in town. *See,* she thought. *That's the problem with gargoyles. They never volunteer information and they never answer more than the question asked demands.*

Gargoyles relied on the scare factor of their appearance to intimidate. Hard to concentrate when 1200 pounds of solid rock covered in leather stood in front of you. Daunting on a good day, gargoyles were downright scary when that was their intention. Most people would be wise to talk to them with their eyes closed concentrating on *what* they said and *how* they said it.

Sade listened to a lot of the magicks with her eyes closed. Eye of the beholder and all that. And yeah, sure, gargoyles were as intimidating as hell when in their normal guise but she'd seen lots of scarier critters. She'd seen her mother the morning after a night of hot monkey lovin' with Oberon. *Before* Tracie put on makeup. She mentioned it to Caleb once. He'd laughed. One day he came in to apologize. Yeah, Tracie was one scary lady with no makeup.

She tapped the pad of her index finger on her lips. Her mind did not want to contemplate something that scared the shit out of the biggest and baddest of the biggest and baddest. And the fact that Crevan didn't know its name? Bad news heaped on bad news. She sighed. Another call to Mathias looked more necessary by the minute. And Sinjen.

Her lungs froze at the thought of him—refusing to pump oxygen for a minute. She so did not want to be alone in the same room with him. She'd rather swab out a drunk tank than face the sexy vampire again. Being solar challenged, both vampires were currently down for the count. She had a six-hour reprieve.

Once she pulled that thread out of the tangle, she mulled over the rest of the information she'd gleaned from Crevan. Who the hell was the crone? And where the hell could Sade find her? Her cell phone sang the theme song to "Cops," an annoying sound on any given day, especially so now.

"Marquis...Yeah, Franks. What's up?...Not a problem. My contact didn't have much that was helpful to say anyway. Go get some sleep. I'll call and leave you a voice mail if I find out anything...Yeah. Catch ya later."

Dick and Jane, not that she was surprised, had both called in sick. Wow. They must really think she was stupid. She'd play with them another time. Irritated at the interruption, Sade concentrated, hoping to find her train of thought. Oh. Yeah. The crone. Who the hell was she and what did she have to do with three dead girls?

The driver rolled down his window and a gust of frigid air swooshed through the cab. Sade shivered. *Damn, it's cold.* She shivered again and huddled deeper into her leather coat. Yeah, it was cold. Cold enough to freeze a witch's tits. Speaking of, Eugenia sure had a set. "Are you a good witch or a bad witch, Eugenia Crowley?" she muttered. "Ding, dong, the witch is dead…but she isn't…and that's the problem it seems."

She looked up, her gaze colliding with the driver's in the rearview mirror. "What? You don't ever talk to yourself? Most days, it's the only intelligent conversation I get." He shifted his eyes to watch the road. She never answered herself. Well, rarely. She glanced out the window to discover the vista of Lake Michigan on her right. Without wondering why she'd suddenly decided on a destination, she leaned forward. "Navy Pier."

Sade had absolutely no idea why she made that request. Maybe if she walked a bit, she could clear her head. Maybe. And now, a few minutes later, she stood in front of the Family Pavilion at the foot of the Pier. Wind whipped off the lake, twisting her coat around her legs. The place looked busy even though the outdoor rides were shut down for the winter.

Pushing through the doors, she headed inside. Warm air enveloped her, thick and cloying with the scent of warm bodies. Wandering into the Crystal Gardens, she shed her coat, her body warm enough now. Centrally located on the east end of the Family Pavilion, the one-acre indoor palm court provided a tropical paradise compared to the frigid weather outside. She paused to read a placard filled with information. Sade hated to admit she was a sucker for trivia. The six-story glass atrium held over seventy full-size palm trees and a variety of seasonal flowers and plants. Dancing "leap-frog" fountains added a rain forest sound to the space.

Despite the heat, Sade kept her blazer on after shedding her leather coat. The last thing she needed was the four stern-looking nuns with their bus-load of students deciding she was a terrorist because she wore a gun on her hip. Dodging through the mob of twelve-year-olds headed toward A-Mazing Chicago, the mirror maze, Sade ducked through the arcade. Her nostrils flared at the myriad scents wafting on the air from the food court. Her stomach grumbled in response to the delectable odors. Unable to remember the last time she actually put food in her mouth, she ambled that direction.

Her stomach and her taste buds waged war, unable to decide between the Tex-Mex specialties at the Twisted Lizard and the brat and sauerkraut dog in the hands of a construction type walking past her. Her mouth watering, she headed toward the counter at America's Dog and placed her order. Used to grabbing food "when and if" while she was on assignment, Sade tossed her leather coat over her shoulder, drenched the dog in mustard and all but inhaled it standing up. Like most cops, she had a cast iron stomach. As she chewed, her eyes constantly moved—watching, assessing, recognizing. Two Goth punks, skateboards under their arms eyed a couple of teen-age girls madly text messaging on their phones. Her nose twitched.

Even disguised by every food scent under the sun, Sade recognized their scent. She swallowed the last of her dog, wiped her lips with a paper napkin, and dumped her trash in a bin as she strode toward the two punks. Brushing past them, she murmured, "Jail bait, especially for the likes of you two." The emphasis she placed on certain words left no doubt that she knew what they were.

"Fuck off, bitch," one of them snarled after her.

Sade stopped dead still. Slowly, she pivoted, her hand catching in her blazer to brush back the placket to reveal a hint of holster on her hip and the badge on her belt. "Don't make me call the king," she replied. Her voice remained conversational, with a hint of warning hiding beneath the tone.

"Yeah, right," the second punk sneered. "Like you have his number."

She caught a reflection of her face in his sunglasses. Her eyes glinted like shards of broken glass. Her scary bitch look. "Actually, I do. I also have the queen's." A slow smirk barely curved one corner of Sade's mouth. "I don't believe we've met. Marquis is the name. Sade Marquis."

The first fae gulped. "Damn," he swore. "What the fuck are you doin' in town?" He glanced at his buddy. "You think Ariel sent us here on purpose?"

Sade's right eyebrow arched. "Well, well. How the hell is ol' Ari doing these days?" Before either of the fae could answer, strong arms circled Sade's waist and soft lips nuzzled through her hair to find the tender skin on the back of her neck. "Move 'em or lose 'em, Ari," she gritted out.

Ariel chuckled, the sound reminding her a bit too much of a snake slithering across sand, but he let her go and stepped around to her side. "Hello, gorgeous. Fancy meeting you here," he purred.

Rolling her eyes at the handsome man, Sade just shook her head. "You know the rules, Ari. And so should they. Hands off the young ones." She held up a hand as all three faeries protested simultaneously. "Human law, boys. They aren't legal 'til they turn eighteen and I don't care how precocious they are or what you fae consider to be the age of consent. That's the rules and you either play by 'em or get the hell out of Dodge."

"Dodge?" one of the fae began. "But this is Chica—" Ari waived a hand and the younger fae immediately shut his mouth, swallowing the word. At Ari's nod, the two punks backed up without another word. Sade snorted— young to a fae was a relative term but they *felt* young to her. As soon as they thought it was safe, they turned their backs and all but fled. The handsome fae at Sade's side tilted his head and flashed a honeyed smile. "Let me buy you lunch...and dinner." His smile turned coaxing. "And breakfast...in bed," he murmured.

Sade tasted his voice on her tongue. Sweet like clotted cream on a blueberry scone—thick and rich and oh so tempting. She snorted, the sound mocking and dismissive. "Not a snowball's chance, Ari." She stared at him a long moment before continuing in an authoritative voice. "So what brings you to the windy city, Ariel?"

The fae laughed. "So now you turn official?" He flashed a winsome smile. "I travel all over for the king. You know that." The man shrugged broad shoulders and Sade could almost hear the women around them sighing.

Nodding, Sade walked away, knowing Ari would follow her. "So," she called over her shoulder. "Who'd he send you to seduce this time?" He did as predicted. A few long strides and he reached her side. She smirked, watching him from the corner of her eye. "Don't you ever get tired of being the king's whore, Ariel?" She hid her satisfied smile as her barb raised the color in his cheeks.

Ari grabbed Sade's arm and spun her around. "Why are you the only mortal who has ever truly stirred my blood?" he demanded. His eyes flashed, a hard glint of anger mixed with frustration. And something Sade couldn't quite name. Longing?

She stared into his eyes, unblinking. "Because I'm the only one who's ever turned you down, Ari, and that just plain pisses you off." She laughed, but it was a bitter sound. Jerking her arm free, she walked away. Ari remained rooted. A few steps further, she hesitated and turned back to face the angry fae. "What do you know about counting crows?"

The fae shook his head, confused for a moment by the change of subject. "Counting Crows? The rock band?" He shrugged. "I can take 'em or leave 'em personally." He gazed around the crowded food court, his nostrils flaring slightly. "I don't detect the scent of wet dog. Where's your pet fleabag hiding these days?"

She maintained her poker face. Ari, like all magicks, wanted the last word. "Still jealous of him? Because he slept in my bed and you could barely get through the door?" Her smirk widened to a snarky smile as she remembered the first time Ariel appeared with seduction in mind.

Dallas, then

SADE THREW OPEN the French doors to let in the soft night air. Unseasonably warm for November, the weather left her restless and unable to sleep. She wandered out onto the balcony and leaned against the stone balustrade. Her fifteenth birthday. The day hadn't been much different from the day before nor was it likely to be any more special than tomorrow. She didn't celebrate birthdays, not any more.

A flicker of sparkling movement glittered in the corner of her eye and she turned her head just in time to watch a magnificent male form materialize. Tall, with defined musculature despite being on the slender side, his sandy hair was sprinkled with what looked like glitter. Full lips, high cheekbones, an aquiline nose—all-in-all a most aristocratic face. Sade stared at him for a long moment.

"Who the hell are you?" she asked.

The man's eyes widened and flashed. He looked like a deer in head-lights. "You can see me?"

Sade looked askance. "Like, duh. Though I guess I should be asking *what* the hell you are, huh?"

"I'm Ari," he told her, flashing a charming smile meant to disarm her.

Quirking an eyebrow, Sade stared at her visitor. Then she laughed as she realized exactly *what* the man was. "Ari Faerie," she chanted. "Quite contrary."

Caleb, in wolf form, had been curled up on the foot of Sade's bed. Hearing voices, he pricked an ear and lifted his head. A low growl rattled in his throat as the ruff on his neck stood up. Recognizing what was out on the balcony with Sade, he leaped off the bed and headed for the door. The faerie tossed a glittering cloud in his direction. Sneezing and pawing at his nose and eyes, Caleb couldn't get through the door before the fae slammed it shut.

Whimpering, he scratched at the door to get it open. Trapped in his wolf form by the faerie dust, opposable thumbs weren't gonna happen. Running across Sade's bedroom to the interior hallway door, he scratched and howled—to no avail. No one came. William was *out* of town, Mathias was *on* the town, and the in-house staff had already retired for the night.

Out on the balcony, Ari was perplexed. Human women had always been easy targets for seduction. Though this slip of a girl was just barely *legal* by human standards—if he stretched the law to the limits, she was certainly old enough for the fae. Yet she stared at him with eyes older and wiser than should have been possible. He stepped a little closer to her. The King's orders had been explicit—seduce her and bed her in short order. Having suffered royal wrath before, he was not about to fail. Reaching out with one hand, he trailed his index finger down Sade's cheek.

Sade continued to stare at him, her expression more akin to a scientist studying some new specimen than a bedazzled teenage girl. She flashed a cold smile. "Tell Uncle Obi-Wan it won't work." Her smile morphed into a smirk. "Now get your ass off my balcony before I open the door and sic Caleb on you."

Her reaction caught Ari completely flat-footed. He'd never actually had to *work* to seduce a human before. He just stood there staring at the girl. Then he realized she'd called the King *Obi-Wan*. He guffawed before looking around guiltily. He tilted his head watching her like a curious bird. A slow smile curved his lips and his eyes twinkled. "Just a kiss, lass," he teased. "Give me a kiss and I'll be away." Let her believe that would be then end of it.

"Ha!" Sade sneered. She turned her back and in two strides, was across the balcony and pulling on the doors.

Caleb, giving up his frantic scratching at the hall door, had returned to sit, nose pressed to the glass. As soon as Sade reached for the knob, he gathered himself, ready to spring. The door had barely opened a crack when he launched and was through the door before Sade or the fae could react.

Ari saw brindle fur and white canines gleaming in the moonlight. He turned and attempted to leap off the balcony. Caleb just managed to catch the fae by the seat of his britches. The material ripped as Ari disappeared with a *pop*. A very proud Caleb padded over and sat down in front of Sade, offering her the material in his mouth. The wolf sneezed as she took it from him. Laughing, Sade sank to the stone floor and threw her arms around Caleb's neck. "My hero." She kissed him on the top of his head.

Later that night, after she washed off the faerie dust, Caleb turned back into human form. He pulled up a chair and settled in front of the doors. Sade was still awake when someone rapped softly on one of the glass panes. Caleb growled and waved the iron fireplace poker he held in his hand. They both heard the muffled curse from the other side and then nothing further.

ARI BLINKED LANGUOROUSLY, staring into her eyes. She knew they'd both shared that memory; she could feel him tiptoeing around the edges of her mind. She smirked. Not one to give up without a fight, Ari had showed up on a regular basis, continuing his attempts to seduce her until Roman arrived. The imposing gargoyle stayed as her full-time bodyguard until her college graduation. Now he showed up mainly to irritate her.

"The mutt still allergic to faerie dust?"

Sade tilted her head, watching the fae. His question had nothing to do with his real thoughts. Even after all these years, he still tried to get her into bed. She sighed, a quiet exhalation slightly deeper than a breath. "It really pisses you off, doesn't it?" A flicker of emotion skittered through the fae's eyes. Fear?

Ariel lifted a shoulder in a negligent shrug far more telling than he might realize. "I failed my king. The only time."

She blinked. Not fear, pain. What had the royals, not known for their good humor anyway, done to Ari to punish his failure? Sade really didn't want to know. She knew he'd been tortured once before. The thought of him suffering because of her made her stomach rebel against the bratwurst and sauerkraut currently camped out there. She raised a hand to touch his arm—an unconscious gesture, but the fae surprised her.

This time, Ari walked away, humming a song under his breath. "Counting Crows," he called over his shoulder. "Interesting group." He hummed a few more bars. "Silences are very telling," he added. "And angels tread where fools shouldn't go."

Before Sade could retort, Ariel disappeared into the crowd. She stood there staring at the spot, knowing he'd dematerialized on purpose and was likely nearby where he could continue to watch her. "Chickenshit," she muttered. An unseen hand brushed her cheek and she shivered beneath the touch.

"I guess you left some feathers in my hand. Was it easier to leave me where I stand, angel?" Ariel's ghostly voice sang in Sade's ear and then was gone. His scent—orange, all spice, and spring rain—lingered in her nose. She could almost taste him on the back of her tongue.

Sade gazed around, looking for the shimmer the fae used to cloak their forms. A hint of glitter led her toward the mirror maze. She caught sight of an odd figure skulking around the entrance. The swirl of a multi-hued velvet skirt with gold coin jangles drew Sade's eyes to a satin peasant blouse with puffed sleeves in a scarlet red, a fringed black shawl lined with goldenrod and a purple scarf tied around a corkscrew mass of bright orange hair. When the woman ducked inside, Sade debated whether to follow. The sounds of a heated discussion kept her waiting at the entrance.

A few moments later, a security guard, one hand firmly gripping the gypsy's biceps, marched the woman out of the maze. "If I've tol'ja once, Angela, I've tol'ja a hundred times. Stay outta da maze!" He turned loose of her and then had to grab her again as she tried to duck under his arm to get back in. Frustrated, he picked the woman off her feet, swung her around and deposited her a few feet further back, facing away from the maze—and staring directly at Sade.

"Bitch," the woman spat.

Sade arched an eyebrow at the wild look in the woman's eyes and the mass of coiling curls escaping from the purple bandana tied to the woman's head. "Hey, lady," she replied, her tone calm but biting. "Medusa called. She wants her snakes back."

The security guard snickered. "Good one," he muttered.

"Ha!" the woman snorted. "Little you know." Her eyes narrowed as she stared at Sade then her look turned speculative. "You need your fortune told?" She wheedled and looked hopeful. "Won't cost much. Just the change in your pocket."

Sade shook her head. "I don't believe in fortunes."

Angela shook her finger. "But you should." She reached out and touched Sade's arm. "Love. Fame. Fortune," she intoned. "All to be yours."

The woman's expression was so sincere Sade laughed. "Yeah, easy for you to say." She pulled away but the woman's grip on her arm tightened like a vise. She opened her mouth to say something really nasty when she realized the gypsy's eyes had glazed over.

In a flat voice, Angela intoned, "Beware the witch that comes in the night. Beware the child with the second sight. Beware the dark man who will not see. Beware the ties that bind. They will not set you free."

Sade rolled her eyes. "What is it with you so-called psychic types? Everything fucking rhymes."

Intelligence flickered in the gypsy's eyes and then her whole body shook. She blinked rapidly before her gaze focused on Sade. "You got some bad mojo following you around," she murmured, wiping her hand down her thigh as though something slimy had rubbed off from touching Sade. Without warning, the woman turned and darted for the entrance to the maze. The guard grabbed her and held on as she squirmed. "But I've got to go in, Silas," the gypsy protested. "She's lost and I'm the only one who can find her."

Silas stood his ground until the woman went limp in his arms. Her face went slack and in the same monotone, she recited, "Little girl lost, between here and there. I can hear her calling. I can feel her fear." Once more, she shook herself like a dog coming out of a pond. "Please, Silas," she pleaded. "She's in there and can't get out." A tear trickled down the woman's cheek.

The guard shook his head. He was adamant even though his gruff expression softened with the sadness he felt. "No, Angela. She's not."

Sade watched the interaction between the two closely. The man glared at her, nothing soft about him now. She pulled back the placket of her jacket to reveal the badge clipped to her belt. Silas nodded at her, acquiescing to her authority. He pulled the gypsy away from the entrance to the mirror maze flashing Sade a *What can I do?* look.

The woman turned to her. "You know," she hissed. "You can see. You can see the others. They took her. Locked her in the maze. Trapped her in the mirrors. I can hear her. I can see her in the reflections."

Sade glanced at the security guard, who shrugged. "Her daughter." He kept his voice calm but she detected the hint of sympathy. "Went missing a couple of years ago. The crazy old bat's been here for the past year, claiming the girl's caught inside the maze." He gently tugged on the gypsy. "C'mon, Angela. Ya gotta go now."

The woman straightened her shoulders and nodded. Without a word, she turned and shuffled away. Sade and the security guard watched until the crowed swallowed her. "She used to tell fortunes out on the pier," he explained. "Had a crystal ball and she'd read palms. The marks liked her. Then the kid went missing and she went loony. Started spoutin' all sorts of dire things."

Sade stared at the spot where the gypsy had disappeared. "Yeah. That happens sometimes." She shrugged. "You do what you can." With a nod in the man's direction, she headed toward the nearest exit. Just before she got to the door, the gypsy woman sprang from behind a plant and grabbed Sade's arm. It was all she could do to keep from reaching for her Beretta.

"You must be careful," Angela whispered, looking all around. "It is the season of the witch and she wants you."

Sade stared at the gypsy. "Why?"

Angela's eyes narrowed. "Once a youthful pair," she recited. "Filled with softest care, met in garden bright where the holy light had just removed the curtains of the night." She stared up into Sade's eyes. "William Blake was a man who knew," she added in a reverent tone.

"Little Girl Lost." Her college requirement to read Blake for English Lit was finally paying off.

The gypsy nodded. "You," she asserted. "Always have been. Always will be unless you get found."

Sade barked a short laugh. "I'm never lost." She pushed past the woman and through the exit, heading back into the frigid January day.

Two crows," Angela called after Sade. "Two crows for joy."

Flagging a cab, Sade slid into the backseat. "What's the deal with crows today?" she growled under her breath. "Central Station," she told the cabby.

"Sure thing, lady," he replied gruffly. "You like Countin' Crows?" he asked conversationally. Before Sade could reply, he turned up the radio— Counting Crows, singing their hit, "Angels in the Silences." The first two lines made her sit up and take notice. Ari had whispered something similar in her ear. She wasn't stupid and when dealing with the magicks, there was no such thing as a coincidence. She leaned forward, listening. The words of the chorus had her knitting her brow. "Waiting for you. All my sins. I would pay for them if I could come back to you. All my innocence wasted on the dead and dreaming."

The song spoke of little angels climbing into bed, whispering as they did. It mentioned those little angels sucking blood, and sins without redemption. Sade wanted a copy of the words but would have to wait until she got back to her hotel room and fired up her laptop. The song ended and she sat back. Witches. Lost innocence. Sucking blood. And sins. She had no choice now. She had to confront both Sinjen and Mathias. The whole case felt very personal again. And Sade didn't like that. Not one bit. Even growing up in the midst of magical folk, she was not one to give in to signs and portents. She didn't believe in a fate carved in stone.

The cab coasted to a stop outside Sinjen's apartment building. Sade paid then climbed out. A gust of wind roared up the street tugging the hem of her long, black coat, making it dance. Icy fingers tried to work their way down her collar and Sade pulled her coat tighter. Nostrils flaring, she looked around.

Magic permeated the air. She caught glimpses of a man attempting to hide in the shadows of a doorway across the street. Her eyes narrowed with the effort to penetrate the gloom to get a good look at him. Her vision blurred and her head swam. "Fuck," she murmured. She had to close her eyes against the induced vertigo. Feet spread apart, she braced for the next attack. When it didn't come in a few moments, she opened her eyes.

The figure across the street was gone. Sade was no longer sure if it had been male or female. A nasty taste coated the back of her tongue, reminiscent of rotten eggs. "Sulphur," Sade murmured. "Bad mojo shit for fucking sure." Magic should have no effect on her. None. Zip. Zero. Zilch. The fact she was still feeling swimmy made her more nervous than she wanted to admit.

Turning on her heel, she stalked into Sinjen's apartment building. A few long strides brought her to the concierge desk. Her buddy, Chuck the doorman, emerged from a door behind the desk, buttoning up his uniform coat. Before he or the concierge could say anything, a young man pushed up out of a leather club chair and approached from across the lobby.

"Agent Marquis?" His eyes darted around the room before settling on her face again. "You might not remember me?"

Sade managed to keep her mouth from gaping as she nodded. "Trey Dandridge." She pitched her voice to match his.

Trey nodded. "May I speak with you?" The pleading tone in his voice tugged at her.

She glanced around looking for a quiet corner. "Uh, sure."

Chuck cleared his throat and Sade glanced at him. "You guys can use the manager's office. Pattycakes won't mind."

Sade's eyebrow almost got lost in her hairline. "Pattycakes?"

Laughing, Chuck looked conspiratorial. "Patek Kakar. He's the building manager. We call him Pattycakes. He's on vacation this week so his office is empty."

The affable doorman came out from behind the concierge's desk and led Sade and Trey down a short hallway. He took out a large ring of keys and unlocked it with a flourish. "Only thing is, no smokin'. Patty hates smoke and has a nose like a bloodhound when it comes to someone blowin' smoke where they ain't supposed t'be."

As Sade stepped into the office, she couldn't get the silly children's rhyme out of her head. "Pat-a-cake, pat-a-cake, baker's man," she recited softly.

Chapter Fifteen

Three Crows For A Girl

*P*AT-A-CAKE, PAT-A-CAKE, BAKER'S MAN. *Bake me a cake as fast as you can.*

Roll it and pat it and mark it with "C" and put it in the oven for CeeCee and me.

Sade tried to hold back the snorting giggle that threatened to erupt. Oh, yeah. She was running on fumes and Trey Dandridge, pale and unshaven, looked truly upset about his fiancée. The fact he'd come looking for answers about CeeCee sans attorney or political handler boded well for actual fact-finding this time. Laughing out loud at a bad pun in her head wouldn't help matters. The kid deserved better. At least for now.

Staring at him, she almost believed he really didn't know CeeCee was dead before last night. In her line of work, a person learned to judge people in the space of a heartbeat. The pause between one heartbeat and the next could be the difference between life and death. She remembered the first time she killed a man in the line of duty. During a smuggling case on the Long Beach docks. He held a gun to the head of a dockworker he'd taken hostage.

She was there front and center when some SWAT macho fuck-up took a shot and missed. Time slowed. Stretched. Stopped. Nothing but silence between those heartbeats. The Beretta 9mm was already in her hand, tracking the perp. She watched his finger tighten on the trigger of the .357

Magnum he pressed against the hostage's temple. The revolver had a double action trigger and hammer.

She had half a heartbeat to squeeze off a headshot and hope to hell she hit something vital enough the asshole didn't jerk that trigger in reflex. The real deal never worked like the movies. The bad guy blew away the long-shoreman's frontal lobe but died doing it, her bullet taking him through the temple. The hostage survived—if you could call it surviving.

Sade wondered sometimes, when she lay awake while the dark pressed down on her like a heavy blanket, if that dockworker would thank her for preserving some modicum of life. Or did he curse Sade's name from whatever was left of his brain? What about his family? She was too big a coward to meet them and find out.

She thought she'd cried that night—didn't really remember. Caleb took her out and made sure she got rip-roaring drunk. She passed out sometime before dawn. Woke up about eighteen hours later feeling like a pride of lions had pissed on her tongue and with a headache the size of a one-megaton bomb going off behind her eyes. Hell, even the ends of her hair hurt. But when she'd been cleared for duty, Sade strapped her weapon back on, tucked her badge in her pocket, and got on with her job. Shit, what the hell else was she supposed to do? She wasn't raised to roll over and play dead.

She took a deep breath, put her own thoughts away, and shut the office door. Sade watched the young man who had preceded her in. He appeared stoic but infinitely sad. She gestured toward the couch and asked, "How did you find me?"

"Lucky guess?" She arched a brow; he looked away. "I did some checking, found out you were hanging around Professor St. John. I figured you'd show up here eventually." Trey scrubbed at his face with his hands. "Is she really gone?" The look in his eyes conveyed a mixture of hope and resignation. Sade nodded, not saying anything.

"Why wouldn't they tell me? Why would they lie and say she'd gone to Madison? Her wisdom teeth? How lame is that!" The boy buried his face in his hands. "Why CeeCee?" The question came out as a lament, the sound of his voice heartbreaking in its torment.

Sade still remained silent. She figured his questions were mostly rhetorical anyway—except for the last one. She wasn't sure if he was asking why CeeCee had been the victim or whether he was actually directing the question to the dead girl.

When Trey didn't speak for a few minutes, she cleared her throat and asked softly, "When was the last time you saw CeeCee?"

He looked up, his eyes staring unfocused at the wall behind her. He blinked a couple of times as if that would fine-tune his memory. "A week ago? I'm not sure. She was at my place and got a call on her cell. She kissed me, said she'd see me in a couple of days, and headed to her office. I figured the Senator was sending her back to DC for something. He...did that sometimes. For the more personal stuff. Then I got a text message saying she'd gone home to Madison. To get her wisdom teeth out. I didn't even know she had wisdom teeth."

Sade chewed on her bottom lip, thinking. "Did you know that Senator McMahon is engaged to Eugenia Crowley?"

This bit of information made the kid sit up. "Genie is engaged?" His reaction caused Sade to wonder—not only the nickname he used but that he seemed genuinely surprised. "He's so much older," Trey mused.

Sade watched the young man, her expression shuttered. "So you know Miss Crowley well?"

Pulled out of his reverie, Trey glanced at her. "Yeah. We all went to the University of Chicago together. When Genie and I graduated, we stayed friends. CeeCee was finishing up some courses she needed. She was a double major—poli-sci and international law."

At Sade's interested look, he continued. "Genie majored in anthropology. I took a degree in business and marketing. I work for the Commodities Exchange. We called ourselves the Fearless Four." Trey broke off. A look of profound sadness washed across his face.

"Who's the fourth?" Sade half-way expected him to name Miriam Goddard.

"Crystal. Crystal Varad. We all met as freshmen and just sort of clicked. People started calling us the Fearless Foursome. Crystal—" Again, his voice broke and he cleared his throat. "We adored Crystal but our families..."

This time, the words trailed off. Sade nodded to him without speaking, encouraging him to continue. "She wasn't *good* enough. Crys was on scholarship and worked but she still managed to carry a full load of classes. Her mother was a gypsy or something."

Sade sucked in her breath at his mention of a gypsy. "What happened to her?"

Trey shook his head. "We don't know. Two years ago, she left class one evening headed to work. She never made it. Everybody said she just took off. That she ran away. We didn't believe it. She loved school. Had a four point GPA. We tried to get the police to stay on the case. They closed it after a week."

He paused to take a breath. "About a year ago, I got a voice mail on my cell. It sounded like Crystal...but not. The only words I could make out were 'mirror' and 'help me.' I thought it was a joke and deleted the message. I didn't want CeeCee or Genie to hear it. They were just beginning to get over Crystal's disappearance."

He remained quiet for a long moment, eyes downcast. "And now CeeCee." He raised his eyes to stare at Sade. "I know who you are, Agent Marquis. I Googled you. I know what you do. What's going on?"

That made her blink. "Googled?" She would have to run a search on herself. *Hope to hell I'm not an entry in Wikipedia.* Sade shook her head, taking a moment to fit all the pieces together. Problem was, they didn't. "I don't know, but I intend to find out," she told him honestly. She offered a sympathetic look. "Trey? Does your father know you're here?"

The guilty look on the kid's face was all the answer she needed. Not only did Mayor Dandridge have no clue what his son was up to, but Trey would be in serious trouble if his old man found out. He didn't have much more useful information and Sade chafed at the need to handle him with care.

She wanted to call Franks and get some information on Crystal Varad's disappearance. And she wanted to track down a gypsy fortuneteller named Angela who talked in riddles and was desperate to get into a mirror maze to find a little girl lost—HER little girl lost. The odds of there being two gypsies in Chicago with ties to a missing girl, especially with the mirror reference were more than Sade wanted to bet on. She repeated a mantra learned early—coincidences and magicks did not coexist on the same plane. She ushered Trey out and stood there in the door of Pattycake's office.

Without warning, her throat constricted as air caught in her chest. She fought to breathe. A vision of her wrapped up in cobwebs, thrashing near the center of a giant spider web as she struggled to get free danced in her mind. Her vision grayed at the edges, narrowed, then blacked out completely. Sightless, she clutched the doorframe. What the hell was happening? She was supposed to be immune to this shit! She lashed out with her hands and legs, trying to kick free of the dream web.

As is the nature of spider webs, though, the harder Sade fought, the more trapped she became. Realizing what was happening, she stopped battling. Forcing herself to relax, she worked one thread at a time on the webs wrapping around her until she had enough room to wiggle out. Running lightly across the web on her tiptoes, she heard dark laughter.

"Soon. You will be mine." A whispered voice promised in Sade's head. "And then there will be no escape."

Blinking to clear her vision, she discovered she was still in the manager's office at Sinjen's high-rise apartment building. "Dammit." Magicks weren't supposed to be able to play with her head like that. The entity behind all of this was far darker and stronger than anything she'd ever encountered.

Glancing at her watch, Sade had to make a decision. The weak winter sun would set shortly and she would have access to both Sinjen and Mathias. She also needed to touch base with Detective Franks. Opting to stay where she was, she called Chicago PD. After a bit of runaround, she got through to the acerbic cop who was now assigned to all three cases.

"Crystal Varad," she said.

"Is that our third vic?" Franks' voice sounded tired through the phone.

"Nope. I take it the ME hasn't made a positive ID on the third one yet?"

"We're still running the missing person reports looking for a match."

"While you're running missing persons, look for Crystal Varad. There would have been a report about two years ago." She could almost feel the sigh in the cop's voice at her request.

"Unless there's some relevance—"

Sade cut him off. "Two years ago, CeeCee Adams, Trey Dandridge, Eugenia Crowley and Crystal Varad were known around the University of Chicago as the Fearless Foursome. Then Crystal disappeared." She could tell by his sharp intake of breath she had his undivided attention. "Now, CeeCee Adams and two others are dead."

"You think Varad went into hiding and she's the one behind the murders?" Franks asked. "Should we put Miss Crowley and the Dandridge kid under surveillance for their protection?" Sade could hear the click of computer keys behind the cop's voice. He paused in his questions but the clicks continued. "Got her. Varad, Crystal. Reported missing by her mother, Angela Varad."

And another piece falls into place.

"That's still an open case," Franks continued. "Girl left campus headed to her job. Never seen or heard from again. Missing Persons moved it to inactive. Case notes indicate she probably flaked out—pressure from school and work overloaded her and she took off for parts unknown."

"I don't buy it," Sade retorted. "From what I've heard, the girl loved school. She was an honor student despite working full time. My source is convinced she'd never run away."

Her brain shifted into overdrive. If Crystal's soul was trapped in some sort of mirror maze, what the hell sort of magick had that kind of power? And how the hell did you catch and neutralize such a critter? As her mind turned over some possibilities, she heard muted voices through her phone.

"Just a sec, Marquis," Franks said and then the phone was muffled, probably against the stocky man's chest, Sade decided. A few moments later, the line cleared and Franks added, "We have an ID on the third vic.

Hannah Stefanos, seventeen. She disappeared three days ago. Her parents just returned from a trip."

"Wait. Did you say Stefanos?" Sade allowed a moment of panic. Not every person with a Greek surname was a dragon, Nikos' presence in Chicago notwithstanding.

"Yeah. Stefanos. She was supposed to stay with a trusted family friend. The friend got a text, allegedly from the parents, saying Hannah was traveling with them after all. It was an anniversary trip for them. A romantic getaway." His voice roughened and she heard him try to clear it with a hard swallow. "She was—" He coughed, the lump still stuck in his throat. "Hannah was special."

Sade recognized the strain and sadness in the Chicago cop's voice but something about the word *special* tipped her off. "Developmentally disabled?"

"Yeah." His voice whispered through the connection.

"Yeah." She sighed, echoing him. "Only the best for our killer." Louder, she added, "I don't need to ask if she was a virgin. Did we ever get a picture of the second vic? There's going to be something special about her eyes."

"What sort of sick fuck are we dealing with?" The cop's anger blasted through the phone.

"I don't know yet," Sade growled and fighting her own anger. "But I'm damn sure going to find out. You got anything else of import?" There was a long pause. "Don't hold out on me, Franks. What do you have?"

He sighed audibly and then dropped his voice to the barest whisper. "You didn't hear it from me, but CeeCee Adams was about three months pregnant and DNA confirms paternity as the Dandridge kid."

Before she could say anything, Franks hung up. Sade stared at the phone for a long moment and then exploded. "Gawdammedmother-fuckin'sonavabitch." Checking her watch, she hit a speed dial number on her cell. It rolled to voice mail on the fourth ring. Sade stabbed another number. A familiar voice answered after the first ring.

"DeVries residence," that oh-so-British voice announced.

"I need to speak to him, Hoskins."

"He is unavailable," Mathias' butler answered.

"Bullshit, Hoskins, Put him on. Now."

"He left explicit instructions, Miss Marquis. He is not to be disturbed."

Sade pictured Hoskins in her mind's eye. Standing there in his striped trousers, vest and traditional morning coat, he would be the very model of a modern majordomo. "Dammit."

"Language," Hoskins interrupted her, his tone chiding and so very uppercrust.

"Stuff it." Her anger leaked into her voice. "You tell him to call me. Like yesterday, Hoskins." She sucked in a deep breath to get her temper under control. "You tell him that if any more girls die because he couldn't be bothered to talk to me, I'll come stake his sorry ass myself." She hit the disconnect button before the butler could make some cutting retort about her lack of manners or her language.

Sade raged silently though she stormed around the office to release some of her pent-up frustration. Her emotions finally spilled over and she could no longer keep quiet. "Mathias, you sorry sonavabitch," she ranted. "You are up to your long, pointy canines in this deal. Somehow. Someway. And you've gotten Sinjen caught up in this mess. And me. And those innocent girls." She paced back and forth.

"Think, dammit. Four friends. The gypsy girl with undoubtedly untapped psychic abilities disappears. And is probably trapped in a fuckin' mirror maze—if not physically, at least her soul. A pregnant congressional aide drained of blood. A college student floating in a fountain of blood, her eyes stolen. A little girl left in a grave, her female organs harvested for their purity."

Sade hit the far wall, pivoted, and paced back toward the door. "Two vampires inexplicably tied together by fate or fortune or both. A self-proclaimed witch with ties to the missing girl and the pregnant one. A witch whose father happens to be a high priest." She kicked at a soft armchair in frustration. "And a partridge in a pear tree." That was her stock phrase for a dead end.

Closing her eyes, Sade rubbed at her temples as the beginnings of a headache throbbed there. Her other hand dipped into her pocket to fondle a small glass square. She'd picked it up at Marie Laveau's shop in the French Quarter. Caleb called it her worry stone. Maybe it was, but rubbing it between thumb and index finger helped her focus.

She felt weary—the lethargy creeping over her more than a simple lack of sleep. This weariness ran soul deep. For the first time in her life—at least the first time she was conscious of the idea, Sade thought about having someone to lean on. She had never leaned on anyone. Not ever. While Caleb had always protected her back, he'd also been a competitor. She could depend on him, but she could never just let go emotionally.

A few men drifted into and out of her life over the years, but nothing permanent. At the moment, she was acutely aware she was on her own—that she always had been. With a flash of clarity, she realized she always would be. What Mathias and the fae had done to her as a toddler changed her. She wasn't quite human but she definitely wasn't magick. She had no dreams or illusions; had never missed them until this very moment. Sade was certain more young women would lose their lives, just as she was certain she could not prevent those deaths.

"Fuck." She spat the word out with no emotion, feeling too drained, too tired to care.

Sade slipped out of the office and headed back toward the lobby and the bank of elevators. Chuck was at his station near the door, and he tossed her a jaunty salute as she punched the button for the elevator. The doors whispered open and Sade stepped inside. The ride up was quiet. She snorted, an inelegant sound. No canned "elevator music" for the residents here.

SINJEN FELT HER coming closer. Closing his eyes, he remembered the first time he had seen her, those long legs gliding across the bare floor of his prison. He smiled as his body reacted. He left his vantage point at the window and crossed the room to await her arrival at his door. He wiped the impatience he felt from his expression. He pictured her hand lifted to ring the bell; opened the door before she had the chance.

Sade looked at him, startled but taking him in, her pupils dilating slightly, the corner of her mouth quirking. He watched her, felt her impressions of him—tall, muscular, ruggedly handsome. Sade didn't stop to think; she simply stepped into him, leaning as her arms circled his waist.

"Honey, I'm home," she murmured, her cheek resting against his shoulder.

He knew she'd meant to make a joke. As she stepped back to pull away, his arms tightened around her. "Yes," he murmured into her sweet-smelling hair. "You are."

He felt her heart stutter-step at his words. Sinjen backed up, moving deeper into the apartment without releasing her. Turning, he bumped the door shut with his shoulder and then, finally, loosened his arms so he could take a half step away. His nostrils flared, drawing in her scent. Gardenia from her shampoo clung to her hair. She smelled of clove and rain, of something earthy like Irish moss, and a spicy musk that reminded him of cloves.

He cupped her right cheek with his palm, his thumb tracing her lips before coming to rest on the beauty mark at the corner of her mouth. He leaned in and kissed her, just the barest brush of his lips yet the touch elicited a shiver. He felt it radiate out from Sade's core. Her eyes closed and she leaned toward him, her chin rising in invitation.

"You have had a trying day, milady," Sinjen whispered, recognizing the pain in her eyes and the dark circles beneath them.

Sade started to laugh but clamped down on it. The little hiccup that managed to escape had the sound of hysteria lurking in it. "Yeah. You can say that again," she muttered laying her head against his shoulder again.

"You have—"

Her brittle laugh cut him off. "Don't be so damned literal, Sinjen." The silky material of his shirt muffled her order.

"Language." He reminded her automatically now, enjoying the game his cautions had become.

"I'm getting sick and tired of people telling me to watch my language," Sade groused. "I'll cuss if I want to."

Sinjen tilted his head and regarded her. "Why would you want to?" he finally asked, truly puzzled.

"Because I can." Her lame assertion had no effect on him.

She tried to pull away, but he tightened the arm still around her waist. His thumb pad brushed across her lips again, followed almost immediately by his mouth. This was no skirmish of his lips teasing hers. His mouth claimed Sade, his tongue licking the seam of hers, asking at first for admission and then demanding it. She didn't resist him, parting her lips and he swept his tongue inside, tasting her as he'd longed to do since first laying eyes on her.

Sade's brain turned to mush as Sinjen kissed her. If his arm hadn't tightened around her waist, she'd have hit the floor as her knees went weak. *Holy crap*, she thought, kissing him back. Her arms circled his neck and she leaned into him.

"Language," Sinjen murmured.

Had she said that out loud? Hormones overloaded her brain, clouding her thinking as her girlie bits all lined up, insisting they be introduced to his manly bits. Pressing her whole body against the hard length of him, Sade growled, "Fuck you."

Chapter Sixteen

Four for a Boy

FUCK YOU. What the hell was she thinking? Fuck her! The best and the sexiest from every preternatural race attempted her seduction at one time or another. Every last one of the magicks, in the right glamour, looked damned hot. Luckily, they couldn't reproduce with humans—which was a very good thing. Otherwise, there would be little halflings running around all over the place. Ariel, known everywhere as the King's Seducer—an actual title within the fae court—never got past first base with her.

The last magick to try—a sexy dragon—still called and texted in hopes of catching her with her guard down. She just thought Nikos Constantine could kiss. If not for a bansidhe attack, she might have been tempted by Nikos. In the end, though, she'd shut him down. All those attempts were to no avail, but here she was in a vampire's arms ready to waive all rights to her virginity.

Hiding the fact she was ready for a horizontal tango remained high on Sade's to-do list. She'd made out with guys before. A lot. Well, okay. A little. Caleb and Roman never let her out of their sight for very long. Not even Ari or Nikos could get her between the sheets. She was not frigid, despite what Caleb thought. She wasn't.

The fact Sinjen had her all hot and bothered at the moment proved her point. Her girlie bits snapped to attention, returning the salute from his manly bits…or *vampirely* bits as the case might be. That meant he'd fed. That bit of lore was correct. Sade once checked with a doctor about it, a prominent cardiologist, in fact. The process all had to do with blood pressure and well…stuff. A twinge of jealousy nipped at her. He'd fed. On someone. Besides her.

"That can be arranged," Sinjen breathed into her mouth.

Sade squeaked. Had he read her mind? There seemed to be a log of that going on. When he continued, she realized his mind was on something completely different.

"But fuck is such a vulgar word for what I want to do to you, Lady Sade." He murmured the words against her cheek as his mouth left her lips and trailed upward toward her ear. His lips paused on the wildly beating pulse under the soft skin of her throat. As he nuzzled, her pulse quickened even more and he smiled. "Will my ice queen scorch me before the night is through?" The word's whispered across her skin.

Once again, Sade's knees all but buckled under his ardent assault. *Damn,* she thought. *All those romance novels are right after all.* That was the last coherent thought she had as Sinjen's arm tightened around her waist. His other hand cupped the back of her head and held her still for the onslaught of his lips and tongue. He angled her head so he could trail kisses down her throat before returning to assault her mouth.

As she melted against him, Sinjen kissed the tip of her nose and rested his forehead against hers. Sade trembled in his arms but it wasn't because she was afraid. No, she would never fear him.

"What a treasure you are," he murmured, his lips nibbling hers as he spoke. "But I fear you think far too much."

Before he could continue, Sade's cell phone buzzed in her coat pocket. With an exhalation that sounded suspiciously like a sigh—something he seemed to be doing a lot of in her presence, he loosened his hold on her and stepped back. His fingers trailed from the back her head to caress her cheek, a gesture elegant and old-worldly. Sinjen's index finger paused at the dimple in Sade's chin, kissing it with a kitten-soft tap.

"Duty calls," he reminded her as she stared blankly at him, completely bemused. Unable to resist, he leaned in to brush his lips across hers one more time.

"Duty?" Sade mumbled, her hand automatically fishing for her coat pocket and the offending phone hiding in the folds of her leather coat. "Oh. Yeah," she added, unable to take her eyes from his face. Sade found the phone, managed to get it to her ear. "Damnation," she breathed into it.

"So I've been told that is what I will suffer." The rich voice that always reminded her of smoke and Sauvignon poured from the cell phone like decanted liqueur. Faintly accented, Mathias's voice held a hint of dry humor. "What is so important that you demand my attention, Sade?" The master vampire's tone changed abruptly. He was all business now.

"Mathias?" Sade pulled her eyes away from Sinjen's face and shook herself, mentally first and then actually shook physically, trying to break the vampire's spell. "You're up..." She floundered, trying to remember why she'd called him.

"It is after sundown. I am normally *up*, as you so succinctly put it," Mathias replied, that touch of humor back in his tone. "I do not have all night, Sade. What dire predicament have you gotten yourself into from which I shall have to extricate you?"

Realizing she would never focus while staring at Sinjen, Sade turned her back to the handsome man who watched her with such fierce awareness of her whole being. The hair on the nape of her neck prickled, and she unconsciously raised her free hand to rub at it. She wracked her brain unable to remember why she had called Mathias. Had she called him? It occurred to her that Mathias sometimes called her before she even realized she needed to talk to him. She stepped further away from Sinjen and her brain started to function again.

Mathias chuckled again, as if he could sense her confusion—and enjoyed the fact she was befuddled. "Hoskins said you called, Sade," he reminded her. "And I believe you mentioned something about 'staking my sorry ass' if I didn't call you back?"

Her brain meshed into gear. "Asking a question and getting a straight answer would do for starters," Sade growled into the phone. The rich chuckle on the other end irritated her to no end.

"I always answer your questions, Sade." An inelegant snort was her pithy reply. The vampire's begrudging sigh spoke as succinctly as Sade's snort had. "Ask," he finally added.

"Kristian St. John." Sade hunched her shoulders as she forced herself not to look at Sinjen. "What debt do you owe him?" Before Mathias could say anything, Sade quickly added, "And don't tell me to ask him. I have. He told me to ask you. I'm asking."

Silence met her question. Utter and complete silence. "Is he with you?" Mathias finally asked. "Of course he is," he added before she could respond. "He saved my life, Sade. He gave up his soul to sustain me so that we could defeat a witch. Sir Kristian was an honorable knight. Ask him about Judge Durand. Ask him why his damned honor is more important than his bloodline." Cold anger curled around the words Mathias spit out.

Sade's brain churned, firing on almost all cylinders now but it only focused on one word. "Witch?" She turned to stare at Sinjen. "Witch? What witch? When? Dammit, Mathias, why didn't you tell me?"

She paused, took a breath, regained her mental balance. "Hannibal Crowley." She dropped that name into a well of silence. She wondered if her cell had dropped the call in the dead air stretching between them before Mathias finally spoke.

"I will call you before dawn." Her godfather's voice sent shivers down Sade's spine and raised goose bumps on her arms. The line went dead with such finality she didn't have to wonder if the call had dropped.

Turning to face Sinjen, Sade studied the handsome vampire for a long moment. He had gone perfectly still—a vampire talent that tended to unnerve most mundanes. His face appeared as serene as a carved alabaster Madonna. Unblinking, Sinjen returned her stare.

"Tell me," she demanded. Only then did Sade detect a reaction and had she not been familiar with vampires, she would have missed it altogether.

The slight flaring of his nostrils and change in the pupils of his eyes was that negligible.

"No."

One word. Cold. Sharp. As biting as an arctic wind. Sade stared back, also unblinking. "I didn't think vampires were afraid of anything." She taunted him, even though she kept her voice soft, her tone almost teasing.

"I will not ever speak her name. To do so is to give her power. She was evil in the purest sense of that word. She is buried. She is forgotten." Sinjen seemed to be trying to convince himself.

"What if she isn't?" Sade hoped to crack the icy façade Sinjen showed her.

"No." He turned on his heel, leaving the word hanging in the air between them, icicles dripping from it. His long, muscular legs carried him in a few short strides to the bank of windows overlooking the glittering lights of the Chicago skyline. "You have not eaten." He dropped his voice lower, enticing her. He would not admit that her fatigue beat at him, that it worried and angered him both. She should take better care of herself.

She tilted her head to regard him like a curious bird. "I'll grab something later."

"No." The difference in his tone and voice made Sade smile. The way he said that one word summed up his commanding presence. She watched his reflection in the glass and saw his returning smile. "You can see me." This time, his voice sounded astonished. And relieved.

Nodding, Sade replied, "Yes." She'd always been able to see a vampire's reflection and she'd often wondered at the myth that they had none. The truth hit her square between the eyes. Vampires had reflections. Hiding it was just one more glamorous trick in a vampire's arsenal.

"Come," Sinjen commanded quietly, turning from the dark vista outside the window to face her. "I will take you to dinner."

Sade thought about refusing but something in Sinjen's eyes gave her pause. She found hunger there...and a loneliness that tugged at her conscience. "Okay," she agreed and was surprised at the look of relief that flickered across his face.

"Good. I was prepared for you to be obstinate," Sinjen replied, his hand at the small of her back urging her toward the door.

Even as he compelled her forward, Sade dug in her heels. "I am not obstinate."

"Yes," Sinjen told her, a hint of humor in his voice. "You are."

Before she could react further, he'd herded her into the hallway, locking his door behind them. Sinjen guided her through the elevator doors when they whispered open. As the doors closed behind them, she wondered about that. Caleb had that uncanny luck too. She couldn't remember ever waiting for an elevator when in the company of a magick...unless the magick was stalling. If that was the case, an elevator took forever to arrive. She silently considered the notion and realized magicks never seemed to wait for a cab, either. Or a table in a restaurant for that matter. "Luck has nothing to do with it," she muttered under her breath, stepping out of the elevator into the lobby.

Chuck hurried to open the front door for them. "A cab, Mister Sinjen?" A jaunty grin spread across the cocky little doorman's face.

"No," Sinjen said, seeming to answer both Chuck and Sade. "We'll walk."

Sade stopped dead still and stared at the vampire. The frigid wind whistled in off the lake and sleet rode it hard, stinging exposed cheeks with its bite. Even as she balked, Sinjen tucked her hand under his arm. She immediately felt warmer.

"How do you do that?" she muttered under her breath. Her only reply came from the knowing smile that briefly lit up his face.

Their brisk walk lasted only a few blocks. A weathered wooden door with leaded glass inserts welcomed them in on a gust of chill wind. Sade managed to grab a quick look at her reflection in a mirror as she passed. Her wind-burned cheeks glowed pink. The wind had tousled her thick hair, teasing it with frisky fingers into a mass of waves and curls some women paid hundreds of dollars for.

The maitre d' smiled and bowed. "Welcome to Beswetherick's" He snapped his fingers and a nearby waiter and busboy hustled into action.

Sinjen took Sade's coat and his own and passed them to a check girl. In a tender gesture that seemed almost out of place, he smoothed his palm across her disheveled tresses. While she gave no outward sign, the heat his touch created scorched Sade all the way down to her toes.

Following the maitre d' but feeling a bit numb, she had enough presence of mind to realize no one in the cozy and crowded little restaurant paid them any mind. Weaving among tables, the three of them headed toward an intimate booth in the back but far away from the kitchen door. She was amazed that a man as handsome as Sinjen could pass unnoticed. Mathias always wanted to be the foci of his world, albeit a mysterious one. And whatever Mathias wanted, Mathias got. Like a good magician's act, Sinjen was all "smoke and mirrors."

Settled into the booth, Sinjen sitting across from her, Sade pursued the train of thought rolling through her mind. People tended to see the magicks with a blind eye, lumping them together as a whole rather than really seeing the individuals. Ariel, Puck, and Oberon were as diverse as Tom, Dick and Harry average human. Mathias had been older—Sade would have guessed late forties to early fifties—when he became a vampire and while not classically handsome, he turned heads. Sinjen had most likely been in his thirties and he was, to Sade's eyes anyway, simply beautiful. She got lost for a moment in his thick, black hair with a hint of wave to it, wondering what it would feel like sliding through her fingers. His wide-set, blue eyes were the color of a high mountain lake reflecting back the sky. His full lips were...

"Stop it," she muttered.

"I am doing nothing," Sinjen's whispered voice rubbed across her skin like velvet.

Sade shook herself. "Oh yeah you are, buster. I recognize a vampire seduction when I'm the quarry of one."

Sinjen smiled, just the barest hint of fang showing. "Do you feel hunted, Sade?"

He looked so damned self-satisfied she wanted to slap him. "No. I've never been prey, Sinjen, despite what most of the magicks would like to think. I am the hunter, not the hunted."

An ubiquitous waiter appeared and looked pathetically eager to serve them. His face fell, though, when he realized that neither Sinjen nor Sade had opened a menu.

"The lady will have the porcini-crusted filet mignon with fresh herb butter, medium, the potatoes Anne, a Caesar salad to start, and a bottle of Loreth Blanc Mazis-Chambertin 2000," Sinjen told the man before Sade could even touch the menu much less open it.

"Excellent choices, sir," the waiter endorsed, all but beaming now. He snatched the menus and bustled off.

Within moments, the wine steward appeared bearing a dark green bottle. With great ceremony, he opened it and presented the cork to Sinjen. The vampire sniffed appreciably and nodded. The steward poured not much more than a swallow into a lead crystal wine flute and handed the stem to Sinjen. He held the glass up to the candlelight and swirled the contents. "If you will notice, Sade, the wine displays a softened crimson color with an orange tint, a sign that it has aged well."

Holding the rim of the glass to his mouth, he sipped the liquid, discreetly swishing it around his mouth and over his tongue before spitting it out into a small silver basin the steward held for him. Sinjen took the proffered pristine linen cloth from the steward and delicately wiped his mouth before handing it back. The vampire regally inclined his head to the man who then poured a full glass, which he set before Sade. Slipping the bottle into a wine bucket and bobbing so low it was almost a bow, the steward backed away from the table.

"Taste it, Sade," Sinjen commanded, his voice soft and inviting. "You will find the wine light, yet complex, with well-integrated berry, smoke, mushroom, and dried leaf flavors." He blinked slowly and watched her from under half-lowered lashes. "Like you, it is elegant, with a clean finish."

She snorted. "Elegant? That's a laugh."

Sinjen shook his head, a gentle motion but with enough force to dribble a lock of hair over his forehead. "Why do you persist, Sade?" His voice chided and caressed at the same time.

Sade fought to keep her hand from reaching across the table to smooth that strand back. A soft murmur of myriad conversations occasionally punctuated by the clatter of dishes filled the restaurant yet she had no trouble hearing and understanding the vampire sitting across the table from her. "Persist in what?" She canted her head to study him. "I am what I am, Sinjen."

"Yes." He used the same tone of voice, but added a hint of challenge. "You are what you are." His hand suddenly engulfed hers and his eyes held her gaze. "Today you are you, that is truer than true. There is no one alive who is youer than you."

Sade stared at him unblinking but lost the battle when she snickered. "Seussisms?" she asked, shaking her head in amusement. She noted the twinkle in his amazing blue eyes. "Be who you are and say what you feel, because those who mind don't matter and those who matter don't mind," she quoted back to him.

She would be the first to admit that she found Kristian St. John utterly fascinating—strictly on a professional basis she quickly assured herself. *Yeah, right*, her libido whispered. She continued to study him. "Curious and curiouser," she murmured. "A man who quotes Shakespeare and Dr. Seuss with equal aplomb is a rare creature indeed."

The padded leather of the booth back was so worn it felt butter soft. Leaning back, Sinjen continued to observe her without blinking. He wanted to know what made her tick, to know what would put a smile on her face. And what would make her cry out his name in the throes of passion.

The way he watched her was a bit unnerving, putting Sade in mind of a snake. A snake looking for a meal. Her nostrils flared. *I'm no mouse or any other meal for him.* She needed to convince herself before she had to convince him. He had a way of unsettling her that was most...unsettling.

A sad smile barely curved the corners of Sinjen's mouth. "And I was equally amazed to find a federal agent who could quote chapter and verse of

Hamlet." He finally blinked. "Would you be surprised to know I have read every book ever written?" His voice held no arrogance for he was simply stating a truth.

Sade looked skeptical. "Every book?" she replied, her eyes twinkling with amusement. "I somehow don't see you as being a huge fan of the romance genre." The pained look that flashed across his face caused her to laugh out loud.

"I stand corrected," Sinjen allowed. "Though I did read a few of Dame Barbara's books."

Searching her memory to put a writer with the name, Sade quietly boggled when she could only come up with one possibility. That was a place Sade wasn't quite ready to hike through. Just as he'd probably read enough books to fill a library or three, he was as likely to have had the same number of lovers, despite his earlier assertions of chastity.

The waiter appeared with Sade's salad. "The wine?" he asked, his attitude both solicitous and toadying. "You do not like the wine?"

He looked so much like a whipped puppy Sade swallowed the caustic remark on the tip of her tongue. Grabbing her wineglass, she took a drink. "See? Fine. It's fine," she began then realized the wine really was excellent. She took a sip and let it swirl across her tongue. "Wow," she murmured. "That's *really* good."

She tasted Sinjen's low chuckle. Chocolate. Melted. Caramel. Hot. And sweet melted ice cream over a hot brownie. Just like a scrumptious dessert, his laugh did funny things to the pit of her stomach and other parts of her anatomy she would rather not think about. Pulling her hand from beneath his, Sade leaned back in the booth, picking around the edges of her Caesar salad with a fork.

"Eat, Sade." Sinjen didn't ask. He ordered, even if his low-pitched voice was couched like a request. "You do not take care of yourself. You do not eat and you do not sleep."

Dutifully taking a bite, Sade briefly lowered her eyes. She missed the gleam of triumph that glinted in the vampire's eyes. Before she realized it, she'd finished her salad and her glass of wine. With an elegant flick of his wrist, Sinjen refilled her glass from the bottle.

The waiter reappeared and surreptitiously removed the salad plate and replaced it with the steak and potatoes Anne, thin-sliced spuds sautéed in butter with onions, sprinkled with feta cheese and then broiled in the pan under an open flame. The mushroom and herb crust on the filet tasted exquisite, and Sinjen relished the look of delight on Sade's face as she sampled it. While he could no longer savor the taste of food, he could 'taste' it vicariously through the expressions on a companion's face.

"How is your investigation coming?"

Chewing, Sade shook her head until she could swallow. "Nope," she asserted. "Not going there, buster. That's a loaded question and the answer is much too complicated to get into with someone who's involved up to his pointy teeth."

Sinjen arched one graceful brow at her, daring her to admit he was still a suspect. He refrained from smiling when she rolled her eyes.

"You know you are. Involved. Besides, you aren't technically cleared yet." She held up a hand to stay his rebuttal. "But you will be. Neither the US Attorney or the DA are looking your direction anymore."

Sinjen nodded. "A bit of a relief though I wasn't too worried. What of the other victims? You are finding a pattern?"

Sade swallowed a bite of potatoes. "I told you, Sinjen. I'm not going to discuss the case with you. Suffice it to say I have more questions than answers."

"Sometimes, the questions are complicated and the answers are simple."

"Another Seussism?" Sade retorted. "This whole fuckin' case is complicated and I have no answers, simple or otherwise." She sighed and put down her fork as if her appetite was gone. "I wish I did."

Once again, his hand slid across the table and captured hers. He gave her a sleepy-eyed smile, ignoring her language. "Then perhaps a less complicated question with a simpler answer. Tell me, Lady Sade. What is it you do for fun?"

Chapter Seventeen

Five Crows for Silver

WHAT IS IT YOU DO FOR FUN? Jeez, talk about answers far more complex than the question. She had fun. Really. She had interests outside the job. No. Really.

"Like what?" Sade sounded defensive and she hated that she did.

"Surely there is something. Cooking? Shopping?"

She rolled her eyes. "I don't shop. Not for fun. Necessity. Yeah. I can shop if it's necessary." Sade stared off into space for a long moment, thinking. "I read. Reports, intel files. Movies. I watch movies. Old ones, anyway. Bogie and Bacall. Katherine Hepburn. Cary Grant. Oohoohooh. Nick and Nora Charles. I love the Thin Man series." She glared as a smirk formed around his mouth. "Shut up. There's nothing like the classics. That's my story and I'm sticking to it." Grabbing her wine glass, she gulped a swig.

And what's up with this "Lady Sade" crap? She seethed inside. Roman was the only man who ever got away with calling her that and only because hitting him felt like hitting granite. The nickname was fine at the age of six but at sixteen? Or now? So not cool. The girls at Holloway would have had a field day. Hell, they had all considered her a freak anyway.

Looking up from taking a bite, she was troubled as she watched Sinjen's face. He'd turned into alabaster again and Sade sensed a deep, angry conflict going on in his mind, layered over with an abiding sadness that almost broke her heart. Without thinking, she reached across the table and cupped his cheek in her palm.

Sinjen, quietly attuned to Sade's moods and expressions, sighed inwardly at the look of sadness that momentarily appeared in her eyes. His heart lurched and he felt a profound need to wipe the look from her face and, more importantly, from her heart. Growing up as she had, Sade was like no other human he'd ever encountered and for all the pain that path brought into her life, she wouldn't be *Sade* otherwise. For the first time in his life, he considered changing a human into a vampire. The thought both shocked and titillated him—and made him inexorably melancholy.

He'd only changed one person, almost eighty years before and he still regretted it, though the man had accepted the invitation issued by the *Concilium Magicae* with full knowledge and a sense of duty. That was the only reason Sinjen had agreed. He would have suffered Mathias' torture had the man been less. He still faced the master vampire's wrath for refusing to change another. But Sade? For her—to keep her with him, he might forget any honor left in his soul.

Her touch startled him from his thoughts but he remained still. She had no words for him but her gesture spoke volumes. His heart actually skipped a beat at the tenderness radiating from her hand. He closed his eyes and surrendered to the feeling, relishing it, absorbing the heat from her skin. For the first fifty years after his change, he'd cursed Mathias's name. For another hundred, he considered himself an abomination in God's eyes. And then one night, a little girl—dirty, bedraggled, and dying—put her hand in his.

England, 1540

"IS GOD PRETTY?" The child stared up at him, eyes sunken back in her skull, her skin dull and ashen.

He shook his head in the negative. "Why would you ask that of me, child?"

"You are an angel, are you not?" Her voice sounded like innocence incarnate. "You surely have seen God. Is he so very frightful?" The girl shuddered as pain wracked her.

Sinjen, unmindful of the ghastly smells emanating from the child's body, gathered her into his arms and lap. He rocked her gently. "No, child," he whispered into her matted hair. "He's not frightening at all. God will welcome you with love into the home you never had on this earth."

The little girl's breathing grew labored and finally stopped. A few moments later, her heart stuttered and ceased beating. And the abomination he was shed blood red tears over the battered body of a street urchin. "I am no angel," Sinjen murmured. "And God has no place for the likes of me, but I am no demon either."

Beswetherick's Restaurant, Chicago

FROM THAT MOMENT ON, Sinjen had come to terms with his exile from heaven. Gazing into the startling green eyes of the woman sitting across from him, his definition of heaven changed. A soft smile quirked one corner of his mouth. "Beautiful," he sighed.

Sade actually blushed then lowered her eyes, looking down at her plate. "I think you have me confused with someone else."

Sinjen reached up and with much reluctance removed her hand from his cheek though he wrapped his fingers around hers. "Finish your meal," he requested, his voice hushed and almost detached. "You have a long night ahead of you."

She actually gulped. Sinjen laced his words with many double entendres he knew she'd catch. He watched her throat for a moment then raised his eyes.

"Work." The word seemed nothing more than a reminder to herself as she spoke it. "That's what I do for fun," she added, looking up and meeting his gaze. "I solve cases. I put the bad guys away and see that the innocent get some measure of justice."

Sinjen smiled though his eyes remained unblinking. "Justice," he murmured, still thinking of the urchin who had died in his arms. "There is no justice for the dead. They are just dead." His voice came out flat, unemotional—completely at odds with the surge of anger swirling in his gut.

"I disagree." Color rose in Sade's cheeks and her voice filled with righteousness. "Somebody has to speak for the dead. Somebody has to pay for the evil in the world. Karmic balance and all that, you know?"

Sinjen's laugh sounded dry and brittle, even to his ears. "Karmic balance? What fools you mortals be!" Sade's eyes sparkled like a broken bottle under a hot August sun. Before she could retort, Sinjen's thumb found her lips. "Shush, lovely. You are a crusader. I acknowledge that. I will not have our meal spoiled by debate on moral righteousness. Eat your steak before it grows cold." He flashed a brazen smile. "And then we shall see about dessert."

He watched her breath catch in her chest and, as if she had to remember to breathe, she drew in a lungful of air and let it out slowly. The woman sitting across from him looked good enough to eat as she took another idle bite of steak and chewed. Sinjen watched, his amusement most likely evident in his eyes though he didn't care. He knew what he would do to her once they returned to his home. Her hair would be tousled again, the color in her cheeks bright.

When they'd walked the few short blocks from his apartment, Sinjen was jealous of the wind. He wanted to be the one to muss Sade's hair and bring that flush to her cheeks. He wanted to hear her panting beneath him, soft little cries catching in her throat as he brought her to the brink time and time again before bringing her to a final climax. He wanted to feel the soft weight of her breasts in his hands, to have her puckered nipples pressing into his palms. Sade's skin would be smooth and soft beneath his fingers and he would make it quiver at his touch.

Sinjen wanted to taste her moans with his kisses as he teased her into hot-blooded arousal. He knew a passionate creature hid behind the façade of the cynical cop. He planned to tempt and inflame Sade until she opened beneath him like the shell unfolding beneath Venus in Botticelli's painting.

Sade finished the last bite of Potatoes Anne, her plate all but licked clean. She was vaguely aware the steak had seemed to melt in her mouth, the crust bursting with flavor against her tongue. Only the heel remained from the loaf of freshly-baked bread and the crock of herb butter that accompanied it was empty.

Sinjen refilled the wineglass then picked the bottle up, holding it to the light so the red wine inside shimmered like rubies—or blood. He offered her the glass. "Drink up, milady," he urged, his gaze riveted on her face.

He held her captive with his intensity. Deep secrets lurked in his expression. Sade couldn't look away—or didn't want to. She wasn't sure. She accepted the glass, raised it to her lips, and took a sip. The wine tasted like liquid rubies. The thought made her smile and in her head, she giggled—a warning sign if there ever was one. Absurdity hit. *What the hell do rubies taste like anyway?* She blinked, keeping her poker face in place, but just barely. "So what happens now?"

Sinjen chuckled softly. "Now that is a loaded question." He watched her mouth a moment before returning his gaze to her eyes. "What do you want to happen now?"

She grimaced. She hadn't actually meant to ask the question out loud. In fact, she wasn't sure she actually had. Even if Sinjen could read her mind, he'd still neatly tossed the ball back into her court. Her girlie bits, every blasted one of them, jumped up and down, squeeing like fangirls at a boy band concert clamoring for his attention. Her libido poised on the brink of mutiny.

The memory of the kiss Sinjen had bestowed upon her earlier returned like a freight train to crash into any moral argument she had left. The slow blink shuttering his eyes only whetted her carnal appetite. "I'm in the middle of an investigation." Sade tried very hard to sound professional and matter-of-fact. "You happen to be a suspect. Dinner was a bad idea. *Dessert* would be—"

Sinjen cut her off with a laugh richer than any confection. "Mandatory," he finished her sentence. He watched her through half-lidded eyes. "What are you afraid of, milady?"

He purred. He really and truly purred at her. Dammit. Every last one of Sade's girlie bits screamed at the same time. They had one demand—that they be allowed to become womanly bits. Despite the hormonal hubbub she suffered, she managed to arch one brow in what she prayed was a sardonic expression.

"Nothing." Oh, but she was inordinately proud she didn't have to clear her throat before managing to get that one word out. Yes, she was. Inordinately. And shocked as hell. She stared at him, almost as if daring him to challenge her. And he did. Sinjen's sleepy-eyed gaze trumped her sardonic brow. In a heartbeat. He didn't say a word; just watched her, the corners of his sensual mouth curling slightly into a beguiling smirk.

After a long, pregnant pause, Sinjen's smile widened. "Come then," he commanded as he slid out of the booth. "We shall see what presents itself."

Dammitdammitdammit, Sade berated her libido, her bits, and all the pieces that clamored for his attention, and then she started on the man himself. *He just fucking dared me to go back to his apartment so he can seduce me.* Spiders and flies immediately came to mind but she swallowed the rest of her wine in one gulp, hoping for some liquid courage to fortify her nerves. Deep down, she knew what was going to happen would be inevitable. Her body knew what it wanted. Even so, she didn't stop fighting.

Plus, the vampire had dared her. Anyone who knew her was well aware of the fact that backing down from a dare was one of her buttons. The whole situation was now a matter of honor as far as she was concerned. Any such challenge had been that way since she'd been a small child. It was stupid. Sade would be the first to admit that dares had gotten her into serious trouble growing up. She managed to set the wine flute on the table without breaking its delicate crystal stem or knocking it over. Sliding across the booth bench, she unfolded her legs from beneath the table and stood up.

Her height remained a continuing source of wonder for Sinjen. That she stood toe-to-toe with him and all but looked him straight in the eye made him smile. He didn't move out of her way. To get around him, Sade would have to brush against him. Realizing her predicament, she froze, going as still as a vampire—no easy feat for a human. Her piercing green eyes bored into his taunting ones. Unblinking, she waged a silent war with him. Being human, she'd have to breathe and she finally did.

"Games," she snorted as she pushed past him. "Fucking vampire games."

"Language, milady," Sinjen chided, his voice made gruff from so many things. He followed in her wake but it was all he could do to keep the triumphant grin off his face. She would not roll over and play dead. Not his Sade. The thought caused him to miss a step, an uncharacteristic gaffe for a man gracefully self-possessed.

By the time he caught up to her, she'd already retrieved her long, leather coat and was shrugging into it. Sinjen paused for a moment, watching the sheer elegance of her movements. He smiled at the incongruity of it. This long, lean woman would never see herself as he saw her. Sade was self-assured, brusque, with no wasted motions. Creatures most humans ran screaming from, Sade stared in the eye, fearless and unflinching. Yet inside, her heart remained as naïve as an untouched virgin.

Sinjen grew hard watching her as he anticipated stripping that same coat from her body. He wanted to strip her bare, open her heart and soul, and make love to her as no man ever had before. The thought left him determined to wipe from her mind the memory of every previous lover she'd ever had. Sade was his. No one would ever take her from him. He glimpsed his face in that moment, shocked at the intensity of his expression. Luckily, Sade ignored him and the maitre d' was too occupied with her to notice.

Without looking at him, Sade buttoned and belted her coat, flipping up the collar to give her ears nominal protection from the wind whipping in off the lake. The maitre d' hurried to open the door before her hand could touch the handle. The spry little man ducked in front of her and managed to get both the door open and out of her way.

Sade never broke stride as she headed out into the frigid Chicago night. The prickling on the back of her neck told her Sinjen followed her through the door, as silent and lethal as any great cat stalking his prey. She didn't like that idea. She was nobody's prey. Lengthening her stride and picking up speed, Sade sought to put some distance between them. If she had any sense, she'd flag down a cab and head either to the police station or back to her hotel. As she debated which destination, she kept walking. Within a few short minutes, a breath of warm air kissed her frigid cheek.

Sinjen trailed behind her for a couple of blocks as he admired the view. He sensed her turmoil but decided to let the woman make up her own mind. After almost nine hundred years, he was a patient hunter. As they neared his apartment building, he caught up to her. Matching his stride to hers, Sinjen was a silent shadow at her side. He turned his head slightly to watch her profile and as she stumbled, his palm automatically cupped her elbow to steady her.

She stiffened, but her reaction wasn't displeasure at his touch. Something else entirely caused her tension and he savored her reaction. He noticed the slight flaring of her nostrils and the movement of her throat as Sade swallowed. Thoughts of what would come tightened his groin and he quickened his steps in response, urging Sade to keep up by the pressure of his hand on her elbow.

Sinjen ignored the woman approaching them on the sidewalk. Hunkered into a down coat, she appeared misshapen, her age indeterminable. The white cane in her right hand tap-tap-tappity-tapped along the sidewalk, and it was Sade who nudged him out of the woman's way. As the three of them passed, the woman raised her head and nodded in their direction.

"Good evening." Her words, muffled by her coat and scarf, whispered across the wind.

"Yes," Sinjen murmured as he glanced at Sade. "It is."

Sade slowed, despite his efforts to urge her on. She stopped, turned to stare at the woman's retreating back. Her whole body tensed. He could feel it even in his light touch on her elbow. He watched her watch the woman. Sade stepped toward the curb as if she contemplated following in order to observe as the woman turned the corner and was abruptly cut off from view by the building. The tapping of the woman's cane echoed hollowly in a sudden lull of the wind.

Tires squealed—a bansidhe's screech of rubber and pavement rubbing together in a hostile meeting. Sade jerked free of his hand and sprinted for the corner. Caught flat-footed, Sinjen lengthened his stride to catch up to her. They rounded the building shoulder-to-shoulder and he matched her stride for stride. A nondescript dark-colored sedan perched nose-in at the curb, the trunk open. Two men wrestled the blind woman, the struggle partially blocked from view by the car. Even as Sade pulled her weapon, one slammed the trunk closed, and both men dove into the back seat from opposite sides. Leaving smoking rubber behind, the sedan bounced up over the curb, narrowly missing Sinjen and Sade. At the last moment, he grabbed her and pulled her out of harm's way.

"Gawdammitgawdammitmotherfuckingpissonthedevilandshit. You made me miss my shot."

He simply stared at her. "I saved you from being injured, Sade." The way she slammed into danger left his heart crammed his throat. He was surprised words actually tumbled from his mouth in any sort of coherent pattern.

She glared at him. "I could have stopped them. Saved that woman."

His hand shook as he brushed the back of his fingers against her cheek. "No. You would have died. And they would still have her. Because I pulled you back, you will be able to investigate and find her." He pointed with a jut of his chin. "She dropped her handbag."

Still muttering curses under her breath, Sade trotted to the large shoulder bag, snagged it and dug through the contents even as her cell phone magically appeared tucked between her jaw and shoulder. Fascinated, yet still quite shaken, Sinjen leaned against the building watching her. How could this woman have such an effect on him?

"This is Agent Sade Marquis, FBI. There's been a kidnapping at the corner of Fourteenth and Federal. Late model, black four-door sedan. Three suspects. Victim is a white female, probably in her late twenties." She dug out the woman's wallet and flipped it open with a twist of her wrist. "Victim's name is Ravena Silverstein. She's blind."

Sinjen tuned out the rest of the information Sade rattled off to the police. He'd noticed the hitch in her breath when she added the victim's handicap. Watching her, he noticed the nuances—nuances humans would miss. He smiled inwardly, careful to keep it from showing in his expression.

His Sade cared, far more than she likely admitted to herself, and certainly more than anyone observing her would realize. Then he recognized the victim's name—Ravena Silverstein, world-renowned concert pianist. Sade tucked her phone in her pocket and continued digging through the bag.

"Sade?" She ignored him. "Sade!" This time, the tone of his voice caused her to look up. Those bottle green eyes glinted under the wan streetlight.

"What?"

"The victim. Do you know who she is?" She continued staring at him then shook her head. The expression on her face revealed nothing of her thoughts so he explained. "She's a concert pianist."

"Oh, motherfuckin'shit no!" She didn't blink. "Please tell me that's a joke!"

He shook his head. "No. The Tribune said just last week after her concert with the philharmonic orchestra that, and I quote, "Her hands are magical."

Chapter Eighteen
Six Crows for Gold

"*HER HANDS ARE MAGICAL?* Oh gawdammutherfuckin'shit-n-piss, they took her right in fucking front of me!" Sade paced up and down the sidewalk, each step a pounding stomp of anger. She grabbed her phone and dialed. "Franks, have you heard!" She didn't ask, she demanded. "Ravena Silverstein. They took her for her hands. We have to find whoever is behind this, Franks, and find them now."

She glared at Sinjen again. She didn't need to voice her thoughts. They leaked out of her riding the waves of her anger. If only he'd let her get a shot off. She would have hit the driver. The pianist would be safe. The kidnappers would be in custody. And she would be hot on the trail of whoever...or whatever killed those girls. But he knew. Had he not acted, she would be lying broken and bleeding on the sidewalk.

In moments, screaming sirens filled the air and squad cars screeched to a stop in front of her. Even as the first officers popped out of their vehicles, her badge glittered in her hand as she issued orders. In her element now, Sade grabbed command and didn't let go. Sinjen simply stood back in the shadows, leaning up against the building at his back and watched. The woman awed him—on so many levels he couldn't even begin to count.

Sade reined in her anger, controlled and channeled it. She issued orders in short, clipped sentences. Do this. Go here. Find out. He was forgotten in the controlled chaos. The detective Sade called, the one they'd met at the fountain arrived. Franks. But like Sinjen, the man simply stood back and let Sade run her course. She was a force of nature. Crime scene people arrived and radios snapped with terse exchanges. She finally remembered his presence and turned to him. Under the street lamps, her eyes flashed and for a moment, looked feral. She stalked toward him, much as she had the first time he'd laid eyes on her.

"You might as well go home."

"No."

"I won't be done until after dawn, Sinjen. I don't think you want to be sitting in the middle of Homicide when the sun comes up." Her eyes softened, just a brief hint of concern, then glinted again as her mouth tightened into a unyielding smirk. "Don't make me play the official business card."

His fingers curled against his palm in the effort to keep from reaching for her. Here, in the presence of her peers. No, he amended. None of these men were her peers. She was so far superior they could not even come close. Within their view, despite how he longed to touch her, to kiss her, to force her to accompany him home, he would not embarrass her.

"As you wish, milady. I leave you to your work." Pleased his voice remained steady, he even managed a smile—somewhat stiff but a smile nonetheless.

Sade stepped closer and he almost lost his control and good sense as her scent enveloped him. Sinjen doubted a trick of lighting softened her face nor did shadows tweak the corner of her mouth into a little smile.

"Go home, Sinjen." Her voice whispered across skin that hadn't felt this alive in centuries. "You can't help."

Curious, he watched her. Sure enough, her expression hardened again and a different emotion flashed in her eyes—regret over the fate of the pianist. While she might feel such an emotion, he felt none. "Haven't quite forgiven me then. So be it. A warning, Sade. I would do the same again. Nothing is more precious than your life." He turned on his heel and walked away, leaving her flat-footed and speechless. He smiled. Even so small a moral victory over Sade Marquis was quite the accomplishment. He turned the corner and abruptly disappeared.

Sade climbed into the front seat of Detective Franks' car, muttering under her breath. He opened his mouth but the one finger she held up stopped him from speaking. "No. It's not him, Franks. Yes, I considered it, especially since there were human accomplices tonight."

"I wasn't going to say a thing, Marquis."

"Yeah. Right."

He chuckled, the sound rattling like dry leaves left on a tree after the first winter storm. "You really believe Ms. Silverstein is our next victim?"

Sade rubbed her temple with one hand. "Yeah. I do, Bobby." She braced as the car jerked to a stop at the red light. Using his first name seemed to surprise the hell out of him. "Whoever...whatever is doing these murders, it's not the run-of-the-mill magick." She caught him cutting his eyes her direction. "Magicks don't willingly work with mundanes, Franks. Control them, yes, but not work with. Those three tonight weren't under any compulsion. Neither was the victim."

Franks snorted. "And you know this how?"

"If I told you that, I'd have to kill you."

"Yeah, right." The cop chuckled, glanced at her and sobered. "Wait. You're kidding. Right?" Her expression never altered and he cleared his throat. After sucking in a deep breath, he blew it out slow and easy, as if steadying his nerves. "You warned me it would get worse." Braking for a right turn, he glanced at her. "How much worse?"

"I wish I knew."

"You aren't boosting my confidence here, Marquis."

"We're cops, Franks. That makes us realists whether we want to be or not. Optimism isn't in my vocabulary. Not at the moment."

The two of them rode in silence the rest of the way to the station. He found a parking place, nosed the sedan in to the curb and killed the ignition before he turned part way in his seat. "So tell me the truth. You know what we're hunting, don't you?"

Sade shook her head slowly from side to side. "I don't. I really don't have a clue and trust me, I even tugged on Superman's cape." He arched a brow at her. "No, you don't want to know. Suffice it to say, the superman in question is one of the oldest and most powerful magicks I know."

"So what did he say?"

"That he'd get back to me." She scrubbed her forehead with the heels of her hands, making circular motions as if that would ease the headache pounding there. "Despite the fact that he would kill me in a heartbeat if it suited his needs, I trust this source, Franks." Her statement got both of the cop's eyebrows wagging. Sade closed her eyes for a moment, filled her lung with a deep breath then slowly exhaled. "In case you haven't noticed, there's been a huge influx of magicks coming to town. And not just run-of-the-mill types, either. Something has tripped their alarms, but none of them seems to know what it is."

Franks stared out the windshield, watching uniformed cops come and go through the front door of the station. "Fuck."

"My sentiments exactly." Crevan. Ariel. Nikos. Why were they here? Sade licked dry lips. She'd only had wine with dinner and her body felt like it was withering up like road kill in Death Valley. She normally drank water like a sailor on shore leave drank beer but she'd been off balance so often on this trip, she kept forgetting that coffee didn't count.

They climbed out of the sedan and strolled almost nonchalantly to the door, neither speaking. Franks trotted ahead to snag the closing doors of an upward-bound elevator and held it for Sade to catch up. She stepped on board and, on the ride up, wondered where Sinjen was. Had he gone back to his apartment like she told him to, or he was he wandering around playing private eye? The doors clattered open and stayed as Franks jammed his thumb against the button on the controls. She stepped out and he leaped to follow her. The closing doors barely missed him.

"Damned vicious." Sade eyed the doors, a wary look on her face.

"No shit. I know a guy who lost his hand just last week."

She laughed, thankful for cop humor, and followed Franks through the homicide bullpen to a cluttered desk shoved back against the far wall. Her nose flared, familiar scents almost comforting in their normality—burned coffee, stale bodies, musty files, a hint of cigarette smoke clinging to furniture and clothing alike.

The muted tones of Steppenwolf's "Born to Be Wild" jangled in slightly distorted digital notes. She pulled her phone out of her coat pocket, indicated with a facial expression she needed to take the call, and backed off a few feet. She swiped her finger across the "Accept Call" bar.

"Please tell me you aren't using Steppenwolf for my ring tone."

"Okay. I won't. Where are you, Caleb?"

"I'm with a horse with no name. What's up with you?"

"A horse—" She rolled her eyes and bit off the rest as she resisted the urge to sigh. "Still walking on the wild side?"

"I'm working. You didn't answer my question, Sade."

"I'm working too. Why?"

"Ripples."

"What the hell is that supposed to mean?"

"Whatever you have stirred up is creating ripples, Sade. Throughout the Veil."

She didn't say anything, mulling over the implications. "The pot was stirred before I got here, Caleb." Rubbing her head, she wished for a bottle of water. "Though considering the preternatural activity in Chicago at the moment, I shouldn't be surprised. Crevan is here. And Ariel and that damn dragon." She held the phone away from her ear as the werewolf's derisive growl echoed from the speaker.

"That should tell you something, Slim."

Slim. Caleb hadn't called her "Slim" in ages. "Are you okay?"

"Nothing I can't handle but you've been on my mind. You're thinking too hard."

"No, I'm not. I'm not thinking hard enough."

"Ripples, Sade. Sometimes you just have to follow them back to find the stone that was thrown in the first place." The sound deadened but for muffled voices and a steady thump, as if Caleb had pressed his cell against his chest while he talked to someone else. "I need to go. Duty calls and all that. Watch your six, Sade. I can't ride to the rescue if something bites you in the ass."

Before she could retort, the connection broke on Caleb's end. Muttering under her breath, she refocused her attention on Franks. He was on his desk phone but waved her to an empty chair. She didn't feel like sitting but sank onto the hard, wooden seat anyway. Closing her eyes for a moment, Sade rolled her head around her shoulders, listening to the creaks and pops.

Ripples. Nothing about this case made any sense and now Caleb wanted her to find the epicenter? As if she could just snap her fingers and *voilà*, the case was solved? At the moment, she needed to concentrate on finding and recovering Ravena Silverstein while the pianist still remained in one piece.

Settled in the chair next to Franks' desk, she watched him work his traps. Confidential informants. Street cops. Detectives. He reached out and touched them all. The fine hairs on her arms prickled so she rolled her head on her neck as a cover to gaze around the room. Nothing. Rubbing the palm of her hand up and down the opposite arm, she pushed out of the chair and paced. The Chicago cop was doing his best. She snagged her phone and started making her own calls.

Two hours later, she'd all but drained the water cooler. Neither she nor Franks were any closer to finding the latest victim. She rolled her head again, this time to relieve the stiffness. She sighed and grabbed her coat. "We both need to sleep. Call me if anything comes up." Franks waved one hand at her, distracted as he continued to work the phone. She shrugged into her coat and headed for the elevators.

FOLLOWING SADE TURNED out to be easier than he anticipated. While standing in a corner of the homicide bull pen and hidden by shadows, Sinjen watched the play of emotions on her face as she talked on the phone. He managed to hear her side of the conversation even above the hum of conversation punctuated by the jangling of telephones that permeated the room. The affection in her voice stabbed him until he realized who had called.

He laughed softly. Jealousy at his age? Rather unbecoming but likely a part of his life so long as Sade remained in it. He watched her, shifting his gaze when she got antsy and looked around as if seeking someone. A patient hunter, he waited, though he knew she would be no one's prey.

He watched all the humans in the room, tensing when someone arrived, relaxing as they left. Considering the hour, this room hummed with conversations and activity. Homicide. Man's brutality against man. He'd seen streets run red with blood. A line, half forgotten from a poem, echoed in his memory. *The love that kisses with a homicide...* George Baker, the poet's name and his words rang hollowly now that Sinjen had tasted that love.

When he was alone again, when he knew Sade was safe, he would initiate his own search for the pianist. Unlike the humans, he was not convinced Ravena Silverstein had been abducted by whatever Sade hunted. Something about the incident seemed just a bit...off. Sinjen didn't need to check a clock. He could feel the passing of time in his bones. He hoped to lure Sade away before sunrise forced him to return to his apartment without her.

As she stood up and grabbed her coat, he smiled. Only one a.m. He all but materialized from the shadows as she stepped into the hallway leading to the elevators.

"Took you long enough."

Sinjen swallowed his laugh. "You knew I was here?"

"I suspected. I caught glimpses of your shadow out of the corner of my eye but you were sneaky enough to stay out of my direct sight." She rolled her eyes. "You're such a control freak, Sinjen."

His laughter spilled out. The elevator doors opened on cue and he pulled her on board. Still chuckling, he didn't look at her on the ride down to street level. He didn't need to. She remained annoyed—resigned, but irritated. Her jaw jutted even as he heard the rustle of her leather coat when she shoved her fists deep into its pockets. The doors open and they stepped off in tandem, their strides perfectly matched. More than a few heads turned to watch their egress.

Out on the street, he stopped and turned to her. His leather-gloved hands gathered the lapels of her coat and pulled them together. In moments, he'd buttoned it up. "The wind is nippy." His murmured words stirred the wave of ebony hair framing her ear.

Before she could reply, a cab rolled to a smooth stop and Sinjen bundled her into the back. He gave the address where the kidnapping occurred and hid his smile at her quick intake of breath. He knew she'd want to revisit the scene and he had his own reasons for a return trip. Once there, Sade leapt out of the cab and began pacing before he could even pay. He leaned against the wall of the building and watched her quarter the block like a hound casting for a scent.

Once more, time tickled his senses. He knew she'd found nothing and was perplexed. He'd found nothing either and felt the same puzzlement. There was a total absence of magic about the place. Which confused him. Replaying the scene in his mind, he would have sworn there was a whiff of oily stench about the kidnapped woman—an odor not unlike sulfur and pine tar. The smell of evil. No trace remained now. He watched Sade for a few more minutes and then stepped in front of her.

"Enough. You are chilled to the bone. Let us go home, Sade." He gave her no room to argue. He simply tucked her arm through his and strode off with her in tow.

Both were breathless as they approached the door to Sinjen's building. Like magic, George, the night doorman, appeared, holding the heavy glass and brass door open for them to sweep through. The door was wide enough they never broke stride as they passed inside shoulder to shoulder and headed toward the bank of elevators. Sade didn't have to speculate if the elevator would open in time since the door slithered open while she and Sinjen were still halfway across the marble-floored lobby.

She preceded him by half a step into the elevator car and the door whispered to a close behind them. Sinjen caught a glimpse of the doorman and the concierge, both with mouths gaping. The concierge fanned herself and George mouthed the word *damn*—stretching it out to two syllables. Yes, the sexual heat he and Sade emitted could quite possible set off the fire suppression system.

Neither spoke on the elevator ride up. As far as Sade was concerned, there wasn't anything to say. Part of her coiled like a spring in anticipation while the other part looked for an escape route. Sinjen's palm burned through her leather-clad elbow with an intensity that would rival summer in the Sahara.

When the doors opened, she hesitated half a moment, Sinjen waiting patiently at her side. She knew then she still had a choice. She could step off the elevator into a great unknown—or she could stay rooted to the spot, ride the elevator back down to the lobby, and grab a cab to anywhere but here. Before she could stop it, her right foot stepped forward, followed immediately by the left, and she was suddenly walking down the thickly carpeted hallway toward Sinjen's apartment.

Sinjen followed her and as she stopped at his door, he came up beside her to insert the key and unlock the door. His arm brushed against hers in the process. His eyes glowed at the quiver he surely felt through her leather sleeve. "Welcome to my home," he whispered into her wind-blown hair.

"Step into my parlor's more like it," Sade retorted but she crossed the threshold, those earlier thoughts of spiders and flies ricocheting around in her head. Then the true meaning of his words sank in. Sinjen had just granted her his protection. Nothing would happen to her here that she didn't want to happen. *Which puts the damned ball right back squarely in my court.* She did not appreciate the turn her thoughts took as her momentum carried her down the entry hall all the way into the living room.

Sinjen hadn't turned on any lights and the uncovered wall of windows framed the wide panorama of the Chicago skyline and the lake. The shadowed buildings created a dark cityscape set with sparkling lights and framed by the sharp contrast of the inky water and black-velvet sky.

Mesmerized, Sade strode across the room to the window wall and stood with her nose only inches away from the thick glass panes. Sinjen walked up behind her and reached around to untie her coat and slowly unbutton it. Her breath hitched in her chest but she made no move to either stop or assist him. Once he had her coat undone, Sinjen pushed the butter-soft leather off her shoulders. Leaning in, his lips found her neck and he teased her chilled skin with gentle nips.

Sade was about to press back against him when the warmth at her back suddenly disappeared. In the reflective window glass, she watched him head back into the entry hall to hang up her coat. A slow smile hinting at her own hunger curled her mouth as the vampire stripped off his cashmere topcoat and hung it next to hers in the coat closet. She gazed out over the panorama again as she waited for him to rejoin her. When he didn't, Sade scanned the room's reflection and then slowly turned around to search the room visually when there was no sign of Sinjen. A few moments later, he emerged from his bedroom. He'd taken off his sport coat and stood leaning against the door jamb. He was barefooted, the crisply starched dress shirt he wore untucked and unbuttoned. She had already been treated to a glimpse of him wearing nothing but a towel but somehow, this debonair picture straight out of a fashion magazine was infinitely sexier.

Sade sighed. He was undoubtedly the most beautiful man she had ever laid eyes on. Her gaze brazenly roamed his body from head to toes and back up again, pausing here and there to savor the view. She watched his nostrils flare in reaction to her perusal and she remembered to breathe.

"Damn," she murmured. "The fae don't have shit on you, stud."

Sinjen chuckled softly, a deep rumbling sound from low in his chest. "I should hope not," he replied, his voice a satiny caress. He held out a hand, palm up, his blue eyes dark with desire and hope. "Come to bed, milady."

Come to bed, milady. That was Roman's line. Always. As a teen, when rebellion bristled in her chest, the gargoyle always patiently waited in the shadows. She might rant and rave, stamp her feet, spit out every curse word in every language she knew yet he waited, implacable and solid. After one such drama-filled example of teen-aged angst, he'd followed her out onto the balcony, lifted his head and sniffed the air. Pregnant black clouds draped the horizon, backlit by jagged lightning. She'd been oblivious to the pending storm.

"Mean people suck, Roman."

"Watch your language, Sade." The gargoyle sighed, even his fabled patience worn thin.

"Why? Boys get to cuss. Why can't girls?"

"Boys should watch their language, too, child," the big magick replied, his tone that of an unruffled schoolmaster. "Only the crassest of creatures resort to using the vernacular."

She'd snorted, the sound both derisive and dismissive, as she continued to stare out toward the storm clouds. That summer had been hot and dry and despite the best efforts of Mathias's gardeners, the grass and foliage around the house remained brittle and coated with dust. The humid air felt thick, the caustic odor of ozone competing with the prevailing acrid odor of dust—a mixture that smelled strangely of gunpowder. Her nose crinkled at the scent. "Why don't people like me?"

"Does it really matter so much?" His voice grated, and he sounded gruff, as if he didn't care.

"It'd be nice to have a date to a dance who wasn't my brother." She ignored the crux of her feelings. "It'd be nice if the gawddammed fae wanted to fuck me because they think I'm sexy. No. They have to be ordered here by Uncle Obi-Wan or Queen Tittyfae."

The gargoyle had recognized the pain behind the sarcastic tone of her voice, so chided her with a look only. He stroked her cheek with one finger. "The time will come, Lady Sade," he assured.

"I doubt that," she'd argued, sarcasm painting each word to hide her fear.

"I don't," Roman replied, the conviction in his words punctuated by a flash of lightning and a boom of rumbling thunder. "Caleb is restless and won't settle until you do. Come to bed, Lady Sade."

Chapter Nineteen

Seven Crows for a Secret

Sade STARED AT SINJEN, unaware she *was* staring. *Damn but why does he have to be so gorgeous?* It was becoming a rhetorical question. *Dammitdammitdammit. What's wrong with me that the only man who makes me feel alive is dead?* Before her brain could overload her body with logic and arguments, she took a few short strides and melted into Sinjen's arms.

With her face buried against his neck, her cheek brushing the slightly raspy skin of his cheek, Sade gave up any pretense at remaining aloof. Her nostrils flared and she took a deep breath, filling her nose and lungs with the vampire's scent. There was no hint of decay or the faint sweetly rotten smell of reptiles some people associated with vampires. Sade took another deep breath and tried to identify the scents—leather, a whiff of ambergris and...something else she couldn't quite pin down. An illusive memory teased her, dancing just out of reach like a moth waltzing with a flame. Sleet spattered against the bedroom window and the memory suddenly slipped into frame.

Rain on a hot summer day in Texas was rare. And when it came, the drops were often huge, splattering the powder-fine dirt and sending up little puffs of dust. That was the scent Sade tried to identify—dry and acrid, the flavor of it settling on the back of her tongue, reminding her of gunpowder. The combined odors made her knees go weak and those rebellious girlie bits cheered, doing The Wave with the precision of a synchronized swimming team.

Sinjen backed into the bedroom, pulling her with him. His palms brushed across her shoulders and her blazer slid down her arms to puddle on the floor. Once she was fully past the doorframe, he picked her up and carried her to the bed. Settling her gently on the silken coverlet, Sinjen knelt beside the bed. His eyes bored into hers as his elegant fingers reached for the first button of her shirt. "Say no, Sade," he whispered. "While there is still time."

She couldn't even blink as she stared into those amazing blue eyes. The emotions she read there rocked her to the very foundation of her soul. In answer, she leaned forward, closing the distance between their mouths. "Yes," she murmured against his lips.

That was all the invitation Sinjen needed. His mouth coerced hers. Slow. Easy. Patient. Even though he wanted, in the best tradition of bodice-ripping romances, to strip her clothes and her defenses. But he didn't. He wasn't alone tonight. She was with him. The fire within could only be quenched by this woman. And he would have her until the sun rose and stole his breath from him.

Not content to lie there passively, she arched into his kiss, her arms circling his neck, needy little noises murmuring from between her lips. His nimble fingers unbuttoned her blouse and slipped it down her arms. Breaking off the kiss, he nibbled the indention on her chin and then sought out the beauty mark at the corner of her mouth. His curious tongue continued to explore, tracing the line of her jaw. Her head bowed back, exposing her throat.

He had to rein in the desire to sink his teeth into that exposed flesh. With great effort, he allowed only his lips to dance across the soft skin. Sinjen kissed the hollow of her throat before following the curve of her shoulder to drag his teeth across her collarbone. She shivered. His mouth alone elicited this reaction from the incredible woman in his arms. What more could he extract from her before the night was over?

Sinjen trailed his tongue down into the valley formed by Sade's breasts. More muscular than plump, they were still full and at the moment, firmly cupped by the black lace of her bra. He paused to appreciate the sight and the irony that the no-nonsense woman sprawled on his bed would succumb to the allure of sexy lingerie.

Sade sighed as his lips and tongue caressed the swell of her breasts. She squirmed and then thrashed her legs as she tried to worm out of her boots. Chuckling, he raised his head and smiled at her. "May I be of assistance?"

Tracing his palms down her sides and along her hips to her thighs, he marveled at the lean curves. Both hands circled Sade's right thigh and stroked down her calf to her ankle. His hands pushed up the hem of her trousers so his fingers could find the zipper of her leather boots. In seconds, the right boot hit the floor with a soft thud. Her toes were curled. His heart leaped. Curled toes—an excellent clue he had kissed her correctly. A few seconds later, the left boot landed next to the right one.

Without asking, he unbuckled her belt and unbuttoned her slacks. Before Sade could swallow a deep breath, he whisked her trousers—badge and holster still attached to her belt—off her long legs. The proprietary smile on his face as he stared was telling. The lace boy shorts hugging Sade's rounded hips matched the bra that cupped her breasts. His heart stuttered a moment and his sharp intake of breath expanded his chest.

"Beautiful," Sinjen uttered out loud. *Mine!* he declared silently.

The predator in him wanted to devour Sade. The Renaissance man wanted to adore her perfect form. The lover wanted to sink into her depths and stay there surrounded by her wet heat for the rest of his days. Sinjen leveraged his body onto the bed, his hard frame halfway covering her lean one.

Sade ran her palms up his chest and then her fingers tangled in his Egyptian cotton shirt. "Too many clothes," she murmured into the hollow under his chin, her lips nuzzling the soft prickles of his shadow beard.

He exhaled, his heart beating in time with hers. Though dead once a vampire surrendered to the day sleep, at least clinically speaking, the rest of the time his body functioned just like a human's. He had to shave, unless he wanted to grow a beard. The same for haircuts. His heart beat and he breathed out of habit, filling his nostrils with scents, his lungs with air. As his erection stiffened to the point of pain, he relished the effect this woman had on him.

Pushing up on his elbows, Sinjen stared down at Sade. A complicated series of expressions danced across her face, her emotions stripped bare beneath his gaze. Her body was pliant, craving his touch as evidenced by the way she pressed against him. Her mind, though, was still filled with thoughts other than him. He intended to change that. "You are thinking too hard, milady."

This woman fascinated him as none had ever before in his long life. Dipping his head, his mouth found one of her breasts, suckling the nipple through the lace. He smiled triumphantly around his delectable mouthful as she arched off the bed and sucked in a deep breath.

"Damn," she muttered, her arms tangled in the tails of his shirt as she tried to circle them around him. "Clothes!" she demanded with a harsh whisper.

Wanting to gloat, Sinjen sat up. In scant moments, his shirt and slacks joined Sade's clothes in a puddle on the floor. "Better?" he teased as he stretched out beside her.

"Much."

He cupped her cheek in his hand and leaned in to kiss her, his mouth gentle on hers. Sinjen traced his palm down her neck and shoulder, trailing it along her arm, raising goose bumps in its wake. Her nipples puckered—an interesting side effect—so he once again dipped his head to taste her through the lace. His hand stroked her arm before sliding to her waist then lower to her hip. Her responses delighted him and he gave up any pretense at suppressing his reactions.

His fingers trailed across her abdomen and paused to caress the skin around her belly button before they nudged aside the satin and lace stretched across her tummy. As he pushed a finger inside her, Sinjen made a surprising discovery—one that had him pushing off the bed and backing way.

Sade, her hair tousled, nipples perked and pressing through the lace of her bra, pushed up on her elbows to stare at him. "Is something wrong?" she asked, as her eyes trailed down his chest, and lower. She blinked and gulped. "Oh. My. You are...wow." Her breath sighed out. Then she gazed at his face and blinked at the expression he wore.

"Why didn't you tell me!" he demanded, his voice harsh. It wasn't a question. Shocked by his discovery, his erection halfway deflated.

"What?" She stared at him, confused by his reaction. And then she assumed the worst. "Y-you don't want me." She whispered the words, praying they weren't true. Watching him, gauging his expression, she knew. And was crushed. Her face flamed, revealing her embarrassment.

Sade sat up, swinging her legs over the side of the bed. Bending, she snatched her shirt off the floor, shrugged it on and haphazardly fastened a couple of buttons. She snagged her slacks and shoved her feet through the legs. Head lowered, her fists gripped the belted waist as the weight of her weapon offered a tiny sense of normality.

Sinjen sank to his knees in front of her. The look on her face broke his heart. His tough cookie wasn't the brassy broad she pretended to be. It was all he could do to stay out of her mind, to discover what terrible emotional trauma had put that pain in her eyes. Despite his best efforts, he still caught the flicker of a painful memory—a lonely little girl sitting on the front steps waiting for so-called friends who never arrived. The moment he pulled back from her mind, all her fears—of not being good enough, of being pretty enough, of being worthy of love, of being loved simply for who she was—surged into her head, and swamped him with their intensity.

Sinjen leaned closer and cupped her face in his hands. He brushed his lips across her mouth, ending with the touch of his tongue to her beauty mark.

"How can you be a virgin?" The tone of his voice revealed the wonder he felt at the knowledge.

Sade's voice held a slightly hysterical edge as she gripped her shirtfront tightly in her fists, holding it closed. "How do you know I am?"

He rocked back on his heels, still cupping her cheek. "I just do. In this day and age? I don't understand how this can be so."

She gulped back a high-pitched giggle. "It's actually rather simple. The only *men* who've ever tried to get in my pants were fae sent by Oberon and Titania to seduce me. I had a seven-foot gargoyle and a werewolf protecting my virtue until I got my first Beretta. It came with a clip filled with both cold iron and silver bullets. Which came in very handy when a fucking dragon decided I should be part of his hoard." Sade pushed him backwards. The mere fact he moved should have told her she'd caught him off guard.

"So fuck you, Professor St. John. And fuck me for forgetting what I am. If you'll excuse me, I'll just grab the shreds of my dignity, get dressed, and get the hell out of here."

He reached for her but she slapped his hand, the smacking sound as sharp as a gunshot. "Look, Sinjen. This was a bad idea. A really bad idea."

She sounded insistent, but he wondered which of them she was trying to convince. "I disagree." He caught her hands, avoiding another smack by doing so, and tugged her down to kneel with him. Reluctant, Sade joined him. Not that she had a choice. While his grip was gentle, he could easily break all the bones in her hands and she knew it. What she didn't know was that he would release her long before that ever occurred. Kneeling there, her eyes were almost on the same level as his and she stared boldly at him. Defiant, she kept her eyes open when he leaned in and kissed her.

Sinjen sent his tongue in gentle exploration of her mouth. His last kiss had been a taking. This one asked, and then answered with its tenderness. Once again, his fingers did their magic and Sade was sans shirt, with her bra joining it moments later.

"I never said I didn't want you, Sade," he murmured into her mouth. "But rather than taking you, I will have to win you slowly. I would not hurt you, milady, in my haste to make love to you."

Her eyes widened and her pulse stuttered. Make love? Not sex? The idea knocked her off center. Her gaze sought his, to see the truth behind the words. He didn't blink as she stared, studying every nuance in the hard planes of his face. Did she believe? Could she? Trust. Hers was hard won but everything in her heart insisted this man spoke the truth.

Sinjen lifted her to the bed and stripped her panties from her hips. Her first lover. The knowledge staggered him. If he hadn't already been on his knees he would have fallen to them in supplication and thanks for this miracle who had entered his life.

She watched him, wary and uncertain. Words whispered in her memory—words Roman once spoke to her as they stood on the bank of the Mississippi River. *"Many will want you, want what you represent, Sade. But for you, there will be only one man who needs. Who needs you. Only one whose heart beats solely for you. Keep your heart safe until the right one comes along."*

This felt so right to her, yet so terrifying at the same time. Sinjen's gaze scorched her bare skin and she fought the urge to cover her breasts and mound. Sade lifted her chin, a slight rebellion against her fear. She would not give in to the dread lodging in her chest. How could he be the right one? A vampire? A man with no heart, no soul? A man like Mathias? She would not run from this despite the very real sense of self-preservation screaming along her nerve endings. Whatever happened here tonight—it would be irrevocable. And she would be changed forever.

Sinjen watched her internal war. What scars did she carry that she was so wounded? He wanted to make love to her. No. He *needed* to make love to her. To love *her*. He didn't believe in soul mates and his life was far too long to fall in love with a human. But he could not—would not walk away from her, or from the blatant, raw need he felt for her. He'd been alone for eight hundred years. He didn't want to be alone for this one night. That's all he would ask from the Universe. He could not ask God, soulless creature that he was. One night with this woman in his arms, loving her. Expecting nothing in return. He waited, on his knees beside the bed, for her answer.

It came when she rolled to her side so she could watch him. She blinked, reached out and touched his lips with her index finger—a kitten-paw touch filled with shyness. "You really want to make love to me?"

He breathed, the constriction banding his chest easing. "Yes."

Sade moved away from the edge of the bed to make room for him. "Then do it, okay?"

Not the most romantic invitation he'd ever received but one that meant more to Sinjen than any he'd ever had or would ever have again. "As you wish, milady." He stretched out beside her and caressed her from thigh to shoulder with a quivering hand. Him, a Templar Knight who had fought the Saracens, who had become a master vampire by the sheer strength of his will. And he was reduced to a trembling fool by a human woman with eyes the color of emerald glass and a spirit more fierce than any he'd ever encountered. Humbled by the depth of his feeling for Sade, he paid homage to her.

Kisses. Slow, pervasive, deeply claiming. His. Always. And he would prove it to her. More kisses peppered against her soft skin that was faintly scented with cloves. He showered attention on her breasts until their areolas were ruched, nipples pebbled. His fingers teased through silky curls between her thighs and were met with creamy heat. He slicked the lips of her sex and he pressed the pad of his index finger against her clit. Her sharp inhalation put a smile on his face.

Sinjen wanted all of her. His greed overwhelmed him but he didn't care. He would wring every last emotion from her before the sun rose. He would swallow her cries for more as he kissed her. He would taste her passion as she came apart from the assault of his mouth and tongue. He would take her for himself, God and the Universe could go to the devil!

As she relaxed beneath his kisses, he slipped one finger into her moist depths. A second followed shortly to be enveloped by wet silk. Her scent intensified—heavy with cloves and gardenias. He drank in her moans as she writhed beneath him, reaching for something her brain hadn't yet defined. He would teach her. He would show her what it was to be loved by a man.

Fingers slid in and out of her sex, his thumb teased her clit. She curled her hips trying to take him deeper, unsure why but instinct driving her body now. Ambegris musk swamped her senses and her breath hitched as she tried to draw his scent deeper into her body. "More," she whispered.

"More." His swollen cock, its tip dripping with his need for her, throbbed as the word echoed in his brain. Her hand groped blindly, found his erection, and her fingers wrapped around it. He gritted his teeth, fighting the urge to pump into her grip. He craved the feel of her hand around him, and the thought of her mouth surrounding him almost made him come. But not now. Not this moment. This was for her. He would teach her how to please him. Some day. Now, though, he would make her scream out her passion. He slipped down her body and his mouth replaced his hand.

Sade couldn't breathe. Sinjen's mouth on her most intimate spot had her wanting to squirm away, or to grab his hair in her fists and grind herself against his face. She did neither, crushing silken sheets in her fists instead. Someone moaned. Was that her? She whimpered in her need to reach for something intangible, something just beyond her experience. The muscles in her legs, braced over Sinjen's shoulders, trembled and she thrashed her head from side to side.

"More," she demanded, her voice ravaged and breathless.

"Yes, more," he murmured against her, the vibrations of his words sending frissons through her body.

Sinjen feasted on her clit and his tongue lapped her before dipping into her vagina. Tension radiated from her and he knew the moment she peaked as her sweet cum flooded his mouth. He drank deeply, his hands griping her hips to hold her still.

Sade's face was slick with tears and she shook uncontrollably. So this was what a climax felt like? This unbearable sense of infinity, of oneness, of...absolution? How could she feel so empty yet so full at the same time? So many questions without answers. She had no understanding of the emotions swirling within her. She groped blindly for an anchor.

Sinjen was suddenly beside her, strong arms wrapping around her, cradling her to him. He kissed her tears away and smoothed his palm up and down her back in a comforting caress.

"Shhh, m'love," he murmured against her hair.

Her head fit the hollow of his shoulder as if their bodies had been carved by a master sculptor and made to match. She panicked. Too much. It was all too much. A sob escaped and his arms tightened.

"Breathe, love. Breathe deeply because I've only just started."

Just started? Sade didn't think she'd survive. He let her rest for only a few moments before his hand found her breasts and his lips her mouth. His erection lay hard and wanting against her hip. He'd been patient long enough. Rolling on top of her, he spread her thighs with his legs and settled between them. The head of his cock kissed her opening and was greeted by silky warmth. He pushed in and swallowed her gasping moan with a kiss.

"Try to relax, Sade. It will hurt until you get used to having me inside."

Her long legs wrapped around his waist, feeling every bit as wonderful as he'd imagined them the first time he'd seen her standing like some modern-day Valkyrie outside his glass prison. Her nicely rounded breasts felt firm in his hands, their weight filling his palms perfectly. Her channel stretched and caressed his cock with silken waves and he filled her completely. His loneliness fled as his senses were swamped by her. Her mouth tasted of her last swallow of wine from dinner. Spice warred with the sweet perfume of flowers as her skin heated, releasing her natural scent.

Sinjen grit his teeth against the urge to pump into her fast and hard, remembering she was a virgin. Holding infinitely still, he gave her inner muscles time to adjust to his invasion. When she relaxed beneath his kisses and caresses, he slowly withdrew. The muscles in her vagina instinctively tightened around him and this time, the groan escaped his own mouth, to be swallowed by her kisses.

Slow and easy, he pushed in and withdrew until she pressed against him, demanding more. Sade squeezed his waist with her legs and feathered her hands across his chest, savoring the play of muscles beneath his skin. She wet her slightly parted lips and watched him through half-lidded eyes. Incredible. This magical creature wanted her. Pragmatism—a product of her upbringing—battled with hope that maybe...just maybe this was real.

Sinjen increased his tempo, keeping time with the pounding of her heart. A wicked smile curved his lips but the expression in his eyes soothed and promised that this was the way of things between a man and a woman. Gods but she wanted to trust him. He drove into her harder and her body responded, opening wider, taking him deeper. She cried out, hips curling and pushing, hands clawing at his shoulders.

"It's all right, Sade. I have you. Just let go. I'll catch you. Always."

And she did. She raced into her climax, bowing her back and rubbing her breasts against the fine hairs sprinkling his chest. She cried out as the pressure built to an unbearable level and then she was falling, her body racked with shudders and tremors, but cradled by strong arms even as Sinjen's shout of triumph echoed and his own climax pumped into her.

Sade just thought her first climax rocked her world. It was nothing compared to this one. She no longer felt detached, above it all, as if floating outside her body. His cock nestled deep inside her, still hard and throbbing as her own inner muscles responded in kind, anchored her to the here and now.

Shivering, he covered her body, almost too spent to move. When Sade fell into a light doze, Sinjen rolled away from her. Gathering up the comforter and sheet on the bed, he covered her, though he stared at her for a long moment, savoring the abraded skin his shadow beard left on her flushed skin, and admiring the tousled waves of her mahogany hair spilling across the pristine white of the pillow. As he watched, goosebumps formed on her perfect skin kissed by the chill air. With one last look, he flicked his wrist and allowed the bed linens to caress her bare skin, hiding her from his sight.

She was his. He had sacrificed and remained honorable for close to a millennium. He had given everything and asked nothing in return. He wasn't asking now. He demanded. Demanded this woman, her heart and soul to be his for now and always. He needed her to fill the emptiness surrounding him, the blackness threatening to devour him with rending claws and teeth. She was light and salvation and by all that was in him, she was his.

With the soft sound of her breathing a solace to his loneliness, Sinjen stood at the wide bedroom window watching the world below him. The storm from earlier had blown inland, leaving the night cold and clear. Though close to dawn, every star in the sky twinkled—pinpoint diamonds flashing against a black velvet backdrop. He gazed up at the sky, knowing he had lied—to the Universe, to God, to himself. One night was not enough. Only one night with Sade would never be enough.

The woman in his bed sighed, a soft puff of air escaping her lungs as she rolled onto her side. With a tap of his finger, Sinjen hit the button next to the window. Massive steel doors slithered almost silently into place, blocking out the view. The sound the security shield made as it slid into place was a faint echo of Sinjen's lonely exhalation. Turning, he leaned his naked shoulders against the cold steel and watched Sade sleep.

"Two of a kind, milady," he whispered. "I fear we are two of a kind. Are we too broken to ever be fixed? Or is there a chance that one is the key to the other?"

Leaving the questions hanging in the enveloping silence, Sinjen crossed to the bed in two long strides and slid in behind Sade, spooning up to her. He buried his nose in her magnificent mane of hair and held her close. Her skin was slick with sweat—hers, his. It didn't matter. She smelled of him and had he been a werewolf, he'd likely have rolled against her, marking her. Claiming her. He knew what he was going to do. He had no hope for salvation once he did it. He didn't care.

For a brief moment, his fangs gleamed like antique ivory and then they sank into the soft skin of her neck. He didn't take much blood—barely more than a taste of her sweet nectar but the sip was enough to make him see stars. His tongue swirled across the two tiny pinpricks in her skin. There would be no sign of his bite by the time she awoke.

Settling Sade into his arms, Sinjen's breathing and heartbeat synchronized with and would forever match hers. Soulless though he was, he held her, cherishing each beat of her very human heart, each breath she took until the sun inched above the horizon—unseen outside the metal curtain but felt by each muscle in his body. He closed his eyes and as his heart and lungs fought to keep working, with a final gasp, he entered the death-like trance that was vampire sleep—*la morte d'aube,* the dawn death.

Sade awoke to darkness though her eyes adjusted quickly. Sinjen's body was still faintly warm but growing colder by the moment. She curled up under the covers, lazy and languorous, like a contented cat. The fact the man next to her in bed was, for all intents and purposes, dead should be upsetting but it wasn't. She was almost relieved she wouldn't have to face him.

"Damn," she muttered as she stretched her legs and sore muscles protested. No light leaked around the edges of the metal shutters covering the windows and only a faint glimmer appeared under the bedroom door. Sade fumbled until she found the switch for the bedside lamp. The light flickered on and she squinted against the brightness. She felt beat up, physically and emotionally but at the same time, everything felt right in the world. Inexplicably so.

Despite swollen and gritty eyes, she studied the vampire sprawled next to her. He'd been spooned around her, almost protectively, until she'd pushed him onto his back. A deeply feminine and appreciative sigh escaped from her parted lips.

He would have been a giant in his time, standing well over six feet tall. Muscular hills and valleys mapped his chest and abdomen, and a feathering of dark hair added interest, especially as it tapered into an arrow shooting down his abs to the dark thatch of hair nestling his now-flaccid penis. A bit embarrassed by her frank perusal, she drew the sheet up to his waist.

A stray lock of his hair tumbled across his forehead. Sade brushed it back with tentative fingers. Her breath caught in her chest as a wave of tenderness assaulted her senses. Her inner muscles clenched, remembering the feel of him as his very personal scent of leather, sweet ambergris, and rain replenishing the earth.

"What the fuck are you doing?" She wanted to scream the question but the words whispered from her mouth, her voice filled with wonder.

With something akin to regret, she rolled out of bed and padded to the bathroom. She found a luxuriously soft robe hanging on the back of the door. In her size. Sinjen's bathroom was well appointed so she found everything an overnight guest might need. Somehow, though, she got the impression the shampoo and conditioner—her usual brand—along with the moisturizing body wash and the "powder soft" deodorant were new purchases for the vampire. Even the little green monster that wanted to know all about his former lovers seemed satisfied the stash had been acquired just for her.

Leaning her hands on the cold marble countertop, she stared at her reflection. Her eyes looked bruised from lack of sleep. Skin on her neck and chest was red from a beard burn and she noticed faint fingerprints that would likely turn to bruises as the day wore on. Under the glaring lights of the bathroom, she wanted to run. Holy fuck but she'd screwed up.

Maybe.

She remembered the way she'd walked into his arms after a really shitty day. The way he'd taken care of her. The way the world shifted when he brought her to her first climax and how complete she'd felt when he finally entered her and they were joined as one.

"One. Maybe it's not such a lonely number after all."

Chapter Twenty

A Secret Never to Be Told

SADE LEFT SINJEN'S apartment secured from daylight and locked the door behind her. Unaccountably, she didn't want to leave and leaned her forehead against the door. Part of her wished she'd blown off duty and climbed back into bed with him, to sleep away the day just so she could be there when he awoke at sundown. She had kissed him goodbye, which was sort of creepy—him being dead and all. But...

Hell. She had a crush on him. Plain and simple. Okay, maybe not so simple. She was an FBI agent. First and foremost and she'd damn well better remember that before things got any more complicated. With luck, she'd solve this case and get back to Washington without a broken heart. Or having to stake one. Because this was far more than a crush and she knew it.

Yeah, but for her? If it weren't for bad luck, she wouldn't have any luck at all. Then the elevator opened for her. And no one was in the lobby to see her leave. Then a cab zoomed up and stopped right in front of where she stood on the sidewalk.

Maybe her luck *had* changed. The cab whisked her to the Hyatt without getting stalled in traffic. Up in her room, she chugged two bottles of water, changed, found succor in a cup of hot, black coffee and now girded for the day, headed to Chicago PD—by way of another miraculously easy cab ride.

Her jacket open to show off both her badge and her weapon and with ID in hand, she swept through the metal detectors at police headquarters without a backward glance. Her luck held as an elevator opened before she pushed the call button. Moments later, she stepped out, paused at the door to the bullpen, and spotted Franks. He looked like he'd slept at his desk. Bleary-eyed, he stared at her.

"Do you just wave a magic wand and get all dry-cleaned or something?" he groused.

Sade didn't smile. "Or something. I take it there were no breaks in the case?"

His hangdog look said it all. Before he could fill her in, his desk phone buzzed like an angry wasp. Franks rubbed a lethargic hand across his puffy eyes and a sound suspiciously close to whimper escaped before he stabbed the button on the intercom. "Franks."

"This is Sergeant O'Toole down in reception." The feminine voice whispered from the speaker. "I've got a woman down here. She insists on seeing a homicide detective. Says her daughter went missing yesterday and she's convinced the girl is dead. Your name is flagged for any reports involving young women. Can I send her up?"

Frank's gaze sought hers, asking for direction. Sade asked the next question. "Marquis, with the FBI, Sergeant. Can you brief us on the facts?"

A rustle of cloth muffled voices on the other end of the line. Sade pictured the cop tucking the telephone receiver against her starched uniform. A few moments later, O'Toole's voice came through clearly. "The missing girl is twenty-four. She's a sales clerk at Macy's downtown store. Mother says the kid was supposed to have dinner with the family last night but never showed up. Turns out she left for lunch yesterday and never returned to the job."

"She have a boyfriend?" Franks sounded bored. Or tired.

Again, the sergeant's voice was muffled for a moment before the line cleared. "Mother insists her daughter didn't date. She went by the girl's apartment. The three roommates claim they haven't seen her since yesterday. Nothing in her room is missing."

Sade exchanged a look with Franks and shrugged. Her gut remained stubbornly silent. Nothing about this missing person report triggered any red flags. "Why does the mother think she's dead?"

"Because I've called her so many times her cell phone voice mail is full!" The open line amplified every shrill word the woman shouted.

The sergeant's calming voice came through as a murmur, followed by a curt. "I'll get back to you, Agent Marquis." The line disconnected.

Once more, Franks' gaze sought hers and Sade shrugged. "I don't know what to tell you. Sounds like a thousand other girls who drop out. Assuming she had her purse with her from work, she could have simply walked away from the job and probably hooked up with friends. Let Missing Persons handle it. They'll kick it up to you if they think the case warrants, right?"

The cop nodded, mulling it over. "Yeah. Probably. My gut is so sour from bad coffee I can't translate a word it's saying."

She rolled her neck on her shoulders, wincing a little at the snap, crackle, and pop. "I know the feeling. At least I've had some sleep. You need to go home, dude. Get some rest. I want to talk to Dick Kowalski and his little friend, Jane."

Franks stifled a yawn. "Haven't seen Kowalski around since that deal at Buckingham fountain." He picked up the stained coffee mug on his desk and stared mournfully at the dregs in the bottom. The next yawn stretched the lower half of his face. "Okay. Uncle." He pushed up out of his chair, the motion heavy and clumsy. "Feel free to camp out at my desk. Or go haunt your own people. I'll see you in a couple of hours. You have my cell phone number. Call me if anything breaks."

Desks, cops, chairs, and file cabinets crowded into a space meant for half the stuff crammed into it. Sade stepped back so Franks could pass between her and his desk and bumped the desk behind her. The cop sitting there glared, rescuing a Styrofoam cup before its contents sloshed across the file spread in front of him. She made an "oops" face at him then turned back to Franks. "You know I will. Sleep. I need your brain firing on all cylinders."

He squeezed by and shuffled toward the elevators. He snagged his parka from an overburdened coat rack, slung it over one shoulder, and disappeared. Sade kicked Franks' desk chair back out of the way and pulled the wooden side chair from beside the desk around so she could sit on it. She snagged the phone receiver, punched numbers, and started working her own traps—reaching out to anyone who might have information, or anyone she could trap into spilling what they knew.

THUMP. THUMP. THUMP. A hand knocked against the layer of ice. Thump. Thump. Thump. Waves bumped against the Lake Michigan shoreline. Beneath the rime, a pale blue body danced to the rhythm of the surf—a faceless chorus girl with no high kicks left in her lifeless limbs. Lidless eyes stared into the weak winter sun.

On the shore, a dog barked, the sound sharp and brittle in the frigid air. The animal dashed toward the pallid shadow, yelped, and retreated. It quivered, nose stretched toward the icy water, one front leg lifted in uncertainty. A shrill whistle rode the wind but the dog remained frozen. It barked again—a sharp yip followed by a rising howl.

"Dexter, heel!"

The dog's howl trailed off to a whimper. He didn't move. His owner approached.

"What's up, Dex? C'mon. It's freezing out here. Let's go home and get warm."

Dexter stretched his nose forward, still hesitant. He whined low in his chest.

The man stepped toward the lake. "What is that?" He spoke the words out loud as he took a dubious step toward the rim of ice. A second step followed, then a third. Very curious now, he edged out. Leaning closer, he peered at the thing caught under the ice. His eyes didn't recognize the ghastly shape at first, though when his brain registered the sight, the contents of his stomach roiled and emptied as he bent from the waist, gagging and wheezing.

SADE STRODE OUT of the elevator, headed for the exit door. She had every intention of getting out on the streets to stir up some of the magicks. Every time she thought she was making headway, she hit a wall. Crevan. Ariel. Nikos. Sinjen. The major magical races had converged on Chicago and there had to be a reason. She gave little thought to the woman perched on one of the worn plastic chairs near the intake desk.

Like a nervous bird, the woman watched each person come and go. She clutched something in her hand and whenever a uniformed officer came too close, she fluttered it at them like a tattered semaphore. That got Sade's attention. She stepped closer.

The woman looked up, her eyes bruised from worry. "My daughter? Is there any news about my daughter?" She held out the photograph as if in offering. "Her name is Eleanor. Eleanor Rigby."

"Oh. Hell." Sade couldn't breathe for a minute. The face of a beauty queen stared at her from the photo. Perfect symmetry. Flawless skin. Angelic smile. Flares erupted in her gut and she swallowed hard to keep from choking on the bile rising in her throat.

Time slowed then seemed to stop. The buzz of conversation and jangling phones, the static snarl of radio transmissions faded to stark silence. The face in the photo stared at Sade, the girl's eyes melancholy and resigned rather than accusatory.

"Agent Marquis?"

O'Toole's sharp tone snapped her back into focus. She dragged her gaze away from the woman and the wrinkled photograph. "Yeah?" Sade glanced toward the desk sergeant. Her eyes narrowed as the cop glanced at the woman then gestured for her to step closer.

"We just got a call," O'Toole whispered, watching the woman through narrowed eyes. "I've already alerted Detective Franks. Civilian called in a woman's body under the ice along the lakeshore. Units are on the way." She slid a slip of paper toward Sade. "Here's the address."

Sade picked up the note and glanced at it. "Any chance I can catch a ride with a unit from here?"

O'Toole nodded and inclined her head toward the door. "A patrol car will pick you up at the curb."

Her stomach churned. She feared they'd find a handless corpse once on scene. Turning, Sade faced the distraught woman again. The hope on the woman's face broke her heart. A warning shiver tiptoed up her spine as she avoided the missing girl's mother. Despite the knots in her intestines, she was convinced the body would belong to the missing pianist, Ravena Silverstein.

Outside, she flipped up the collar of her leather coat and shoved her hands into her pockets. Pacing back and forth, she chided her gut and did her best not to picture the despair plastered on the woman's face. Ravena Silverstein. That case had to be her focus. She knew the body at the lake would belong to the blind pianist. Without a doubt.

The patrol car rolled to a stop in front of her and she jumped into the passenger seat. Running Code Three with lights and sirens, they arrived at the lake in record time. Yellow crime scene tape fluttered in the stiff breeze as Sade approached the edge of the strand. Ice, whipped into peaks and jagged edges by wind and water, rimmed the sand.

Members of Chicago PD's Marine specialty unit, zipped into black and orange vulcanized suits, cut into the ice with a power saw. A black body bag stained the dirty white shoreline. Unmoving, feet spread, her body braced against the wind, she waited. Seconds crawled into minutes and the whine of the saw grated on her nerves.

Eventually, divers and tools did their jobs. The cap of ice was lifted, placed on plastic sheeting, and preserved—not that any real evidence likely remained. The group of onlookers—cops, firefighters, a couple of EMTs—surged forward. The ice cracked ominously and everyone froze. Sade stepped forward, completely undaunted. Everyone else stepped back, leaving her standing there alone—a somber shadow against the frozen waves. Unblinking, she watched as the divers lifted the body.

"What the fu—?" One of the divers choked back the expletive.

The corpse's hands remained intact. Sade's gut roiled. "Fuck." She finished the man's sentence. Mindful of the slippery conditions, she scrambled to the black body bag. One foot slid out from under her as she tried to stop and the shocked diver grabbed her arm to steady her as Sade stared at the recovered body.

Lidless blue eyes stared skyward. Bare muscle and tendons wrapped a skull bereft of flesh. Small pieces of skin left on the body flapped, loose and waterlogged, like that of a butchered chicken. Body shape and type didn't fit Ravena Silverstein, which opened a door to other possibilities—possibilities Sade did not want to consider. The woman sitting in the waiting room at the police station might as well be standing next to her on that frigid shoreline. Sade knew. And she alone would have to atone for that knowledge.

"You need to see anything else?"

She looked up at the harsh voice. A man in a full biohazard suit stared at her, his face circumspect. "Beyond the obvious, any idea of cause of death?"

He stared at the body stretched out by his feet. Sade noticed the twitch under his left eye but his voice sounded noncommittal. "The ME will have to decide after the autopsy." He glanced up at her, his face awash with anger. "Find this sick sonavabitch." The words hovered in the air between them.

Sade dipped her chin, her head bobbing once in a hard jerk. The man knelt, flipped the top of the bag over the dead girl. The zipper rasped as he pulled it around to lock her inside. A cold shiver traversed Sade's spine, leaving a trail of goosebumps that had nothing to do with the weather in its wake. "Helluva time for someone to walk across my grave." She muttered the words but the investigator from the ME's office glanced her way. Backing up, she gave the crime scene people room to move in.

Time dragged the noon into afternoon. The victim's body had been removed at last. The divers loaded up their gear and departed. The technical investigators stowed their gear and rolled up the crime scene tape.

As the sun set behind the skyline, Sade turned her back on the scene. She easily picked out Sinjen's building. He would be awake now. Her heart clutched and stuttered. Her entire being ached to feel his arms around her. She closed her eyes, leaning back against the cold wind sweeping in off the lake so she could remain upright. For a brief moment, she could almost feel his arms circling her waist, could almost hear his voice whispering in her ear.

Come home, Sade.

If she had any sense at all, she would get one of the patrol units to take her back to Homicide. Franks had called to say he was there rather than coming to the scene. The mother in the waiting room wasn't waiting any more. She closed her eyes and resisted the urge to rub her temples. No one had ever accused her of being a coward, but at that moment? She couldn't do it. She couldn't face the agony that came from the complete devastation of a mother's world.

Come home to me.

"Yes." She breathed the word but as soon as her psyche acknowledged her plans, her heart felt lighter. One of the cops approached and he watched her, his expression expectant. "You must be my ride. Will you drop me at Central Station? The apartment building."

He nodded. "Not a prob."

They walked to his car in silence. He turned the ignition as they settled into the front seats and he cranked the heater as the motor caught and smoothed out. Sade stared out the window, picturing the scene as it had appeared earlier. The officer stared at her.

"What?"

"Sorry, ma'am."

She turned to face him. "You're staring. Why?"

He blushed and muttered something sounding like an apology under his breath. She watched him until he cleared his throat. "I heard you were some hot-shot medium or magical or something." She didn't blink and he gulped. "You know, like a witchy woman."

"Witchy woman. Uh huh." The words almost stuck in her throat. She arched a brow at the cop and he tugged at his collar.

"Guess not, huh? But you are some sort of preternatural expert, right? That's why you're here? Because, damn. If a human is murdering these girls I don't even want to think about how evil this sonavabitch is."

She started to speak then closed her mouth. Opened it again. Closed. Angry words gathered, ready to spew forth. She cleared her throat, choking them back. "So. Let me get this straight. If a magick is behind these murders that makes it somehow less...evil?"

He nodded, his enthusiasm annoying her to no end.

She bit her tongue quite literally. After several deep breaths, she continued. "In other words, you expect a magick to be capable of something this terrible? You believe they have no conscience?"

Like a bobblehead doll, the cop nod-nod-nodded, a grin splitting his face.

Sade bit her tongue again. Arguing with the idiot would do no good. "You do realize I came here to clear Professor St. John of the murder charge?" His head immediately stilled and he cut his eyes her direction. "And that he has been cleared?" He gulped. "But to ease your mind, magic is involved. I'm just not convinced it's one of the preternaturals behind it. They have rights, too, Officer..." She paused to check his nameplate. "Officer Brown. Just like humans. And unlike humans, preternaturals very seldom kill just for the thrill of it."

Sinjen's building loomed up ahead and the cop steered toward the curb, applying the brake a bit hard so the vehicle bucked to a stop. Chuck, the doorman, bustled over to open the car door. Sade continued to stare at the cop.

"Thanks for the lift. You remember what I said." She slid her legs out and stood. Chuck closed the door and the car peeled out, leaving the stink of burnt rubber behind.

"Evening, Agent Marquis." Chuck tipped his hat and hustled to grab the door to the building.

She swept inside, her cheeks burning as the hot air splashed against her face. She wondered if Chuck had been watching for her, upon orders from

Sinjen. The elevator dinged, the doors sliding open, and she never broke stride entering.

Upstairs, Sinjen waited in his doorway, her questions answered. He knew she was coming. Brushing past him, she stopped just inside the door. He removed her coat and hung it in the coat closet then drew her closer to the windows.

"You are chilled." Three words but his voice embraced her like a warm blanket before his arms encircled her and pulled her close.

Sade didn't mean to, tried to tell herself she was just tired—though tired wasn't the word for how she felt. Weary. Worn out. Drained. Jaded. Not even those adjectives came close. For whatever reason, she leaned into him and closed her eyes. The tension from the day seemed to drop away. Then her stomach growled.

"You need to eat. I will fix you something."

"You cook too?"

"A man needs something to fill the hours."

As he puttered in the kitchen, she relaxed in the overstuffed armchair and watched. Her idea of cooking involved a cell phone and take out. In what seemed like no time at all, he served her Lobster Florentine with a salad of winter greens in a light vinaigrette dressing.

"And a gourmet at that," she muttered around a bite.

Sinjen laughed, his eyes twinkling with mirth as he watched her eat. "I am a man of many talents."

She gulped and almost choked. Swallowing, she managed a strangled, "Yes. Yes, you are."

"As soon as you finish eating, I will remind you of some of the other things I can do."

The food on her fork dribbled off as her hand shook. Sade stared into his eyes and swallowed hard. Again. His gaze focused on her throat, watching the muscles work. Then he swallowed. Hard. The look in his eyes turned predatory. He took the fork from her and laid it on the plate. With one finger, he traced the line of her jaw from chin to ear and then cupped her cheek. Leaning closer, his breath teased her lips. "Time for bed, Lady Sade."

She sighed. And wanted to kick herself. She was not some character in a chick flick. Not an hour ago she'd stood over the faceless body of a young woman. Now, as Sinjen urged her to her feet, the dichotomy struck her full force. Weak-kneed, she leaned against him and savored the feel of his arms sliding around her waist. Before she could react, he'd scooped her into his arms and simply held her cradled there. "You will tell me later what has you so distressed. First, we will learn anew how to please each other."

He carried her into his bedroom and laid her on the bed, kneeling beside it as he did. Without a word, he slipped her blazer off her shoulders. Deft fingers disarmed her then quickly unbuttoned her blouse. Her belt, boots, and slacks soon followed. Left in nothing but her bra and panties, Sade resisted the urge to cover her chest with her arms. For all her boldness when dressed, the hungry look on Sinjen's face undid her, pulling forth a shyness not felt since her teens. Her throat felt scratchy and her mouth dry. She swallowed again. His eyes focused on the spot where her pulse throbbed in time to each beat of her heart.

"I want to taste you."

His voice washed over her, raising goose bumps. She knew what he wanted. Each throb of blood in her veins urged her to let him. With a soft exhalation, she closed her eyes and tilted her chin, opening her throat to his pleasure.

She felt his fingers trace across her ribs and hips then snag in her panties. He whipped them off. Her eyes flew open as he spread her knees. He kissed along her inner thigh, which caused the hair on her arms to prickle. A soft breath of air chilled her most private of places but the tongue that followed warmed her in ways guaranteed to bring a smile to her face—if her memory of the previous night was reliable.

"Mmmmm." He sounded so satisfied there between her knees, lapping and tasting her. Sade laughed. She couldn't stop the sound burbling up from her chest. Oh, yeah. He wanted to taste her all right! Well, that was a game two could play.

Later, she watched him through half-lidded eyes. He stood, still as a gargoyle, staring out the window across the lake and city. He turned away from the view. His expression, fleeting though it was before he schooled it, twisted her heart.

"You care about them."

Her statement puzzled him. "They were killed to fulfill some senseless purpose. Life is too precious not to care about those who lost theirs needlessly."

Sade patted the space beside her. "Come back to bed, Sinjen. We can't solve their murders tonight. And I can't make up for all the lonely nights, but for right now, for this one night, we can celebrate life."

His enigmatic smile gave nothing away as he slid in beside her. She melted into the arms he held open, her arms twining around his neck as she kissed him. Her tongue teased his lips and as his mouth opened, she caressed his incisors with it. Sade felt his shiver all the way down to her toes. Sinjen rolled her over onto her back and she spread her legs as he settled on top of her. His weight felt like it belonged. She wrapped her legs around him and arched her hips.

"Be still." His order hissed into her mouth. She smirked but he kissed her before she could retort. She let her body respond. "You are incorrigible." He growled against her neck and her skin prickled as his fangs grazed the skin above her pulse point.

"I am, yes."

Her fingers wrapped around his cock and lined the head up with her entrance. He surged into her, filling her. Her vision narrowed and then fled completely. Floating in a sea of darkness, she remained anchored by Sinjen's body. Small flashes of light flared behind her retinas as her body and emotions collided. Sade lost all sense of time, of place. She knew only pleasure as Sinjen braced above her, his body driving into hers over and over. Eventually, his body stilled, and he rested against her. She kissed the soft skin under his chin and felt him shudder. Moments later, he murmured something about his weight crushing her and rolled away, but gathered her into his arms. Sated and content, she drifted off to sleep.

"Why are you the only woman who completes me?"

The words whispered across her psyche and she wondered with the part of her brain still cognizant if she simply dreamed them.

Sinjen held her, felt their heartbeats pulse in tandem and fought his basest urge. A battle he lost a breath later as he sank his fangs into the side of her neck. He rested his cheek against hers. She'd wanted to celebrate life. He would bring only death. But he drank anyway.

DAWN. She felt it as sure as if she'd been turned. Memories flooded and she reached up to touch her neck. Nothing. The skin wasn't even tender. A dream then, though one far more vivid than normal. Lower spots, tender and swollen from Sinjen's attention reminded her of the reality of her evening. His body still warmed hers so he hadn't been *gone* long. She touched his lips with the tip of her finger. Bending, she brushed her lips across his.

"Damn you." The words came out more as a plea than a denial. "I have no time for any man."

Rolling away, she pushed off the bed and padded into the bathroom. After her shower, she discovered a drawer with a suspicious bit of lace hanging out. She found several pairs of Victoria's Secret panties and bras, all in her size and preferred design. "Dammit, Sinjen." She glared at her reflection. "You really know how to get under my skin, don't you?"

Back in the bedroom, she stood staring at the lifeless man on the bed. Leaning over him, she pulled the comforter up over his shoulders, brushed the thick, black hair off his forehead, and kissed his lips.

"Why are you so damn beautiful?" With a sigh, she straightened. "And why is the world so ugly?" Everything in her—every sinew and nerve—begged her to throw off her clothes and crawl back into bed with Sinjen. But duty called. The souls of all those girls pressed close, seeking resolution. It was up to her to find it for them. Squaring her shoulders, she pivoted on her heel and headed out.

Sweeping off the elevator and across the lobby, Sade pushed through the heavy glass doors before the doorman could react. Stepping into the cold, gray morning, her nostrils flared even as the hairs stood up on the back of her neck. She snorted. "I love the smell of magic in the morning."

That was the last thing she remembered—that and the stench of burnt rubber from screeching tires. And the coppery taste of her own blood.

Chapter Twenty-one

Eight Crows for Heaven

BLOOD. He would forever have the blood of good agents on his hands. He hated making *the* call when one went down in the line of duty. Hated the anger and the pain spewing back at him by mourning families. Today had been no different. The war against evil was not without its casualties.

The door to his office *snicked* but he didn't turn around. Only his secretary moved that quietly. Two walls of windows framed picture postcard views of Washington from the White House to the Smithsonian. George Bailey continued to stare out across the vista, his thoughts morose despite other pressing business.

"Any word yet?"

"No, sir. Don't worry. Agent Marquis can take care of herself."

His shoulders lifted and fell with his deep inhalation. "I'm worried, Alice."

"I know, Director."

The spry, little woman joined him at the window and offered a cup of steaming coffee. He took it from her but didn't drink. Alice Cooper. What would he do without her? Of indeterminate age, she'd outlasted four directors and would likely occupy her desk in the outer office long after he hung up his badge. She barely topped his elbow and perhaps weighed a hundred pounds fully dressed and dripping wet but her small frame contained a dynamo of energy. He glanced down at her then returned his gaze to the window. In silence, they watched dirty gray clouds chase across the dull winter sky.

"She's not like the others."

"She's human, Director."

"And that's the problem, Alice."

"You didn't think so when you picked her for the job."

"She's mortal. Like the rest of us."

"She's also uniquely qualified, Director." Alice turned her head to look up at him, her expression serious, her gaze probing. "Why are you having second thoughts?"

"This whole thing stinks like a political setup to me."

She laughed, a short bark of sound that ended with a snorting giggle. "Director, this is Washington. Every move we make is a political setup. But you have to trust your instincts. You trusted Agent Marquis long before you ever knew about her unique abilities. And you trust the team you created."

"But can she trust them? When push comes to shove, Alice, where does their allegiance lay? What have humans done for them? We're so much fodder for the magicks and you know it as well as I do. What keeps them from simply enslaving the human race and taking over?"

Alice nodded toward the busy streets streaming with traffic. "Think about it, Director. Do you really believe they want to rule that? All that noise? All those emotions?" She turned to face him, rocking up on her toes as if she could look him eye-to-eye. "The magicks know what the British didn't realize way back there in 1773. You can't keep us upstart Americans in line. Somebody somewhere will always get a wild hare about freedom. The magicks don't want to spend their time policing the ranks. They'd rather enjoy their lives. Humanity is messy."

She turned to face the window again and George compared their reflections in the window. He looked massive and ungainly compared to Alice's compact form. And, he felt messy and a bit rebellious at the moment. A smile crooked one corner of his mouth.

"I see your point."

She patted his arm. "I'll let you know as soon as Agent Marquis checks in, Director. Is there anything else?"

"Any word from the desert?"

"Not recently. But then you know Agent Jones. He is rather independent about these things."

George closed his eyes and rubbed his palm over his balding head. When he opened them, he blinked quickly as he realized only his reflection showed in the glass. He glanced over his shoulder just as Alice slipped out the door and it closed behind her. "How the hell does she do that?" His rhetorical question hung in the air.

How the hell did his secretary do any of the things she did? She ran his office with frightening efficiency and he'd be lost without her. Two thick manila files, having appeared as if by magic, now marred the pristine surface of his desk. He settled into his chair. Marquis would be okay. She always was—by luck or divine intervention. Yes, most likely heaven had a hand in her fate. He hoped so anyway.

With a tired grunt, he opened the first file. The life of a bureaucrat left him pining for fieldwork and part of him envied his agents working in the trenches. Out there, the battle lines were clear. Here, politics and politeness ruled the world. He crashed a big fist down on his desk, shaking the sturdy mahogany enough the now lukewarm coffee in his cup sloshed over. He mopped at the spill. If Alice discovered he'd made a mess, there'd be hell to pay.

ENSCONCED BEHIND HER DESK, Alice slipped a cell phone from her blazer pocket and glared at it, her distaste plain. She managed to find her contacts, scroll through them to the one she sought, and stabbed it, hoping the call would go through. Modern technology did not like her and she pined for the simple days of manual typewriters and rotary phones.

When the buzzing in her ear stopped, she spoke softly. "He is worried, yes, but I diverted his attention for the time being. Heaven knows the situation needs to resolve soon." She listened for a moment. "No, I have him under control. We need do nothing in that regard." After another brief pause, she added, "I am positive. Do what needs to be done. I will keep a lid on things here." She stabbed the phone again, cutting off the call.

Alice dropped the phone in her pocket and pushed back from her desk. Her feet swung free of the floor, her chair cranked to the upper limits of its hydraulics. With care, she slid forward until her feet touched the plastic mat under her chair and she glided over to the window. Dusk came early to Washington in wintertime. She longed for the brighter days of spring, days when cherry blossoms fell like snowflakes and perfumed the air with hope. Winter, to her old bones, simply felt like hell.

HANNIBAL CROWLEY HUNG up the phone, the expression on his face as bitter and cold as the wind howling off Lake Michigan. He turned to the man cowering across the room and stabbed his finger in that direction. "Do something!"

"What?" Dick Kowalski's voice quaked with fear. "What do you want me to do, Master? She's a federal fucking agent." He took a deep breath. "You should never have involved the vampire!" Emboldened, he pressed home his point. "That's what brought the bitch here. There was no point. We could harvest what we needed easily, with no suspicion cast our way. It was a mistake."

Crowley's face paled. His nostrils flared below eyes widened so the whites showed—not in fear but in anger. "How dare you."

The priest's voice whispered through the air between them and Dick shuddered as his arms prickled and stung like a thousand tiny knives cut and slashed at his skin. A door creaked and the pain immediately lessened as Eugenia entered the room.

"Father? What's going on?" Her voice trembled and she looked as wan and ethereal as some fake ghost from a bad Hollywood movie.

Kowalski shivered. He had a bad feeling about all of this. He didn't presume to know the Master's mind but he suspected Eugenie Crowley was a very large part of the plan. As he watched, the girl seemed to transform before his eyes. Her color returned—two bright red splotches on her cheeks, almost as if she ran a fever—and her hair snapped and crackled with static electricity. Her eyes remained on her father and he was eternally grateful she wasn't looking at him with the calculating stare she turned on the other man.

"I asked you a question, father."

Crowley seemed to melt from his daughter's heated gaze. "Nothing for you to be concerned with, Eugenia. Are you feeling better this morning?" His tone was meant to sound placating but to the cop's trained ears, the Master sounded almost afraid of the girl. He stepped back into a corner to watch.

"But I am concerned, Father. Why is this FBI person so concerned with Alex? And us?" She marched up to her father, leaving scarcely a hand's width between them. "And why didn't you tell me about CeeCee?"

Kowalski watched Crowley swallow, his throat working hard as if he had a suddenly dry mouth and there wasn't enough spit. He'd always thought of the Master's daughter as a sheltered weakling. The thought he'd been wrong had him worried.

"I didn't want to distress you, Eugenia. You should be resting, dear. I need to prepare for the ceremony. You will need all your strength to assist me when the time comes." The high priest took his daughter's hand and brought it to his mouth for kiss. "Your destiny is written in the sands of time, Eugenia."

She smiled at the top of her father's head as he bent over her hand and the cold, calculating look on her face shocked Kowalski and scared the shit out of him. He wondered who was truly in charge—high priest or witch. That skittering shiver crawled up his spine again, raising the hair on his arms. Maybe it was time to cut his losses and run. He refocused his attention only to discover both father and daughter stared at him, their faces twin masks.

"You have your orders," the two said in unison. "Do not fail us."

Shaken all the way to his boots, Kowalski turned and fled. His heart pounded against his rib cage all the way down in the elevator, and he could barely breathe around its hammering rhythm. "What the hell have I gotten myself into?"

"HEAVEN HOLDS NO PLACE FOR FOOLS."

"What do we know of heaven, fae?" The gargoyle's voice grated in the frigid January air. "Not one of us shall ever grace those gates."

Ariel shivered despite his fur-lined coat. "I never knew you to be a pessimist, *Le Vieil*. You and your kind have perched upon the pediments of great cathedrals for centuries. Why would the human god not open his arms to welcome so faithful a servant?" What passed for gargoyle laughter assaulted his ears. The sound resembled rocks being ground beneath a grist stone.

"We are not mortal, nor are you, Ariel. Or had you forgotten in your thrall of all things human?"

He bristled at Crevan's insinuation. "I serve my king and queen, gargoyle, and thereby my people."

The gargoyle laughed again. "Need I remind you of their interference?"

Ariel blinked and unconsciously rubbed his ass where Caleb's teeth had once come much too close for comfort, there on Sade's balcony. "And what of that of the gargoyles?" Two could play this game and he was pleased his voice held a hint of challenge in its tone.

Crevan stretched to his full height, leathery wings popping to their full width. Ari hid his triumphant expression. He'd touched a nerve, obvious by the gargoyle's intimidating display.

"Ever have the gargoyles acted as mediators and protectors, fae. We have prevented wars among the magicks. Always have we sat on the side of justice. We know our duty and remain steadfast." He peered down. "Frivolity and seduction are the purview of the fae."

Ariel bristled again, but bit back the angry outburst on the tip of his tongue. Crevan's jab was well aimed. He'd been ordered to seduce Sade almost from birth and he'd been instrumental in her repeated abductions as a child. In her teens, it became a game of wits between he and the werewolf. Sometimes Caleb won. Sometimes he did.

He remembered standing on Sade's balcony while Caleb, trapped in wolf form, scratched at the door, the game of tag between the two them ongoing. He popped in and out at all hours of the day and night. Sade would turn over to find him sitting on her bed watching her sleep with Caleb muzzled and shut in the bathroom.

Ari hated to admit it, but he enjoyed the verbal sparring in which he and Sade engaged. She was droll and sarcastic with a quick, dry wit. Notorious for loving and leaving his human conquests, he never actually stopped to talk with them. Until Sade. Her continued rebuffs of his advances gave him the opportunity to get to know her as a person and not just another sexual victory. They even became begrudging friends. And remained so. Hell, she'd pulled his butt out of the fire not long ago in New Orleans.

But back when she'd been a girl, he'd appeared on her balcony one night and got the fright of his life. Seven feet of granite-carved muscle blocked his entry to Sade's bedroom. "Ariel," the gargoyle's voice echoed in the night air.

He'd backed up a couple of steps and acknowledged the other magick. "Roman." He'd hated the soft squeak surrounding the first syllable of the gargoyle's name.

"Tell Oberon the girl is under my protection," Roman rumbled. "And remind Titania of our pact."

He'd nodded, turned, and quite frankly fled, Roman's chuckles following him *between* as he winked out. The night Roman showed up, the game ended for all intent and purposes. Until Sade grew up and joined the FBI.

Ari stared up at Crevan. "I almost found heaven. Once."

"There is no heaven for the magicks, Ariel. Not even in the arms of a mortal. Be thee warned, fae. A great darkness is coming and if the *tödlich* fails in her quest then may we all pray for hell."

"Pray for hell? That's crazy, Crevan. Why not pray for the unattainable? Why not pray for the mythic heaven of the humans?"

"Do you know what comes, Ariel? Does the Seelie Court remember the dark and twisted landscape of before? Time is not on our side in this, fae, and I fear that our fate rests in the hands of a mortal. Believe me when I say that hell would be preferable to the evil existence dictated by she who comes.

"Oh, hell."

Chapter Twenty-two

Nine Crows for Hell

"**O**H, HELL."

"Yeah, ain't it though?"

Franks stared at the ME. "Her face was skinned off? Like…literally?"

"Isn't that what my report said? Along with much of the rest of her epidermis."

"Well…yeah…but…"

"But nothing. You have one very sick serial killer running through the streets of Chicago, Detective." The brusque doctor gazed out toward the hallway. "You didn't bring that scary Fed with you?"

Bobby shook his head. "No. She hasn't checked in yet." He didn't want the ME to know how much that fact distressed him. It wasn't like Marquis. He'd fully expected her to be camped at his desk impatiently waiting on him that morning when he arrived in Homicide. Not only wasn't she there but she wasn't answering her cell phone. He'd tracked down the street cop who gave her a lift from the murder scene at Lake Michigan. The cop insisted he'd dropped her off at Central Station and she'd gone inside the apartment building—the building where Kristian St. John lived. Stale coffee burned up his esophagus and he swallowed hard, hoping to keep the acid reflux under control. This was a helluva time for her to go MIA.

"Are you listening to me, Detective Franks?"

Startled away from his thoughts, he nodded. "Yeah. You'll have the final report for me in a few days. Thanks, doc."

He hustled out and once he was away from the antiseptic odor of industrial cleaning fluid and formaldehyde that never quite covered up the stench of death, he grabbed his cell and hit redial.

"Marquis. Leave a message."

"Dammit, Marquis, where the hell are you? It's after four. Call me. Like yesterday."

He dug in his pocket for the roll of antacids he habitually stashed there. He peeled back the wrapper to dislodge the last two tablets, tossed them into his mouth, and chewed. His stomach growled but the burning sensation behind his breastbone eased slightly. Progress of a sort. Bobby hoped he still had a full roll hidden in his desk. He needed them, like now.

Dispirited, he headed back to his office. With any luck, he could get through the rest of the day without another body showing up. He laughed, the sound dry and brittle. "Who the hell am I kidding? This is Chicago." The best he could hope for was no more mutilated girls. The skinless body on the slab at the morgue would haunt his dreams for a many a night. So would the look on her mother's face when he'd delivered the news that morning after a positive ID.

"You owe me big time, Marquis." He remained pissed that he'd had that duty alone. He'd been counting on the Fed to go with him to interview the girl's mother. And they still had no leads on Ravena Silverstein's whereabouts. No one called demanding ransom or anything else from her manager. In fact, her manager seemed rather nonchalant about the whole situation.

Bobby's instincts still bristled over that deal. He didn't doubt Sade's version of events and the physical evidence at the scene backed her up. The whole damn thing stunk worse than a week-old corpse. He'd been a homicide detective for too many years to believe in coincidences. Despite Marquis's unshakable belief in St. John's innocence, he wondered. What were the odds their next victim would be snatched off the street right in front of the vampire and a federal agent?

He found a space on the street in front of headquarters and parked. Pushing through the front doors, the noise and scents washed over him. He tossed a salute to the desk sergeant and was about to head toward the elevators when an altercation broke out. A woman with crazy hair and wearing crazier clothes threw punches into the chest of a uniformed security guard. Bobby stepped closer thought the big guard didn't appear fazed by the woman's attack.

"Settle down, Angela. I told you'd I'd bring you here. Don't get mad at me 'cause that woman ain't here."

The woman stopped battling the bigger man and whirled, her colorful skirt swirling while the coins on her belt jangled. "You!" She stabbed her finger at Bobby. "You let her get away."

He backpedaled a few steps. "Let who get away?" He glanced at the security guard hoping for enlightenment.

"Angela here is lookin' for that lady FBI agent. They talked the other day at the Pier. Angela had a vision." The guy rolled his eyes and gave a slight shake of his head. It was obvious he thought the woman was as batshit crazy as her hair. "I'm Silas Miller. I work at the Pier. Angela here is one of our regulars."

Bobby knew what that meant.

"Snow white, rose red, black as midnight."

"What?" Bobby stared at the woman. She'd gone slack and likely would have collapsed to the floor if the big guy hadn't grabbed her arms. Her eyes glazed and lost focus.

"Hands of magic, yet no sight, beware the tiger burning bright."

Bobby decided Silas was right. This woman was a candidate for a straightjacket yet her rambling riddle intrigued him, especially that last line. If she was referring to Ravena Silverstein, what the hell was the reference to a tiger? He vaguely remembered a poem he'd had to read in high school but as far as he knew, this case had no tigers.

The woman blinked rapidly and then stared at him. "My daughter. She's lost."

His spirits drooped even further, if that was possible. Another one so soon?

"You did not find her in time and now her soul has left the mirror."

A smidgen of information niggled in the back of his memory. "You're Angela Varad?" Amazed he'd pulled that out of his ass, he watched for her reaction. She nodded. "What do you mean, Ms. Varad?" At this point, nothing would surprise him anymore. "Agent Marquis told me about your daughter but I need *you* to tell me now."

The security guard released Angela and she took a step toward him. "Crystal is gone. Her soul fled before the horror of what is to come. She tried to warn us but it is too late. The season of the witch is here." She looked around, her eyes looking wild and unfocused again. She stepped closer, her gaze now narrowed on him. "Where is the one in black? The one who can see what others cannot?"

Puzzled, he stared at her. "You mean Agent Marquis?" She nodded, one short bob of her head. "I...don't know. I haven't heard from her today." He had a very bad feeling about all of this and wished he'd stopped for more antacids.

"The dark will swallow her whole if she fights the light."

Bobby's stomach roiled and he now doubted there were enough antacids in the drugstore to soothe his ulcer. "Do you know where she is?"

The woman shook her head, a vehement motion that sent the wild curlicues of her hair into a mad dance. "Into blackness she has gone. The horror will possess her and we are lost." The last word trailed off into a wailing moan as the woman sank to the floor. "All is lost. Little girl lost, never to be found. Little girl lost, forever to be bound."

The hairs on Bobby's arms and on the back of his neck prickled. He looked around, nervous and apprehensive. The room was silent, every eye in the place fixed on the little drama playing out. He was no hero and the woman's words scared the shit out of him.

She looked up at him, eyes glistening with tears. "If she does not remember her home and heart, we are doomed."

"Who? Marquis?"

"Little girl lost, between here and there. Little girl lost, never was, never will be."

Crumpling to the floor amidst the colorful billows of her skirts, Angela looked like a wilted flower. The big security guard squatted beside her and touched her tear-stained cheek with infinite tenderness. She jerked away from him. "Shhhh, Angela. It's me, Silas. C'mon, honey. Let's get you up and I'll take you home." She didn't fight as he stood and pulled her to her feet. Silas glanced over. "Sorry 'bout all this. She seemed real lucid when she asked about that FBI lady."

Bobby's answering smile did little to alleviate his sadness. "S'okay, Mr. Miller. You don't mind looking after her?"

"I been lookin' after her since Crystal disappeared, Detective. I figure I can do it a bit more."

Silas led her away. As soon as they disappeared through the exit doors, the hum of conversation returned. Phones jangled. Radios squawked. And Bobby felt like a chunk of time had been carved out and flash-frozen. "Heaven help us." He muttered the plea but stopped in his tracks as an old man replied.

"Heaven's deaf when Hell plays in the band."

Dallas Now

MATHIAS DE VRIES, the cuffs of his tailored Egyptian cotton shirt carefully rolled to bare his forearms, rubbed his temples. The phone jangling from somewhere deep within his home irritated him to no end. He'd risen early, anticipating calls and messages. He'd cast a wide net and expected to tug on many lines this evening. Heavy draperies shrouded the tall windows of his study and the lethargy of day sleep clung to his bones. He stared at the flames as they undulated like dancing girls in the grate of the fireplace. His nostrils twitched. Even all these years later, he could still smell her blood— and that of the man who'd hurt her.

Caleb. Though still a pup, the werewolf protected Sade and stayed by her side afterwards. Stayed and comforted when none of the humans in his household would. He heard Hoskins' measured step passing by in the hallway. He'd taken measures after that day, measures to ensure his staff's loyalty. He closed his eyes, the scene in his memory as fresh as the moment he'd pulled it from Caleb's mind all those years before.

Dallas Then

THE TUTOR GRABBED the pup by the scruff of his neck and pulled the now snarling animal across the floor. "You will not interrupt my lessons again, you scruffy mongrel." Caleb's feet scrabbled to find purchase but the cold tile was too slick for paws. He twisted and turned trying to bite the man but the human had his hands fisted in the thick fur of the pup's neck. Caleb fought, claws scrabbling madly for purchase, as he was dragged across the floor anyway.

Sade screamed, running behind the man. "Let him go!" She begged, tears streaming down her face. "Nooooo," she wailed. Sade ran to the door and flung herself in front of it, blocking it with her body. Spread-eagled, she pressed back against the door. "I'm gonna tell my dad," she yelled. "I'm gonna tell Uncle 'thias."

"Move, you brat," the tutor commanded. "You are a seven-year-old child. I am an adult and in charge of you. Who do you think they'll believe?" When Sade didn't budge, he turned loose of Caleb with one hand and grabbed Sade's arm. He jerked and Sade went flying. Her head hit the corner of the marble fireplace hearth with a sickening thud.

Sade woke up as Caleb frantically licked her face. When she touched her head and her fingers came away bloody, she started to cry. Hoskins finally arrived. As he came into the room, he saw the child covered in blood, Caleb's muzzle dripping with it, and the dead tutor. Afraid, the butler backed out of the room. None of the staff would enter to check on Sade. William was out of town; Mathias not yet awake.

Sade whimpered. "It hurts an' I feel like I'm gonna throw up."

Caleb sat beside her and she put her arms around his neck, leaning against him. With that contact, her nausea quieted. He whined and nosed her with infinite care. He'd done what he could to protect her but he didn't understand why none of the humans had come to help Sade. Finally, the shadows lengthened in the room and before long, Caleb heard footsteps and caught a scent that was all too familiar.

Mathias swept into the room, took one look at the scene and grabbed up Sade. He pulled back his foot to kick Caleb but Sade screamed. She wrapped her hands around the vampire's neck, sobbing. "Noooo." She managed to get the word out. She swallowed hard and managed a sentence. "Caleb helped me." More sentences came out. "Mr. Tetters hurt me. It was Mr. Tetters." Tears streamed down her face. "Don't hurt Caleb. He's my friend. My only friend." She slumped against Mathias's shoulder, unconscious.

When Sade awoke later, Caleb was nestled at her side, his chin resting on her chest. The little girl curled her hands into his fur and he nosed her chin gently, his expressive golden brown eyes liquid with worry. Sade smiled. "I love you, Caleb," she whispered. Caleb's tail thumped against the bed as his ears flicked forward.

The door to the bedroom opened and Mathias came in. He sat on the edge of the bed and stared down at Sade and Caleb. "Mr. Tetters has been...dismissed. You will begin classes Monday at Hollowday Academy. I am sorry, Sade, that none of the staff would come to your aid. That situation has been rectified and will not occur again." Mathias leaned over and kissed Sade on the forehead. "Sleep, child. Your father will be home tomorrow." In one graceful move, Mathias was on his feet and striding toward the door. He stopped about halfway and turned back to the bed. He regarded the two lying there for a long, unblinking moment. "You did well today, Caleb," the vampire allowed. The pup's tail wagged madly.

Dallas, Now

"INDEED, CALEB. You have always done well. Would that you were at her side now."

The phone on his desk chirped, indicating the call came in on his private line. Very few had the number and not even William was allowed to answer it. He snagged the receiver before a second ring.

"What have you learned?" No preamble. No greetings. He had no time for the niceties of society tonight. His eyes narrowed as he listened. "Keep me informed." He slammed the receiver against the phone in a rare display of temper. His skin prickled, marking the passage of the sun. Winter, the vampire's blessing. The short days invigorated them while the dog days of summer drained their energy.

A short tap on the door ended his musings. "Sire? You have a visitor."

Visitor. Mathias refrained from laughing. Hoskins refused to consider the reason for his visitor's presence. Sade, ever pragmatic, labeled the young women who arrived for a brief time before disappearing back into anonymity of human society far more succinctly: Flavor of the Week. A sardonic smile tugged one corner of his mouth. Sade asked him once what blood tasted like. She'd been quite earnest and curious.

"Do people taste different?" she'd asked.

He assured her they did and she'd giggled at his descriptions. Society girls hoping for a rich husband tasted of mimosas and white wine spritzers, he'd told her. Mathias grimaced. Now, they tasted of appletinis and cosmopolitans. He preferred richer flavors and "hunted" accordingly. Hoskins tapped again. "Mr. DeVries?"

"Send her in, Hoskins." He glanced over his desk and shuffled a few pages, covering them with folders. He rose from his chair as a tall woman strolled through the doors. Hoskins bowed slightly and shut the door behind her.

"You're up early, Mathias." The woman's voice sounded husky, with hints of Sauvignon wine.

His nose twitched. Barely after four and she was already drinking wine? This evening would be his last taste. She'd be gone before morning, sent off with a generous gift and his thanks but no promise and no memory. She waited just inside the door, her eyes half-lidded for a sultry look. Fiery red hair, swept off her neck in a fetching up do, gleamed in the firelight and the skin of her neck and upper chest glowed. The low-cut cashmere sweater she wore cupped her ripe breasts like a lover's hand. She had seduction on her mind but he had far too much on his for bedroom games tonight. The only thing he wanted to sink into her were his fangs.

Mathias stepped around the massive mahogany desk and positioned himself in front of it. He leaned his hips back against the edge and folded his arms across his chest, and crossed one ankle over the other, his pose relaxed. "Come here."

She did, her walk a slinking parody of a hunting cat. She stopped a whisper away from him. "Hello, lover."

Her words puffed out on a sighing exhalation, her breath brushing across his muscular forearms. He no longer trained with a sword, using other, more modern means to remain fit. She leaned closer, her tongue flicking through her parted lips in invitation. He didn't move.

"What? No kiss?" Her eyes widened, showing surprise and perhaps resignation as well. She blinked then leaned closer so that her breasts brushed across his bare arms as her lips pressed against his mouth.

He uncoiled and with one hand in her hair, he pulled her head to the side, tilting it so the skin over her carotid artery throbbed with each beat of her heart. He bent his head, his lips nuzzling the spot and she sighed. As he sank his fangs through skin and vein, she went limp in his arms.

Mathias drank deeply, his hunger unsated. Once he finished, the woman would be moved to a luxury hotel where she would awake in the morning, money in hand and her bill paid for a week's vacation, with planted memories about how she arrived there. He closed his eyes, savoring the dark taste of her blood. Her skin paled but he continued to drink, sucking hungrily, out of control.

Some small shred of sanity remained. Poison, it whispered. He raised his head. The room wavered like heat waves on a hot, August day. His grip on the woman loosened and she slipped to the floor. He caught the edges of his desk, and propped his weight there, moments away from joining her on the thick Persian carpet covering the polished wood beneath it. Who? How? He was a master vampire, millenniums old. No mere mortal could trick him this way. He shook himself like a great bear come out of a river. Mathias threw back his head and roared.

"The devil take you, you bitch!"

Chapter Twenty-three
And Ten Crows for the Devil's Own

"**W**HAT THE DEVIL is going on here?" William Marquis stood rooted to the floor as his brain attempted to process the scene before him. The most current woman installed in the guest suite lay slumped on the floor of Mathias' study looking so wan he could see the blue trails of her veins beneath her translucent skin. Two trickles of blood flowed from a spot beneath her jaw, down her throat and chest to stain the pale pink sweater.

Next to her, Mathias crouched like a rabid animal, hunched and wild-eyed. Blood stained his chin and his teeth protruded over his bottom lip.

"Mathias?" William took a cautious step forward, giving him just enough room to close the door so none of the staff could see. "What's wrong?"

The man he'd worked for most of his life, who he considered his closest friend, stared up at him with a face drawn and haunted. The vampire's throat worked and his mouth opened, closed, and opened again as if he tried to form words. William stepped closer.

"No." Mathias raised his hand but the effort involved was too much and it dropped to his side. He swallowed and worked his mouth until words finally emerged. "No closer. I hang onto control by a thread."

"What's happened to you, Mathias?"

"Poison." He slumped back, eyes closed, chin resting on his chest.

"What? How? Who? I…I don't understand. What do I do?" William crept closer, peering at the vampire he trusted with his life. "Do…do you need my blood?" The words tumbled out before he could even think about what he offered.

"Not yours, my friend." Mathias was weakening. Each word came out as a growl as he clung to control by his fingernails.

"Then whose, Mathias? I…you're dying. I can't sit here and do nothing."

"Rom."

William stared at him, thinking his voice had trailed off before finishing the name. "Rom? Roman? You need Roman here? I…I don't know where he is, how to get in touch with him."

Mathias shook his head. "Romulus Jones."

William shuddered. That was a name he hadn't heard in twenty years. He straightened and moved behind the desk, his steps reluctant. He jerked open a drawer and pulled out a well-worn leather book. Opening it with a sense of reverence, he stared at the old-fashioned handwriting before flipping through the parchment-like pages searching for the correct name and number. Finding it, he reached for the phone and dialed.

"Put on speaker." Mathias sounded breathless, his words forced from his mouth with effort.

William pushed the speakerphone button and the electronic "brrrng" of the ring tone echoed against the snap and crackle of the fire.

"It's your nickel." The gruff voice answering the phone sounded familiar.

"Mr. Jones, I'm—" Raucous laughter cut off his introduction.

"Well, now. Talk about a blast from the past. How're they hanging, Billy-boy?"

"Jones."

"Mathias? That you? Dude, move closer to the speaker. I can hardly hear you. What's shakin'? Still plagued with them damn faeries?"

"I need you, Rom. Come now."

Clothes rustled on the other end of the phone line and William pictured the werewolf sitting up. "Am I walkin' into a hornet's nest, ol' son? Should I bring reinforcements?"

"Bring Amelia."

"Oh, hell, man. On my way!"

The speaker hummed.

"Tell Hoskins."

William hurried back around the desk. He stared down at Mathias and shuddered. Pain radiated from the vampire through his sunken eyes, his skin gray and stretched taut over his skull. He rushed from the room, sick to his stomach with fear.

"HOSKINS!" His panicked shout echoed through the house. The ubiquitous butler arrived behind him on silent feet.

"Sir?"

He jumped, his heart beating too fast as he tried to breathe through the shock. "A guest will be arriving shortly. Show him to Mr. DeVries' study immediately." A smirk curled the butler's upper lip. "Mr. DeVries summoned him." He watched the smirk deflate and felt heartened by it for some strange reason. He executed a sharp about-face and marched back to the study.

Mathias hadn't moved. William knelt beside his old friend and reached for him, intending to help move him to the leather couch.

"Do not touch me."

He fell backwards, his heart skipping a few beats. "I…I'm sorry, Mathias. I thought to make you more comfortable."

"My control hangs by a thread, William." The vampire's eyes remained closed, as if the act of opening them was too much. "I would not hurt you, old friend."

Maneuvering with great care to avoid touching Mathias, he regained his feet and moved around the vampire's legs to check the woman. She wasn't breathing and he gagged. When he could breath without his stomach roiling, he said the words out loud. "She's dead, I think. What do we do now?"

"Wait for Rom."

Romulus Jones. William tasted that bitter name. The werewolf first appeared when Sade was a baby. Mathias had turned the nursery into a bower fit for a princess and a lovely young woman was hired as her nanny. And then Sade disappeared—the first time. The household staff turned out in force to search the house and grounds for the child but she seemed well and truly gone. None of the staff would confess to seeing a thing. William could only wait until Mathias awoke.

When the vampire awoke, the staff was sent to search again. Mathias suspected that someone at the Seelie Court, if not Oberon the High King himself, was behind the child's disappearance but without proof, he couldn't petition for redress. The vampire made a few phone calls and the doorbell rang just before midnight. Rom Jones. Werewolf.

ANSWERING THE DOOR, the butler stared down his very British nose at the scruffy man standing in the wan glow of the porch light. Making a mental note to check the wattage of the bulb in the fixture, Hoskins sniffed and turned up his nose. "No soliciting." He looked and sounded imperious.

"Y'all called me, old son," the man growled, his eyes flashing strangely in the pale light, like an animal caught in the light.

The butler stepped back, flustered as he recognized the man who stepped inside. Tall and lean, his shaggy, gray-streaked hair brushed against cheeks covered by several days' growth of beard. The faded red flannel shirt he wore was tucked into stained jeans, ripped at the knees. The man's worn work boots, caked in mud, left smudged outlines on the polished white marble of the foyer.

"You!" Hoskins sniffed in disdain. "Your presence is required in Mr. DeVries study." He pointed an imperious finger toward the back of the house. "I presume you are capable of finding your own way?"

As Rom passed, he stopped and pressed against the man wearing an impeccable morning coat and starched white shirt beneath it. Jones sniffed once, arched an eyebrow, and whispered into Hoskins's ear. "Still nippin' d'good stuff, huh, Hoskins?"

Sputtering, the butler slammed the door and stormed off to his sanctuary in the butler's pantry adjacent to the kitchen, tossing a haughty "Harrumph" over his shoulder as he exited.

Jones padded deeper into the house, literally following his nose. He pushed through the study door without knocking. "What the hell is so all fired important you dragged my sorry ass into th'city, Mathias?" Jones growled and then blanched. "Damn, ol' son. Hang on." He dropped to his knees and leaned toward the vampire, griping his arms. "Hold still. And hang on. Mellie's on her way."

He looked up at William. "That British nancypants stormed off t'pout. Go wait by the door for Mellie t'get here. She's a...specialist." His eyes glinted in the firelight and a golden flash flickered momentarily as he turned his head, giving him a feral look.

Shocked by the gleam, William took a step backwards. "What is she?" he murmured, almost afraid to hear the answer.

"I tol'ja. She's a specialist. Now go wait for her." In the blink of an eye, Jones stood next to William. "Just a minute there, dude." He leaned in and sniffed the front of William's shirt. Then he sniffed behind William's ear. The human's eyes widened as he bent over from the waist and sniffed his crotch.

"What the blazes are you doing?" William sputtered, stepping back angrily, his hands cupping his groin. "That's just...obscene."

Jones sank back beside Mathias. "He's clean, not that I figured otherwise. Get t'the door Billy-boy or we'll have t'be callin' that daughter of yours to come investigate Mathias's demise."

William choked back a gag, turned and ran into the hall, shutting the door behind him. Pacing the front hall, he fretted about Mathias, the reason for his poisoning, and wondered who—or what—he waited for.

In the study, Jones laughed at the human's precipitous retreat, the last notes of his laughter almost a howl, one that sounded full of sadness rather than glee. "Dammit, Mathias. Who the hell would wanna poison you?" He nudged the woman's lifeless body with his toe. "And use a mundane t'do it. There just ain't no honor no more." He offered his arm. "Take a drink, guy. Take the edge off 'til Mellie gets here."

Mathias shook his head. "We don't know if the poison will spread that way. I need you to find who did this, Rom."

"You know I will, Mathias." His voice almost rang with the sincerity of his words. Not formal, but a vow nonetheless. "You still feudin' with the fuckin' fae?"

The hint of a wan smile ghosted across Mathias' face. "I may have grown soft, Rom, but...what is it you often call them? Those damn pixies? No. Not Oberon. For all that he is, he would not stoop so low as this. Can you track who did this?"

Rom nodded. "I'll track 'em, Mathias. And we'll deal with 'em." He nudged the woman again. "Where'd you find 'er?"

"Where one finds such of her ilk. She was pliable and that may have been the problem." His chest rose and fell as if he took a deep breath. "If someone in this house..." He closed his eyes, out of breath.

"I'll take care of it, Mathias. You have my word. We've ridden a lot of rough roads together. I'm not gonna kick you off the wagon now." He glanced at the antique clock on the mantel. If Amelia didn't arrive soon, Mathias wouldn't make it. "Any chance it was Titania? That's one bitch who holds a grudge until she gets even. I still don't wanna start a war with the Glitter-flitters but damned if I'll let 'em get away with this shit."

Mathias shook his head. "Neither do I, Rom." The admission came reluctantly. "Our old feud was laid to rest years ago. No. I suspect other, darker forces at work. Forces with human assistance."

The hair stood up on the back of Rom's neck. "Fuck," he muttered. "I got a really bad feelin' about this."

The study door swung open on well-oiled hinges and a slip of a girl crept in. She bobbed her head in Rom's direction and studiously ignoring the dead human, knelt between Mathias' out-stretched legs. "I came just as quick as I could." Her voice sounded as child-like as she looked.

Mathias shuddered and his fingertips clawed his palms as he fisted and unfisted his hands. Rom tensed, ready to intervene if Mathias attacked the girl. "Can you do anything, Mellie?"

She held out her hands palms down and seemed to touch Mathias from head to foot though her hands hovered above him. Eyes closed, face serene, she appeared a study in concentration. Rom held his breath. Amelia was a well-kept secret, a one-of-a-kind jewel in a world filled with magical treasure. As he watched, the girl paled and her hands shook. She moaned, a faint wail of sound riding a soft sigh.

"This is bad."

"Can you fix it?"

She touched her fingertips to the vampire's chest, just above his heart. "Yes."

The one word, though spoken in a hushed voice, rang in the quiet room. Rom took a breath. He might hate vampires on principal but Mathias always treated the packs with honor. He was a rare breed and Rom did not want to lose his calm counsel. "What can I do?"

She didn't look at him, remaining focused on Mathias. "Find the one who did this." She glanced at the woman's body, dismissing it with her next statement. "And store that somewhere."

"Done, baby girl." Rom stood and moved around the girl and the vampire. Bending from the waist, he grabbed the woman's arm and hoisted her body over his shoulder. He paused at the door. "Call me if you need me, Mellie."

Rom almost bumped into William Marquis in the hallway but the human leaped back out of his way.

"Where are you taking tha....her?"

"Gonna put her on ice. That big freezer still in the basement?"

Slightly horrified, William cleared his throat and gestured down the hall. "I'll show you the way."

Once that chore was disposed of, Rom sent William to gather up the staff. He had the scent of the poison and the spell in his nose. If any member of this household had a hand in poisoning Mathias, he would sniff them out. Literally.

A few minutes later, everyone had gathered in the formal dining room. William stood nominal guard at the door while the staff occupied the opulent chairs, nervous and unsure. Out of pure cussedness, he started with Hoskins. Unfortunately, the snooty butler came up clean. One by one, Rom worked his way around the table. Maids. Gardeners. Kitchen staff. One man fidgeted in his seat, pale and nervous. The chauffeur. Rom's nose twitched. He glanced over at William. The man had noticed the driver's behavior too. A stench reminiscent of rotten cucumbers and dead flowers caused him to sneeze. Fear and guilt.

"Y'all just sit tight, hear? Mathias will be in shortly."

The chauffeur blanched and his throat worked furiously as he tried to swallow. Oh, yeah. He was as guilty as sin. Silence blanketed the room broken only by the occasional sniffle or rustle of clothing as one of the humans shifted in their seat. Rom watched his suspect, anticipating the man would bolt sooner or later.

Sure enough, he did the moment Mathias strode through the door looking as mean as only an angry vampire can. Rom caught the guy by the collar of his uniform jacket and held him high enough his booted feet dangled a couple of inches off the floor.

"The rest of you are dismissed." The vampire's voice was all the more menacing for its restraint.

The staff fled, ducking past Mathias with downcast eyes and hunched shoulders. Even Hoskins. Rom almost laughed but refrained. He shook the chauffeur again instead. Mathias stalked toward them and the man struggled, gnashing his teeth in the process. An instant too late, Rom figured out what the man was doing. Foam bubbled from between the human's lips, his eyes rolled back in his head, and he went limp.

"Aw, hell."

"Indeed, Rom. I suspect we shall all have a taste of hell before this is ended."

"Well, shit."

Chapter Twenty-four

A Murder of Crows

OH, SHIT. Did she say that out loud? Her head pounded, the pain a thundering echo that left her deaf and blind. Sade opened her eyes. She thought. Pitch black wrapped her in a stifling blanket and she couldn't tell if her eyes were open. Reaching up, she brushed a fingertip across her lashes. Yeah. Eyes were open. She gulped in a deep breath, partly to ensure she was still alive, partly to make sure there was air to breathe. Her heart thudded in her chest—slow, turgid beats with an eternity between each one. Her nostrils flared as she sucked in another breath, her lungs laboring to process the oxygen. Sparkles erupted behind her blind eyes and an explosion of light filled the space around her. Air whooshed from her lungs. Her heart stuttered. And stopped.

If one's past really played out in the heartbeat between life and death, Sade figured she was done for. Figures appeared in the blazing light, nebulous at first then solidifying. She was so not ready to walk into the light. She squinted at the scene, waiting. Crystalline, as if encapsulated in a snow globe, she saw a dark-haired woman sitting in a car, tense, unsure, watching.

Oh, god. The last time she'd seen Caleb face-to-face. The night he told her he was leaving her. That night in Alexandria. She forced air into her lungs. She'd been crushed after Caleb shut her out. Never mind she was the one who walked out the door and closed it behind her. Angry at the memory, she kicked out and her booted foot connected with something solid.

"SHIT!" That hurt. She wasn't dead. Yet. She forced air into her lungs as sparkles formed behind her eyes. She closed her eyelids. Darkness consumed her. Not once, not in her entire life had she been afraid of the dark. Until now. Memories intruded. Hurtful scenes of her childhood. Real and imagined slights. And searing pain. Too much. She couldn't deal with it. Eyes squinted against it all, one tear squeezed out between her lashes and left a hot trail down her cheek.

"Fuck this. I don't cry!" She railed against her confinement, hands and feet pounding and kicking against the solid confines of her prison. Light exploded in her head.

"Pay attention!" A disembodied voice snapped like a whip, flaying her frayed nerves.

"What the fuck?" Her words echoed hollowly and she winced, her ears bruised by the sharp echo of her voice.

"The answers you seek are within you, Child."

Very few people called her "Child" and this voice was not a familiar one. "Who are you?"

Silence greeted her questions. She didn't believe in God. Not really. When asked by a college roommate why she didn't, Sade had answered, "Because God doesn't believe in me."

Roman chastised her soundly for that. "Your arrogance astounds me, Child."

Princeton. Four years of her life spent with Caleb and Roman in dogged attendance to her. Memories tumbled like the sparkling flakes in a snow globe. Scenes of her and Caleb squabbling like the siblings they'd become, slinging comfortable arrows at each other...

"You throw like a girl!"

"Yeah? And you smell like a wet dog!"

"You're a sadist, you know that?" Did she say that out loud or was the echo in her head? And who had she directed that question to? "There's a reason I hated that Wonderful Life movie, you know. An angel showing the nice man his life? Showing him all the bad things that would happen if he'd never been born…pure crap. And bah humbug. I hate Christmas too."

At least the pomp and circumstances of the holiday, she admitted. Presents were cool but dressing up and dealing with the relatives and social toads trying to get in good with Mathias was a pain in the ass. She snickered, remembering the Christmas dinner when Caleb changed at the table. One moment, he was a clumsy sixteen-year-old boy, the next he was sitting next to her chair trying to lick his balls.

Only Mathias and Aunt Polly noticed, the rest of the guests bespelled by Mathias to forget. The old woman looked like a dowager queen as she reigned over the event. Sade knew her as Aunt Polly though she'd been introduced to the guests as Dame Apolline, an old friend of the family. There were old débutantes at that dinner too, each one hoping to seduce Mathias. He'd always said débutantes tasted of mimosas and white wine spritzers. He much preferred the rich, earthy tones of a good lager, a single malt scotch, or a dark red Cabernet Sauvignon. At the time, Sade had gagged and called the women who periodically appeared in the household his Flavor of the Week.

Silence stretched, cloaking her in sensory deprivation. She wondered if she'd gone mad. Then she wondered if she were dead and this was Purgatory. Alone with nothing but her memories for eternity? Oh fuck no!

Hours might have passed or only seconds. That throbbing pain pulsed without mercy and rainbow prisms of light danced behind her eyelids. Against the sparkling display, black letters danced like mad marionettes. F. B. I.

The FBI. Her home away from home. The one thing that gave her life meaning. She had no friends there, but she damn sure had respect. She kicked out her foot and winced as it connected with the solid wall. She didn't need friends. Friends didn't last. Roman was gone. Caleb had abandoned her to walk on the wild side. Hell, even Ariel only wanted to get into her pants. Nikos didn't count. She hadn't known him long enough to consider him anything more than a pain in the ass. Once she stopped amusing him, he'd move on. Her chest swelled with indignation. Eventually, Sinjen would leave her. Or she would leave him.

Her chest felt like a steel band was squeezing all the air out of her lungs. She gulped back panic. Air. She needed air! She beat against her prison until she could no longer breathe. The darkness swallowed her again.

Sade awoke with a start and sat up. She banged her head so hard, sparkles of light danced in the dark. "Gawdammotherfuckinsonavabitch!" Her heart raced and her chest felt like a jackhammer pounded against her ribs as she waited for someone to tell her to watch her language but only silence greeted her expletive. She blinked in a futile attempt to clear her vision of the prisms. The rainbows focused into pinpoints assaulting her senses as sure as any laser beam. She blinked to clear her vision. Angels. With teeth—little pointy teeth they gnashed.

"Blood," the tiny angel lights sang, their voices off-key and screeching worse than any nail scraped across a blackboard. "We want your blood. We want your sin. We're waiting for you…"

She batted at them, her knuckles scraping across the rough stone surrounding her. "Owww." Closing her eyes, she sucked one bleeding knuckle and wanted to laugh at the cacophony her action invoked. "If I can't see you, you aren't here." She just wished she could plug her ears to protect her hearing from the god-awful caterwauling.

"You are really pissin' me off!" The lights dimmed and silence blanketed her. She blinked. Her vision cleared for a moment but then her heart stuttered. A part of her brain wondered if battery cables could jump-start it. In the dark, those figures whirled and her stomach churned. "Oh, fuck no," she shouted. Or thought she had. "I am *not* going to throw up!" Somewhere beyond the swirling dervish of lights, laughter echoed.

Waltzing figures, candlelight, and then chaos as Caleb leaned in to whisper, "You really know how to make an entrance, Slim."

Her nose filled with the cloying scent of roses. Her lungs expanded painfully then deflated with a whoosh. Sweat trickled between her breasts. The memories flashed between throbs of pain, pausing each heartbeat, turning the thrumming blood in her veins to turgid sludge.

"You have always been a thorn in my side."

"Who the hell are you?" She had just enough breath to spit out the question. "Yeah, that's me. Always a thorn in someone's side." The words echoed in her head. She was too weak to spit them out. Her heart beat once more then settled into a dull ache.

Thump....thump....thump. Was that her heart? She fought to wake up. She was a fighter—always had been.

"Is that what you did, Sade?" Her father sounded resigned and terribly sad. He didn't turn his head to look at her. "Punch them in the nose?"

Sade nodded. "I did. And I won, Dad. I came out on top."

"It's not always about winning, Sade,"

"Yes, Daddy," she told the darkness. "It is. It's always about winning when you are right." Her lungs refused to inflate. "No, dammit. I'm not giving up." She sucked hard, willing her chest to rise. "I am going to win!" Sparkles blinded her for a moment as her brain struggled to function.

Gasping. The sound of tortured lungs struggling to expand. Was that her? Stabbing pain erupted behind her eyes as her heart forced out a beat. Her vision narrowed, fixed on one single light as the darkness filled her lungs. Her heartbeat no longer echoed in her ears. She watched, detached, floating above, looking down on the scene, as if she were omnipresent— hearing, seeing, privy to thoughts and emotions of those she watched.

"Well, crap. Do I have to relive my potty training now?"

One heartbeat. Breathe. Must breathe. Her will melted into the darkness.

"Pay attention!" That voice boomed and echoed like thunder. "This is the day for which you have lived."

Like an old movie, what she thought was a memory flickered against her closed eyelids.

Titania stared at the toddler deposited in the middle of her bower. The child was almost too beautiful to be human but there was absolutely nothing magical about her. The little girl blinked up at the queen, her heart-shaped face solemn, eyelashes long and dark below a cap of curly-soft chestnut hair.

The fae queen leaned down to stare into the child's startling green eyes. A pudgy hand grabbed a fistful of Titania's platinum tresses.

"What is it?" the queen mused. "What power do you possess that you have enchanted two such powerful creatures as the High King of the Fae and a master vampire centuries old?" She tried to straighten up but the toddler's fingers tangled in her hair. As cold and cruel as Titania could be, this time she gently disengaged the child's hand. She moved away from the bed, pacing back and forth. After a bit, she stopped and stared down at the trusting child. "That they would risk war for you? It is beyond comprehension." She murmured the words in wonder before pacing again.

Titania just didn't understand. The child was no changeling. She was simply human. A lovely child to be sure, but she was *human*. What was so special about humans anyway? She had never understood the magicks' fascination with the creatures. They were frail, loud, dirty, and short-lived—at least in comparison to magical folk. For three years, she sat back and watched Mathias and Oberon wage their war. The child on the bed had logged more travel miles than most astronauts. She had been kidnapped and snatched back only to be kidnapped again. Transported to that dimension, rescued and hidden in a different one only to be spirited to another. Back and forth, neither side able to hide or keep her from the other for any length of time.

"You are not worth the devastation a true war would leave in its wake, child," the queen told the toddler, her tone and demeanor solemn. Sade blinked once, her serene expression never changing, her green eyes sparkling like neon on the Las Vegas strip. "And those bull-headed jackasses will decimate the magical folk without a second thought." Again, Sade simply stared, looking wise beyond her years. Titania tilted her head and stared at the baby, horrified by the thought just entering her head.

"No," She breathed out her denial. The queen approached the bed again, never taking her eyes from the tot. She finally picked up the child, holding her at arms length. Looking deep into Sade's eyes, Titania dropped all pretense of glamour. The baby cooed and blew bubbles through her lips. The queen almost dropped her. "Aye, by all the Old Ones." She swore an ancient oath under her breath. "They've marked you. Both of them, the fools. They have sewn the seeds of our destruction." Biting her lower lip, she lowered the child to the bed and stepped back.

Walking to the sliding glass door, she pulled it open and stepped out onto the balcony. She let out a shrill whistle. A few minutes later, she heard the beating of leathery wings pushing against the dry desert air. A creature more comfortable on the pediments of a church than a Las Vegas high rise settled onto the balcony.

"I am not a dog, Titania." The gargoyle's voice grated like rusty hinges.

"No, Roman, you are not," the faerie queen agreed. "You are a Sentinel. Have you any idea what they have done?"

The creature nodded his massive head. "They created a human immune to magic."

Titania threw up her hands in disgust. "They have. We cannot kill it, can we." It wasn't a question.

Roman chuckled, a sound more like gravel being crushed than laughter. "No. You cannot kill the child, Queen Titania. And I do not mean that in a moral sense for you are known as a cold and calculating ruler who is capable of a deed most foul. Carrying the marks as she does, while she is not immortal, I do believe she is immune to any of the lethal arts you could throw at her." The gargoyle's deep voice resonated through the room.

The queen paced from the bed to the balcony and back again. He stood, stone-faced and patient. She finally stopped in front of him and looked up at his craggy face. "Take her back to Mathias," Titania decreed.

The gargoyle's expression didn't change. "Are you sure?" He didn't move until she nodded, then he asked, "What of Oberon?"

Titania shrugged, the rise and fall of her shoulders an elegant gesture. "I will deal with the king. This ends here and now. Return the child."

Roman didn't wait for her to change her mind. He scooped up the child and wrapped her in a fuzzy blanket. Cradling Sade in one arm, he strode through the door to the balcony and without a backward glance, he launched into the starry sky, his wide, leathery wings beating strongly.

The little girl wrapped one arm around his neck, tucked her head into his shoulder and said, "Ruv ru, Romo."

The gargoyle's face finally changed expression as a ghost of a smile curved his lips. "Love you more, Lady Sade."

No. I love you more…

No more.

Chapter Twenty-five

Nevermore

NO MORE, not if he had his way.

Sinjen hated the smell of magic as it swirled through the air as thick as smog. Despite the cold, he stayed on the balcony outside his bedroom, sniffing the wind, sorting through the various scents as deftly as a werewolf. From the band of trees in the park below his balcony, a murder of crows cawed, their chilling calls echoing off the tall buildings.

He did not believe in soul mates. As he no longer had a soul, such belief appeared to be an exercise in futility. Nothing had occurred in all his long years to make him a believer. Yet the first time he saw her—walking with that long-legged glide of hers into the room holding that infernal glass cell in which he had been confined? Those snapping green eyes, the jut of her stubborn chin, the beauty mark begging him to kiss her full lips. His heart knew her immediately. As did his body.

Each night thereafter, upon waking, he could feel her. He knew her moods if not always her thoughts. And when the two of them finally came together, he knew her body, her desires, as well as he knew his own. Lying in his arms sated and warm, he could touch her innermost thoughts though he refrained. She would not have welcomed the intrusion.

But now? Now, there was nothing. He had no sense of her. It was as if Sade never existed. When he concentrated on her, there was only a cold, empty void. Someone had taken her and hidden her so effectively he could not find her.

To act in anger was to act imprudently. He knew in his heart her very life and soul was threatened. But if he could not find her, he could neither protect nor rescue her. He now regretted his decision. Had he marked her more completely, he would be able to find her no matter what. His damned honor stayed his desire to do so. He had come close but declined at the last moment even though he had begun the process. To mark her fully without her knowledge, without her permission would have put an insurmountable barrier between them. But now, as he paced the dark confines of his rooms, he wondered which would be worse—Sade hating him for eternity or Sade lost to him for eternity.

Given the tension of their last meeting, when Mathias had called Sinjen before the *Councilium Magicae* to turn another human to become the Legate of New Orleans and he'd refused, Mathias would ignore his call. He had to try anyway. To lose her because he did not do everything possible was unacceptable. He retrieved his cell phone from his pocket and punched in the numbers. Three rings later, the connection crackled.

"DeVries residence."

"Tell Mathias that Kristian St. John requires his assistance. Tell him that if he values her life he will come immediately. Tell him that where there was once heat and warmth and passion there is now nothing but a dark, icy void." Sinjen paused, drew a long, shuddering breath. "Tell him," he told Mathias' man, "that there are no more secrets. There is a debt to be paid." He hung up the receiver without waiting for a reply and stepped inside.

He pushed the door closed, turned on his heel and marched into the living room. His measured stride carried him to the wall of windows that overlooked the vista of the Chicago skyline glowing against the frigid night sky. He stared out, then closed his eyes and forced himself to relax. Sinjen cleared his mind; opened it to the cosmos. He waited. The touch came a moment later. He grimaced. Touch was perhaps a misnomer. The demand was more like a padded hammer blow.

Leaning his forehead against the cold glass of the window, he forced his mind to allow the inquisition. A vampire could never deny his sire entry—to do so meant pain, a great deal of it. Over this great a distance, he could only exchange vague ideas with Mathias. Sinjen focused his thoughts on the distress he felt over the fact he could not *touch* Sade, that he could not feel her life force. The compulsion pressing against him suddenly withdrew and Sinjen wasn't surprised when his phone rang a few moments later.

"Where is she?" The cultured voice with the faint traces of old Europe in it sounded unaccountably weak.

"I do not know, Mathias." At wit's end, Sinjen brushed his fingers through his hair, leaving furrows combed through its length. "I would not have called you if I could reach her."

"Reach her? Did you mark her?" The weakness he'd noted before disappeared.

Sinjen had realized shortly after meeting the long-legged fed that she carried not only the mark from Mathias, but also some sort of ensorcellment that stank of fae. Master vampires were territorial and Sinjen was not surprised at the tone of Mathias's voice. He took a deep breath. "I didn't need to." He almost smiled at the dead silence that fairly crackled through the phone held to his ear. As one of Mathias's children, Sinjen recognized his sire's mark on Sade and touched her through it. By sampling her blood, he strengthened the tie they already shared but if he had fully marked her, he would not be having this conversation.

"Why was she with you?" Deceptively soft, the tone Mathias used spoke volumes.

Surprised by his sire's swift change of subject, Sinjen sighed. "As she told you, a series of murders and disappearances. Young women." He didn't suppress the shudder that ran through him. "Young women with talent. The stench of magic is everywhere. The air itself is heavy with evil." When Mathias didn't reply, Sinjen waited another few heartbeats. "I sense the Witch's hand in this, Mathias. But she is well and truly buried, yes?"

On the other end of the line, Mathias rubbed his eyes. He would admit to himself that he'd been worried when Sade had not called him before dawn, nor had she called during his day sleep. His research had not left him with peaceful thoughts during his short daylight hours. In fact, he had remained awake for over an hour past sunrise in order to talk to her. And now, with his attempted assassination, he had no choice but to face the facts.

"No," Mathias finally acknowledged. "Her tomb was found. That fool, Crowley, discovered where we trapped her. It took him years, but he has managed to transfer her crypt. The final seals have not yet been broken but I fear it is just a matter of time."

Sinjen stilled. He knew the Witch; knew what she would do to live again. He had witnessed the ritual. That abominable ceremony had been the final crack in his sanity. Sir Kristian St. John, Knight Templar, Defender of the Faith, had knelt before the creature of the night who shared his dungeon and bared his throat for the vampire, Mathias DeVries, to take his blood— and began his unwitting conversion to soulless.

The Witch laughed when the two knights confronted her. But together, the vampires, ancient and newly turned, managed to trap her, binding her with old magic and new faith. Her final shroud had been Sinjen's jupon— the white tunic with the crosses of the Templar Knights embroidered on it. He gave up his soul to stop the Witch and now she was back. Any human who chanced to see him at that moment would have quaked in fear.

"Sade." Fear gnawed deep in Sinjen's gut as he whispered her name.

"Yes." Mathias affirmed his worst fears. "I am flying into Midway Airport. I will see you there."

The dead connection hummed in Sinjen's ear and he finally clicked off his phone. His eyes remained riveted out the window. Off across the park, a dark shadow obscured the lights of the skyline. Sinjen stepped out onto his balcony to meet the leather-winged creature soaring his way. The ancient being touched lightly on the balcony railing and then stepped down onto the floor, gracefully folding his wings.

"*Le Vieil,*" Sinjen greeted the gargoyle by his title but kept his voice noncommittal.

"Sir Kristian," the Old One replied. "You know what has happened?"

Sinjen stared at the gargoyle for a long moment. "She is gone."

The gargoyle settled on the balcony, turning to face the city, his wings folding almost flat against his long back. When he squatted, haunches not quite touching the floor, knees bent to his chest, he could still turn his massive head and look the vampire in the eye.

"Not gone. Taken," the Old One corrected. "There is evil awakening. An evil older and more malevolent than most." The gargoyle's voice grated like rough edges of granite grinding together. "You have brought this upon her," Crevan accused. "You and Mathias."

A heartbeat of time passed. Three. Ten. "No," Sinjen denied. "A human with greed in his heart and the mistaken notion that he is stronger than magic has done this. The evil was buried, sleeping where none should have awakened it." His voice turned colder than the winter wind sweeping in off the frigid lake. "We knew not how to kill it so it was not destroyed." Regret dripped off his words, forming illusory stalactites in the arctic air.

Crevan nodded his head and Sinjen could almost hear the sound of stone rubbing against stone. "Evil cannot be killed. It can only be dispersed. Not even the old one knew this."

Sinjen nodded. His sire, Mathias, was referred to as "the old one" by other magicks. It wasn't an appellation such as the *Le Vieil* title that had been bestowed upon Crevan. Mathias was simply one of the oldest known vampires. What the humans did not know and did not understand was that the magical races had lived for millenniums with an uneasy peace and mutual respect for the abilities and cunning of the other races.

Every magick was susceptible to something. While they were hard to kill, they could be. Sun was the bane of vampires. Oh, they could be staked and beheaded, but that didn't really kill them. It took the sun to cleanse their particular stench from the world. With the fae, it was cold iron. It poisoned the blood and leeched the magic from them and once the magic was gone, they could be killed like any other mortal. Silver did the trick for werewolves and water for gargoyles. Sinjen knew of a stretch of the Seine River that was hazardous to boat traffic when the water level was low. The riverbed was littered with the lifeless hulks of drowned gargoyles, their stone features scrubbed plain by the water. Other, lesser magicks each had their own Achilles Heel.

"Can you find her?" Sinjen didn't move, remaining as deathly still as the gargoyle.

Silence stretched between them for a minute, then five. Ten minutes. An hour. Neither supernatural creature moved yet each was infinity aware of the world around them. Lights on the skyline frolicked in a mesmerizing pattern, flicking on and off in a dance to which only the lights knew the choreography. Both creatures were seeking, each in their own way.

"She is still among us," Crevan finally affirmed, his voice holding echoes of the sepulcher in their depths. Sinjen stood stock-still, so immobile he could have been made of granite himself, as he waited for Crevan to continue. "The evil surrounds her, eclipsing her light." The ancient gargoyle turned his head to stare at Sinjen. "Look for the void. That is where you will find her." With that, *Le Vieil* pushed off his haunches, stepped to the balcony railing and launched into the dark sapphire sky.

"Where go you?" Sinjen called after the gargoyle but he received no response. He watched until he lost the hint of shadow that marked Crevan's passage. Turning on his heel, he headed inside. Snagging his cell phone, he made a call. A limousine would be waiting by the time he arrived downstairs.

Retreating to his closet, Sinjen dressed for battle. He pulled on leather pants, thick yet still supple enough that they fit like a second skin. A white silk undershirt, long-sleeved and form-fitting provided a layer between his skin and the thick leather jacket he shrugged into. The jacket fell to mid-thigh and had wrist-hugging cuffs.

From a chest stored in the back of the closet, Sinjen dug out a bundle of folded leather. Shaking out the hooded cape, he set it aside as he reached back into the chest and extracted a long parcel wrapped in oilcloth. Untying the binding, Sinjen unrolled the wooden sheath with the steel hilt extending above it. This was the sword he carried at his side as a Knight Templar. This was the sword he used to help Mathias dispatch the Witch. Even now, he couldn't bring himself to say her name.

He unsheathed the weapon and swung it experimentally. His hand fit the pommel like a lover's embrace. The blade was three feet of polished Toledo steel, forged by one of the finest sword makers in a region famous for its fabled blades. As was fitting a Templar, the blade was plain, an elegant two inches wide tapering finally to a slightly dull and spatulated point. This sword was made for the cutting and slashing inherent to fighting armored opponents, not for stabbing. The guard was a simple cross shape looking vaguely like a thin bow tie. The birch grip was wrapped with leather cords, the pommel topped by a humble, round beveled peen.

He settled the sword back in its sheath and laid it atop his cloak. Bending over, he pulled on leather boots, thick and stiff yet still fitting him like well-worn gloves. Dressed now, Sinjen belted the sword on and settled it at his hip. He shrugged into a cashmere topcoat, draped the cloak over his arm and headed out. He locked his apartment door then strode purposely down the hallway and straight onto an elevator as the doors opened, never breaking stride.

Down in the lobby, Chuck had the front door open and ready as he came off the elevator. The limousine waited at the curb, its engine idling, the back door open. As he passed through the door, Chuck hurried to the open door of the limo to close it after Sinjen disappeared inside. The doorman barely stepped back from the curb before the big automobile accelerated away and smoothly joined the line of traffic coursing down the street.

The black limo slid through the gates to the private jet area at Midway Airport. The vehicle idled, throwing up a cloud of exhaust into the cold air, while a sleek executive Lear slowly taxied to a nearby hangar. The ground crew placed chocks at the wheels as the engines whined down to a high-pitched hum. The plane's door opened, stairs unfolded, and one figure, his black cloak whipping around him, stepped down onto the tarmac. Sinjen opened the back door and Mathias settled in the seat next to him. As soon as the door closed, the limo pulled away, headed toward downtown Chicago.

"Does Hannibal Crowley have a church?" Mathias asked without pre-amble.

Sinjen shook his head. "He has what he calls a 'congregation' and a group of hangers-on. He stays in a suite at the Drake. But I know of no temple where he conducts his rituals."

Mathias, his mouth tightening in acknowledgement, stared out the window as if lost in thought. "Trying to hide in a mantle of respectability, I suppose." Lights flickered beyond the smoked glass. After a moment's reflection, he retrieved a cell phone from the briefcase he carried. He hit a speed dial button and waited only moments before ordering, "Addresses of any property that can be traced to Hannibal Crowley." He paused for a moment. "Or the Institute for the Study of Ancient Entities."

Sinjen tried not to snort. "His tax dodge?"

Nodding in response to the question, Mathias listened to the voice droning through the phone. "None?" The older vampire looked incredulous. "That cannot be. He must have a lair somewhere."

Fighting his rising sense of panic, Sinjen thought about how one went about tracking a man who appeared to have no property. He mulled over the information Sade had given him. His eyes met Mathias's and knowledge slid into both their eyes as they silently traded information.

"Contact your friends at Customs," Mathias barked. "I want the address of any shipment from Turkey delivered to Crowley within the past five years." He ended the call with a flick of his thumb and stared at Sinjen. "Did you report her missing to the authorities?"

Sinjen nodded. "But only after contacting you. Luckily, there were wit-nesses who saw her leave my building after sun-up. I called the CPD detective she has been working with. He, too, is worried. And expecting us."

Once again, Mathias perused the scenery rolling past. Thirty silent minutes later, the limousine parked in front of the main Chicago police station. The driver double-timed around the vehicle to open the curbside door. Sinjen emerged first and took up a protective stance. Old lessons were never forgotten. A minute later, the older vampire appeared.

"We will find Detective Franks here." Sinjen disliked the necessity for this action, but under the accords reached after the Big Rip, they needed human authorities to lend legitimacy to their quest.

Patently aware of the sword belted around his waist but hidden under his coat, he fell into step with Mathias. Even though it was evening, a steady stream of people flowed in and out the front doors of the building. Like the Red Sea before Moses, the crowd parted and the two vampires swept into the building. Neither of them slowed down at the metal detectors, brushing through the gates without a backward glance. Though alarms went off, no one seemed to notice.

They approached the bank of elevators side by side. Three elevators opened simultaneously, two of them spilling out people. The vampires entered the empty one. No one got on with them, despite the huddle of people waiting. The car ascended, slowed to a jerky stop, and the doors opened. They disembarked, still shoulder to shoulder, and Sinjen pointed out Detective Franks with a glance.

Franks, along with everyone in the place, looked up as the vampires entered. The detective shivered and his respect for Sade climbed a notch. She didn't even blink when facing the magicks. The unknown vampire with St. John exuded so much power, the hair on the back of his neck prickled like he'd stuck his finger in a light socket.

Sinjen made introductions and began an explanation of their concern but was interrupted when Mathias' cell phone rang.

Mathias listened for several minutes. "The large one," he finally said. "Where was it delivered?" He listened again. "A warehouse on the Southside?" He glanced at Franks and the detective nodded, already punching in the number for dispatch on his desk phone. "Address." It wasn't a question. He listened then commanded, "Call me if you find anything else." Mathias ended the call as he advised, "The six thousand block of East Eighty-Third Street. Crowley took receipt of a rather large shipping crate three years ago at that address."

"Rather large?" Sinjen stared at his sire.

"The customs manifest listed the contents as imported tile and restoration building materials. Four tons worth. From Turkey." Mathias arched one eyebrow at Sinjen.

"The fool." Sinjen spat out the words, not relishing their taste in his mouth.

Franks checked a map. "Damn," he muttered. That's twelve blocks away from Oak Woods." The two vampires turned to him for clarification. "Oak Woods Cemetery. Marquis and I caught a homicide there."

"Four murdered." Sinjen answered Mathias's silent question. "Plus a disappearance about the time Crowley took receipt of that crate and the recent disappearance she called you about." He closed his eyes a moment. "The woman kidnapped in front of Sade and me. And now Sade."

"Two more," Mathias murmured. "The Witch needs two more sacrifices." He faced the cop. "Crowley has a daughter?" Franks nodded. Mathias turned cold eyes to Sinjen's stricken face. "And Sade." Mathias stabbed Franks with a glare. "We will go with you."

The detective opened his mouth to argue the policy on civilians participating in police operations—for about two seconds and then he admitted defeat. "What killed CeeCee Adams, Miriam Goddard, Hannah Stein, and this latest girl, Eleanor Rigby, has more power and magic than I want to face." He opened his desk drawer and took out a spare clip for his pistol. "Even with silver bullets. You guys sound like you know who's behind this. Want to give me a hint?" The vampires exchanged inscrutable looks.

Mathias lifted his shoulders in an eloquent shrug. "The Witch is evil in pure form," he explained. "She had been buried and, we believed, forgotten centuries ago. Hannibal Crowley discovered her prison and brought her here. If she gets free, heaven help us all." His eyes glittered like coal crushed into diamonds when he glanced toward the window. "We must act immediately. While Sinjen and I can withstand some daylight, we will be significantly weakened once the sun rises."

He gave the humans no opportunity to argue, turning on his heel and heading for the elevators. Sinjen followed while Franks and a couple of uniformed officers scrambled to keep up.

They emerged onto the sidewalk in front of the building to find several patrol cars parked behind the limousine. The figure lounging against the limo's back door raised the hackles on the back of Sinjen's neck. Mathias just smiled.

"Ariel."

"Mathias," the fae acknowledged, adding, "I am here to help."

Sinjen opened his mouth for an angry retort, but Mathias's voice in his head cautioned him to hold his tongue. "What have Oberon and Titania to do with this?" Mathias stared at the fae, anger showing as a brief flash across his features.

"They also recognize the danger, Mathias. The Witch must not be resurrected. That you and your protégé were able to contain her was a feat beyond the skill of most magicks. She has lain in wait all these centuries, drawing power to her. It will take more than the two of you or the human police to defeat her this time."

Franks, and the human cops wisely remained silent, though the detective's chaotic thoughts spilled into Sinjen's mind. *Blond surfer dude? But a magick. That's good, right? Not scared of the vamps and they're freaking terrifying. Don't ever want to piss them off. Reinforcements are good, yeah. We might pull this off.* The human's mind blanked for a moment and then was filled with the memory of Grant Park and a fountain filled with a million gallons of blood. *We're dead meat.*

Sinjen understood the sentiment but refused to despair. To do so meant giving up on Sade and he would not do so. Mathias and Ariel ducked into the limo while the humans sorted out into other vehicles. Sinjen stilled, shifting through the currents wafting through the night, and then joined the other magicks when he found no trace of Sade.

With emergency lights blazing, the convoy headed south on Michigan Avenue, their destination some ten miles away. Crossing under the Chicago Skyway, a cold chill raised Sinjen's hackles. Seeking with his inner senses, he touched…nothing. Off to the left, he saw a large, ornate building with a dome and Moorish façade, but they zoomed past and the feeling subsided. Minutes later, they arrived at a nondescript warehouse. A large armored van, its diesel motor growling like a pissed-off werewolf, idled there along with several more patrol cars.

"SWAT team," Franks explained as he met the three magicks on the sidewalk.

Mathias nodded. "They will deal with any humans inside. Leave the rest to us." While his voice remained soft, the command was implicit.

None of the humans argued. The SWAT team, with well-rehearsed precision, entered the building and began their search. Ten minutes later, they called an all clear. The building was empty. Franks looked helplessly at Mathias who simply stared out into the dark. Sinjen did the same—and he met the same blankness as he faced the north as he'd felt en route to the warehouse.

Look for the void. That is where you will find her. The ancient gargoyle's words echoed in Sinjen's mind. "The Moorish looking building," he demanded, whirling to face Franks. "Several blocks back. What is it?"

The detective looked perplexed but one of the district cops spoke up. "You mean the Arcadian Theater? Up on Seventy-Ninth Street." He turned and pointed. "We get calls there all the time. It's being renovated and the contractors complain about stuff going missing constantly."

The three magicks exchanged glances and Franks whistled in wonder. "Four tons of Turkish tile," he exclaimed. Before he could suggest checking it out, all three magicks had disappeared. Just like that—literally in the blink of an eye. Franks yelled over to the SWAT commander as he sprinted for the patrol car. "It's at the Arcadian."

THE MAGICKS MATERIALIZED across the street from the impressive edifice. Ariel drew a deep breath into his lungs, expanding them fully before a coughing fit choked off his air. He spat and sputtered until he could take a shallow breath. That the vampires chuckled did nothing to alleviate his discomfort. "You have smelled her stench before. Why didn't you warn me?"

Mathias' expression twisted in contempt. "The place reeks of her evil, yes. Crowley has cloaked it best he could. Is there a crack we can slip through?"

Ariel stepped into the street and approached the other sidewalk. The air sucked at his steps so that he had to drag each foot as if trudging through knee-deep mud. Finally standing by the front doors, he panted and had to wipe sweat from his brow. Glancing over his shoulder, he called in a quiet voice, "Give me a minute." One moment he was there, the next a glimmer of shadow wisped into the air.

A short time later, he reappeared next to them. "The old goat outfoxed himself." He all but rubbed his hands in glee. "Someone left a window cracked around back, second floor, and the magic leaked. I can get in. As for you two, wait for the humans." His grin stretched wider. "The place is warded against magicks—especially vampires and gargoyles but the fae? Not so much. And humans not at all. The cops will have no trouble going through the door. Just be sure *they're* the ones to touch it not either of you. Once I'm inside, I'll let you know the layout."

Ari faced Sinjen. "I love her too, you know. We'll get her out." Turning to Mathias, he flashed a jaunty salute. "If you have reinforcements, now is the time to send up the bat signal." Before either vampire could retort to the fae's jibe, he winked out, leaving only a faint trail of glitter in his wake.

"Relax, Sinjen. The fae love to torment. It is part of their endearing charm." Sarcasm was plain in Mathias' tone.

The passage of time weighed on Sinjen's psyche like shifting sands in the desert ready to swallow a man whole. While only minutes passed, dawn drew ever closer. He muttered something under his breath that sounded much like Sade's favorite expletive. "I'm not waiting, Mathias." He stepped off the curb, determined to cross the street but an iron hand gripped his biceps.

"Wait, Sinjen. The mundanes will be here soon enough. Let the fae scout out the situation. And we await our own reinforcements."

He quirked a curious brow at the mention of reinforcements but the sound of leathery wings hovering above preempted his question. The grumble of a diesel engine masked the sounds and moments later, headlights swept across them, bathing them in stark clarity. Uniformed officers tumbled out as patrol cars slowed and stopped. The back doors of the SWAT vehicle flew open with such force they clanged against the sides of it. Men in black spewed from the shadowed interior like living bile.

Franks held a hurried and whispered conversation with Mathias and the SWAT commander. Sinjen watched chaos become cohesion as the cops assaulted the old theater with military precision. Once they breached the main doors, Sinjen surged forward, Mathias at his side, shadows fading into the light.

Chapter Twenty-six
Say Goodbye to Yesterday

SHADOWS FADING INTO LIGHT? Was it possible? Sade blinked, realizing the pitch black of her tomb showed a faint line where sides met roof. She wasn't afraid of the dark; she was all too familiar with what lived there. This was different. This was terrifying. The air felt oily, with a thick stench that coated the back of her tongue with every shallow breath she sucked in. She gasped, elated when her lungs filled despite the taste. Unsure if she'd dreamed or experienced the sensation of dying, she didn't want to repeat it again.

Gingerly, she groped around her. Her fingertips scraped against rough stone. The skin on her hands was raw and tender. Her right foot ached and she vaguely remembered kicking something very solid with it. Refusing to surrender to fear, she explored the space enclosing her—a prison entirely too coffin-like for her peace of mind. She'd been laid out flat on her back but did have room to curl her knees to her chest and put her feet against the top. She gave a push, gratified when the lid seemed to give a little. Relaxing, Sade listened for any activity outside of her prison. Either the rock was thick enough it muffled all sound or she was alone.

"Well," she muttered. "There's no time like the present." Gathering her strength and focusing on her bent legs, she pushed with all her might. The stone lid moved. She tried again. And again. At this rate, moving the lid would take her much more time than she probably had. Squirming like a contortionist, Sade managed to turn over and get her feet under her. With her back bowed and hunched, she tucked her chin and braced her shoulders against the lid. Counting to three she exploded with all the force she could muster. The lid flew off and her momentum carried her upright. She squinted against the sudden flare of what seemed like a thousand flickering candles.

Dropping to a crouch, she took a defensive stance. Only her eyes and the top of her head showed over the side. The room appeared to be empty. She was alone. Climbing out of the stone sarcophagus where she'd been imprisoned, Sade suppressed a shiver. "This is just fucking creepy."

The room stank as she sniffed the air, testing it like a hunting dog seeking the scent of prey. Old blood and decomposing flesh. Her stomach clenched and Sade fought down the bile rising in her throat. Pain pounded in her head again. Carefully, she lifted a hand and felt around her skull. No bumps. No blood. Drugs then, she decided. A door opened and she froze. For the space of a few heartbeats, a group of people stood silhouetted by the bright light behind them.

"Good evening, my dear Miss Marquis," Hannibal Crowley said jovially. "Welcome to the shrine of Sahirah."

Welcome to the shrine of Sahirah? Yeah. Right. That sounded more like *Welcome to my parlor.* Only one problem—she was the fly and the spider's menu listed her as the main entree.

She assessed the situation as instinct and her training kicked in. The square, tower-like room with soaring walls several stories high was capped by a dome. Candles flickered everywhere, casting grotesque shadows against the walls. Mosaics depicting some really nasty looking creatures covered every flat surface. The wide door through which Crowley entered vomited people.

As her eyes adjusted to the flickering light, all her suspects were lined up: Hannibal Crowley and his daughter, Eugenia; Mayor Dandridge; Senator McMahon; Mr. and Mrs. Thurston, the pushy matron and her milquetoast husband from the party. Detective Dick Kowalski was there, standing next to a woman wearing a tailored suit. If Sade had to guess, she'd bet the woman was Jane Rinehart, the ADA who tried to frame Sinjen. She'd only seen the woman from the rear as Rinehart had slipped out of Crowley's party. More bodies pressed in behind the key players, each person jockeying for a position to watch the proceedings. She lost count at twenty-five.

"Dammit all to hell." Anger and regret battled in her gut when one more woman joined the group, her white cane tapping on the tile floor with a ratta-tat-tat that echoed in the chamber. Ravena Silverstein. Sade wanted to kick herself. She'd been chasing her tail looking for the concert pianist. And another young girl fell through the cracks while she did. Her eyes narrowed as she clamped down on the outrage singeing her lungs. Later she could indulge in guilt and anger. Right now, she had to save her own life.

A large metal urn stood in the center of the room, halfway between Sade and Crowley. A thin tendril of oily smoke curled up from the mouth of the massive amphora. The crowd watched the sooty coil, mesmerized as if a cobra writhed above a snake charmer's basket. She stared at their faces, repulsed by the looks of lust and greed plastered there—all accept Eugenia Crowley. Her features appeared slack, her eyes dull and lifeless, as if she'd been drugged. Sade had a really bad feeling.

Crowley flashed a gloating smile at her. "So nice of you to join us, Agent Marquis."

"Yeah?" Sade kept her tone conversational, even though she wanted to wipe the smirk off his face with her fists. "Seems I don't have much choice in the matter." She stared at each person in the room but they all ignored her, their attention focused on the ancient jug. Runes, or hieroglyphs—she wasn't sure what to call the markings—circled the perimeter of the floor, some drawn or painted, others worked into the tile. Even as she looked for a way to escape, reluctance to step across the outside frame of the design added to her unease.

Crowley showed no similar disinclination. He stepped closer, drawing his listless daughter with him. Sade noticed what she thought was a low bench on the far side of the urn. Crowley settled the passive Eugenia onto it.

He wore a ceremonial robe made of black satin with appliquéd runes on it. His daughter wore similar attire though blood red in color. Crowley's vestment shimmered in the candlelight, catching the eye and holding it hypnotically. Sade shook her head to clear it. The scent of incense now wafted through the room as if to mask the stench that still made her want to retch if she breathed too deeply.

"Six," Hannibal intoned, turning his back on Sade and facing his followers. "Six sacrifices have been made."

Damn. There's one we didn't know about. She'd already chalked up Crystal Varad's disappearance to this loony cult. Crystal, CeeCee, Miriam, and Hannah were all victims of this madman. And the girl who disappeared the morning after Ravena Silverstein—the one Sade ignored, concentrating on a kidnapped woman who was part of the game. She ran the numbers through her head. Six was a magic number...nine more so—three times three. They needed three more sacrifices. She made herself focus on Crowley's next words rather than that damnable robe.

"We have before us the Vessel," Hannibal proclaimed. "My daughter has lived for this moment. She will become the living goddess. One more sacrifice and the offering will be complete. Our Mistress Sahirah will be reborn to walk again among our midst in all her grandeur and majesty."

Sade blinked. Forget magic number nine. She could guess the seventh sacrifice. Seven was a very bad number, powerful in a dark way. However, unlike the poor unfortunate girls murdered before her, she had a few weapons at her disposal. Using one of those, she reached out with her mind. And met a blank wall. When she'd needed them before, focusing on memories of Caleb, Roman, and Mathias created a thread of communication. But there was nothing. No sense of them. Or herself.

Switching to Plan B, she glanced around looking for something she could use as a weapon and an exit. Too many people blocked the hallway and that was the only door she could see. As Crowley chanted an incantation, the whole group moved into the room and fanned out along the walls.

All of them looked slack-jawed and dreamy-eyed as they succumbed to Crowley's invocation. Even Sade swayed in place. Once she realized what was happening, she forced herself to stand still. To counteract the thrumming mantra, she sang the first song that occurred to her—the theme to *Gilligan's Island*—in her head. Her senses cleared by the time she reached "three-hour tour." Just to be safe, she put the tune on continuous play loop in her mind.

She watched Crowley bend over the inert form of his daughter. Eugenia lay on the bench, her head hanging off one end, her arms crossed atop her breast. The smoke seeping from the urn appeared more substantial now, as thick as a man's arm. It undulated in time to Crowley's chant.

Sade shivered. "Helluva time for someone to walk over my grave," she muttered. It wasn't the first time she'd had the feeling while working this case and she was getting damn tired of it.

Two men separated from the group. They approached and she spread her stance, ready to fight. As they reached for her, someone behind her looped a chain around her neck and yanked. The men grabbed her, holding her immobile while a woman bound her from neck to ankles with the rest of the chain. The men lifted her and carried her to another stone bench near the urn. This one was higher off the floor, with a solid base, and as they draped her across its cold top, she guessed it was an altar.

Sade lay there thinking furiously. She caught a flicker in the corner of her eye, like a handful of glitter tossed in front of an open window. Hiding her relief, her expression never changed when Ariel materialized beside her. Sade was the only person in the room who could see him.

The fae eyed the chains that bound her with amusement. "Gold?"

Sade's eyes narrowed. "What? You wanted fuckin' iron? Get me free, Ari. Right now!" She hissed the words.

"As milady commands." The fae chuckled then touched the various strands of chain with his right index finger. His lips mouthed a silent conjuration and in seconds, the chains loosened then fell away completely.

Sade watched the crowd. Their attention remained fixed on Crowley. Slowly, with a great deal of care not to attract notice, she swung her legs off the altar and was about to stand up when Crowley turned around. He held a long, wicked-looking knife in his hand.

"How—?"

She didn't give him time to finish his question. Sade launched off the altar and caught the priest around the waist in a flying tackle. Her momentum carried them to the base of the urn. She grabbed Crowley's wrist, fighting for control of the knife. As they thrashed on the floor, they rolled against the urn. It tilted ominously but appeared to settle as they rolled away. Within moments, they lurched back.

"Help me! HELP ME!" Crowley screamed.

The two men who had bound Sade stirred and shook their heads to counteract the hypnotic trance. As they fought the compulsion, Crowley gained his feet, pulling Sade up with him.

"Ari, the crowd." Sade yelled, panting with exertion between words.

She stepped into the priest and twisted, holding his arm out in front of her as she backed into him. Crowley stumbled. He grabbed Sade but only succeeded in pulling her off balance too. They fell backwards into the urn and it rocked again, this time tipping precariously.

In slow motion, it toppled over. The grated lid skittered across the floor as the amphora crashed against the mosaic tile surface. A thick, viscous fluid oozed out of the jar to drip onto the floor. The substance touched one of the runes and flared, setting free another tendril of smoke. This one joined with the first, twining together. Like a macabre finger, the twist of smoke poked at the motionless figure swooning on the bench before it.

As if he finally realized something had gone wrong, Crowley stopped fighting. "No! No," he ordered. "She is not the sacrifice. She is the Vessel." He released Sade and took a purposeful step toward his daughter.

The smoke hissed. "Ssssshe issss not. Sssshe issss ssssacrifice." With prescient intelligence, the black vapor turned its thickening head to face Crowley and Sade. A tendril split from the main body and stabbed in their direction, too much like a finger for Sade's peace of mind. "Herrrrrr. It issss with the fatessss that ssshe be the Vessssel. Ssssshe issss sssstrong."

Sade stepped back, shaking her head from side to side, one hand raised as if she could ward off the entity undulating toward her. "This so isn't going to happen."

Several things occurred all but simultaneously. Hannibal lifted his arm and pointed a .45 automatic pistol at Sade, his index finger flexing on the trigger. She had a split second to wonder where the hell the weapon came from before Eugenia sighed. One of the girl's hands flopped toward the floor as her slack mouth sagged open. The smoke jumped from the spilled urn to the girl's mouth and disappeared.

The window at the top of the dome shattered and two winged creatures soared through the broken glass as the weak sunlight of pre-dawn glittered among the pieces of falling glass. A SWAT team, dressed in black BDUs with combat helmets, bulletproof vests, and carrying automatic weapons followed two men cloaked in black leather through the wide arching doorway.

Sade watched the scene unfold in slow motion. She swore she could actually see the bullets leave the barrel of the gun Crowley clutched in his hand, watched as they came seeking her flesh. She tensed, waiting for the wet slap of metal impacting skin to burrow into muscles and organs. Before the bullets reached her, a streak of gold passed in front of her, jerking backwards as three bullets slammed into it.

"The Witch has taken the girl," Sinjen yelled. "She must be killed before the evil can take her." He surged forward. "We can contain her there and bind her as we did before."

Crevan's grating voice rang out. "The Witch will only rise again. She cannot be destroyed. The evil that she is must be dispersed somehow." He swooped low with the intent of snatching Eugenia's body but he was distracted when Hannibal randomly fired the remaining bullets in his pistol then threw it at the gargoyle. The priest rushed to his daughter's side, now brandishing the ceremonial knife. Crevan veered off with a curse. "Beware the blade. It is bespelled."

"We will bind her and then worry about destroying her." Mathias shouted, his voice rising above the melee.

The SWAT team and regular cops herded Crowley's followers back into a corner though they kept a nervous watch on the aerial ballet performed by the two gargoyles. A stench unlike any Sade had encountered before filled the room. She'd dealt with week-old corpses bloated by the heat of a south Texas summer that smelled better.

Eugenia Crowley's body deflated like a balloon, the skin drying out and covering her skull like shrink-wrap plastic. Smoke erupted from the girl's death head smile, dancing from one rune to another until it came to rest on one that vaguely resembled the lazy figure eight of Eternity. The column of smoke stretched toward the ceiling, thickening and taking on substance.

Hannibal Crowley stood over the desiccated body of his daughter, knife clutched his hand. "Noooo!" He screamed, oblivious to the swirl of oily smoke that snaked from Eugenia's body.

Ariel, visible now, stumbled back after taking the bullets square in his chest. Sade caught him but the fae's weight bore them both to the floor. He looked up at her, his eyes an opal swirl of colors, his face gray with pain. "That was incredibly stupid," he murmured through clenched teeth.

"Yeah," Sade agreed wryly. "It was." She never took her eyes off the entity swaying in the shaft of sunlight streaming in from the dome.

It cannot be destroyed. It must be dispersed. Sade considered Crevan's statement, turning it over and over in her mind as she watched the amorphous smoke take further shape. *How did you kill Sahirah before?* Sade asked, reaching for a tenuous mind link to the vampires.

"Do. Not. Say. Her. Name," Mathias spit out between gritted teeth. "We didn't," he added in answer to Sade's unspoken question. "We caught her feeding—just as she was doing here. We killed that body before she could and trapped her inside it."

Sinjen took up the tale. "We bound the body in gold and silver chains then wrapped it in my jabot. The crosses emblazoned on it held what the gold and silver could not. Mathias then laid a binding on it and we entombed her in living rock."

That worked for Sade but she knew it would only be a matter of time before someone else just as power hungry and stupid as Hannibal Crowley found the Witch and tried to release her again. Once again, she turned Crevan's words over in her mind. The glimmer of an idea formed. The evil that was the Witch had to be absorbed somehow and then dispersed. Sade instinctively knew that neither vampire could do this. For all their noble intentions, they were still on the dark side of the line. She glanced at the fae bleeding in her arms. Faeries straddled the line—more gray than white, though compared to the vampires, their power came from the light.

She blinked, realizing there were no magicks made strictly of light. There could be no taint on the soul when dealing with Sahirah's evil. And that's when the answer slapped her in the face. It took a soul to deal with this kind of evil. It took a soul to absorb it and change it and spit it back out like the sick bile it was. Magic would allow the evil to collect, to fester, to grow even more powerful. Yet without magic, the evil would consume its host.

With the sudden clarity of pure inspiration, Sade knew exactly what needed to be done. She had been born—had been bred no matter how inadvertently for this one moment in time. That long-ago conversation between Roman and Titania made sense now. She was unique among humans—wholly human but touched by both the light and the dark sides of magic. She wouldn't survive. But neither would the Witch. Sade's arms tightened for a moment around Ariel. "Thank you, my friend," she murmured softly before she brushed dry lips across his mouth. "By saving my life you have saved them all."

"What the bloody blue blazes are you planning to do, Child?" Ari tried to sound assertive but his voice hissed out, not much more than a tortured whisper.

"The only thing I can," she told him. "If you die, I'll haunt you through all the Realms," she added as she carefully propped him against her tomb and moved away.

Scooting back, Sade put more distance between her body and the hypnotic tendril of vapor coalescing into something less nebulous. It looked solid and substantial now. She didn't have much time. She would have to strike while Sahirah was still in this transient state.

Sensing what Sade was about to do, Sinjen stepped forward. A sudden blaze of sun through the portal in the domed ceiling blocked his way—a prison bar of light stretching from wall to wall. Despite the danger, he gathered himself to dash through the beam. Already weakened, he would more than likely die, but he would stop Sade from her course of action. She would live. She had to live. But even as Sinjen watched, he saw Sade tense. He couldn't reach her physically in time so he sought her mind. Their gazes locked and he caught only an echo of her thoughts.

"...*always love you*," Sade's voice whispered in his mind as she prepared to act. Abruptly, he was shut completely out as she focused entirely on her task. In the blink of an eye, she leaped at the column of smoke swaying before her. In a second blink, the smoke was gone and she lay in a crumpled heap on the stone floor.

"SADE!" Sinjen roared his defiance to heaven. The light in his mind that was Sade had disappeared—snuffed out as quickly as a candle flame left in an open window. Her trajectory had carried her to the brink of the sun's radiance. Every fiber of his being fought to reach her side but Mathias held him, his arms like iron bands around Sinjen's waist.

"Stop, Sinjen. Think, man. Suicide solves nothing."

Shaking and barely able to stand, he nodded dumbly. His feelings for this human woman rocked him to his core. Where had the depth of them come from? He'd lived for close to a millennium, stubbornly alone. Until Sade strode into his world all long-legged assurance, all brittle obstinacy covering a heart full of compassion. Would he walk into the sun rather than live without her? The thought held appeal. She was the light in his darkness, heat to warm the ice incasing his heart. He buried his face in his hands and remained standing only because Mathias held him upright.

Every other person in the room, human and magick alike, stood in frozen silence, stunned by what they'd just witnessed. Cold air swirled into the room from above, and aided by the sweeps of gargoyle wings the stench of evil receded from the room. Slowly, Crowley's disciples shook off their stupor, left dazed and traumatized by events.

Detective Franks recovered and took command. Issuing terse orders, he waved a couple of his uniformed cops forward and they arrested Hannibal Crowley, double-checking the handcuffs they put on him.

Emergency personnel moved in gingerly, keeping wary eyes on the magicks present. Ariel lay propped against a stone sarcophagus. Roses of red blood blossomed on his shirtfront. The Senator and the Mayor were both handcuffed as EMTs triaged the civilians, some who had sustained superficial injuries when the gargoyles broke through the dome sending shards of colorful stained glass raining down.

A pair of female paramedics picked their way through the debris to get to the fallen fae. They knelt beside Ariel, studiously ignoring Sade's body. He flashed a cocky grin at the two. "'Tis only a flesh wound, sweets," he quipped right before passing out.

Roman and Crevan had landed and now moved toward Ariel. "Cold iron," Roman rumbled at the paramedics. "Your medicine won't help. We'll take him to his people. They can heal him if it's not too late." Crevan easily gathered the fallen fae in his arms and launched into the air, soaring up to the dome and through the broken window at its apex.

Sunlight spilled through the hole and glittered on shards of glass littering the mosaic floor then faded to a soft penumbra as clouds obscured the morning sun. Roman knelt beside Sade and gathered her limp body into his arms, cradling her against his chest. He stood in one smooth motion and carried her over where the two vampires waited back in the shadows.

Sinjen collapsed to his knees. Mathias stood behind him, a solid hand resting on his shoulder. No words were spoken aloud between them though thoughts flew fast and furious. Each blamed himself for Sade's demise; each wondered what else could have been done to save the woman they both loved.

Sinjen looked up and raised his arms, silently asking the gargoyle for Sade's body. Roman relinquished her into his keeping. "We must get all of you to safety." Roman hid his emotions in action. He turned to Detective Franks. "Is there a loading dock? Or some egress where an enclosed van could be maneuvered? Mathias and Sinjen cannot be exposed to much more sunlight."

Franks called the SWAT commander over. When asked, the man nodded. "Bay in the back alley," he said. "Big enough a van could pull in and park."

Mathias stepped forward. "Sade is human. She will need to go to the morgue to fulfill the legal requirements of human law. We will accompany her and stay beside her during our day sleep. She is not to be touched until we awaken." His voice remained neutral but power vibrated around him.

Franks exchanged a look with Roman. "Don't want to overstep or anything and I damn sure don't mean to be funny, but could we put them in body bags to protect them during transport?"

After a flurry of phone calls, and a short wait, Franks escorted the magicks, Sinjen still cradling Sade, from the altar room. Wending through the magnificent Art Nouveau architecture and decoration of the old building, their path circuitous to avoid patches of sunlight, the group made their way to the backstage area of the main theater. A door opened and they headed down a short flight of stairs. Three gurneys, with opened black plastic body bags spread across each one, awaited their arrival.

Mathias exchanged a disgusted look with Roman while Sinjen relinquished Sade to the final embrace of sterile plastic. He hesitated, fingers combing through her hair, brushing it off her forehead. Bending, he placed a kiss between her eyes, another on the beauty mark that would never again punctuate her expression, and the last one on her lips.

Roman zipped up the bag, waiting to complete the task until Sinjen and Mathias climbed onto the other gurneys. Franks gingerly zipped the vampires inside. Reluctantly, he zipped up the sides of the bag but refused to close it completely over her head. Neither of the transporters argued. They loaded the three gurneys and looked at Roman for instructions.

"I will fly," he informed them. "Should they not arrive safely, you will have me to deal with."

The two men exchanged uneasy glances, secured the back door and hurried around the van to climb into the cab. They cautiously pulled out into the alley and at a very sedate pace, headed toward the Cook County Morgue up on West Harrison. Roman launched into the sky to follow.

Still standing in the bay, Franks turned to the SWAT commander. "Fuck," he swore softly.

The commander nodded. "I don't know what the hell that thing was in there, but that FBI agent saved every last one of us."

Franks nodded. "No shit. But how the hell are we gonna explain what happened to the FBI. They don't take kindly to losing agents."

The SWAT officer shrugged. "Make the ME do it."

IN THE MORGUE, the gurneys holding the three black body bags sat side by side, untouched and undisturbed. The massive gargoyle pacing the confines of the room ensured that. Outside, the sun slowly traversed the heavens. Roman was a creature of the earth. He knew exactly where sun and earth aligned.

Restless, he waited. An hour before sundown, he unzipped the body bags containing Mathias and Sinjen. The old master awoke shortly after. Mathias sat up slowly. He glanced at Sinjen before his eyes slid to the third bag.

"Any sign?" Mathias spoke in hushed tones.

"None." Roman hid the profound sadness in his heart though the word grated from him.

"What word from the Seelie Court?"

"*Le Vieil* arrived in time. Oberon and Titania were able to revive Ariel after Merlin removed the bullets."

Mathias rubbed his eyes. "Would that Merlin had been here."

Roman stared at Sade's face, still uncovered by the body bag. "He would only have accomplished what you and Sinjen did all those centuries ago, Mathias. And the wizard's magic could do nothing to help her. This is a battle only she can wage."

The entrance doors whispered open and a kid with a shock of blue hair sauntered in. White iPod earphones piped music straight to his brain and he sang along, "Just sit right back and hear this tale, the tale of a fateful trip."

He almost stumbled into Roman as he gaped at the distinguished man sitting on the gurney. He gulped, stared wide-eyed, and back-pedaled as Sinjen sat up.

"Whoa, du-uude," he exclaimed. "Undead. In my morgue. Awesome!" When he backed into Roman, he whirled and got a real look. "Day-ang." He breathed, eyes wide and mouth gaping. "Gargoyle. Dude, can I get your autograph?"

Roman stared, unblinking, and the kid scrabbled backwards but stopped when he noticed the body bag on the third gurney. "Whoa. That a vampire too? I mean, like did you convert her or something and you're waiting for her to rise? Cause, like, dude, if you're not, that body needs to be put on ice before it starts to—" He never got the rest of his statement out. Sinjen came off the gurney and wrapped one long-fingered hand around the kid's throat, holding him off the floor so that his feet dangled.

Daaah-la-lah-laah dah-daah-la-aaaa! Daah-da-la-la-da-laaaa.

The infernal tune played over and over like a broken record. She wanted to scream. This had to be infinitely worse than any form of Chinese water torture. Dark surrounded her again. She liked the dark. Really interesting things hid in the dark. Things like...like... She couldn't remember. She felt herself blink. It was an interesting sensation. She blinked again. There was something else she was supposed to be doing.

Breathe.

She thought about that. Considered it.

Just breathe, Sade.

Sade? Who was that? She blinked again. Something coiled inside her—writhing and hissing. She swallowed. The thing inside her didn't like that. It tried to crawl out. The infernal tune played in her head again and the thing cringed. Her stomach churned, bile rising and burning. She took a breath, her chest rising and falling.

"Breathe, Sade!"

"Fuck you."

Sinjen would have cried in relief if he'd already fed. Even so, one blood-red tear trailed down his cheek.

Sade groaned and tried to sit up. "Oh god. I'm gonna be sick." She moaned.

Sinjen fought to get the body bag open all the way so she could sit up but the zipper snagged. He grabbed her shoulders and turned her as she retched. Black bile spewed out on the floor and splattered on his boots. Sade heaved again. More viscous liquid spattered on the floor.

Waves of nausea continued, wracking her body as it purged itself. Finally, black turned to green and then the heaves turned dry. Sinjen held Sade, pushing her hair back off her face. Her body finally empty, she managed a weak, "I'm sorry." Trembling, she tried to breathe. *Too tired,* her brain said. *Too much.* Sade's eyes rolled back in her head and she let out a dying sigh.

"Noooooo!"

Chapter Twenty-seven

Day is Done

Washington, DC: FBI Director's Office

GEORGE BAILEY LISTENED intently to the voice on the phone. "Yes,
Mister President," he managed to interject. "I understand. Yessir. With
honors. Understood. Good night, Mister President." He hung up, swiveled
his chair to face the window. Leaning back, he watched the sun sink into
the Potomac. "Dammit, Marquis," he growled. "You just had to go and be a
hero." The Director couldn't hold back the quiet sigh that followed.

Las Vegas: Ariel's Condo

THE FAE STRETCHED CAREFULLY, wincing a little as healing skin pulled
tight. A few moments before, he'd been enjoying the filtered sunlight of late
afternoon as it cast a golden glow across his balcony. A garden of potted
plants screened what little metal had been used in construction. Ari had a
broad view of the Vegas Strip—or would have if *Le Vieil* wasn't currently
blocking the view. The old gargoyle eclipsed the balcony and didn't leave
much room for Titania and Oberon. The queen had settled on a second

chaise lounge while the king stood behind her. Ari eyed his visitors warily, keeping his face blank.

Le Vieil stared at Titania. "The King's Seducer did what he could, Queen Titania. Had I not been there, he would have died. The so-called high priest used cold iron, not silver," he chided, his voice grating like gravel under tires. "He took the bullets meant for the Child and had Merlin not been nearby, Ariel would not have survived."

Ariel glanced over at his regents. "I seem to remember a time when the two of you wouldn't have minded seeing her dead...or broken upon my shaft."

Queen Titania snorted, the sound inelegant and crass. "Things changed."

Ari refrained from rolling his eyes or muttering under his breath, keeping his court mask firmly in place.

"What's done is done, Titania." Crevan conspicuously ignored her title. "The Child of Men was the only salvation. She sacrificed herself without thought. Without hesitation."

The fae queen sniffed. "That the mongrel had a noble bone in her body galls me."

Oberon's hand settled on his queen's shoulder and squeezed—none too gently. "Enough, Titania," he commanded. "As *Le Vieil* said, what's done is done. Hindsight is always twenty-twenty." He glanced at Ariel. "Are you well enough to attend the ceremony?"

Ariel grimaced. "Do I have to?" He whined, trying his best to look pitiful.

Titania snorted again. "The day an elf can command me—" Oberon squeezed her shoulder again, stopping her complaint mid-sentence.

"That elf happens to be President of the United States. We will have a delegation in attendance. The Witch might have conquered us all had she survived." Titania opened her mouth to speak again but Oberon silenced her. "She was pure, unadulterated evil, Titania. Her greed and hungers were legendary. Had she been left to gather her minions, the final battle would have been epic. Do you not remember the tortured landscape from before?"

He inclined his head to Crevan. "The Seelie Court will be represented in Washington. I have already responded to the President's invitation."

"As will all the magicks, your majesties." He turned to the injured fae. "Lord Ariel. I leave you to heal." Turning gracefully, despite all his bulk, Crevan stepped to the balcony rail and catapulted into the late afternoon sun. Within three wide beats of his wings, he had disappeared.

Ariel turned to his monarchs and tried once again to look pitiful. "Do I have to?"

"YES!" Titania and Oberon commanded simultaneously.

Chicago: Sinjen's Apartment

THE LAST RAYS of the setting sun faded from the sky. Sinjen rolled back the metal curtain and stood staring out the wide glass door, watching as shadows gathered and crept across the dark navy expanse of Lake Michigan. He sighed as a slightly off-key voice sang in the background.

"The mate was a mighty sailing man, the skipper brave and sure. Five passengers set sail that day for a three-hour tour."

"Desist!" he growled, the sound meant to menace. He did not turn around.

"I'm trying," a husky voice replied. "I can't get that gawddamned song out of my head."

"Language," Sinjen chided, his voice filled with resignation he didn't feel.

"Fuck you." The epithet was a sultry invitation.

"The doctor says you are not strong enough." His voice betrayed both his concern and his longing as he gazed at the room's reflection in the glass.

"Fuck the doctor. Come here, Sinjen. I need you." Her voice sounded plaintive.

He hesitated a moment before turning to face the bed. She laid there, her dark hair a tangle of waves staining the pillow. His chest tightened at the sight of her.

"Please?" Her bottle green eyes gazed up at him. "I want you." When he didn't move, she gave an exaggerated sigh. "Your attitude could do serious damage to a girl's ego."

Sinjen stared at the woman in his bed, his head tilted to the side like a hawk watching its prey. "How are you feeling?"

"I'm fine," she grumped. "But for that stupid song in my head. I think my brain is going to explode if I can't get it out." The corners of her mouth quirked into a sly smile. "If you make love to me, I won't sing it anymore." One brow arched in eloquent testament.

"Tempting though that might be—" Before he could finish, the woman launched off the bed and into his arms.

"Shut up and kiss me," she murmured against his lips.

"As you wish, milady." Sinjen wrapped his arms around her, carried her back down on the bed, his lips finding the tender spot just above her carotid artery.

Several hours later, a cell phone shimmied across the nightstand's polished surface. A naked arm snaked out from under the covers and patted the table in a blind search for the offending thing.

"Ignore it," a deeply satisfied male voice murmured.

"I can't. That's the bat signal," an equally satisfied female voice replied. The hand finally found the phone, grabbed it, and pulled it under the covers. "Uhm, yeah, hello. This better be good."

"Sade? Caleb is missing."

The Exciting New Series from Silver James:

The Penumbra Papers
Cases from the Shadow's Edge

Penumbra: Etymology: New Latin, from Latin paene almost + umbra shadow

Welcome to the Penumbra Papers. Buried deep within some anonymous warehouse outside of Washington, D.C., there is a wooden box with mystical markings branded into its sides…Oh, wait. Sorry. That's the Ark of the Covenant. My mistake.

The Penumbra Papers actually sit buried in a bottom desk drawer in the office of the Director of the F.B.I. Within its pages, the forces of light and dark dance through shadows which humans had only glimpsed before the dawn of the new age. Since the arrival of the new millennium, all manner of preternatural folks intermingle with humans in ways mysterious and magical or…criminal.

Maybe it was it was the stray star, The Flyer, aligning with Mars. Or the hole in the ozone. Whatever happened in the year 2010, all hell broke loose. Literally. It turned out that there really were monsters under the bed and the things that went bump in the night were bigger and scarier than anyone could imagine. Vampires. Faeries. Gargoyles. Werewolves. Witches. Creatures of legend and nightmare. Overnight, reality took on a whole new meaning.

Vampires. Ghouls. Faeries. Ghosts. Werewolves. Creatures of legend and nightmares. Overnight, reality took on a whole new meaning. And that's where Sade Marquis enters the mix. An FBI agent with an X-Files mentality, she was handpicked to fill a new slot within the Bureau – Preternatural Liaison Officer with the MAGIC Unit. It's Sade's job to deal with all the bad nasties.

The world's best and brightest from every discipline—physics, theology, anthropology, chemistry, to name only a few—all tried to explain the rip in the cosmic curtain. Sade has her own theory. The monsters have been here all along, flying just under the radar of normal perception. They've been masquerading as mundanes—their term for humans. Of course, Sade knows the truth of the matter. Her boss doesn't need to know she was raised by a master vampire or that her pet "dog" shifted into a boy the night of her twelfth birthday. That's Sade's secret. She has a lot of them and she is very, very good at keeping secrets. Which makes her very, very good at her job. And that makes the magicks very, very afraid of her. As they should be…

Coming Spring, 2014
THE DEVIL'S CUT – Penumbra Papers #2

Caleb Jones. He gets furry once a month. Or more. He has a nose for magic, which comes in handy as a special agent with the FBI's MAGIC Unit. Caleb goes undercover to investigate a Mexican drug lord, the death of a Border Patrol agent, and a couple of missing werewolf "pups." Along the way, he discovers a devil's playground as he tracks a set of Native American relics.

Colorado Bureau of Investigation crime scene technical investigator, Adele Kincaid, is processing the evidence in a series of baffling murders. They all have one thing in common—Native American fetishes. As she works her angle, she bumps into a most interesting man, but one who raises her hackles. Figuratively speaking.

When the two go missing, Sade Marquis is called in to help with the search. She brings reinforcements in the forms of a pesky fae, a persistent dragon, and a gargoyle Sentinel. The devil's in the details and Sade swears it doesn't get much better than this.

Available now

THAT OL' BLACK MAGIC

Along with her FBI partner—and werewolf best friend—Caleb Jones, Special Agent Sade Marquis is sent to New Orleans to investigate the murders of several high-ranking magicks. The Big Easy is neutral territory so Sade must find and arrest the culprit before war breaks out between the Realms. Things look up when the gargoyle Sentinel, Roman, a permanent fixture in Sade's childhood, arrives to keep the peace. Maybe.

The investigation is hampered by Sade's faerie nemesis, Ariel—the King's Seducer. Oh, and then there's the new dragon in town, Nikolas Constantine. Sade can't decide whether to arrest his ass or admire it.

When guilt and innocence come to play in the French Quarter, it'll take Sade's brand of crazy to sort it all out.

Keep Reading for more Extras!

SOUNDTRACK
SEASON OF THE WITCH

Music is a large part of my creative process and this is especially true with The Penumbra Papers. If you are curious about my play list, here's the soundtrack by chapter/scene. All rights to these songs belong to the composers, lyricists, artists, and/or recording companies. I've listed them for informational purposes only. If you are interested in buying these songs, please visit THE PENUMBRA PAPERS (http://silverjames.com/-penumbra-papers/soundtracks-and-playlists/) for retail buy links to various outlets.

Chapter 1 – Hello, Darkness

Genesis: The Boxer Rebellion: Semi-Automatic

Chapter 2 – Charlie Foxtrot

Briefing: Daughtry: There and Back Again

Sade hits Chicago: El Perro del Mar – Walk On By

Chapter 3 – SNAFU

Licensed Driver: Imagine Dragons: Working Man

University Quad: Brussup – To Zero

Chapter 4 – Just Blow

Sade's Theme: Roxette – She's Got the Look

Caged: 3 Doors Down – When I'm Gone

Chapter 5 – Three Hour Tour

Riding in luxury: Hunter Hayes – Where We Left Off

Memories: Sting – Someone To Watch Over Me

Meeting the Crowleys: Ace of Base: All That She Wants

Chapter 6 – Déjà Vu
Suspects: Paul Banks – The Base

Calling home: Daughtry – Who's They

Chapter 7 – Promises, Promises
Sinjen's Theme: Nickleback – If Today Were Your Last Day

Going home with Sinjen: Stone Sour – Wicked Game

Chapter 8 – Danger Will Robinson
Betrayed: Adele – Set Fire to the Rain

Reflections: A Thousand Years – Sting

Chapter 9 – Blood and Turnips
Fountain of blood: Queen – The Show Must Go On

Chapter 10 – Nothing to Fear but Fear Itself
Aftermath: Toad the Wet Sprocket – Pray to your Gods

Chapter 11 – Coward of the County
Clash: Natalie Maines – Take it on Faith

Chapter 12 – Doctor Who?
Graveyard: Cold Specks – When the City Lights Dim

Chapter 13 – One Crow for Sorrow
Meeting the Old One: Daughtry – Maybe We're Already Gone

Chapter 14 – Two Crows for Joy
Ariel's In Town: Daughtry – Crawling Back to You

Crystal's Story: XXXX – Heart of Gold

Chapter 15 – Three Crows for a Girl
Details: Counting Crows – Angels in the Silence

Sinjen's Welcome: Gary Clark Jr. – Things Are Changin'

Chapter 16 – Four for a Boy

Things That Go Bump: Lindsey Stirling – Shadows

Dinner Conversation: Dinner: Chris Medina – What Are Words

Chapter 17 – Five Crows for Silver

Games: Metallica – Nothing Else Matters

Chapter 18 – Six Crows for Gold

Missing Caleb: Phillip Phillips – Gone, Gone, Gone

Scene of the Crime: Brusspup – Break Emotion

Jason Aldean – Don't You Wanna Stay

Chapter 19 – Seven Crows for a Secret

Wanting You: Kerli – Chemical

Together: Patty Griffin – Not Alone

Lonely Walls: The Civil Wars – Dust to Dust

The Claiming: Damien Rice – 9 Crimes

Chapter 20 – A Secret Never to be Told

On Thin Ice: Lana Del Rey – Summertime Sadness

Taking Time: Emily West – Head On

Chapter 21 – Eight Crows for Heaven

Washington Games: Roxette – View From a Hill

Gatherings: Lifehouse – Unknown

Chapter 22 – Nine Crows for Hell

Visions of Death: Jon Heintz – God in the Machine

Chapter 23 – And Ten Crows for the Devil's Own

Saving Mathias: Jon Heintz – Ashes

Chapter 24 – A Murder of Crows

Where in the World is Sade Marquis: Neverending White Lights – The Warning

Follow the Light: The Tenors – Lead With Your Heart

Chapter 25 – Nevermore

The Hunt: Imagine Dragons – Radioactive

Chapter 26 – Say Goodbye to Yesterday

The Fight is On: Toad the Wet Sprocket – Hold her Down

Sacrifice: David Cook – Light On

Eternal Wait: Daughtry – What About Now

Chapter 27 – Day is Done

Raise Your Hands: Kim Taylor – Lost and Found

Don't forget the award-winning Moonstruck series

Blood Moon
(Moonstruck Book 1)

Army Major Hannah Jackson knows where the skeletons are hidden at the Pentagon and now she's been tasked with keeping the secrets of Army Special Sci Ops Unit 69—the Wolves—and their secret is a doozy. That a civilian corporation wants to exploit the Wolves is a matter of pressing concern.

Sergeant Major Ian McIntire doesn't trust Hannah as far as he can throw her—and that's quite a ways considering he's an alpha werewolf. The woman is a pain in his butt and with the Blood Moon coming, the unit needs to complete their mission and get home before tempers flare. While she might know most of their secrets, the one she doesn't know about the moonstruck Wolf might just get them all killed.

When a covert operation goes wrong, Mac must trust Hannah to save his men—and his heart. Secrets, lies, and betrayals are more personal under the full moon, but when a Wolf loves a woman, he'll do whatever it takes to keep her safe.

Warning: Pursue an alpha Wolf at your own risk. Hot sex, bad words, and action of the blood and guts kind will ensue.

Bad Moon
(Moonstruck Book 2)

Former Army sniper Michael Lightfoot lives a simple life as a forest ranger in Wyoming. The job fits his need to run wild when the moon is full—until two special wolf pups are kidnapped, along with Dr. Liz Graham, the wildlife biologist who makes him want to howl.

The last thing Michael expects when he meets the feisty doctor is to be moonstruck, but the alpha Wolf has more on his plate than just convincing Dr. Liz to love him for who he is. She's being stalked by mercenaries who stole two wolf pups for an unknown faction. Now, with her life in danger, he must reveal his true self to save her. Reuniting with some of his old Army Special SciOps unit, Michael takes on the corporate raiders who want more than just his hide—and Liz's expertise.

Secrets, lies, and betrayals are more personal under the full moon, but when a Wolf loves a woman, he'll risk heart and soul to keep her.

Warning: When a moonstruck Wolf meets his mate, hot sex will ensue. If his mate is threatened, bad words and violence of the blood and guts variety will definitely occur.

Hunter's Moon
(Moonstruck Book 3)

Dr. Jacey Randolph just might be crazy. A rescued wolf is more than he seems and his ability to get into her head—literally—makes her doubt her sanity. After the death of her husband in the Gulf War, she returned to the family ranch to run an animal sanctuary. Bad enough she has to fend off advances from the local sheriff, but now she's turning into some sort of Dr. Doolittle. Except she doesn't talk to animals, dammit.

When Colonel Joshua Harjo, an old friend of her husband's, shows up on her doorstep with a wild tale that the wolf is actually Marine Captain Nathaniel Connor, Jacey must make a leap of faith—and jeopardize her heart—to get involved with the wolf and a group of former Army SciOps soldiers in full rescue operation mode.

Secrets, lies, and betrayals are more personal under the full moon but when a woman loves a Wolf, he can do no wrong. And Jacey Randolph is not about to let a little thing like a band of mercenaries keep her from the Wolf she loves.

Warning: Explosions, death, and sex go hand in hand when a group of Wolves and their women fight for their existence.

Wolf Moon
(Moonstruck Book 4)

Sean Donaldson, former combat medic and demolition expert, answers an SOS from an old Army buddy and rides smack dab into the middle of a conspiracy. Murder and kidnapping are just the tip of the iceberg. Going undercover with a biker gang seems the quickest solution but Sean's best intentions are complicated by Annie Simmons and her son, Cody.

Annie is a waitress at the Half Dollar Bar and Grill just scraping by to provide a better life for her son. She doesn't want a man in her life, especially a scary dude like "Boomer," the big biker who steals a part of her heart. What she doesn't know about the lies he's told can hurt her…and put Cody in danger.

Secrets, lies, and betrayals are more personal under the full moon but when a Wolf fights for his heart, he'll risk his life to make sure the family he loves survives.

Warning: When it's the month of the Wolf Moon, anybody who gets between a moonstruck Wolf and his mate deserves what they get. Blood, sex, and four-letter words dead ahead.

Bride's Moon
(Moonstruck Book 5)

When the remnants of Special SciOps Unit 69, the Wolves, reunited to save a group of soldiers used as lab rats in a secret experiment, Colonel Joshua Harjo never expected to command the covert government unit again.

Someone near the top wants the 69th back on active duty and Harjo is tasked with making it happen, along with keeping the men the Wolves rescued top secret.

Amy Rouse is the best "cat herder" around and she's recruited for administrative duties with the new unit, a job with perks—Wolves and their commanding officer, Joshua Hargo, the man of her dreams. Amy didn't count on murder, mayhem, and a redheaded Deputy US Marshal to complicate her life.

Secrets, lies, and betrayals are more personal under the full moon, but when a man loves a woman, nothing will stop him from tying the knot.

Warning: The road to romance is never smooth and a runaway bride might just jinx a highly sensitive operation.

Rogue Moon
(Moonstruck Book 6)

Rudek Tornjak is a Wolf without a pack. A man scarred by his past, he prefers it that way. While living in the shadows of the French Quarter, whispers of treachery and betrayal reach his ears—along with accusations implicating him in unthinkable acts. He comes out of hiding to confront his accusers only to discover he's under a death sentence. On the run, he encounters Isabelle Fontaine, a woman with a past of her own she'd rather keep hidden.

Family is everything to Izzy and she'll do whatever it takes to keep hers safe. Crossing paths with a shadowy corporation and a rogue Wolf puts the people she cares about in jeopardy—not to mention her own life and heart.

Secrets, lies, and betrayals are more personal under the full moon, but when a betrayed Wolf fights for his honor, no one is safe—not even the woman he loves.

Warning: Doubt a Wolf's honor and you'll get a serving of hot blood and guts to go.

Acknowledgements

I know the voices in my head aren't real. But sometimes? They have really good ideas! So I write them down. With luck, people will then read my words. This book is for all the people who have read a book, enjoyed it, and let the world know. It's also for people who have read a book and hated it. The point is to read a book!

I also want to thank the usual suspects. They pretty much know who they are by now. Without them, I might never leave the world of my imagination.

This is a book special to my heart and without Keiran, Kelly, Traveller, Cherry, Liza, Beth, and Janet, I might not have seen this project all the way through. Thank you, my friends.

Last but definitely not least, I have to recognize my readers. Each email, Facebook comment, tweet, and visit to my website convinces me that maybe I can put a bunch of words together and tell a story. One last caveat: Any and all mistakes are my own.

About the Author

Silver likes coffee and walking on the dark side. Okay. She loves coffee. LOTS of coffee. Warning: Her Muse, Iffy, runs with scissors and can be quite dangerous. An award-winning author, she's been a military officer's wife, mother, state appellate court marshal, airport rescue firefighter and forensic fire photographer, crime analyst, technical crime scene investigator, and writer of magic, mystery, and mayhem. Now retired from the "real world," she lives in Oklahoma and spends her days at the computer with two Newfoundland dogs, the cat who rules them all, and myriad characters all clamoring for attention. She writes dark paranormal thrillers, time travel romance, and light contemporary romance with a kiss of suspense.

To find out more about Silver and her books, visit her website: www.silverjames.com. She loves to connect with readers on Facebook (https://www.facebook.com/pages/Silver-James/122400874477832) and Twitter (https://twitter.com/SilverJames_).

Other titles by Silver James

The Penumbra Papers:

That Ol' Black Magic – A Penumbra Papers Novella

Moonstruck:

Blood Moon – Book 1

Bad Moon – Book 2

Hunter's Moon – Book 3

Wolf Moon – Book 4

Bride's Moon – Book 5

Rogue Moon – Book 6

Novellas:

Café Midnight

From the Wild Rose Press:

Faerie Fate

Faerie Fire

Faerie Fool

Class of '85 Reunion Series:

Fairy Tales Can Come True

Promises, Promises

Dearly Beloved Series:

Best Laid Plans